# Counterpoint

## SONG OF THE FALLEN
### BOOK I

RACHEL HAIMOWITZ

Riptide Publishing
PO Box 6652
Hillsborough, NJ 08844
www.riptidepublishing.com

Counterpoint (Song of the Fallen, Book I)

Cover Art by Simoné, www.dreamarian.com
Editor: Tal Valante
Cover Design, and Layout: L.C. Chase, lcchase.com/design.htm

ISBN: 978-1-937551-20-9

Second edition
February, 2012

Third edition
December, 2012

Also available in ebook:
ISBN: 978-1-937551-19-3

# Counterpoint

## SONG OF THE FALLEN
### BOOK I

RACHEL HAIMOWITZ

RIPTIDE PUBLISHING

# TABLE OF Contents

*For my dear friend and editor Tal Valante,*
*who let me play in her sexy, sexy sandbox.*
*I found treasure buried there.*

*And also a dead parrot.*

*But mostly treasure.*

# Chapter One

$A$yden awoke to wrongness.

He shoved his furs aside and tuned his inner ear to the forest's song—the bass hum of the trees, the trills of insects—a thousand points of sound merged in near-perfect harmony. He sniffed the air as he listened, detecting nothing but a faint whiff of last night's cook-fire, the loam of the forest floor, the comforting scents of the massive red cedars and the stream running by his campsite.

And *there* was the wrongness, the faintest whisper of jagged notes worming through the forest song. Had a human dared to cross into their lands?

Ayden's lips pulled back from his teeth in a grin entirely void of humor.

*Time for a hunt.*

He unwove the branches of his shelter with an impatient mental hum and stepped out into the first light of day. A second sound reached his ears then, a physical one this time: dull hoof beats and snapping branches, faint but rising by the moment. The approaching racket might be nothing more than an animal on the hunt, but he dare not take that chance.

He stooped to grab his kit, lashing his furs to his satchel and slinging it and his fighting sticks across his back. Then he dropped a sleeping dart into his blowpipe and once again cast both inner and outer ears to the ruckus rushing closer, closer . . .

And sighed, relieved, when he recognized the sound for what it was: a pair of wild boars tearing down the path to his campsite. He lowered his weapon and tuned his other hearing to the boarsongs, churning crescendos of urgency and blind rage. They were almost upon him already. Ayden spun a soothing melody in his mind, a half-forgotten lullaby, and sent it to weave through the boars' frantic tempos—

The two boars emerged into the clearing, drawing to a halt not two feet before him, heads bent and hooves pawing at the earth.

"What haste, fierce ones?"

Of course they couldn't understand him, but it felt good to use his voice again.

Not surprisingly, the boars responded about as intelligently as most people would: one snorted, and the other one squealed.

The squealer took a hesitant step forward and to the side, then stopped again. Its gaze shifted from Ayden to the path beyond and back. Ayden closed his eyes, tried to hear what the boars were hearing, what was driving them forward so urgently. And there it was again, the *wrongness*, just a whisper yet but a precursor, he knew, of a powerful wail to come: the Hunter's Call, summoning beasts to twist with hate before siccing them upon the human realms.

"Ah." Ayden opened his eyes and nodded at the boars. "I'd not discourage you from such a noble task, but you must know the humans will kill you?"

The squealer took another step forward. This time, the snorter joined him.

Who was he to argue with that?

He stepped aside. Freed of his influence, the boars bolted across the clearing and disappeared back into the dense wood.

Ayden took off after them at a hard run. He followed them for hours, even though he knew with fair certainty where they would go. Indeed, they did not disappoint.

The sun had crested the sky by the time they reached the boundary between the elven and Feral lands, where a foot-wide crack cut through the forest like a fatal wound. No life grew near the fissure for twenty paces, the very earth scorched into volcanic rock and great sheets of muddy glass. No elf had crossed the fissure for nearly three centuries. The boars, however, trotted over without pause, drawn inexorably by the Call that wailed like death in Ayden's inner ear.

Ayden stopped short, loath to set foot or toe upon the deadened earth.

Instead he found the tallest tree at forest's edge: a massive red cedar, its trunk as big around as twenty of him and its lowest branches a good dozen paces overhead.

"I don't suppose you'd offer me a hand up?" he asked, placing a hand upon the trunk and trying to coax a branch to bend within his reaching.

Alas, this tree had sung its melody unchanging for over two thousand years, and it had no interest in shifting for a whelp such as he—never mind that he'd seen a century or eight himself.

Ah, well. He hadn't really thought it would. He fished his steel bearclaws from his satchel, buckled them onto each boot and hand, and started up the trunk the hard way.

Long minutes later, sticky with sap and quivering with fatigue, Ayden broke through the canopy. He dug his farseer from his satchel and peered through the lens. From this new vantage point over a hundred paces high, he could see south across the cultivated human lands for nearly three leagues, and the same distance west across the forest canopy of the Feral lands into the Myrkr Mountains. A few leagues southwest, in the direction the boars had gone, he spotted a dozen crowned eagles gliding over a low mountain peak. No, not just gliding . . . they were circling as a pack, wingtips splayed like fingers on a massive hand.

Crowned eagles never flew in flocks, could barely tolerate each other even when mating. He could hear the *wrongness* pouring from them in pounding, discordant waves.

Command would wish to know of this. Ayden balanced himself between the trunk and two narrow branches, letting them take his weight, and focused his mind on forming a signal cloud. 'Twas no easy feat for him, a naturally adequate musician at best, to hear the cloudsong so far away and amongst so much noise from the forest below, but at last he detected faint threads of it, high notes jittering chaotic and fast in the upper sky, and he shaped them with his mind into clear lines and measures. Above him, three clouds merged into two and formed the symbol for Ferals and a navigational marker.

He held them as long as he could, gritting his teeth against the strain. But his clouds drifted quickly, and a moment later he gave up, panting, and let them scatter. No matter, though; Command would have seen the signal immediately and understood.

The Surge was building.

Having done all he could for now, he turned his thoughts to a meal, and water, and setting up camp for the night.

Climbing down the massive cedar was, to Ayden's chagrin, nearly as taxing as climbing up it had been, and it didn't help that the Call was growing more strident by the hour. Halfway down, a small herd of caribou bucks in full rack raced by his tree and crossed the border. As he reached the ground, a squirrel whizzed by, and he could not help but wonder what harm such a harmless creature could possibly inflict. But the Hunter's Call would not draw it for nothing; surely it had *some* purpose.

'Twas not his concern, though. His empty belly, on the other hand, was very much so. Fortunately, he knew these woods well, and before an hour had passed he'd gathered a feast of mushrooms, huckleberries, wild onions, miner's lettuce, and hazelnuts. There was no water source nearby, but 'twas easy enough, even for him, to draw it from the moist air; he untwined the dewsong from the airsong and guided the trickle into his upturned mouth until his thirst was slaked. He drew more to fill his canteen, then climbed back up to the first branch of the cedar he'd scaled before and unrolled his furs. If he slept on the ground this night, he might very well be trampled. Besides, 'twas best to be prepared should something go wrong: should the Surge for once flow into elven lands, or should the humans, in their desperation or foolishness, try to cross the border themselves.

Ayden woke early and alone, wondering what was taking the others so cracking long. Had they not seen his signal? Or were they simply too lazy to travel through the night?

Regardless, he would be well prepared when they arrived. He emptied his bladder, foraged a quick breakfast and a large store of extras, and packed his kit before the sun had cleared the horizon.

Back atop his cedar, he coaxed the leaves and branches to weave into a hunting blind large enough to camp in. From this perch, he had a clear view of the nearest human village a league to the south, and several leagues of their land beyond it. To the west, he could see a few leagues across the Feral woods until the ridgeline cut his view. He spent the morning watching them both, enjoying the solitude and the late summer weather, the many-layered forest song drowning out the worst of the *wrong*.

He was jarred from his peace round noon by the urgent clanging of bells to the south, and he snapped his farseer toward the human village, where both the temple bell and the bell atop the Surge fortress were ringing madly. The human occupiers of that sorry patch of borderland were dropping tools and baskets in the fields where they stood and scrambling toward safety. Half a league to their west, a mismatched couple of Ferals—a caribou buck and a wolf—were racing toward them. He couldn't hear the humans screaming this far off, but he liked to imagine that they were.

The Ferals were gaining quickly on a man and a woman who'd been working a distant field; the humans with their two weak legs could never hope to outrun the four-legged Ferals, but they were certainly trying. The man's longer stride carried him ahead of the woman, but he paused, ran back to grab her hand, pulled her forward again. How foolish and sweet: they'd die together.

From the east rode two archers on horseback, but Ayden doubted they would make it on time.

And indeed they did not. The woman faltered up a steep hillock, and the Feral wolf caught up with her. She crumpled beneath its lunge without a fight, and Ayden gave the wolf a silent cheer for meting out swift justice.

The male—the stupid fool—stopped again, looked back. Probably screamed the woman's name. Ayden couldn't make out his expression or hear his song from here, but clearly he was torn. By the time he realized there was no helping the woman and began to run again, the Feral buck had gained on him. The man took but ten steps before the buck, as large in its twisted form as a plow horse, gored him through the back and tossed him aside. The man hit the ground with the grace of a soldier and rolled to his knees despite the gaping hole in his chest. Ayden watched him pull something from his belt—a knife, he thought, from the glint of sunlight—but the man died before he could use it.

The Ferals trampled his body as they charged past, but didn't savage it. Instead they raced toward the two riders, then veered off to tackle a man who stood paralyzed in the fields. Ayden fastened his farseer onto him and cursed. 'Twas only a scarecrow. He could see that even from here; how did they not? The cavalry was closing in on them from behind, and he found himself waving the Ferals along—he would have called out to them if he were closer, foolish as that was—but he had no hope of swaying their course. The Ferals charged, leapt, knocked down the scarecrow and sent its head flying.

Then the mounted archers reached their range, and they felled the wolf with two shots through the head that even Ayden had to admit were impressive from horseback. The Feral buck turned and rushed them with lowered antlers—gods, Ayden hoped it wouldn't hurt the horses—but the riders re-nocked their bows in time to take it out.

It was over.

Or not: a third creature, so small that Ayden had missed it before, took a flying leap and scurried right up the leg of a rider. It was on his face before the man could reach for his knife, and he fell from his horse, batting wildly at his head. The other soldier dismounted and killed the Feral rodent, but his companion lay unmoving now, either unconscious or dead. Hopefully dead. That made three kills to three for the Ferals—a definite win. After all, wild animals bred much faster than humans.

The excitement died down after that. The one surviving soldier rode back to town, the bells stopped clanging, the humans returned to work, and a group of men built a pyre for the dead. A lone Feral hawk watched them all as carefully as Ayden did, but none of its friends came to join it.

Speaking of friends, Ayden was growing rather impatient with the tarrying of his own. He gathered his strength to form another pair of signal clouds, just in case, then settled in to wait for the next attack.

The scouts arrived about an hour later. Ayden couldn't see them—they must have been muting their lightsong—but he could hear four of them moving through the forest long before any sound reached his bodily ears. He climbed down to greet them, and found them waiting for him by the time he reached the ground.

Except they were still invisible.

Show-offs.

Ayden looked directly at the space where he knew the one in the lead to be, and a grin crept up his face despite his best attempts at annoyance. "I can *hear* you, you know."

The forest before him rippled into the shape of a familiar, smiling elf.

"Afi Kengr," Ayden said, grasping forearms in greeting. "By the fallen gods, what took you so long? And where are the rest of you? Or does the Council not deign to concern itself any longer with such business?"

Afi smiled back. "Always so impatient, you are." His three companions, still invisible, spread out to form a perimeter. "Do you know how far we had to travel? And we daren't ride with the Call so strong—'twould be a shame to have our horses go running right out beneath us past the Crack."

Ayden conceded the point with a chuckle.

"Anyway, the rest aren't far behind. But you're right about the Council, they have grown complacent. I have toenails older than some of the boys and girls they've sent this time. But tell me: how far have the Ferals progressed?"

Ayden reported what he'd seen so far, then invited Afi up his tree to take a look. For Afi, of course, the tree bent its first branch. Ayden shot him a dirty look, but stepped up beside him all the same.

"Fret not, my friend," Afi said, slapping Ayden on the back. "Another few hundred years of practice and they'll bow for you too, I know it. Shall we race to the top?"

Though Afi didn't wait for an answer before leaping to the next branch, Ayden grinned and cried, "You're on, old elf!"

He beat Afi to the top by half a dozen paces.

Once in his hunting blind, they sat back, scanning the landscape and waiting for the rangers to arrive. To the west, a wake of vultures had joined the eagles on the updrafts over the Myrkrs.

"Gods, how can you stand the *noise*?" Afi asked, pressing his hands to his temples as the Call ratcheted up another notch.

Ayden shrugged. "You get used to it."

"The view is worth the price, though."

"Indeed. Will you stay?"

The old scout shook his head. "Command has other plans for me."

Ayden knew better than to ask what they were. Instead they settled into companionable silence, one eye to the Ferals and the other to the woods behind them.

Their waiting ended half an hour later, when the clutch of junior rangers arrived in a hail of stomping boots and rattling foliage and nervous chatter.

"Ah, younglings." Afi sounded fond.

Ayden pulled a face. "I was *never* that green."

Yet Afi's clamped, twitching lips told a different story. "Come, greet them," the old scout said, cutting off Ayden's indignant response. "'Twould do you good. You've been out alone for too long, my friend."

Ayden snorted. "Climb down a hundred paces for the pleasure of their prattle? I thank you, no."

Afi shrugged. "As you wish."

"Signal if you need me," Ayden called to Afi, who'd started his way to the forest floor. Afi threw a teasing wave, the kind that said he'd have no need of young whelps, and continued on his way down.

The treetop seemed very quiet when he disappeared into the foliage below.

Four days in, and Ayden's little nest had become quite cozy. Below, the greenwood rangers grew ever more restless, their nerves scraped raw under the constant barrage of the Call. They worked hard to conceal it, Ayden credited them that: they whiled away the waiting with stick fights and patrols, blowpipe competitions for range and accuracy, and anxious bets on when the Surge would finally crest. Ayden sparred with them only once, for after he routed all challengers, none would face him again. Afterward, he ventured down only in short bursts to gather intelligence and food. The invitations to stay aground he ignored. The one trembling, brave request to join him in his blind he glared into a stuttered apology.

He probably enjoyed that more than he should have, but the chatter and bravado of novices a quarter his age frayed his patience more than even the Hunter's Call could. Ella would have disapproved. Crack it, Ella would have presided over their silly contests and stroked their pride and soothed them with songs at night. He snorted at the idea, but he couldn't quite erase the smile at the thought of his little sister.

So back into his blind he went, blissfully alone, watching Feral birds arc across the western sky when he detected a hint of deep familiarity above the *wrong*.

Ella?

Ella! What was she doing *here*?

In the face of his sudden urgency, the cedar branches bent and shifted beneath him, passing him to the ground in moments. Ella was waiting for him with a soft smile that belied—and nearly disarmed—his concern. Still, he gripped her by the shoulders and asked, "What's wrong, sister? What brings you here? Is everything all right?"

She plucked his hands from her shoulders and held them in her own, shaking her head indulgently. "Always thinking the worst, Ayden."

"For good reason," he said, thinking on that *other* time she'd come to find him on patrol, nearly three centuries past, with the news of their father—

Ella poked him in the belly, and when he glared at her, she flashed him that cracking cheeky grin and asked, "The new rangers, how do you find them?"

"*Young*," Ayden said.

She smiled as if expecting his rancor. "Do be patient with them, brother. No doubt they will learn much from you."

"Yes," he drawled, "perhaps in the next hundred years I might succeed in teaching them the value of silence, but I am not hopeful." And speaking of silence . . . "You never answered my question. What brings you here?"

Ella straightened up. "Why, my love of you, of course."

"I see. And the real reason?"

"I'm going to see Chaya."

"What, *now*?" He gripped her shoulders, scarcely resisting the urge to shake her. "The Ferals are gathering; you'd be a fool to—"

She knocked his hands away. "They never hurt us, you know that."

"But the humans are on high guard now, and they *would* hurt you."

"Not Chaya," Ella insisted, thrusting forward into his space. He wondered if she realized the challenge she was issuing. Probably not. "She's my friend and I trust her."

Ayden covered his eyes with his hands, held them there until she tugged them away.

"I am *not* blind *nor* a fool, thank you very much." Her indignation gave way to sadness as she added, "The human I go to see is dying, not dangerous."

"That is what mortals *do*, you kno—" Ella eschewed the usual belly poke for a halfhearted belly punch, cutting him off. He scowled at her. "Your presence won't change a thing. Go home, Ella."

He tried to turn her round, but she held her ground. "No."

"Ella . . ."

"I said *no*, Ayden. I'll not let her die alone."

Ayden let loose an exasperated sigh. Wherever had she learned such stubbornness? He realized that short of binding her, he would not be able to stop her. Though he had to admit, that idea did have its merits . . .

She poked him in the belly again. "Stop that. It's not for you to command me, brother. I am not one of your rangers, if you'll recall."

"Yes, how silly of me to have forgotten." But in fairness, it seemed he had; she would go with or without his permission, so they might as well part on amicable terms. He offered her a resigned smile.

"I forgive you," she said, perfectly grave, though a smile was twinkling in her eyes. She stood on her toes to kiss both his temples. Then she was gone, off at a trot toward the human-elven border as if 'twere perfectly harmless: nothing more than some scribbled line on a disused map.

"Come back before the Surge crests!" he called.

"I will," she called back, not even bothering to turn her head.

"And don't forget to mute your song!"

Her laughing response was a blast of notes so loud that every ranger in his seeing winced—she'd have blazed like the sun to a human's eyes—but then she went virtually silent, and he trusted her to stay that way for the duration of her foolish excursion.

He watched her go until he could no longer discern her through the trees. As he turned back to his cedar, he saw where she'd been standing a single small flower, pink-petaled and perfect, reaching toward the sun. Just like Ella, he thought: always grasping for things she could never have.

Back in his perch, Ayden tracked Ella's progress through the human lands with his farseer. Between the clamor of the Call, the forest song, and Ella's deliberate muting, he'd expected to lose all sound of her, and was pleasantly surprised to discover himself attuned enough to track her all the way to her human's house. He kept watching and listening even when she disappeared inside. From time to time she emerged—fetching water from the well or wood for the stove—a bright, distant figure in the powerful lens of his farseer. A farseer that, strictly speaking, should have been trained on the gathering Ferals ... Ayden resisted the twinge of guilt between his shoulder blades and kept watching the village.

And for that he thanked the fallen gods in a great, panicked rush when he spotted a pack of human soldiers, spread out a league beyond the village and heading straight for it.

Only centuries' experience with conquering battle rage held him back—and just barely—from hurling himself down the tree and into action. Instead, he readjusted his farseer with shaking fingers. Ten men at least, though from this distance 'twas difficult to discern one from the next. They were slinking through the far field, making faint ripples in the wheat, their steps slow and measured. But that worked to his advantage: he could try to head them off before they reached the village.

Of course, they might not be coming for Ella. The Ferals were on the prowl, after all, and the humans were responding in kind.

But if they *were* coming for her ...

He mapped a quick path and memorized the landmarks, then scrambled down from branch to bowing branch. As soon as his feet struck the forest floor, he was racing toward the border and across it for the first time in over two hundred and fifty years.

Ayden ran as he'd never run before, the forest parting a trail before him. He stayed within its safety for as long as he could, but soon the trees thinned and made way for fields of wheat and soy. Before stepping out into the open, he spent precious moments calming his mind and clamping down upon his song until it faded to the softest of whispers; humans could not hear elfsong, but they perceived it as a soft illumination that would betray him. He despised the sensation of binding himself, and the world round him seemed somehow *less*, but 'twas nothing compared to the thought of a world without Ella.

Even muted, he still possessed the use of all his hearing, and he cast out his senses in search of the soldiers as he sprinted across the fields. He found excitement, eagerness, hatred and anger, confidence and a touch of fear: men on the hunt for a dangerous trophy. Ayden bared his teeth. They had no idea how dangerous their hunt had just become.

He reached the muddy outskirts of the village and slowed to a stop amongst a copse of apple trees near the human's home. Ella's song was wrapped round the dying human's like a swaddling blanket, soothing even to Ayden, though he dared not let it calm him. Instead he cast out his senses once more, his blood rising in his veins as he noted how close the soldiers had come. Too late to head them off, and no time to warn Ella without exposing them both. But surely she'd sensed him by now, and could hear his fear.

*Hide*, he thought. She might hear it and understand.

Then the time for thoughts was over.

He climbed the tallest tree in the orchard, a measly ten paces to the top, and braced himself to balance without his hands. Through his farseer he spotted the soldiers a hundred paces off, moving quietly down the dirt road. Closer now, he counted nineteen men.

He grabbed a fistful of darts—the lethal ones, not the sleepers— dropped one into his blowpipe, and put it to his lips. Eighty paces. He begged the tree for all he was worth to hide him well, for once the soldiers spotted him, he would lose his main advantage. The leaves and branches rustled softly, closing him in.

Sixty paces.

Fifty.

Ayden blew the first dart, aiming for the rear line in the hope that the soldiers ahead wouldn't notice. The man slapped a hand to his neck, and Ayden planted darts in two more soldiers before the first one even hit the ground. A fourth soldier folded a second later, but then a cry went up and the whole contingent crouched behind their shields, shouting amongst themselves to find the marksman. Ayden took out two more before a sharp-eyed soldier spotted his perch, and before he could reload again, a hail of crossbow bolts chased him from the tree.

Discovered now, he unleashed his bound song with a satisfied growl and called up a fierce gust of wind, but the bolts were too fast and heavy to be swayed much. One skimmed his left arm as he ducked behind the trunk, ripping a burning furrow into his flesh.

He heard shouts of "Elf!" and "Get him!" and "Watch out, sorcery!" as he dumped his kit and jumped to the ground, wondering how by the fallen gods he would best thirteen men armed with crossbows now that he'd been seen. He sang to the wind for a greater gale and it complied, kicking up pebbles and debris and hurling them in violent spirals.

The soldiers shouted in fear and huddled behind their shields again. But this parlor trick wouldn't hold them at bay for long; he needed to act quickly before they flanked him.

*Storm*, he thought. He'd show them a *real* storm.

As another salvo of bolts *thunked* against the tree that sheltered him, Ayden sucked in a breath and sought out every sizzling, snapping note in the air around him, in the dirt at his feet and even within his own body. He summoned them together into a tight, sparking ball of sharp notes and frantic tempos and hurled it at the soldiers.

Panicked screams, then shrieks as his ball lightning burst through the front soldier in a crackling fit of fire and smoke, arced off to a second and a third, regrouped and attacked a fourth. Ayden fought for all he was worth to hold it together, but he couldn't stop it from flowing through the fifth man's feet and into the dirt.

Six dead from his darts, five from his lightning; that left eight more between Ella and safety. He sang out to summon a second ball, and two soldiers turned tail and fled. But the remaining six found their courage and charged him.

His lightning was building too slowly. Desperate, Ayden pulled his daggers and threw, felling the two men in the lead from ten paces out.

He was running out of weapons. He whipped up the airsong round him into a smoldering crescendo, too hot for the humans to press through. Their fear screeched like untuned strings in the music of the battle as they fell back again. The grass round him caught fire, and he let it burn as he struggled to call together the charged notes once more.

A second ball lightning coalesced in his hands and surged forward with a clap of thunder, stopping the heart of the soldier it hit. Ayden urged it on, but his mind-voice cracked and the lightning went directly to ground.

He had no strength left in him to form a third. His legs buckled beneath him and his vision swam, but even as his knees hit the ground, his hands found a dead branch and snapped it in two—he'd dropped his fighting sticks with his kit, so these would have to do. His left arm throbbed where the bolt had grazed it, and his hand was slick with blood, but he had nearly eight centuries of practice on these vermin and if he could just . . . get . . . up . . . he knew he could take on the three who remained.

He was just getting one foot beneath him when something sharp slammed into his back. It knocked him face down into the dirt, ripped the air from his lungs. His first thought, before the pain hit, was of Ella; he prayed like he'd not prayed in over two hundred years that he'd bought her enough time to reach safety. His last thought, before the world went black, was that he'd miscalculated: there had been *twenty* men, not nineteen, and he'd overlooked the one who had scouted ahead.

# Chapter Two

Not for the first time this week, Freyrík wished his brother were here. Well, not *right* here, right now, in his bedchambers with—

"Oh, *Highness*!" Lord Jafri threw his head back, planted his palms on Freyrík's belly and sped his rocking across Freyrík's hips. He was lovely, Freyrík had to admit, with those dark round eyes and black hair, bronze skin slick with sweat, sculpted arms trembling with exertion . . .

Arms, Freyrík reflected, that had earned their beauty wielding the sword. Not even sons of Earls were spared from the Surge Wars. At least Jafri would command his own company this time—

"Just like that, Highness," Jafri breathed.

Freyrík wanted to comply but didn't know what *that* referred to, since Jafri was doing all the work. Oh, he *wanted* to want the man, to lose himself in the tight, eager body atop him and the silk sheets below. To forget, just for a moment, the darkness and death encroaching upon his people. Only in scattered skirmishes yet, but not for long—he would have to mobilize the army soon. And as if that weren't trouble enough, the contingent in Akrar had captured an elven spy, though not before the creature had single-handedly killed four-fifths of them. His men could barely hold one front against the darkers; if elvenkind meant to rekindle aggressions, Farr Province might not survi—

"Highness?"

Freyrík snapped back to the present and realized that Lord Jafri was staring down at him, worry pulling at his lips and creasing his forehead. He'd stopped moving. Freyrík's member had gone limp inside him.

"Are you well, Your Highness?" One hand slid up Freyrík's chest and settled hesitantly over his heart. "Is it . . . have I displeased you?"

Freyrík sighed and curled his hand over Lord Jafri's, giving it a gentle squeeze. "Of course not," he said. Then, because he could ill afford to worry about the easily-wounded feelings of someone who'd given their arrangement more meaning than it deserved, he tugged Jafri off his lap and said, "'Tis just the war. I find it hard to attend my own pleasure when so many lives will soon be lost on my orders." *Or lost to my errors.* He'd dispatched scouts and soldiers to the elven border, but he could scarce afford to divert them from the fight with the dark beasts. Had it been the right choice?

"You worry overmuch, My Prince," Lord Jafri said.

Freyrík shook his head. 'Twas impossible to worry too much when the entirety of his brother's kingdom—and all the Empire beyond—stood so very near the precipice of extinction.

Lord Jafri knelt at his hip and leaned in, looking up at him with dark eyes made darker by the low light and his desire to please. His breath ghosted over Freyrík's member. "If you would permit, Highness, I would ease your tensions . . ."

He bowed his head, mouth open, but Freyrík nudged him away and stood. "My thanks, Jafri, but I must rise and meet the day." He felt compelled to add, "Perhaps tomorrow," though he knew he shouldn't have. Tomorrow would be no less taxing.

Jafri bowed his head and stood. "Shall I fetch your groom?" he asked, sorting through his clothes and carefully avoiding Freyrík's eyes. Upset, then, though for wounded feelings or foiled ambitions, Freyrík knew not.

And what beneath the great shadow of the gods had planted *that* thought in his mind? Most people desired him for their own ends, true, but Lord Jafri had *never* shown . . .

Freyrík poured some water into his washbasin, splashed it across his face. "Yes, thank you."

". . . Shall I leave?"

"That might be best," Freyrík said, but kept his tone kind. "If you would summon my secretary on your way, I'd be most grateful."

Freyrík heard Jafri's footsteps on the carpet, and his bedroom doors open and close. Only then did he allow his worry to surface. 'Twould not do to air his fears in the presence of his people—not even a paramour. But he *could* share his worries with the Aegis. He could ask for an emergency recruitment from the inland provinces; he was certain the Aegis Exalted could draft at least a battalion for him. Or rather, for his brother.

He would write Berendil, then, and ask him to appeal to the Aegis in person. 'Twas why his brother spent so much time at High Court, after all; that it pleased his third wife, a daughter of the Aegis, was but a secondary gain. Yet on days like this, Freyrík wished he weren't alone in the outlands, with a regency on his hands and a Surge on the brink of cresting upon his borrowed lands.

But he would manage, as he always had. He had his brother's confidence, his people's confidence—befang it, if one listened to the clergy, he had a godly right. And Berendil would be home in another month and back on the throne where he belonged.

His groom returned from what Freyrík suspected was an interrupted breakfast to bathe, shave, and dress him. He felt poorly for having recalled the man so soon after dismissing him, and gave him 'til evening to spend as he wished. Then he settled into his private study to write the letter, but he had barely penned his opening salutations when his secretary interrupted: the elf-catchers had arrived with their prize and were awaiting his pleasure in the Great Hall.

Freyrík entered the hall through the antechamber behind the dais, his secretary in tow, and took a moment to compose himself in the private alcove. Even from there he could see the abandoned tables, still strewn with the interrupted breakfast of the court. The guards had cleared the room, or else his guests and relatives had retired to safety of their own accord. The flock of servants darting round the edges of the hall, removing half-eaten dishes to personal trays, seemed to vacillate between terror and awe. Freyrík's enmity for the elven warrior deepened at the sight of his court in such disarray, and he found himself eager to confront the creature. He strode out into the Great Hall proper.

And froze halfway down the dais stairs, nearly tripping over his own feet.

There beside the runner at the bottom of the stairs, shackled and flanked by two soldiers, stood a creature of stunning beauty, made even more so by the glow of elflight. Freyrík should have expected this—he'd seen his share of elven slaves serving at High Court and sold off in the markets—but nothing in his past could have prepared him to see, at this moment, a *female* elf.

Particularly one so young and small, a wispy maiden as light and lovely as dandelion down and surely no more threatening. She could not have killed sixteen of his men; the idea was preposterous.

A young sergeant stepped forward and clicked his heel in sharp salute. "The elven prisoners from Akrar, Your Highness."

Prisoners, plural? Yes, the elven woman's eyes were fixed upon a male across the runner, hanging bloody and beaten between two soldiers, his head slumped so low that all Freyrík could see of him was messy dark hair and a crossbow bolt jutting from his shoulder blade.

Freyrík turned back to the sergeant. "You call this one elf? There's no light about him."

The sergeant flushed but said, "He is, Your Highness." He grabbed a fistful of the elf's hair—nothing but cowlicks, Freyrík noted with amusement, for all the gravity of the occasion—and jerked the prisoner's head up. "Glow for your prince!"

Freyrík's breath caught as he looked upon the creature's face, so very like the female's: his eyes the same shade of green, his cheeks and lips and chin the same dazzling arrangement and shape. He was harder than she, in the lines about the jaw and brow, and darker as well—black hair to her red, bitterness and rage to her fear. And he stirred something within Freyrík that the female never could, that his sometimes-lover had just failed to, something immediate and hot and primal in a way he could never permit.

The elf blinked, squeezed his eyes closed, pried them open and turned them upon Freyrík. His exquisite face—too pretty by half to be human, surely—twisted into a sneer. He licked blood-caked lips and growled, "He is not *my* prince."

"Ayden, don't!" the female cried—apparently she had more sense than her companion—but it came too late: the sergeant slapped his open palm against the crossbow bolt and shouted, "I said *glow*!"

The elf threw his head back and screamed, and then suddenly he *was* glowing, much brighter than the female, so bright that Freyrík had to shade his eyes even as his personal guards rushed to shield him with their bodies. The soldiers holding the elf dropped him with startled yelps and cradled their hands to their chests. Freyrík smelled burnt flesh. Guards and soldiers trained blades on the creature, and one of the scalded soldiers kicked him hard enough to flip him onto his side.

"*Enough!*" Freyrík roared.

Every mouth in the hall fell still and every human head bowed in supplication. In the new silence, he could hear the female weeping "Please, stop!" over and over. Sometime during the uproar, she had torn free of her guard and knelt beside the male, who now lay curled as tightly as one could with his hands shackled behind him. He was bleeding all over the fine mosaic floor, his face twisted with pain so profound that Freyrík wondered if he even realized the female was there, focused upon him as though he were the entirety of her world.

He motioned his guards aside with a nod and added, calmer, "We are *not* brutes. There will be no more violence in this room today—" he looked pointedly from the soldiers to the guards to the elves and back, "from *anyone*. Is that clear?"

He was answered by a grudging chorus of "Yes, Your Highness" and a desperate, longing "*Please!*" from the female elf as a soldier dragged her back to her feet.

Another moment, and the struggle went out of her. She turned watery eyes to him and said in a voice watery to match, "Please, Sir Prince, he's badly hurt. He needs my help."

The female's distress seemed to rival even her companion's pain. "What is your name, child?" Freyrík asked, despite the distant certainty that this "child" had outlived him many times over.

"Ella," she said, and then with a little sniff, "Daell." Her companion shuddered, moaned, and her eyes darted back to his bloodied form. "Please, Sir Prince," she begged, "'tis my fault, all of it. Ayden was only protecting me. Please, let me go to him."

And truly, how anyone could ever deny this creature a single thing he had no idea, for he found himself nodding at the soldiers to let her go despite vague thoughts of sorcery and sixteen dead men.

The soldier holding her looked imploringly at the sergeant, who in turn looked at Freyrík. "Your Highness?"

It seemed his soldiers feared the same: lethal magic unleashed upon their heads. Yet if she were capable of such, would she not have struck already? A lifetime of war made it difficult to remember that not everyone had it in them to kill.

He looked upon Daell, so full of compassion, so very *feminine* in every way, and said to the soldier, "Let her go."

The instant the soldier loosed his grip, Daell threw herself to her knees beside her . . . brother? father? husband? *Gods, does it matter?* Ayden, she'd called him; beside Ayden. She coaxed him onto his stomach with soft words and shackled hands. For a moment, Freyrík wondered if she were a healer, but 'twas quickly evident from her wide-eyed faltering that she was no such thing. 'Twas equally evident that if love alone could mend bones, Ayden would be whole again in moments.

Daell closed her eyes, and the glow about her intensified. The soldiers retreated a step, and the guards who'd hastened to shield him earlier made to do so again. Freyrík stopped them with a curt wave. He would wager his life that the only harm on Daell's mind was the harm that she meant to undo.

She opened her eyes, the green half-lost behind a blazing silver aura, and wrapped trembling fingers round the blood-slicked bolt. Even through the elflight, Freyrík could see her blanch, and he stepped forward to catch her if she swooned.

She bent her head to Ayden and whispered, "Forgive me, brother"— well, that answered *that* question—and wrenched the bolt free.

Ayden screamed, and Freyrík shuddered in sympathy, wanting to hold *him* too, to silence his cries with a kiss and soothe away the blood and the hurt.

He stopped himself by main force of will, turned sharply, and took the throne.

Daell clamped her hands atop the gushing wound, her elflight growing brighter yet, and Freyrík could have sworn he'd heard . . . music? But then Ayden screamed again, and Daell cried out, "I'm sorry! I'm sorry! I don't know how it's supposed to sound!" She wiped at tears with the back of her wrist but still left a bloody smudge on one perfect cheek. "I can't . . . I don't know the bonesong, Ayden. I can't fix it if I—"

"Ella."

She fell silent at that single hoarse whisper, and no wonder, Freyrík thought, for though it brimmed with pain, he heard strength there to match. Ayden flexed his fingers behind his back until Ella—Daell— calmed slightly and grasped them in her own.

Freyrík, and indeed all his wary men, were held in such silent thrall by the unfolding scene that the elf's rasping voice seemed to echo through the hall: "Peace, Ella. Listen to the other one."

The meaning of this conversation was lost on Freyrík, but it seemed that Ella—Daell, befang it—understood, for she nodded and laid her head against Ayden's uninjured shoulder, closed her eyes and breathed deep for several long moments. "I hear it now," she whispered, her lips curling into a soft, secret smile that Freyrík suspected most men would kill to own. "I hear it."

Then she sat up and placed her hands atop Ayden's wound, and the both of them blazed so brightly that Freyrík saw spots clear through his clenched eyelids.

When he felt it safe to open his eyes again, brother and sister were sitting side to side, Ayden hunched over Ella's lap and Ella leaning upon his back, each looking for all the world like the only thing keeping the other from falling. Freyrík startled at the sight of Ayden's shoulder through his rent shirt, smooth skin lying whole atop sculpted muscle.

His gaze turned disbelievingly to Ella's hands, then to her face, where it stuck and would not come loose. She seemed too exhausted to speak, but she made known her gratitude with shining eyes and a graceful nod.

It occurred to him for the first time to ask, "And what of you, child? Are you hurt?"

Even as she shook her head, the sergeant stepped forward and bowed his own, saying, "No, Your Highness. I took great care to see her unsullied for you, though 'twas quite the test of forbearance, if one may say."

Freyrík clenched his teeth, and Ayden tensed in his sister's embrace, but Ella herself showed no signs of dismay. The innuendo seemed to have sailed right past her, gods be thanked for small favors.

He relaxed his jaw enough to say, "You showed wisdom, sergeant," and bit back the following *Else I would have extracted payment in flesh and blood and seed.*

The sergeant grinned wide beneath the perceived praise. "She's of fine stock, Your Highness, and never to grow much older. If one may be so bold as to wish you many a year of her pleasurable services, or the joy of the healthy coin she'll fetch at High Court . . ."

"One may not," Freyrík said curtly. He knew the man was angling for a reward, but that didn't stop his anger from rising, nor Ayden from sitting up and turning horrified eyes upon him.

"Sir Prince?" Now Ella was looking at him as well—not with fear, but with the shocked uncertainty of someone who'd not considered their future. "You mean to hold us in your service?"

The word, polluted by the sergeant's innuendo, sounded profane upon her lips.

Freyrík shook himself and set to explain that no, of course not: they were to be sold to the midlands, where the nobility had time for such frivolities as elven slaves; he had a war to fight, you see.

But somehow, the word "Yes" fell from his lips.

Ayden's stare felt as sharp as a blade at his throat.

"I understand," Ella said—except she obviously didn't—"You have spared our lives, and shown mercy. I would show my gratitude—"

"Ella, quiet!"

Ayden's voice, low and whip-crack sharp, drew Freyrík's gaze to him. The elf gazed back, his eyes clear and nearly free of the pain that had crippled him before. Freyrík shuddered under that stare as a warm, buzzing trickle formed in his chest and sank deep into his belly, where he stopped it by sheer force of will. But he knew that Ayden had seen through him; the revulsion on the elf's face was shadowed only by his desperation.

"Please, Prince," he said, and Freyrík heard how much it had cost him, to address him with such respect. "She doesn't know what she's saying. Please, let her go. She has done you no harm."

"No." Freyrík shook his head, more to clear it than to deny the request. "That is beyond my purview." And beyond his will, truth be told; ah, but he could tell the elf was seeing through him again.

"Then I beg of you," Ayden said, anxiety giving way to resignation, "whatever *service* you demand, demand it of me. If you—"

The elf paused, swallowed hard and dropped his gaze to the floor. Freyrík waited, spellbound, with a patience he'd never afforded his own men. When Ayden looked back up, there was steel in his eyes of a kind Freyrík knew well: a warrior's commitment to a hopeless battle.

"If you keep her safe," he continued, "I will do anything you ask of me. *Anything*. Do you understand?"

"Yes," Freyrík breathed, his head bobbing of its own accord despite all the blood fleeing from it in a rush. His hands clenched on the armrests of the throne. "Yes."

He cleared his throat and turned to his guards, fixing his gaze upon them lest it wander and lead him astray. "Take Daell to the north tower. See to her needs. She is to be accorded every hospitality as befits a lady."

Ella startled and sought out her brother's eyes, even as a palace guard tugged her from the floor. "Ayden?"

"It's all right, Ella. Go."

The bleakness in his tone made Freyrík glad he'd taken care not to look at him. He made the mistake of looking at Ella, though, and found her pleading eyes fastened upon him.

"What of my brother, Sir Prince?"

"He will fare well as long as he honors his promise," he said, keeping his tone deliberately soft to mitigate the harshness of his words. "And as long as you mind your conduct."

She seemed to believe him, for she nodded, and made no objection as the guard saw her off. Two more guards peeled away from their posts to follow. Freyrík bit back an imprudent chuckle: an escort of three was at once insufficient and far too cautious.

The sergeant reclaimed Freyrík's attention by clearing his throat. "Apologies, Your Highness, but . . ." He hesitated, bowing deep. "Isn't that a terrible danger?"

Freyrík exhaled sharply through his nose. *Patience. Not everyone had the benefit of High Court education.* "Those rooms were built of cut stone centuries ago," he said. "She cannot work her sorcery within their walls. 'Tis nature that answers to elven magic, not that which has been molded by human hand."

And oh, how the High Court gentry reveled in that fact.

"Besides," he added, "she would not risk her brother's life. And you—" he turned to Ayden, quenching his desire with an iron fist. "Soldier-killer. Your sister's life lies in *your* hands. Do take care not to murder anyone else if you can help it."

"Then do not give me a reason," Ayden growled, and though still he was slumped on floor, he reminded Freyrík of nothing more than a darker wolf.

Freyrík chose to ignore him, turning instead to the guard at his right. "The elf and I have much to discuss. Bring him to my chambers. See my attendants removed to safety, and post guards. I'll be along shortly."

He turned back to Ayden, taking measure of the pride in his eyes. "There will be no need for irons now; am I not right, elf?"

He'd meant it as a challenge, a test—one he'd expected Ayden to fail. Yet to his surprise, Ayden merely nodded.

The guard clicked his heel and hauled Ayden off the floor, much less gentle than his counterpart had been with Ella. Ayden winced, and Freyrík snapped, "Careful. He belongs to me now; I am the only one to decide if he is to be harmed."

"Apologies, Your Highness," the guard said, deferential but grudging. This once, in memory of the sixteen dead, Freyrík overlooked his tone.

Lord Commander Hákon entered the Great Hall with fresh guards in tow. Had Freyrík truly been so enthralled that he'd failed to notice the Captain of the Guard slipping out? Regardless, he was grateful for the reinforcements; with a flick of his wrist, he dispatched four of them to escort the elf.

With both elves gone from his sight, he once more deemed himself in full possession of his faculties. He nodded to the waiting soldiers, who were clearly disgruntled by the turn of events, and called forward his secretary.

"Lord Lini, see to it these men are rewarded for their courage: six months' pay, and a year from their conscription. Find out which of the dead had wives, and send two years' pay to the widows, along with my condolences."

Lord Lini acknowledged the order with a slight nod of the head and a "Yes, Your Highness." Beside him, the soldiers' bitterness gave way to elation: they chorused their thanks and clicked their heels in salute like a herd of stomping bulls.

Freyrík pressed his hand to his forehead, hoping to still his thoughts in the ruckus, but 'twas not to be. Finally he said, "Leave, all of you. Lord Lini, I would not be disturbed until morrow."

He retreated to his public office off the Great Hall, nodded to the attending page to shut the door, and sank into his chair. *Thank the gods, solitude at last.* He poured himself a glass of wine and peered into its depths, swirling it round and round without drinking.

What beneath the great shadow of the gods had he just gotten himself into?

# Chapter Three

reyrík struggled over his map table for a long hour, deploying and re-deploying figurines of the contingents he hoped the Aegis would send. A scattering of red pebbles represented the recent darker attacks: small groups of twisted animals that had terrorized some outlying village before dying at the hands of a patrol or some eager farm boys. Soon there would be more beasts—hundreds, thousands, breaking in a great wave upon his lands. The numbers wouldn't square no matter how he moved the figurines. Men would die in force.

Gods, he needed more troops. And not some hastily drafted merchants' sons, but practiced soldiers. Warriors like Ayden.

Now *there* was a fearsome weapon, if only he would strike where Freyrík pointed him. The creature had slaughtered sixteen trained men within moments; if he were unleashed upon the witless darkers, what grand devastation might he wreak? He would resent being used, true, but his sister's wellbeing would make fine incentive. Freyrík grimaced as he measured that gambit against the virtue of honor, but the numbers on the map table decided him. He would do what he must.

And what of the threat of a second elven war? He was inclined to believe what little he'd heard of Ella's tearful story. After all, his garrisons had received but this one alert of elven trespass, and only because some sharp-eyed grain merchant had watched the fair visitor since boyhood and never seen her age. That the merchant also claimed Ella had spelled his widowed neighbor, perhaps even brought about her death, Freyrík was less inclined to believe.

But the fact remained that an elf had been stealing regularly into his villages for decades at least, and another had just crossed over in open hostility for the first time in over two and a half centuries. Perhaps 'twas wishful thinking to believe that Ella and Ayden really were alone, and not the heralds of new hostilities between elves and humans.

Well, there was only one way to find out.

The four guards posted outside his rooms saluted sharply as Freyrík approached with his own personal guard of four. He stopped a hairsbreadth from his door and took a fortifying breath. No matter what greeted him beyond, he must keep his faculties tightly reined. The elf would be a challenge. Already he knew Freyrík's weakness toward him, and if he were anything like Freyrík, he would exploit it quite thoroughly.

Perhaps, then, he should delegate the interrogation to someone else, someone less involved—

*No.* He recognized this for cowardice and sliced its head clean off. This was *his* duty to perform, and if anything remained sacred in this befanged age, 'twas duty.

A protested command and a sharp rebuke saw that his personal guard, who would gladly shadow him into the befanged privy during his annual spell as prince-regent, remained in the hall. Then, feeling a bit ridiculous with eight armed men at his back, he threw open his doors.

And was greeted with an almost comic sight.

Ayden was sitting stiffly in a highback chair at the center of the drawing room. Around him, six more palace guards stood bristling with drawn weapons, their eyes glued to the elf as if he were a darker snake poised to strike.

Freyrík's military instincts reared. He scoured the elf with a stare, but all he saw was an exhausted, wounded creature, sitting straight through force of pride alone and masking his tension with a strained sneer. Some far-sighted guard had washed the blood and filth from him, or rather doused him with a few bucketfuls of water, from the looks of it. He'd been given a fresh pair of breeches, thank the gods, but no shirt—so much for Freyrík keeping his thoughts in check. All that expanse of fair skin, that lean, muscled torso . . .

The guards snapped to attention when they realized who had entered. Freyrík yanked his stare from the elf and turned it to them, but he spared them no words, merely raised an eyebrow and waited. One by one, the guards sheathed their weapons sheepishly.

"Leave us," Freyrík said when they were done, and at their obvious hesitation he added, "Wait outside." *With the other eight guards*, he thought, and clamped his lips tight; the Prince Regent did not *chortle*.

But the sight of Ayden's thin amusement sobered him. He caught the elf's eye with a hard stare and said loudly, "If he harms me, kill the girl."

Ayden's amusement disappeared with the twitching of a muscle in his jaw, the clenching of hands in his lap. Rage and fear subsumed the bravado in his eyes, but otherwise he made no move. In his mind, Freyrík offered him a quick bow of respect for his restraint.

When the room emptied, Ayden slumped in his chair, unwilling or unable to keep up the pretense anymore.

Freyrík surveyed him for a long moment. "You look like a man convinced he's about to be tortured."

Ayden's eyes narrowed. "Aren't I?"

"The choice lies with you," Freyrík said, though he could hardly imagine this creature choosing any but the most difficult path.

Ayden held his stare a moment longer, then bowed his head—less an act of contrition, Freyrík suspected, than a shielding of expression. He wondered what hidden emotions had graced those rich green eyes, for they blazed only with suspicion when Ayden looked up again.

"What have you done with Ella?"

"Her needs are being seen to, as with any guest in this house." In fact, a battalion of footmen and maids were still busy transforming two officers' rooms into a lady's apartment in the north turret; Ella herself was asleep in a third room, so soundly that even the bellow of a darker bull wouldn't wake her. Freyrík knew; he'd tried before coming here. "I am a man of my word, elf. Your sister shall not be harmed as long as you obey me."

Ayden's nod was nearly too slight to see. He sank further in the chair, and for a moment Freyrík feared he'd spill to the floor. He stepped closer unthinkingly, knee to knee but not quite daring to touch. Ayden tensed under his shadow and pressed back against the chair, hugging crossed arms to his chest. The motion called Freyrík's attention to a soaking bandage on the elf's left bicep, and he reached for it with a frown, but in the space of a blink the elf had captured his wrist in a startling grip, fingers digging into the tender space below his thumb.

Freyrík just barely swallowed a shout for the guards. Now was not the time to show fear or weakness. Nor was it the time for a flexing of sword-arms; pride would quickly turn this bloody. Nay, he would campaign on the battlefield of wit and will instead.

"Thus fares the promise of an elf," he said, forcing a wry smile despite the growing threat of his thumb coming out of joint.

Ayden bared his teeth in a quick, silent growl, but a moment later he let go of Freyrík's wrist. He still flinched when touched, but did not object when Freyrík pulled his arm up to examine it.

The elf's skin seemed to smolder under Freyrík's fingers as he carefully worked loose the bandage, exposing a gash that no longer bled but still looked raw. When he leaned in, the scent of the elf hit him like a lance to the chest: blood and sweat and the roads, yes, but also a strong hint of forest loam and fallen leaves riding in on his quickening breath.

Only when Ayden squirmed did Freyrík realize he'd closed his eyes and nearly touched his lips to the elf's shoulder. He straightened up to see Ayden panting hard through his nose, teeth clenched, head turned resolutely away.

Freyrík cleared his throat. "Is this my men's doing?"

"Yes," Ayden spat, but before Freyrík's anger could flare at his guards' disobedience, Ayden added, "When they captured me." He glanced back with an echo of his previous sneer. "Your men have poor aim, Prince."

"Hmm." Freyrík was more concerned about his own discomfort as he tried to rebind the wound without touching skin to skin, grateful for the many layers of formal clothes he wore. 'Twould not do for Ayden to think he was aroused by the sight of the wound, when in fact it was the wiry muscle, the smooth skin, the intimate angle between shoulder and neck that fascinated him so—

And shouldn't he be interrogating the elf?

"Does it hurt?" he asked.

At this Ayden jerked away from Freyrík's hold. "Why would you care?"

Well asked, Freyrík supposed.

He took a subtle step back, putting some distance between them to clear his head. 'Twas a blessing the elf could not know how disconcerted he truly felt, or how reluctant he was to ask his next question, which would almost certainly lead to . . . unpleasantries.

Another moment of silence, and Ayden sat up straight and defiant. "I grow weary of you, human. Ask your questions, do with me what you so clearly wish to do, but gods be cracked, hurry up. Even *I* grow old waiting for you to come to the point."

Freyrík huffed, amused despite himself. "Very well. As you're so eager to oblige, you may start by telling me who you are."

Ayden blinked. And blinked again. Squared his shoulders and said, "I am Ayden *barn* Vaska *barn* Alarra *barn* Oneisi *barn* Hilmir *barn* Tívar the Blessed."

Freyrík gave him a mock bow. "Your recital does honor to your forefathers."

"Fore*mothers*, you tone-deaf imbecile."

Mothers? Truly? Or was the elf merely taunting him?

"Well, human? We are introduced. Are you satisfied?"

"Not so easily," Freyrík said, feeling his groin tighten at the double meaning. "Tell me more."

"What more would you know?"

*You*, Freyrík thought, and *Everything*, but his mind got hold of his tongue in time, and instead he said, "Start at the beginning."

Ayden's eyebrows arched high above his wide green eyes. "Do I look a storyteller to you? Choose a better question."

Freyrík bit back a smile. He *had* chosen his question carefully; surprising, really, how few could answer it without fluster. But, "You forget yourself, elf. 'Tis not for you to command me. I *will* have your answer."

"I've no answer to give."

Freyrík unsheathed his dagger and held it up to Ayden's eyes. "Then you leave me no choice but to carve it from you by blade."

He had anticipated a number of different responses to this threat—including the possibility of attack—but it had never occurred to him that the elf would simply throw his head back and laugh.

"Oh, *human*," Ayden said, pushing the dagger away as if 'twere a child's toy, "you cannot lie to an elf! I can *hear* your feelings!"

Startled—nay, rattled to his very core at the mere *possibility* of such power—Freyrík stiffened as his mind raced through everything he'd felt since he'd entered the room. Amusement, arousal, anger . . . no doubt the elf could sense his current agitation, too, if the creature spoke true. He wanted to punch the smirk clear off Ayden's face, but 'twould be foolish to let the elf strip him of control. No, if Ayden could truly see through him, he would simply have to match emotion to action.

"You hear my feelings?" he said quietly. Then he lunged into Ayden's space, grabbed him by the chin and pressed the tip of the blade between his collarbones, just hard enough to draw blood. "Then hear me when I say that I will do what I must to protect these lands. You will tell me who you are and why you've come here, and I will know if *you* lie. Do you hear *that*, elf?"

Ayden held his stare as a single drop of blood rolled slowly down the dagger's blade, and Freyrík cursed under his breath, bracing himself to follow through.

But then the elf jerked his head away, sagging as if the tiny puncture wound had drained him of all his fluids and air. "Fine. You may have my story; it is of little consequence. But I will allow you to kill me and Ella both before I betray my people."

Freyrík nodded his understanding, one warrior to another. Then he took a step back, resheathed his knife, and settled against the sofa to listen.

Ayden knew not what to make of the human's question. He felt like he'd been dropped in the middle of an open field: no visible paths, all directions equally open, and the gods knew what pitfalls lay where. He had no intention of tripping, though, or of leading the prince anywhere significant. In fact, if he were feeling stronger, he'd have taken grim satisfaction in wearying the human with every minute detail of his childhood—from the name of every plant he'd discovered, to the song of every animal. No, better not to mention elfsong at all.

Yet he had to start somewhere.

"I grew up in Kappi Dómr," he said, skimming two centuries with that single statement. "My mother is an artist, a painter; she holds such love for frivolous things. My father was an—" advisor to one of the Fallen, but no, that would prompt difficult questions, "—a great elf."

He prattled on about his life, leading the prince in meaningless circles. The human, fallen gods be praised, never tried to steer him toward subjects of greater import. He spoke of joining the army to his mother's crushing protests; of taking two decades' leave to travel the known world, as the young were wont to do; of following his family to the Council's seat at Rád Dómr in the time of the Great Peace.

"Which, of course, you humans had to ruin with your betrayal," he couldn't help but add.

The prince hardly seemed contrite as he said, "So your people claim."

Anger trumpeted through Ayden, driving the weariness from his muscles. "What else would you call murdering the Council in cold blood?"

"A convenient lie," the human said easily, but before Ayden could jump to his feet or whip up his song into a wounding heat, the prince's own song flared harshly. "And what would you call giving birth to a race of dark beasts that have spilled our blood ever since?"

Ayden felt his lips twist into a cold smile as he said, "Justice."

He winced as the prince's song crashed upon his inner ear in a cacophony of drums and shrieking strings. "But the Ferals are not our doing!" he cried over the mental noise. "'Twas Nature herself who raised the Hunter's Call against you!"

The prince's song gradually folded back round him, and Ayden felt a traitorous stab of admiration as he realized that throughout the rage, the prince had remained motionless but for tensed muscles and quickened breath.

"So your people claim," the prince repeated coldly. "But 'tis of no import now. On with your tale, elf."

Ayden stifled a groan and turned his weary tongue back to his stories of nothingness. He skipped his father's death in the War of Betrayal— 'twas too private, and still as raw as the wound in his arm despite near three bitter centuries' passing. Instead he spoke of his dispatch to the front lines of the war, of being captured once before ("You hold no candle to their skills of persuasion, Prince"), and of returning to border patrols when the war was ended, this time with skills enough to tread alone. His voice softened when he recounted Ella's antics and strange beliefs about humans, and that brought him to her last, fateful crossing of the border.

"The rest of it you will need to ask of your men," he finally said, "for I spent much of these last days senseless."

The prince nodded once, pursed his lips. His thoughts, no doubt, were circling round and round Ayden's story, searching for discrepancies and exploitable slips. Yet he would find none. Ayden had been too careful.

Perhaps the prince had reached the same conclusion, for his song lost its predatory edge, relaxing into fascination and slithering back toward arousal—and crack it all, what was it about Ayden that the human found so appealing, anyway?

But then the prince gave himself a shake, and the timbre of his song changed once more, determination riding in afresh on every note. He stood and stepped too close for comfort. Ayden could not help flinching back, though he scorned himself for it. His neck protested the sharp angle it took to return the man's stare.

"So. Your people spy often on our movements."

"We do not *spy*. We merely watch the border to ensure no foolishness on your part."

"Indeed, and I'm merely having a charming discussion with a new friend."

Ayden choked on his response, half snort and half snarl, but managed to hold back reckless words. As furious as the prince made him, he had to admit the man was clever. Besides, a war of sarcasm would get him nowhere; best stick to logic.

"Humans have already tried to flee the Ferals into our lands. What will stop them from demanding passage with drawn swords next time? In our place, would you not wish to be prepared?"

The prince made no reply, but his song wavered, and Ayden could tell his last question had hit the mark.

"And yet *you* are the one who's crossed the border now," the prince said. "Perhaps your people think differently, but under Aegean law, 'watching' and 'trespassing' are as different as man and elf."

"I told you, I only went to save Ella from your soldier beasts."

"Indeed." The prince thankfully paced away, then turned back to him. "Let us revisit that part of your tale, where by your own admission your sister has been stealing across the border for over a hundred-year."

Ayden groaned and closed his eyes. He needed to sleep. Crack it, he needed *salt*. "She was only visiting with friends."

"Ah, my apologies, I'd forgotten. These friends, then, what have they been telling her?"

"How should I know?"

The prince strode up to him again, and crack it all, but again Ayden failed to control a flinch. This time, the human's hands—strong and battle-hardened—gripped the backrest of the chair on either side of Ayden's head. The prince leaned in until his forehead nearly touched Ayden's. How could a man's eyes be such a clear blue?

And just how addled was he now to be thinking such things?

"You trifle with me," the prince said, and from this close, his low voice reverberated through Ayden's flesh and sent a shiver clean through him. "Do not. What did your sister want with them?"

Ayden swallowed, shuddering when the motion drew the human's stare to his throat. "Just . . . to meet them. To learn their ways, perhaps. She makes no sense to me either, human."

The prince lingered in Ayden's space, breathing hard of Ayden's own air, one wavy lock of hair tickling Ayden's left cheek. Ayden could see nothing beyond the man's face, strangely handsome in its brutish, stubble-roughened way, and gods but he wished it gone that he could think beyond the hunger wailing like an infant in the prince's head.

The prince licked his lips and swallowed hard, his throat muscles flexing. Ayden fought an overwhelming urge to twist away, knowing that any moment now the prince would grab his head and force a kiss—

But instead the human wrenched himself away and took two long strides from the chair, putting his broad back to Ayden. Ayden breathed out a shaky sigh and scrubbed at his face with both hands, not sure what brought him more relief: the distance now between them, or that the prince at last seemed to believe him.

. . . Or not. The prince whirled back and pinned him with an unyielding stare. "How many other spies have crossed the border?"

"What? Ella is not—!"

The human's hand lashed out like a scorpion's tail, and pain exploded in Ayden's cheek a second before he crashed to the floor, dazed. He'd not even heard it coming.

"At last, the human shows his teeth," he mumbled round the blood in his mouth, regretting it almost as soon as he'd spoken. Another such blow would surely render him unconscious . . . though for the answers he'd given so far, perhaps that would only benefit his people. "I'd begun to think you had none, *Prince.*"

He heard clothes rustling, and braced himself for a kick that never came. When he glanced up, the prince was coolly putting the chair aright—he must have knocked it down when he'd fallen.

"Get up, elf."

Gladly, Ayden thought; but his ears were ringing and the floor was churning beneath him as if seized by an earthquake. How long since he'd last eaten, drank, slept rather than lay unconscious in the back of a moving cart? How much of his blood had been spilled, how much of his mind's voice spent by singing out for that lightning?

How much longer could he keep this up?

He couldn't sense the prince's song over the faint roar in his mind, but he certainly did sense the hands on him, strong fingers pressing deliberately into the wound on his left bicep, hauling him off the floor and back into the chair. A whine of fear wormed through his own song, but he wrestled it down.

The human leaned in closer, cheek to cheek, his unrelenting grip making Ayden's eyes water. "It appears teeth is all you understand," he said, hot breath puffing across the shell of Ayden's ear. "I do not wish to harm you, elf. But do not mistake that for me not knowing how."

Another squeeze, and pain sparked white-hot from Ayden's shoulder to his fingertips.

"Now," the human said over Ayden's cry, his tone as sharp with restrained rage as the fingers digging into Ayden's wound, "you will answer me, or I shall take this conversation to Ella. Do I make myself clear?"

Whatever fear Ayden felt for himself seemed suddenly insignificant, a mere drop amongst his sudden rush of panic. He nodded furiously.

Yet still the human clawed at his wound, and pain crested into agony that left him moaning on every exhale. "*Speak aloud* when you answer me. Do I make myself clear?"

"Yes," Ayden panted, barely able to spit the word out without unleashing the scream welling behind it. "Yes!"

"Good."

The pressure disappeared at last, though the pain lagged long behind, stubborn and unforgiving. Ayden watched the prince flick blood from his fingers and swallowed hard to keep dry heaves at bay. He knew not if the nausea swirling in his mind and gut was his or the human's. Both, he suspected.

The human's voice drew Ayden's attention back to his face. "How many spies besides Ella?"

Ayden recoiled, reeling with helpless frustration. "How can you think her a spy! The only reason she crossed—"

The moment the words left his mouth, the human was atop him again, his knee in Ayden's groin and one hand round his throat, the other hand tearing back into his wound. Ayden thrashed, screamed as white flame scorched through nerves and sinews, fanning into his head and back as he arched against the prince's hold like an overdrawn bow.

"How many!"

"None! None would care enough to do it! The only elf foolish enough to bother with your beastly lot is a—" he choked on a watery gasp as the fingers round his arm tightened "—is a sweet girl who believed there was something worth saving in your traitorous race!"

His unspoken words hung between them: *And look what her compassion bought her.*

The prince's fingers fell away and Ayden sagged, shuddering and panting. When the tremors faded, he lifted his right hand—the left one would no sooner obey him now than the writhing tongue of fire it currently resembled—to wipe the wetness from his eyes. He could hear nothing of the prince's emotions over his own howling pain, but he thought he'd glimpsed in his eyes . . . Well, he wasn't quite sure *what*, really. Cautious belief, he thought, and regret, and . . .

And gods crack the brute for being able to gaze upon Ayden in all his abject misery—such as he had caused, no less—and still envision pleasures with him. He was staring again as if transfixed, standing far too close, reaching out to touch . . .

Ayden jerked back, and the human startled too but in the opposite direction, leaving a good two feet of space between them. The human turned abruptly, poured himself a glass of water from the pitcher on the tea table, and downed it so quickly that Ayden thought—hoped—he would choke.

Gods, but the water looked good.

The human poured another glass and turned back, caught Ayden staring as it was halfway to his lips. He eyed Ayden shrewdly, then brought the glass back down and rolled it between his palms, back and forth, making the water slosh gently with a murmur of music fit for the fallen gods themselves—and may they crack the human *again* for playing on Ayden's thirst.

Though 'twas fitting punishment, perhaps, for Ayden betraying his thirst in the first place.

He ripped his eyes from the water glass, but they landed instead on the prince's lips, glistening with moisture, on the prince's tongue that darted out to catch a stray drop . . .

"Well?" Ayden choked out, forcing his gaze up to the prince's eyes. "You have your answers, human. Are we done here?"

The prince took a sip of water, heedless of Ayden's blood smeared all across the glass. "No, not yet. Tell me, how many elves infest the woodlands at our border?"

Ayden found the direction of that question frankly terrifying. This human's people outnumbered Ayden's by orders of magnitude. If the human ordered a raid into elven lands, not even his people's elfsong and knowledge of the forest would prevent a great many deaths. He must put a stop to this, right now.

"Thousands."

The human's hands tightened round the water glass, and a shiver of fear like tiny cymbals crashed across Ayden's inner ear. "What manner of warriors? Swordsmen? Archers?" A pause, then, "Sorcerers?"

"As I am: all three and more."

That was clearly the wrong thing to say, for the human slammed the glass down on the tea table and leaned in close, grabbing Ayden by the hair and snarling into his ear, "What did I say about your lies!"

Ayden shoved him away in a fit of fury to match the human's, but then forced himself still, horrified by his action. "Well what did you expect of me!" he demanded. "I told you I would not betray my people."

"And I told you," the human growled, fisting Ayden's hair again and pulling his dagger from its sheath, "that I would stop at nothing to protect mine."

The blade nestled behind the shell of Ayden's ear and Ayden froze, holding his breath as cold steel sent a shiver down the side of his neck. This time, the human's song grated with equal parts disgust and determination.

"You may heal quickly, elf, but I doubt even you can grow a new ear."

He had the right of that. Ayden swallowed, and the fine muscles behind his ear moved against the blade. He closed his eyes; the pain he could endure, but not the sight of his own ear falling to the carpet.

"Tell me, when do your people march on mine, and in what force?"

He heard each word acutely—never was one's ear more keen than when it might be hearing its last—but their joined meaning eluded him, for his mind rejected its absurdity. Yet that *was* what the human had asked, was it not—when elfkind would launch a second war?

That was the secret he meant to pry from Ayden at any cost?

Ayden burst into laughter.

Thankfully, his response shocked the human into releasing him rather than cutting off his ear.

Ayden sprawled back in the chair, laughing so hard he could barely breathe. "Oh, human!" he wheezed, nearly choking on the tension as it drained from him. "Is that your fear? That we'd invade your lands?"

He looked up into the prince's face through teary eyes, and the affronted scowl there nearly undid him all over again. Gods, he was past tired, to be laughing at a time like this.

Especially when the human clearly found no humor in his words. In fact, the prince's song was whipping into a steely crescendo that would surely climax in violence—

But even in the face of that, Ayden could not stop. He held up a placating hand, begging a moment. "Do you believe," he gasped out, "do you truly believe we have nothing better to do than trouble ourselves with your pitiful, dying race?" He managed to contain himself to a snicker, a few hiccups, and added, "Especially when the Ferals do so well on their own? No, human, they do not need our help!" He wiped at leaking eyes and shook his head, his whole body trembling with laughter and the effort to contain it.

The human studied him in stony silence for many long moments, jaw clenched and face pinched. Ayden's dismissal of his fears had clearly insulted him, but wending through the prince's anger was relief so profound that Ayden felt it as his own. Or maybe it really was his own; the gods knew he hadn't been looking forward to being carved up like some grass-eater destined for the supper table.

"Are you quite finished?" the human asked, but though Ayden nodded and bit into his fist, still he snorted once, twice, a third time, his shoulders twitching in restraint.

The human sighed, lifted his eyes to the ceiling and shook his head, but his anger was fading. Perhaps he realized that Ayden could no sooner control this now than the human could control the weather. Or perhaps the human's own relief was making him a little giddy too, though it did not show on the outside.

He did, however, pick up the glass of water and thrust it against Ayden's chest. 'Twas the last thing Ayden had expected, and he fumbled and nearly dropped it. But once his hands had wrapped round the glass, he chugged the water in a single breath. It was gone impossibly fast—surely the glass held more than that?—and did nothing for his thirst but bring it to stark, demanding attention.

At least the drink had drowned the laughter, but his body continued to betray him, for now he found himself holding the glass out in a silent request for more.

The human jerked his chin at the pitcher and said, "I know not the ways of your lands, elf, but under this roof, a prince does not wait upon a prisoner."

That nearly set Ayden laughing again, but he was too focused on his needs, now that the human had given him leave to indulge them. Yet when he stood, the floor bucked beneath his feet and sent him stumbling to all fours, the glass flying from splayed fingers and rolling across the carpet.

He glared up at the human, daring him to speak so much as one mocking word. But the prince merely pinched the bridge of his nose and shook his head again, then stooped to pluck the glass from the floor. He refilled it and handed it to Ayden, who gulped it down eagerly.

The prince was peering at him as if seeing him for the first time. "Have they fed you at all this past week? No, of course not. I'll have something sent up."

Ayden dropped his scathing reply in favor of a loud protest when he was scooped off the floor (or rather, he thought he protested; 'twas hard to concentrate with the water sloshing so in his stomach), but he was too weary to struggle against the strong arms that cradled him—fallen gods have mercy—to the human's chest.

They passed through a set of double doors he'd not noticed before and into a cool, shuttered room. A moment of dizziness, and Ayden found himself dumped on the edge of an oversized bed. The mattress dipped under him, softer even than the roving-stuffed bedding waiting for him back home.

"Don't bleed on my sheets," the prince warned as he disappeared through yet another door.

Ayden wondered how he was supposed to control that, even if he'd wanted to. 'Twas the prince's fault that he was bleeding again, in any case. Gods, but he was tired! How sweet it would be to lay his head upon the pillows, close his eyes and simply—

The human returned with a water basin and fresh strips of linen, took a seat by Ayden's side, and started washing his arm as if he weren't the one who'd mauled it in the first place.

Ayden's clouded thoughts and weary tongue refused to reconcile, and so all that made it past his lips was, "Why?"

"You've told me what I need to know," the prince said, trading the sodden cloth for the linen and rebinding the wound. His hands moved deftly, but even their light touch left Ayden stupid with pain after the damage so recently done. For a moment, whatever words spilled from the human's mouth flowed right past his ears.

"... no threat to me now." The prince tied off the linen and smoothed a hand over Ayden's shoulder, down his arm. Something shifted then within the human, and his hand lingered a moment too long. A song of need—the first hesitant touch of the bow to a violin's deepest strings— slithered like a millipede through Ayden's head. He fought the urge to recoil.

"Eat and rest, Ayden," the human said—and Ayden did not, for one moment, miss the sudden use of his name—"and I promise you that our next meeting won't be the slightest bit unpleasant."

# Chapter Four

The elf had fallen asleep, or perhaps unconscious, before Freyrík finished washing the blood from his hands. He seemed nearly swallowed by the bed, pale limbs a striking contrast to the burgundy sheets upon which he lay, body tucked tight into one corner and twitching with the occasional shiver. Freyrík longed to cover the poor creature, but he knew better—touching such a warrior in his sleep would be as wise as poking a sleeping darker bear. But watching was safe. And my, how lovely Ayden was with all the spite and hatred smoothed from his face, with the pain and anger fallen away.

*And with his befanged tongue stilled . . . at least from speech.*

Freyrík suppressed a chuckle and peeled himself from his bedside before the urge to join the elf overwhelmed him. He ordered food sent up, simple things that would not upset the elf's stomach after standing empty so long. Then he dismissed all but four guards, two within his drawing room and two in the hall, and left for his public office.

'Twas time for the midday meal already, but he doubted he could eat—he was exhausted, jittery with a wholly inappropriate but undeniably ferocious sexual charge, and shaking from a battle high despite having wielded no sword. Ah, but that wasn't exactly true, was it. He'd simply wielded a sword of a different kind. He liked to think he'd won.

'Twas a shame the cost of victory was so high.

But that was behind him now, never to be dwelled upon again. No, now he would share his better self with Ayden, perhaps even manage to teach him that not all humans were—how did that quaint epithet go?—a beastly lot.

And he would take great satisfaction in proving it, in seeing Ayden writhe in pleasure beneath his hands and mouth and manhood, in erasing all memories of harshness with the care and generosity of his love.

His brother would call him a soft-hearted fool and suggest—again—a wife or a new consort. Yet the man surely knew by now that both would fail to satisfy.

Speaking of Berendil . . .

Freyrík picked up a quill and a palm-sized square of parchment designed for carrier by pigeon. It left little space for niceties, but he possessed the well-practiced hand of a scholar and could fit much onto such notes.

*My Dear Brother,*

*I fear I must begin with grave news: a Surge gathers. Reports of darker attacks have come all week from Eine and Háls. They are small yet, but you and I know only too well what lies in store. The next cycle shall see much human blood spilt.*

*The battle maps tell a grim story. I cannot hope to protect the whole of the western foothills, and without more troops, I fear this wave may sweep right past us and break upon the midlands at last.*

*Brother, we must have men from the Aegis, four battalions at least. Infantry and archers, cavalry and falconers and fighting dogs. I know the Aegis is hard-pressed against the Council of Eight, but you must help him impress the danger upon those soft-bellied fools.*

He paused, stared at the empty inch of parchment remaining: large enough to inform Berendil of the elves, but too small to explain why they should not be sold, at least of yet. Nay, no need to worry his brother over a situation well in hand.

He bent his head over the parchment again and penned his parting salutations:

*I count the days until the Harvest Festival and your return. Your people miss their king. I miss my king.*

*May the gods bless you ever strong and wise, dear brother. My eternal love and fealty to the Aegis Exalted and to you, my lieges.*

*Freyrík*

He dusted the ink with pounce, rolled the letter into a carrier tube, and summoned a page to see it off to the aviary.

"By fastest bird," he instructed the messenger. "Then summon the Council."

They would wish to know what he'd learned.

"Counselors!" Freyrík shook his head and pursed his lips in rebuke lest they twist into an unbidden grin—twelve of the most distinguished military and civilian minds in all the Farr kingdom, all turned to gossiping scullery maids by mere mention of the elves. "Look, I have told you all there is to tell of the creatures, and I would remind you that more pressing issues are at hand."

The air of amusement fell away quickly as Freyrík turned their discussion toward the gathering Surge. His generals huddled round the map table while he spoke of the numbers and readiness of current forces, potential plans, supply lines, coin to fund the campaign.

"Additional forces from the midlands should arrive—" if even but one god took mercy upon their bedraggled race "—just in time for the cresting. We shall reconvene in three days' time to lay down our final stratagem. I would prefer," he added with a flat smile, catching each councilman's eye, "that when my brother comes home, he still has a kingdom to rule."

He dismissed his generals then, sparing them from the day-to-day affairs of state, keeping only his secretary, the Lord Chancellor, the Keeper of the Privy Purse, and the handful of dukes currently residing at court. Talk moved toward the blessedly mundane: harvest yields, the Harvest Festival, tax collection, the annual conscription list, and the wedding of his niece to the second prince of Kali, to further cement the crucial friendship with their neighboring kingdom. Despite the tedium, Freyrík meant to set all the kingdom's affairs in order before his brother's return for the Festival.

The Council dispersed for the evening meal, but Freyrík excused himself from the Great Hall dinner, for he desperately needed some time alone. All throughout the Council meeting, thoughts of Ayden had crowded his head, and he'd kept them at bay with a steel fist. But now they threatened to flood his mind with the force of a mental Surge. At least *these* thoughts were far from dark . . .

"Your Highness?"

Freyrík turned to the familiar voice. "Lord Commander. Were you not headed for the Great Hall?"

The Captain of the Guard hesitated, then gestured toward a side chamber and said, "A word if you would, My Prince."

Freyrík pushed back thoughts of Ayden sleeping in his bed, eyelashes casting fan-shaped shadows upon high cheeks— "Of course," he said, and if his voice was harder than he'd intended, well, so were other parts of him.

Commander Hákon sent away the page manning the chamber doors with a single glance, then closed them behind him. Another moment of hesitation before he turned back to Freyrík, then, "I beg forgiveness if I give offense, Your Highness, but I feel I must know your plans toward the elven prisoners."

Freyrík allowed his eyes to close, only for a moment, as he entertained his plans for Ayden: gently undressing the elf, washing every inch of him in his own tub, trailing wet fingers with kisses . . .

But he was fairly certain the commander's concerns lay elsewhere. He cleared his throat and said, "My plans, Commander Hákon?"

"As you've said, Sire, this battle will not turn in our favor. The elves could buy us much if we—"

"Nay, Commander. The Aegis will support us, as he always does. And I've other plans for the elves."

Commander Hákon bowed his head. "I would not begrudge Your Highness any pleasure, nor 'tis my place to do so. But if one might suggest . . ." He paused, and it occurred to Freyrík that a man whose guidance he'd trusted since childhood now seemed incapable of looking him in the eye. "Keep him for a short while, Your Highness, sate your desires, and then sell him to the midlands."

Freyrík chuffed, shook his head. As if he could ever sate his desires with a creature such as Ayden in a short while . . . or even a long while. He had no intention of pursuing that line of thought, however, at least not now. "You mistake me, Commander. My plans would see the male elf in battle with us."

Commander Hákon's head snapped up, eyes wide and mouth agape, but he possessed the discipline to hold the worst of his shock from his tongue. "Does Your Highness not think that dangerous?"

"He does not," Freyrík said shortly.

Commander Hákon bowed his head again, but his eyes found Freyrík's nonetheless. "What then of the female? She alone could fetch—"

"No," Freyrík snapped, clenching his jaw against thoughts of Ella passed from one nobleman's bed to the next, forced into debaucheries he doubted she even possessed the vocabulary to describe. "She is my hold on the male. She will remain here."

Freyrík could have sworn he heard the commander's teeth gnashing. "Should we not at least take them to High Court to have their magic bound?"

Again Freyrík shook his head. "I would entrust such valuables to none but my closest advisors, and you are all needed for more important matters just now—the coming Surge, for example?"

"'Tis true, Your Highness, but my first concern is for your own wellbeing—"

Freyrík silenced him with a raised hand. "I appreciate your dedication, Commander." And no doubt Berendil had warned him that any harm befalling his little brother in his absence would be revisited upon the commander tenfold. "Now I must also demand your obedience in this matter. I hold the elves tightly reined, and the male *will* serve in battle."

The commander pulled himself straight and clicked his right heel. "Yes, My Prince."

"Good. I daresay we'll find him more valuable than a hundred armored horses. And I assure you that when the Surge has ebbed, if there is still a need, I will take them for binding myself."

Commander Hákon bowed his head once more, and Freyrík nodded his dismissal, anxious to make good his escape at last. But, "Lord Hákon?"

"Yes, Your Highness?"

Freyrík paused, debating his words, and finally settled on: "One would keep this discussion private. The Council will be notified of my plans in the fullness of time."

And there would be the darkers to pay when that happened, no doubt. But in the meanwhile, Freyrík had other plans with which to concern himself. He barely waited for the Lord Commander's confirmation before exiting the chamber and heading for his office, and if he chose the public one instead of the private study in his rooms, 'twas merely because he wished to peruse some documents of state.

Three hours later, Freyrík was still pouring over his papers, though to claim he'd accomplished three (or even one) hours' work would be a falsehood. His mind turned again and again to his rooms and to the pleasures that awaited him there, but he kept telling himself 'twas important to give Ayden time to recover from the fury and the pain of the interrogation. Surely the elf needed more than a simple afternoon's nap.

But in his calmer moments, he recognized this as an excuse. The truth was that *he* did not wish to face Ayden's fury and pain. Nor was he yet prepared to face his own response to the elf, for though a part of him believed he could keep a hold of himself, another part of him did not— and did not wish to, either. And 'twas unhealthy, perhaps even unnatural, how often and how thoroughly his thoughts veered thus. He could not afford such distractions.

Perhaps some time and distance would cause them to lessen. Perhaps he should sleep this night with Lady Drífa and their newly toddling son instead. *That* was where his mind should be: on the future of the kingdom.

Ayden stopped pretending at sleep and sat up in bed as soon as the prince had left the bedroom. 'Twas perhaps one of the hardest things he'd ever done, fighting the pull of soft mattress and warm blankets, the false security of the canopy overhead and the curtains waiting to be drawn down the sides. But as he'd lain there with his eyes closed and his senses taut and quivering, night-terror images of what he'd soon endure in that very bed plagued his mind.

He couldn't stay there another second.

But that didn't mean he couldn't make himself comfortable elsewhere. He forced himself to his feet, then grabbed the blankets and sheets and pulled, stripping the bed to the mattress and forming a nest in the far corner of the bedroom. Two walls to his back, body cocooned once more in soft warmth, he closed his eyes and fell instantly into darkness.

He came awake startled and groping for a weapon that was not there, but the lack of it didn't stop the guard who'd entered the room from starting and drawing his own sword. Ayden wondered idly what would happen if he shouted "BOH!," but the fair certainty it would end in his swift and violent death held him back from experimenting.

"Food," the guard said with the typical eloquence of his kind.

Ayden followed him to the drawing room, where a tray sat on a tea table. He didn't trust even his ravenous appetite to withstand the loathful stares of the guards, so he picked up the tray, cursing his trembling hands, and carried it back to the prince's bedroom. 'Twas with fair pleasure that he gave the door a little kick behind him, closing it upon the guards' half-hearted protests.

Once alone, he let the tray clatter to a bedside table and tore off the plate covers. A bowl of strained broth, another bowl with cooked oats, and a third one filled with a watery mash that smelled like apples and tasted the same when he dipped in a finger to try it.

No salt anywhere.

"Gods be cracked!" he shouted, hurling a silver plate-cover against the wall. It landed with a great clatter but stubbornly refused to dent. He nearly followed it with the whole of his tray, but held back for the surety that no more food would be coming—and that his hunger would compel him to his hands and knees, licking oats from the cracking walls.

He clenched the bowl of broth in his hands, brought it to his lips and forced himself to drink slowly lest its contents revisit the tray. Then the oats, then the apples, all seasoned so well by hunger that he fair moaned at the taste. The food didn't soothe the trembling in his limbs, but it left him warm and full for the first time in many days. Tired, too; he fell asleep again moments after returning to his nest.

Again he woke with the abrupt awareness of someone near him, and again grasped for a missing weapon. This time, the visitor did not startle. Thought it was perhaps inaccurate to call the prince a visitor in his own bedroom.

The human was leaning against a nearby dresser and staring at him as if lost in a waking dream. He smelled of horses and exertion and summer heat, his hair windblown and his eyes flashing hungry and tired in the rosy light of the setting—no, *rising*—sun.

Had Ayden slept straight through since yesterday?

And fallen gods help him, but where had the human been?

"How are you feeling?" the prince asked as Ayden scrambled out of his cloying nest.

"I will feel much better when I have news of Ella," he said, aware of a sudden of his half-nakedness and wishing he'd thought to filch a shirt.

"She is well cared for. Her rooms are all but ready, and she is much the better for her rest, last I heard."

Ayden glared at him and ground out the words one by one, like crushed glass. "Last you heard?"

The prince smiled in sharp sympathy. "I've not been by to see her, if that's your concern."

Ayden closed his eyes and sighed out his relief.

"And what of you?" the prince asked, a hint of amusement coloring his tone. "Did you find my bed lacking?"

"In appeal, yes," Ayden snapped, and had the satisfaction of watching the prince flinch.

. . . But he was not here for his own satisfaction, and he must never forget that. "Look, I'm . . ." The word *sorry* would not quite pass his lips; he thought it likely never would. "This is new to me," he said instead.

The prince rocked on his heels, guilt underscoring the motion with a soft, mourning lilt. "'Tis small consolation, I know, but I had breakfast brought up." He waved toward the drawing room. "Will you join me?"

Though Ayden wanted nothing less than to break bread with this man, he found himself still ravenous, too tempted by the offer to refuse it. So he followed the prince through the bedroom and into the drawing room, doing his best to ignore the two guards by the door, the servant by the far wall spinning an overhead fan with a system of ropes and pulleys, the two gentlemen-in-waiting standing at the ready for the prince's every whim.

A tea table had been moved into the center of the drawing room, two chairs tucked beneath and two trays waiting atop it. The prince waved him toward one, and though Ayden sat grudgingly, he did not wait for the prince to sit as well before attacking his meal. 'Twas the same bland fare as earlier, though this time the cooked oats were sweetened with maple syrup and the soup was dotted with vegetables. Still no salt, but it curbed his hunger if not his tremors.

He'd nearly finished his soup when he heard the prince clear his throat. Ayden paused with his spoon halfway to his mouth, but only for a moment; whatever the man wanted, it could wait until he was finished with his meal.

"*Ahem*," the prince said again, quite conspicuously.

Ayden put down his spoon with a sigh. "What," he said, noticing for the first time that the prince had not even removed the cover from his plate yet, let alone begun to eat.

The prince raised an eyebrow. "Are you godless creatures, truly? Do you not pray over your food?"

"We pray in *silence*," Ayden lied. When the prince continued to stare as if he were some recalcitrant child, Ayden slammed down his bowl and shouted, "Don't! Don't you dare sit there and pretend you're better than us."

The prince's hand flew up, clutched round his eating knife, and Ayden reared back in his chair. But the prince's eyes were focused over Ayden, not on him, and when Ayden turned he found two guards standing close, pikes leveled and ready to strike. At their prince's wordless command they dipped their heads and backed away.

Well, so much for insulting the prince in front of his subjects. Ayden wondered why the prince had bothered to call them off, but perhaps he merely wished to finish his meal in peace before he had Ayden punished. So be it—he'd endured whippings that would have killed a man, and he doubted the prince had the stomach for inflicting anything half so bad. And if the prince thought that delaying the sentence would add to its cruelty, then he had much yet to learn about his new slave.

But the prince merely said, "Claiming superiority was hardly my intention." He laid his left hand flat atop his heart and touched the fingers of his right hand to his bowed forehead. Then he uttered a soft, clear prayer of thanksgiving—in flawless Ancestral tongue.

Ayden felt his eyes widen and he stared straight at the prince's face, now graced with a gentle smile. "The *Behn Thakka?*" he breathed. "How do you know of such things?"

"You speak my language," the prince said, lifting his head and shaking his linen napkin across his lap. "Is it truly so surprising that I would speak yours?"

"But *nobody* speaks the Ancestral tongue." Well, that wasn't precisely true: the eldest of the elders did, and the priests and the poets. And the military, for intelligence and reconnaissance, but that was best left unsaid. "The language of our day-to-day lives is the Trade tongue, same as yours."

Though of course the prince would think of it as "his" tongue, rather than "theirs"—typical human arrogance.

"Ah," the prince said, "but I have long been a fan of the elder master poet Fehgir, and there *was* no Trade tongue when he first put ink to parchment." He laid one hand atop Ayden's where it rested on the table, and shifted in his chair until his left knee was pressed up against Ayden's right. "You elves have quite a way with the language of the forest."

A half dozen sharp retorts rose to Ayden's tongue, but there he forced them to remain, just as he forced his hand and leg to stay unmoving beneath the prince's touch. *Think of Ella*, he commanded his muscles and nerves, *and give the prince no need to turn to her for satisfaction.* And certainly, by the way the prince was touching Ayden, looking at Ayden, singing out to Ayden, satisfaction was foremost on his mind.

Was he expected to return the prince's gesture? Somehow he'd never anticipated how different reciprocation would be from endurance: as different as song from silence. He wasn't sure he could sing back without cracking.

But the prince removed his hand from Ayden's, cleared his throat, then cleared it again as if he'd failed the first time to dislodge the desire so obviously wedged there. "Yes, well, I suppose we can discuss elven poetry another time. I've trained since the first light of dawn with my falcon and steed; I've worked up quite the appetite."

Appetite*s*, plural, Ayden thought. His own had left him by now, but he went back to his soup anyway, steeling himself to serve as the prince's dessert. And just how, he wondered, could one possibly go about preparing for *that*?

And by the gods, what was that glorious smell?

The prince had pulled the cover from his meal, and what wafted forth drew the whole of Ayden's being: fried potatoes and hard-boiled eggs, dark brown bread with pots of jam, sliced fruit and a handful of flaky pastries. 'Twas the eggs and potatoes he craved, both so heavily salted that he could sense it from across the little table.

The prince clearly noticed, for he touched Ayden's hand again, which was clutched now round his spoon as if round the hilt of a dagger. "You should not eat such things after going so long without. My apologies, Ayden, for I did not mean to tempt you."

"No, you don't . . ." Ayden stopped, swallowed, panting softly; his mouth was watering so hard he was afraid he'd drool. "You don't understand. 'Tis not the food, 'tis . . . I need . . ."

"Yes?" the prince asked, curiosity and concern twining through both his tone and his song. "What is it, Ayden?"

And crack it, but why was it suddenly so hard to *think*? He could not tear his eyes from the prince's plate. "Salt," he breathed. "I need salt."

The prince speared a grape with his fork and asked, "Whatever for?" before popping it in his mouth. If he was surprised by any of this, he hid it well.

"For . . . Because . . . I just do," Ayden said desperately. "'Tis an elven need."

"Truly?" the prince asked, this time spearing a potato, his manner and expression the very picture of nonchalance. "I have known many an elf in my youth, and none have ever claimed such a need."

"More slaves?" Ayden choked out, struggling to force down his sudden, boiling anger.

The prince nodded. "The Aegis keeps many. I was fortunate to attend his training academy as a boy. I remember an armory packed end to end with weapons forged in magic by his prized elves—blades so strong they never broke, never dulled. In fact, my own sword and armor were forged thus." The prince took another bite of potato and said, "But this does not interest you. Answer me true, Ayden, and I may give you what you crave."

Ayden hesitated, scrubbed a hand through his hair. 'Twas not that he feared the humans would use this knowledge to call forth their own lightning, for they were both deaf and mute to the songs of nature. Nay, he feared betraying his weakness so thoroughly. His unthinking reaction had already alerted the prince to his needs; if he confessed the truth behind them, the prince might take care to deny him salt for the short remainder of his life. Of course, the prince might deny him regardless, simply to *get* the truth from him.

He did not doubt the latter. As for the former . . .

"Salt has a song to it," he blurted, praying he'd chosen right. "Short and snappish, like lightning. Other things have it to a lesser degree. Your people cannot hear it, of course."

"Of course," the prince murmured with a trace of amusement. But his eyes and song were riveted to Ayden, keen with interest. Almost as thirsty for this knowledge, Ayden thought uncomfortably, as he had been for . . . other things, earlier.

"Yes, well. When I was doing battle with your men—to protect my sister," he added on the side of caution, or perhaps of accusation, "I threw lightning at them."

"Threw lightning?" the prince repeated as if tasting foreign words. "They said . . . But I thought they were only . . ."

Ayden gave him a sardonic smile. "Not this time, Prince. I was . . ." He debated confessing it, but he'd confessed worse these last two days. "I was desperate. It was a desperate defense, and it stripped the song of salt from the earth around me and from my very body." He held out his shaking hands between them for the prince to see. "Only the faintest of whispers remain."

The prince's song was deep and restless: thoughtful, Ayden guessed, and concerned. "I know some animals will lick salt from rocks," he said, nodding as if to himself.

Ayden bristled at the comparison, though he knew damn well he'd be on all fours with his tongue out if he saw a mineral rock on the ground now. "Your own body requires it just as much," he returned.

"Is that so," the prince said, bristling as well—though at the comparison to an animal or to an elf, Ayden wasn't certain.

Ayden stared pointedly at the prince's plate.

"I see," the prince said, his gaze raking over Ayden's face and held-out hands. "And if I were to allow you to renew this, this salt song, what is to stop you from using it in such a way again?"

'Twas lucky that Ayden's jaw dropped with incredulity, else he might have spat out a reckless retort and doomed his plea.

His glare must have spoken for him either way, for the prince nodded and said, "Ella, of course. Very well."

Ayden expected him to summon one of the handful of lords and servants who quietly attended the prince's rooms, but instead—and much to his surprise—the prince merely picked up his own plate and scraped the eggs and potatoes onto Ayden's tray.

"If this is not enough, you will tell me," he said, and then picked up his fork and knife and started in on the remainder of his breakfast.

Given salt at last, Ayden ate nearly without chewing, feeling his strength flowing back by the moment. Not even the human's stare resting heavily upon him could spoil this appetite. But still he craved more, even after he'd swiped the last of the residue from the plate with his finger.

"Is there more?" he asked, knowing—and not caring—how entitled the question sounded. If the prince meant to hold him against his will, the least he could do was tend his needs.

But when he looked up, it was to find the prince tense and at the ready, right hand curled round the hilt of the dagger sheathed at his hip. The guards and even the servants in the room had grown similarly wary and alert. Now that he thought to listen, he could hear their fear, their resolve to protect the prince at all costs . . . but from what?

His own hand tightened round his spoon (they had not trusted him with a knife), but he immediately forced himself to put it down. "What?" he demanded. "Do my manners offend so greatly, *Your Highness*?"

"You're glowing," the prince said, his voice and song sharp with the same cutting edge as yesterday, when he'd determined to pry Ayden's secrets from him.

Ayden awaited elaboration that never came. "Yes," he said finally, feeling like a fool for stating the obvious. 'Twould have been comic but for the prince's grip on his weapon. "I *am* elf. Or have you so soon forgotten?"

"You have glowed before only when striking with your magic."

*Oh, for the blessing of the—* "Because I was weak! What you see as aura is . . ." He tossed his hand, frustrated at the need to explain the most basic facts of life. ". . . Just me. Harmless song. As natural to us as breathing. But as breathing takes strength, so too does this. I was dying before. I could barely 'breathe.'"

A sharp note of surprise wrenched his stare from the prince's sword-hand to his startled gaze.

"I would do nothing to risk my sister's safety," Ayden said, slow and emphatic. "I did not lash out, even as you tortured me"—he felt, more than saw, the prince flinch at his bluntness—"and I will not do so now."

The prince held his stare a moment longer, as if trying to hear Ayden's song despite his deafness, then nodded. "I believe you," he said, and all round him Ayden felt the tension drain away. "And yes, there is more."

Again Ayden expected the prince to call over a servant, but instead the man rose and walked to an end table by the sofa, from which he plucked up a palm-sized silver dish full of chestnuts, roasted and rolled in salt.

"Leave us," the prince said as he retook his seat, the dish cradled in his hands. Though his command had been neither loud nor forceful, the guards and servants left his room in moments. Ayden was instantly sorry to see the fan-puller go, but with his strength returned, 'twas a simple thing to reach out to the air fragments round him and lull them, *andante*, into a cooling tempo.

The prince waited 'til the last man had closed the drawing room doors, then plucked a nut from the dish and held it out. When Ayden made to take it, though, the prince pulled his fingers just out of reach, and only moved them forward again when Ayden dropped his hand.

Ayden sighed and tried again, and again the prince pulled back.

"What manner of teasing is this!" Ayden demanded, banging the table with his empty hand.

"'Tis no tease," the prince said, the very picture of sincerity. Still his fingers hovered before Ayden's lips. "Come, eat it."

And that was when Ayden understood: the chestnuts were meant to be dessert for them both.

He let his hands fall to his lap, where they balled, unseen, round the strange fabric of his borrowed breeches. Then he leaned forward and parted his lips, letting the prince place the nut on his tongue.

He could not help what happened next, the craving was still so strong: he closed his mouth and sucked the salt away, and damn if the prince's fingers weren't still between his lips.

The prince made a little noise that Ayden suspected was distinctly unprincelike, and did not reach for another nut until Ayden pulled his mouth away from the intruding fingers.

Rather than reach across the little table to offer the next nut, the prince slid his chair over, pressing his leg to Ayden's. Ayden licked his lips, still hungry enough for salt to ignore this closeness with no more than a frisson of annoyance. And if the prince wanted to construe his quickening breath and the way his eyes closed at the taste of salt on his tongue as an answering song of arousal, well, all the better for him.

The little silver dish was nearly empty by the time the craving had left Ayden. He leaned back and licked his lips clean. The taste of the prince's fingers had been salty in itself and not so wholly terrible, but he made a point to chase it from his tongue with a long drink.

"Enough," he said when the prince offered another chestnut, his tone harsher and his full import clearer than he'd intended.

'Twas with much relief that the prince merely nodded, making no argument. Instead he swallowed hard, rubbed his still-moist fingers across his own lips in what struck Ayden as an unconscious gesture of longing, and then stood from his chair. The bulge in his breeches was impossible to miss.

"If you'll excuse me," he said, shifting his stance and then shifting again, "I'm afraid I have business to attend. We'll continue this later."

*How tragic,* Ayden thought, and *Good riddance,* but to the prince he said none of those things. He merely nodded and watched the human go.

# Chapter Five

Already a bird had flown in from High Court with a message from Berendil, and the very sight of it instilled Freyrík with dread. Surely the Aegis could not have forced a call to arms through the Council of Eight so quickly? Reluctantly he unfurled the small note, crammed end to end with his brother's jagged scrawl. Why Berendil hadn't asked his quill hand to write it for him, Freyrík could not guess; no part of it spoke of private things.

*Dear Rík,* the letter began, *Aegis beat you to the trumpet call. Started wringing the Council's ballocks (and purses) a week after I arrived. Sending 2 battalions: ½ cavalry, 1½ infantry. All armed and armored. 500 falcons, 100 dogs, 2 contingents of trainers. Kit and food for thrice as many. 100 spare warhorses, 20 new elf-forged weapon/armor sets. Wife if you want one.*

Freyrík laughed, wondering if that were the Aegis's joke or Berendil's, even as a sick hollowness spread through his guts at the numbers.

*Arrival in 15 to 18 days via Góz River; cutting it close I know, but best course if they need be rested to fight. First Wife returning with separate escort approx. 2 weeks hence. She is well but misses home. Love, Berendil.*

'Twas two battalions short of Freyrík's hopes, half the reinforcements he'd trusted the Aegis to raise. Damn the midland provinces and their foolish release laws; it seemed half their able-bodied men paid their way free of conscription each year, and even more cravens paid free of reserve duty. Of course, their coin made possible the spare food and kit, but what good were provisions for an entire battalion if he had only a contingent to feed?

Still, any reinforcement was welcome. He would make do with what he was given.

. . . Or perhaps not. Four hours later, he conceded that no amount of inventive repositioning could reduplicate two battalions. Each Surge seemed to grow vaster and more violent than the last, while their own resources dwindled.

Well, they would fight with what they had, and even so they would endure. There was simply no other option. He would pass the news along to the Council and meet with them two days hence; let twelve wiser heads ponder on this challenge for a time.

As for himself, he'd had enough of hopeless puzzles for one day. Lunch in the Great Hall had come and gone without him some two hours past; his rumbling belly and the throbbing ache behind his eyes were becoming fierce distractions. 'Twas time to lay his planning to rest for a while and take tea in the gardens, perhaps watch his middle sons spar. Both were too young to take the battlefield of yet, gods be thanked, as was his eldest, away at the Aegis's academy. They would not die in this Surge, or likely the next; but what of the one after that, and after that, and after that...

Freyrík shook his head. Such were dangerous thoughts in the face of his duties. Yet he wondered if his father had thought the same, and his grandfather, and—

Sometimes he wondered at how hopeless it all seemed.

But there would be one bright spot in his day, at least. Tonight, he told himself—tonight he would lay with Ayden, and share with him all the pleasures he knew how to give.

Ayden spent his day staring out the window, watching the sun crawl across the sky and fair torturing himself by envisioning over and over what would happen when the prince at last returned. He hoped to whittle away the horror of it by constant thought of those cold, possessive fingers on his skin, unwanted lips pressing to his own, the weight of that muscled body atop him, the burn of the prince's cock in his arse and the baying of lust in his ears. He could endure it, at least he thought he could, if the prince would only take his pleasure and be done with it.

But he doubted 'twould be that simple.

Though he'd met the prince only yesterday, already the man had surprised him too many times. His candid concern for his people. His knowledge of the *Behn Thakka* and his talk of elven poetry. He didn't strike Ayden as the kind to enjoy an indifferent partner. No, the human might well expect him to be willing, if not eager. And Ayden had promised to obey his every demand.

But he'd not meant that. Not that. How could he ever . . .

Perhaps if he closed his eyes and ears and pretended hard enough, he could trick his body into thinking the prince were Leifi or Ástir, and dwell not on memories of the one dead on the battlefield and the other parted with harsh words. He'd not lain with a male in nearly two hundred years, but one scarce forgets such pleasures, and the prince's body would surely feel the same beneath his hands: smooth skin and thick muscle, hard cock and firm arse. Cooler, though; humans burned dull, barely kindled and quickly extinguished. Could he bring himself to pretend at eagerness for such a touch?

He would find a way. To protect Ella—*anything* to protect Ella.

By the time the prince returned to his bedroom, the sun had nearly set, and Ayden was ready for him. He stepped away from the window and forced himself to bow his head. "Prince," he said. It was the first word he'd spoken since morning, and it came out rough.

"Ayden," the prince returned, a soft smile quirking his lips.

He looked tired, sounded fretful to Ayden's inner ear. But beneath that—*of course*—was a high, thin thread of desire, curling round Ayden's skin like fingers. He ground his teeth and swallowed, forcing a smile.

Neither of them spoke or moved.

The silence grew painful.

"I trust you're well?" the prince asked at last, as if Ayden were some visiting dignitary, and not a prisoner he'd tortured just the day before.

"Oh, yes," Ayden said, smiling sharply. "'Tis my favorite pastime: being locked in a human's rooms."

The prince winced, and so did he. He'd not meant to be sarcastic; he could not afford to drive the man away, not when "away" amounted to Ella. And crack his tongue for not finding the words to undo the damage . . .

"Well, at least 'tis a *nice* bedroom," the prince said with a desperate smile.

Ayden forced his lips to twitch up. "That it is."

Relief chimed like bells all round him, as if the prince thought some silly banter could possibly mend what ailed them. He waved in Ayden's general direction and said, "I see you found my shirts?"

"'Twas cold," Ayden lied. "I hope you don't—"

"Quite all right, 'tis proper to be dressed for dinner anyway. I had some sent up. Won't you join me in the drawing room?"

And *that*, fallen gods be blessed, was one request he could indulge eagerly enough.

Except that of course the prince insisted on hand-feeding him, and of course the prince's fingers found need to explore past his lips with every bite he took. At least the food was decent this time—better than decent, in fact, despite being spiced with *human*. Ayden cleaned his plate and some of the prince's as well, once the prince had declared himself sated. Dessert was a rich chocolate cake the likes of which Ayden hadn't tasted since before the war, for the cocoa bean did not grow in elven lands. He thought he could be excused, then, for licking frosting from the prince's finger with such enthusiasm.

Once the last bite was gone, the prince's hand, no longer occupied with food, draped itself across Ayden's shoulder and began to stroke. "I have seen many an elf," the prince said softly near his ear, "but never one so compelling as you."

Ayden barely refrained from asking, "Truly? Is *that* the best you can do?" But he had only to think of the prince speaking thus to Ella, and his resolve to see this through was hardened. Besides, he sensed neither deceit nor empty flattery from the prince—only desire, lust, cautious delight. The man, oddly enough, was telling true.

The hand on his shoulder slid to his chest, skimmed across the exposed skin of his throat. He swallowed hard beneath the prince's roving fingers.

"You're so warm," the prince whispered. "Is that . . . normal?"

"I feel normal," Ayden replied, mirroring the prince's touch. His heartbeat quickened and he bit his lower lip to stifle his desire—let the prince notice that, and not that his desire was to squeeze his fingers round the man's throat.

The prince leaned into Ayden's hand and closed his eyes, laid his cheek upon Ayden's shoulder and pressed his nose and lips to Ayden's neck, sniffing deeply. Ayden froze, every muscle in his body locked against this unwanted intimacy; even his hand stilled where it lay between the man's collarbones.

At last Ayden could stand it no longer and leaned away, covering his retreat by taking the prince's face in both hands, as if to study or perhaps to kiss him. The man's stubble scraped against his palms.

The prince licked his lips, caught one between his teeth and let it slowly pull free. "Would you . . ." He curled his fingers round Ayden's, gently freed his head—not that Ayden resisted—and stood from his chair, still holding Ayden's hand. "Would you come with me now?"

To bed, he meant, Ayden could tell. He nodded, wondering at the prince's timidity. Certainly there was no call—nor any hope—for the man to woo him. Why, then, was he trying so hard? 'Twas doubly frustrating for the time it took; Ayden wanted nothing more than to get this over and done with.

It seemed, then, that he would have to make it happen himself.

He walked them both the short distance to the bed, then freed his hand from the prince's and began to strip himself of his human clothes. The breeches first, for he found them stiff and uncomfortable, the cut too confining and the fabric too heavy for the summer heat. Then the shirt, riddled with buttons at the cuffs and all down the front that made removing it a cumbersome nuisance. At least his wound was finally healing; he felt only the slightest twinge of pain when he pulled his left arm from the sleeve.

Yet the twinge of embarrassment, even shame, that came with the loss of the shirt was far from slight. He fisted his fingers in the material, clinging to it for another moment; then he tossed it aside, beyond temptation. 'Twas not as if he'd never been naked before others, even if they had been lovers or fellow soldiers and not—

No, think nothing of that. Do what you must.

He lifted his feet one at a time to peel off finely-woven socks and a silk undergarment. Bare now as the forest in wintertime, he kept his gaze to his feet for a moment, schooling his face into careful blankness before looking back to the prince.

The prince's expression was equally frozen but certainly not blank, his eyes traversing Ayden's skin as if a dream he feared to lose upon waking. "By the gods," he whispered, reaching out with an unsteady hand to trace his fingers across the ridges and planes of Ayden's stomach, rather more pronounced now than they had been at the start of this accursed week.

Ayden's breath caught at the touch and his muscles contracted away from the prince's fingers, but he forced his feet to remain in place.

He sucked in a deep breath, then another, praying the prince would construe his aversion for nervous desire. Though if he kept balking . . . He tried to step into the prince's caress, yet when those cold fingers trailed low across his hip, toward his thigh, his traitorous feet lurched backward, carrying him out of reach.

"Ayden?" the prince asked, and the way he looked up at him then, with wide and tremulous eyes, reminded Ayden of nothing more than Ella as a child, her heart at his feet, handing him some craftwork and waiting, just waiting for his praise.

Crack the man anyway for being so gentle. Why could he not simply *take* what he wanted, force Ayden's hand so that Ayden would not have to extend it freely? 'Twould have been more bearable that way. More compassionate.

The irony of that did not escape him.

The prince let his hand fall to his side. "Am I not pleasing to your eye?"

His confusion was so genuine that for a moment Ayden felt sorry for him, despite his galling assumption that all the world would bed him at the first opportunity.

"You are," Ayden said with an ease born of honesty, taking in the prince's bright blue eyes, his wavy hair the color of cattails that grew by the Loekr River, his robust warrior's frame. But looks were by no means the beginning and the end, and slavery could bring ugliness upon the fallen gods themselves.

Still the prince stared up at him with imploring eyes. "Is this not done among your people then—to bed man with man?"

"We take no mind of gender," Ayden said. "When you live as long as we do, you cannot always be and do the same without going mad."

The prince nodded, sat heavily on the bed, pulled his eyes away from Ayden's bared flesh and dropped them to his own lap. "Perhaps 'twould be better," he muttered, "if I found you some nightclothes."

"No," Ayden said quickly, wrangling his feet back under control and forcing them to shuffle forward. "No, I want—" He cut off short, wondering at the power of words to choke as surely as smoke.

The prince's song sharpened, desire now shadowed by something deeper that Ayden couldn't place but hoped was merely lust. "You want . . . what?"

"This," Ayden said desperately, accenting the word with a forward step, then another. "You. Isn't that what all your subjects wish? To bed the handsome prince?"

The question faded from the prince's eyes, and the deeper notes in his song—not lust, crack it, but wariness and disappointment—swelled to drown his keening desire. "*You* are not one of my subjects. And have I not proven already that I can see through your lies?"

"No, I wasn't—!"

"You despise me still," the prince said, "though your fate here is hardly my fault, though I've shown you such mercy and kindness as I could, treated you as equal when I could. I'd hoped— I *hope* to change your feelings in time, but do not insult me by pandering to mine. Rest easy, Ayden; I will take my pleasures elsewhere tonight."

"No!" Ayden planted a firm hand on the prince's shoulder as he tried to stand. The prince looked surprised—half wry, half murderous; he was clearly unaccustomed to commanding hands on his person—but remained on the bed. "No," Ayden said again. "You are wrong. I don't take well to slavery, 'tis true. But in absence of my freedom, I would take whatever . . . pleasure . . . you are gracious enough to offer. Please," he said, caring not at all that he was begging.

He felt the prince's resolve begin to waver and pressed upon it harder yet, caressing the prince's cheek with his thumb and adding, "If I must be your slave, then I beg of you, Prince: permit me this small respite."

The prince closed his eyes, leaned into Ayden's touch. But then something shifted within him, and he slapped Ayden's hand away and demanded, "What manner of teasing is this?"

'Twas no coincidence, Ayden thought, that he had chosen to spit Ayden's own words back into his face.

The prince stood, and this time Ayden daren't press him down again. "You *do not want this*!"

"I do!" Ayden shouted, throwing his arms wide before the prince, shamelessly displaying his nakedness. "I do! Here I am—do with me what you will!"

"What I will? What I *will*? My *will* is clearly beyond your comprehension!" The prince stared at him, breathing hard for a long moment. Ayden dared not break the silence, not even as the prince pushed past him and strode toward the doors. "As I said, elf, I shall take my pleasures elsewhere."

"Wait!" Ayden shouted, finding his tongue at last and rushing after the prince. He gave hardly any mind to his nakedness as he burst into the hall, and remembered the guards only when their arms blocked his way, restraining him. Even in his panic he could not help but notice a hand squeezing his naked arse, or the powerful wave of lust and the backbeat of smugness that accompanied the violating touch.

"Prince, please!" he cried, straining against the guards' grips until he felt something tear in his healing wound. "You promised you wouldn't hurt her! I've kept my word! You *promised!*"

The prince froze mid-step, his song growing cold and fierce in the space of a heartbeat. When he whirled round and marched back toward Ayden, the force of his . . . fury? indignation? outrage? . . . was so overpowering that Ayden staggered back from the guards' grips and braced himself for the blows to come.

The prince planted his hand in Ayden's chest and shoved him so hard he went sprawling to the carpet. He heard the doors slam shut; then the prince was dragging him by the arm, off the floor and into the bedroom, where he spun him round and pushed him again. Ayden slammed back against the edge of the bed and landed on his arse once more, but at least this time his fall was cushioned.

"How *dare* you!" the prince shouted, shaking Ayden by twin iron grips on his shoulders.

"I'm sorry!" Ayden cried out. "I *tried* to give you what you wanted! And 'twas not my place to question you before your men, I know, but please, please don't hurt Ella!"

The prince's face scrunched up in disgust and he gave Ayden another hard shake. "You . . . *You* . . ."

Gods help him, he'd angered the man speechless.

"What kind of man do you take me for!" the prince demanded. "You think that I would— that I'd— Gah!" Another hard shake, and yet strangely, when Ayden flinched, the prince's grip on his shoulders loosened. "Is it easier for you to hate me, if you can think me a raper? Must you hold onto your hate so tightly to survive here? Am I truly so cruel?"

Ayden said nothing, altogether too stunned by this turn this of events to form a reply.

The prince released him, scrubbed both hands across his face and let out a tired sigh. "I did not take you against your will, even as you claimed to want me. I would certainly not take Ella. Despite what you clearly wish to think, I am no dark beast."

Ayden looked up at the prince and opened his mouth to speak, but still no words would form; relief had clogged his throat.

"Nor do I lack for eager company," the prince added with a pointed stare. "There are as we speak three Lady Consorts most anxious to bear me sons. I will go to one of them, *as I was doing*, and shan't trouble you again."

Ayden swallowed round an errant urge to apologize and nodded mutely.

"But you must listen," the prince said, dropping to one knee before Ayden and gripping his forearms. 'Twas profoundly uncomfortable to have the prince's face so close to his naked lap, even if the human looked only into his eyes.

"There is much hatred here for you," the prince said, his voice low and urgent. "Nobody must know of this kindness, do you understand? For if there is any hearing of it, I shall have no choice but to disprove it with a contrary demonstration."

Ayden nodded once more, wondering where his tongue—typically his weapon of first resort—had gone off to.

The prince stood and stepped away, a small, sly grin twitching at his lips. "Now I must stay awhile, for appearance's sake." He retrieved Ayden's breeches and shirt and handed them over. "I will find you some nightclothes. Meanwhile," he added, his smile growing wider, "feel free to shout whatever obscenities may rage upon your tongue."

"For appearance's sake?" Ayden asked, gratefully shrugging into the unbuttoned shirt.

"But of course." And then, "I don't suppose you play chess?"

Ayden felt his lips flap soundlessly once again. What in the name of the fallen gods had happened here? All the world seemed suddenly a dream, for in what waking world would a prince deceive his own people for the benefit of a slave?

Yet dream or no, he'd be a fool to pass this mercy by; he would play for as long as the prince allowed it. 'Twas a simple thing to do—he need only picture the prince with Ella, undressing her, touching her . . . "*NO!*" he screamed, loud enough to carry halfway across the castle. Then he added, considerably softer, "for no one has ever taught me how."

The prince had startled, but now he laughed and waved Ayden through the double doors to the drawing room, where a large marble chess board sat upon a table in one corner.

"Do sit, then," he said. "I'll even let you play the darkers; they strike first."

*And last*, Ayden thought, taking his seat at the board and shaking off his confoundment, gathering his wits to trounce the human at whatever game he offered.

# Chapter Six

Freyrík snuck back into his rooms after an early breakfast and a surprisingly lively attempt to bolster his bloodline with Lady Sefi. He took a seat at the map table in his private study, planning to work the whole of the day there, where none would trouble or interrupt him.

Clearly, he'd forgotten to take Ayden into account.

"You're losing."

Freyrík startled at the soft voice just behind his shoulder and turned to find Ayden towering over him. When had the elf woken? And how had he dressed and traveled from the bedroom to the study without making a single sound?

Ayden stepped up to the table beside him and tapped a finger against the map, between a handful of darker figurines at forest's edge and a human contingent at the crest of a hill. "I thought the game was played on tiles, not terrain."

"This is no game," Freyrík snapped, knocking Ayden's hand away, and two of the human units along with it. He righted them quickly, praying 'twas not an evil omen.

"You're still losing," Ayden said.

"Then help me, if you're so clever!"

"There is no help for you." Ayden strolled over to the settee against the far wall and threw himself down in a lazy heap. "Is there breakfast?"

Freyrík couldn't help but laugh at the gall of him. "Are you quite serious?" And before the elf could answer, "Never you mind, of course you are. I will feed you when you do as you're bid."

Ayden took an apple from a bowl of fruit next to the settee and crunched noisily.

"You test me, elf!"

"Nay, prince," Ayden said round a bite of apple. "I surely daren't."

Freyrík slammed down his quill and stalked over to Ayden, hauled him off the settee and snatched the apple from his hand. "Leave!" he barked, then added, "Not you," when Ayden tried to extricate himself.

The one servant manning the study scuttled out quickly, closing the door behind him.

When he was gone, Freyrík dropped Ayden back onto the settee but did not loose his grip on the elf's shirt. "Have you so soon forgotten what I told you, elf? These walls have eyes and ears—"

"We call them 'people,'" Ayden said, "though I suppose you high-borns don't think of them as such."

Gods, how Freyrík wanted to smack the snideness right off his face. "Neither do you," he said, "and do not try to pretend otherwise. You'd slaughter us all if you had the chance."

Ayden's answering silence gave him less satisfaction than he'd thought it would.

"Tell me, Ayden, must I beat it through that thick skull of yours that these *people* may wag their tongues if they see me indulging your insolence? To them you are a dangerous beast—a slave, an animal to be broken by the whip."

"And to you?" Ayden asked.

"To me you are a fool, for I offer you kindness, and you piss on my father's grave."

For a long moment Ayden held his tongue, but then he wrenched free, threw himself back on the settee and crossed his arms. "I will not be broken, by whip or otherwise."

"No," Freyrík said, "I don't suppose you will. But you need not if only you *listen* to me! I have no desire to possess your spirit"—and yes, perhaps that was a little untrue, and he suspected Ayden knew that—"but you must learn the rules of this house and your place within it."

"Must I learn to dance and sing for you, as well?"

Freyrík bit his tongue against the rash words this creature seemed so routinely to incite. "What's done is done, Ayden," he said instead. "You cannot be free, but you can have a comfortable life here. Any other lord would ride you to death trying to break you. I too could demand the world of you—and have I not your word that you'd give it?—but instead I offer you and Ella what I may to ease the pain. Rage upon me in private if you must, but darkers take you, *obey* me."

Ayden scowled, still looking distinctly churlish, but after a moment he nodded.

"Good." Freyrík took a step back, offered Ayden a flat smile. "Now I will order you breakfast, whatever you wish, and then you will make good use of those tactical skills you flaunted so well at chess, for tomorrow I must bring my Surge plan to the Council."

Ayden's eyes narrowed, and he opened his mouth to speak, but Freyrík cut him off with a raised hand. "And before you ask, I know you'll give these plans your very best effort, because our fate is your fate—you will be fighting beside us."

Ayden shot to his feet, shouting, "I will do no such—"

Freyrík shoved him down again and shouted right overtop him, "What did I just say!" He sighed, pinched the bridge of his nose. "I grow weary of threats, Ayden; I much prefer kindness. But if you wish me to have you beaten, you need only ask." 'Twas clear to him Ayden's surprise that he hadn't been disciplined already. Less clear was why Ayden kept pushing him into it against all attempts to the contrary. "And if you fear not for your own hide, then fear for your sister's. You *will* fight at our side, end of discussion. Now come, we have much work to do."

He reclaimed his seat at the map table and waited—*patiently*—while Ayden dragged over a chair and slammed it down across the table from him. Freyrík tried not to think of the damage to the carved wooden legs. But the elf was studying the map, at least.

After a moment, Ayden sighed deep as the Dalr Canyon and asked, "What's the scale?"

"Each tile is a hundredth-league. It represents . . ." Freyrík bent down and rummaged in a map chest, pulled out a stiff leather roll and unfurled it over a less-crowded corner of the table. "It represents this space here," he said, circling his index finger above the matching area. "This map is a half-league per tile."

"Is your league the same as ours?"

Freyrík shrugged. "'Tis the distance a man can walk in an hour."

"Are you quite serious?" Ayden asked, and did not give Freyrík a chance to respond before adding, "Never you mind, of course you are."

Freyrík glared.

"What if a short man and a tall man each walk for an hour?" Ayden continued, leaning back in his chair and stretching his legs. "How would you choose which measurement is right?"

"Ayden."

"Or if one man is lame?"

"Ayden . . ."

"Or if one is walking up a steep—"

"Ayden!"

Ayden shut his mouth and put his hands up in a silent gesture of contrition, but Freyrík couldn't help himself; he said, "And I suppose *your* league is just perfect, is it?"

Ayden shrugged—a flawless, infuriating mirror of Freyrík's own manner. "'Tis eight hundred rods. Up hill, down hill, tall elf, short elf, lame elf . . ."

Freyrík blinked. Blinked again. And finally, grudgingly, said, "Oh."

"Though I'll admit it does take most people about an hour to walk it."

Freyrík opened his mouth to reply, but indignation pressed his thoughts into a wordless huff. "If you're quite done mocking our ways, may we concentrate on what matters now, please?"

The shadow of a smile on Ayden's lips seemed to say, *Why not? I've had my fun.*

He pulled the overview map out from under Freyrík's fingers; Freyrík allowed it with a grimace. Perhaps the elf would see something new there, though he doubted it, as many times as he'd studied these maps himself. He'd even ridden these lands on horseback, from the forested slopes at the edge of the darker territory, through the foothills of the Myrkr Mountains, and into the grassland valleys some sixty leagues west of the castle walls.

"What are these?" Ayden gestured at a cluster of red pebbles on the detail map. "Feral forces?"

"Darker attacks. They've been heaviest at Eine, Tveir, and Hals," Freyrík said, pointing out the three villages that straggled along the foothills. "And so the Surge will all but certainly crest upon one of them, as history has taught us . . ." He rubbed his eyes, then his temples. "Or upon all of them at once; there's no telling. And therein lies the heart of our weakness. If we—"

"It matters little where they plan to strike," Ayden said distractedly.

Freyrík's head snapped up, a sharp retort on his tongue, but he held it back, held back his very breath when he saw the fierce look of concentration on Ayden's face. The elf was staring at the map fit to burn holes through it, and Freyrík could all but see the thoughts darting behind his eyes: odds weighed, courses of action studied and discarded, and maybe, *maybe* some new genius that would swing the battle in their favor . . .

But whatever Ayden had been thinking, it seemed to escape him between one blink and the next.

Freyrík slumped over the map and cradled his forehead in one hand. "You're a fool to disregard their target. *Everything* rides upon it." He tilted his head to survey the three pebble-choked villages for the thousandth time. "Look: If I deploy troops to intercept the darkers at Eine, and the Surge instead crests upon Tveir, then we'll have missed it. Tveir will be ravaged, and by the time we catch up to the darkers they'll have spread across the borderlands and into central Farr. Do you see the matter now?"

Ayden grunted. 'Twas an absentminded sound, which Freyrík chose to take as positive.

"And yet on the other tray of the scales," he continued, "if I deploy in all three villages and the Surge crests upon only one, 'twill sweep through our thinned defenses like a darker bear's claws through leather armor. Now, if I had four new battalions from the Aegis instead of two . . ." He shook off the foolery of wishful thoughts. "But no, 'tis clearly no longer an option."

The noise that escaped the elf's throat this time was closer to a growl. Freyrík looked at him sharply, suspecting that it expressed more glee than concern, but Ayden hardly seemed to be listening. And truly, why had he expected some revelation from a member of the race who had birthed the darkers in the first place?

He returned his attention to the board and swept up the human figurines like so many gambling stones, forcing his mind to the loathsome but inevitable conclusion.

"I *could* deploy at two villages, though only barely. At least then, if the Surge crests upon all three, only one need be sacrificed. 'Twould cut the invasion by two-thirds, and if we chase the remaining third inland quickly enough, we may contain it before too much blood is spilt. Unless . . ."

He sighed again; 'twas the same old argument, the same old sacrifices, the same old choices year after endless year. "Unless the Surge crests upon the one unmanned village, in which case the darkers would strike central Farr at full force. 'Twould take us ages to round them up, and the gods know how much havoc they could wreak in the interim. And if I *am* to deploy at two villages, which one do I sacrifice? None holds more tactical value than—"

Ayden thumped a hand down on the map and said, "Stop your prattling."

Freyrík started at the bold-faced insult, his hands curling into fists. But then he realized how softly Ayden had spoken, and how without malice, and he saw that spark of excitement in Ayden's eyes again. Freyrík's hope kindled in response, eager as a child. And as easily disappointed, he cautioned himself; who knew what vitriol the elf was preparing—

"Look here," Ayden said, in what struck Freyrík as another conscious echoing of his own manner. He held out his hand, and after a moment of confusion, Freyrík realized that he was asking for the human figurines. Another moment, this one of reluctance, and Freyrík placed them in the elf's palm.

"You need not abandon any of them," Ayden said, busily arranging the unit markers. "Rather than deploy within a village, deploy here."

Freyrík felt his hope draining as surely as the blood from his face. "That's two leagues into darker territory," he said. "See this line here? That's the border between—"

"I'm not a fool," Ayden snapped. "I can read a map."

"And yet only a fool would suggest we venture into darker lands! There is strong magic afoot there, and it bears us grievance. Have you not seen the great fissure in the earth?"

"Oh, I have. But it is *this* great fissure that interests me." The elf tapped his finger in the center of the figurines he'd positioned in a horseshoe, on a tile so crowded with elevation lines that they nearly formed a solid bar. "'Tis a box canyon, is it not?"

"Yes, but—"

"But nothing. Shelve your foolish superstitions and save your soldiers' lives." He gave a feral smile that Freyrík was fast learning to dread. "Or not; it matters little to me. You can play cups with your villages or you can fight the Ferals right," *tap*, "here."

"Yes, I see," Freyrík drawled. "Because fighting *outside* the village forts, on enemy soil no less, will spare so many of my men."

The elf nodded. He even seemed sincere.

"They'll be ripped limb from limb out in the open!" Freyrík stood away from the table, tore his hands through his hair, paced in two tight circles before stopping to point an accusing finger at the elf. "If this is your notion of help—"

Ayden threw his hands up in defense, or perhaps placation. "Have you never fought out in the open before?" he asked, but though his words and face were guileless, Freyrík knew befanged mockery when he heard it.

"Have you ever *seen* a darker grizzly? Larger than a carriage, and with a great many more teeth and claws! Shields and armor do little against such threats—the only way to stop them is from atop sturdy battlements, and even then 'tis a desperate wager."

"You have sturdy battlements here," Ayden said, pointing at the box canyon, "and from all three of its ridges you can loose arrows in a driving rain upon the Ferals."

Freyrík rolled his eyes. "A brilliant stratagem, truly. And how, pray tell, do you propose we *get* the darkers to join us there? Shall I dispatch an invitation by bird?"

A slow, sly smile spread across Ayden's face, and this time, Freyrík sensed not a hint of mockery therein. "Why, you lay down a trail of crumbs, of course."

Ayden yawned as a servant came to clear away the remnants of their late lunch. He was worn down with recovery and painstaking planning, and drowsy with rich human cooking—an array of delights he'd not tasted since the War of Betrayal had begun. Strange—and foolish, nay, *dangerous*—that he'd indulged in such laxity behind enemy lines.

The prince took notice of his weariness—the prince took notice of nearly everything, it seemed—and suggested a break. "Perhaps you wish to nap?"

"No." Ayden heaved himself to his feet and crossed the study to the bedroom, aiming for the window. What he needed was exercise and sunlight, two things he'd seen precious little of this week. And though it chafed him raw to ask permission for such a simple thing, he said, "Might I take a walk instead?"

Behind him, the prince's song struck a discordant note, though the man followed him anyway. "'Tis not safe for you to wander the grounds without me."

"Come along, then." Ayden turned to him and made a sweeping gesture toward the study. "We're finished here, have been for an hour or more. All we're doing now is shuffling stones from one pile to another and back."

The prince huffed through his nose, and his eyes, still fixed on the map table through the open study doors, narrowed as if to squeeze out one last insight from their notes and overlays. "Perhaps you're right," he said after a moment, rolling his head from side to side. "Perhaps a walk would clear my head."

Yet still he paced back toward the study, staring at the map. Ayden admired the man's dedication (though he'd sooner shoot himself with a poisoned dart than admit it aloud), but his sun-starved skin wanted, *needed* to go outside.

"You shuffle stones, Prince," he said again, and the way the prince eyed him then made him wonder if anyone else ever dared speak to him so. "And surely the burden of planning does not rest solely on you? Leave some challenge for your generals and advisors."

The prince's stare flicked to the window, and a warble of longing to match Ayden's own flared through his rigid song. Almost . . . Ayden held out his hand and wiggled his fingers, suffering the idea of touch for a higher cause. Of course the prince took the bait; a smile broke out across his face, and a hum of nervous lust twined through his longing as their fingers touched.

The handholding didn't last beyond the bedroom, fallen gods be thanked, for apparently 'twas all fine and well for the household to believe the prince raping him, but intolerable to hint that the prince might be fond of him.

The prince's guards fell into step round them as they left the apartment, and servants and soldiers bowed deep as they passed them in the halls. Ayden heard many a hateful feeling tossed his way, but only respect, admiration, and love for the prince. 'Twas the sign of a fair ruler, even he had to admit . . . in the privacy of his own mind.

Three corridors and one flight of stairs later, their little group stepped, blinking, into the sun. Ayden paused just past the threshold, closed his eyes and threw his head back, sucking in fresh air through his nose and reveling in the touch of the breeze upon his skin.

A thousand songs clashed and twined in the air: the staccato clicking of sparring pikes, the scream of iron under a blacksmith's heavy hand, the whinnies of frightened colts, and the chatter of lords and ladies enjoying the open space; but also the joyous songs of trees and shrubs, birds and insects, and the vital melody of bodies at eager work. 'Twas a cacophony profound and beauteous all at once.

He opened his eyes and looked round the enormous bailey, spotting from where he stood a stable and riding ring, a barracks, a smithy and workshops. Human males practiced in training yards, and overdressed women rested on marble benches or strolled along the gardens and fountains and statuary. 'Twas lovely enough, though neither as green nor majestically wild as the Hall of the Elders where he'd first sworn his liegance to the elven army, first learned to fight for all he loved.

A wave of longing fit to drown him crested through his heart, but he rode it with skill and forced it back from whence it came; this was not his first battle away from home, nor his first time caught behind enemy lines. Brooding would do him no good here. He should count his blessings instead—he could almost believe he was fortunate, in fact, to have fallen into the hands of this particular human.

"I thought you said you wanted to *walk*," the prince said, nudging him from his reverie with his shoulder.

"Actually," Ayden said, feeling his muscles swell with life after so long shackled by injury, "I'd much rather run. Shall we race, Prince?"

And he took off like a dart from his blowpipe before the prince could answer.

He heard a dramatic sigh behind him, and a shout—"No, leave him be! He can't go far"—then the sound of boots stomping in the grass, the tread both heavier and slower than his own but certainly no less determined. He tossed a look over his shoulder and saw the prince, head down, running full bore. Oh, the human could make chase all he wanted. Ayden grinned and kicked up his pace.

He was moving so swiftly now that the wind gripped at his clothes and hair, and his feet pounded out a hymn upon the earth as air surged through his chest in counterpoint. The sun was hot but he carried his breeze along with him, rustling the bushes and trees in his wake. He hadn't moved like this in far too many days, and he'd forgotten how strong he was, how much endurance he possessed, how joyous life could be without thought, only motion—how simple it was to outrun all the trouble and bother of the world.

Except he wasn't alone this time. He could not run where he pleased, for he carried Ella in his mind with every step, like a chain stretching back to her rooms, heavy for all that it was loved and willingly carried.

And to think that only moments ago, he'd been foolish enough to consider himself nearly fortunate.

He realized he'd slowed down when the sounds of the prince, struggling mightily behind him, gained in volume. Ayden gritted his teeth and redoubled his pace, running now for spite. A quick glance over his shoulder revealed that the guards in their dress armor had long fallen away and that the prince, rapidly losing ground, was waving for him to stop. Ayden pretended he'd not seen it and set out on a new circle of the bailey, passing by the hard-winded guards and their murderous glares. The prince's song grew faint and distant behind him, and Ayden allowed himself a feral smile; even in recovery, he'd run this human into the dirt in the span of a league, and he'd quietly scouted the whole of the bailey along the way.

A sharp turn by the western wall brought the prince into his sight, flushed and floundering like the fool he was. But perhaps Ayden had made too much the fool of him, for the prince had already proven his prickliness toward public shows of disrespect, and this . . . this humiliation was *certainly* public. He staggered to a halt, weighted by the thought of losing the privilege of the bailey.

Well, so be it. He would no more sacrifice spite for privilege than he'd break under the whip. If the prince thought to control him this way . . .

But the impulse to run had deserted him. He plopped down by a pear tree, settled against the trunk, and asked the tree to share its fruit. It obliged with a contented hum by dropping a pear into his upturned hand.

By the time the prince reached him, panting like a racehorse, Ayden was nibbling at what remained of the fruit's core.

"Enjoying yourself?" the prince asked, folding in half and dropping his hands to his knees.

Ayden flashed him the familiar mean smile, unwilling to so much as consider an apology. "Oh my, yes," he drawled, and he may or may not have accidentally-on-purpose tossed the pear core onto the prince's shoe.

The prince, alas, ignored the offense against his footwear. He was practically beaming as he straightened up, blue eyes aglitter with the force of his smile. "Indeed! It's been many a year since I've run for the joy of it. I'd forgotten how exhilarating a footrace could be."

Suddenly Ayden didn't feel like smiling anymore. "Exhilarating for you, perhaps," he said. "For me 'tis cruel mockery, when to run reminds me only that I cannot run free."

He'd meant the words to hurt the prince, but they bit into his own heart with potent truth. His earlier elation now pained him all the more for casting light upon the bleakness in which he was living. And if his satisfaction at blighting the prince's pleasure wasn't quite complete, well, slaves had to make do with whatever satisfaction they could find.

The prince regarded him a long moment, and Ayden hated that he could make no sense of the shifting song behind the man's eyes. But finally the prince said, "Let us return to my rooms, then, if you find this taste of freedom so intolerable."

Ayden squashed his protest between clenched teeth. The human was watching him as if waiting for something, perhaps the very denial on his tongue. So that he could throw it in Ayden's face? No. Let him wait.

The prince shook his head and turned away, though he soon realized that Ayden had no intention of rising from the pear tree, and turned back. Now his body was singing anger loud and plain, for all that he covered it with a smooth mask.

Ayden climbed slowly to his feet, looking round the bailey for what would probably be the last time and wondering what new punishment he'd just earned himself. 'Twas well worth it, though, if the prince would finally start acting as he should: a soulless brute rather than this confusing amalgam of entitlement and unrelenting kindness.

# Chapter Seven

'Twas a relief to be inside again, out of the public eye, especially when said eye had been looking upon him askance. Freyrík had given himself up to the run with rare youthful abandon, but after its disastrous end, he'd become acutely aware of what a spectacle he'd made of himself in sight of his court.

And now the elf was trailing him shrouded in sullenness again, as if Freyrík had been the one to cloud their afternoon. Gah, the ungrateful *gróm*! 'Twas beyond him how someone could turn every gesture of kindness upon its ear. Captivity could make anyone bitter, but surely Ayden knew his actions would only incite Freyrík's anger and squash his instinct for compassion. Whyever would the elf choose to bring such pain upon himself?

They arrived at his rooms, and though two pages opened the doors before them, Freyrík drew to a stop. Perhaps he should simply ask Ayden, for he could see no other way to—

The elf ducked past him and entered the drawing room first, as if he ruled sovereign over Farr.

Freyrík gaped after him, heat rising in his cheeks as the guards' and pages' stares darted between him and Ayden, equally incredulous. Of all the befanged insults to give! 'Twas enough to make a man rage despite all efforts to the contrary, which in turn made him rage even more.

Yet he was a strategist himself, and darkers take him if he'd allow a churlish elf to maneuver him into a corner. He reached for the doors and pulled them shut with a crash.

"There," he said to the hall guards, as if he'd meant all along to exile the elf to his rooms. "See that he makes no mischief."

They clicked their heels with renewed respect and fell into position, two of them cracking open his doors and slipping into his rooms with sheepish expressions, as though loath to undermine his grand gesture.

And Freyrík found himself stranded in the corridor of his own home.

He could not remain standing there, so he walked away, though he had no idea where he was headed; only that he was far too livid for working or thinking or resting or even fucking, which left only fighting or talking. He tried to envision entering Lord Lini's rooms and sharing his woes over a glass of port.

Fighting it was, then.

If his personal guard wondered why they were returning to the bailey so soon after leaving it, the four shadow-like men made no sign. Freyrík thought to pick up a practice sword and trounce the training cadets one by one—'twould be a good opportunity to visit with his sons, if nothing else—but halfway across the bailey, he realized that his feet had carried him to the north tower rather than the practice fields.

Of course. Who better to council him on Ayden than Ella, and if she dared to repeat his words, no one would take heed of her. Not that he thought the lass so spiteful or foolish.

She'd been given the second- and third-floor rooms in the tower, Freyrík knew, and judging by the guards atop the second-floor landing, that's where she currently was. He fervently hoped 'twas her drawing room and not her bedroom as he approached the door.

The guards unlocked it at his nod, but still he knocked before going inside.

"Come in, Sir Prince," Ella called from beyond the door. He shook his head and smiled at the quaint salutation, giving up on wondering how she knew it was him almost before he began.

When he opened the door, a cat dashed in between his legs—and where beneath the shadow had *that* come from?—nearly tripping him and mewing indignantly, as if 'twere somehow his fault. He puzzled but briefly over the animal, his mind instead turning to relief as he saw that this was indeed Ella's drawing room, and that she was awake and fit for company.

Well, *almost* fit. She was barefoot and dressed in a robe of South Sea silk, sitting before a narrow window, gazing out over the moat and orchard and the outer walls beyond them while stroking a kitten curled in her lap.

"Sir Prince?" she said, and Freyrík realized she'd risen to her feet, displacing the kitten.

He meant to gather his faculties, but now that she'd turned toward him, he glimpsed on the windowsill an astonishing assortment of butterflies, all flexing their wings as if to reclaim her attention. He realized that more were flitting about the room, and found himself wondering how a darker butterfly would look.

Did butterflies even have teeth?

"Prince Freyrík?"

Manners prevailed where concentration had not, and Freyrík snapped his stare to her and gave a slight bow. "Lady Daell," he said, remembering at the last moment to use her proper name.

"Do you bring news of my brother?"

He snorted, half exasperated at the thought of Ayden and half amused at her question, then held up a placating hand when her eyes narrowed. "He is well," he said, walking over to the chair across from hers. "'Tis only that his first question is always of you, as well."

His answer seemed to please her, for a smile dawned upon her face; Freyrík was captivated by it as he took his seat, and so it came as quite a shock when, a heartbeat later, a terrible screech filled his ears and something sharp raked across the seat of his breeches. He leapt away, and so did the cat that had occupied his chair, bristling and hissing. Freyrík almost reached for his sword before his mind caught up with "*Not* darker."

Tinkling laughter filled the room.

Freyrík scowled at Ella as he sat in his now cat-free chair, but 'twas difficult to be angry at such a sweet girl. Especially now, trying as she was to stifle her giggle with her fingertips as she retook her seat.

"I'm sorry, Sir Prince," she said, the amusement in her tone giving way to sincerity and perhaps just a touch of worry. "I didn't mean—"

"Oh no, child," he drawled, "worry not. The gods know your brother has no trouble laughing at my expense."

She dropped her hand from her lips, which had settled into a faint smile. "Ayden, he brings you much grief?"

"Yes." Freyrík sighed, leaning back as much as he dared in the delicate ladies' chair. "He reminds me at every turn of how despicable I am, how slow and weak, how tainted all my motives are." He realized what he'd said, what she'd last heard of him, and added quickly, "I've not . . . hurt him."

Well, not like *that*, anyway.

Ella was scooping up the feline he'd startled—that had startled him, rather—and paused to eye him over its tawny head. "I did not think you had," she said, cradling the cat against her chest. It purred as happily as most any male would to find itself pressed against such a bosom.

Freyrík quickly drew his eyes higher, to hers. "Where did all these cats come from?"

"They are your rat-catchers, Sir Prince. I'm told dozens roam your halls." She scratched the cat between its ears and added, "But I do not think you came to speak to me of cats."

"No, I did not."

And why, pray tell, *had* he come?

"Ayden is . . . bitter," Ella said.

Freyrík's hand clenched atop his thigh. "And you are not?"

She shook her head slowly.

"Why?" he asked, cringing at the sharpness of the word even as it left his lips. "Why don't *you* hate me?"

"Because you are wedged between two tall cliffs and can go neither left nor right, forward nor back. I know you cannot free us. Your people would tear us *all* to pieces if you tried. 'Twould be easiest for you to sell us, and most profitable too, but you have not. Nor have you killed us, or thrown us in the stocks or the dungeon, or used us for your pleasure, though you clearly have eyes for my brother. You have in fact done all you can—at every turn and at great expense and effort—to make our captivity as comfortable as possible. Well," she shrugged, "at least my captivity. But I can hear into the hearts of men, Sir Prince, and yours sings pure in my ears. There is blood on your hands, but it sickens you; you only do what you must for your people."

Freyrík stared at her, overcome by warmth—and yea, even love, though not of the familiar sort—at being so cleanly and openly understood. And frustration as well, that she who'd been shunted aside to these rooms could see so clearly, while her brother remained so obstinately blind.

Ella was regarding him in turn, and Freyrík wished he could hear emotions as Ayden claimed to do. She seemed . . . hesitant, or perhaps conflicted. But finally she gave a firm nod, shooed the cat off her lap and smoothed her robe.

"Ayden knows these things well," she said, "but his mind is sometimes silenced by his heart. And he cannot bear to lose control; that is the difference between he and I." She paused for a moment, instinctively stroking the tawny feline as it jumped back into her lap. "If you wedge me between two tall cliffs, I would hang a portrait on each and call them home. If you wedge Ayden, he would spend the next thousand years carving a stairway with his blade, one grain of stone at a time, until he could call himself free."

"I do not wish to be carved," Freyrík said darkly.

"Nor have you a thousand years. So you must give him the stairway he seeks, if you wish to earn his friendship."

Freyrík opened his mouth to ask what god could ever hope to accomplish that when Ella added, "Only promise me you'll not harm him if he fails to see the goodness in your heart. I believe you would not, but you must promise."

Freyrík bowed his head. "I give you my word as Crown Prince of Farr, Lady Daell."

She stood then with a nod, scooped the cat from her lap and deposited it in Freyrík's before he could object or lurch away. He didn't quite dare to move as the feline mewed, spun in a circle, kneaded at his thigh (with claws, befang it!) and then sprawled across both legs, purring away. He'd never held these creatures before, never bothered to touch them—a superstition perhaps, ill feelings left over from their dark cousins.

"Pet him," Ella said. "It will soothe you both."

And for one mad moment, Freyrík dared to think she spoke not only of the cat.

Freyrík returned to his rooms with a light heart, his very blood singing a challenge to Ayden's obstinance. The two guards in his drawing room looked distinctly thunderous, and he could easily see why: a servant had brought by a tea tray, and it seemed Ayden had eaten both their sandwiches and sweets and was now lying across the sofa in the drawing room with his dirty boots on.

Freyrík swallowed a grin that would have tipped his hand, newly excited as he was to clash with Ayden on *this* battlefield, kindness versus spite, with Ella's words still glowing in his mind. He ignored the elf completely and crossed over to his private study, where he unlocked one of the map chests with the key tucked into his collar and rummaged through the scrolls. Battlements, ground level, second floor, secret passages—gods forbid, not that one—ah, there. He snatched up the parchment and strode back to the drawing room, then dropped the scroll across Ayden's chest.

Ayden acknowledged him with a lazy turn of his eyes in his otherwise still head, not lifting a finger to move the scroll from his chest. But if

Freyrík was learning anything from Ayden, 'twas patience, and he knew the elf's curiosity would eventually get the best of him. He crossed his arms and waited.

"Your guards threatened to beat me if I ate your food," Ayden said.

"I see you listened well."

Ayden's smile was all teeth. "'Twas an empty threat. They fear to touch me, all of them."

Metal jingled and cloth rustled behind Freyrík, where the two men in question must have shifted in place.

"Truth be told, I forbade them to harm you," Freyrík said, feeling rather sorry for them upon reflection. "They will act when it matters."

"Yes, yes," Ayden said. "So you've claimed."

There followed a long silence, Ayden seemingly content in it, and Freyrík assessing and discarding plans for his next move. Finally he struck upon a promising one: he kicked off his shoes and made a great show of taking a seat on the sofa—on top of Ayden's shins, for lack of free space.

Ayden pulled his legs in at the last moment, and Freyrík sank into the cushions, stretching out his feet to a nearby stool. He raised an eyebrow at the elf, who was nearly folded in half on his back and glaring furiously. Then, for the master's touch, he patted his lap in invitation for Ayden to rest his feet.

Ayden stretched back out, but only to kick at him. Or so he tried, at least; Freyrík captured the elf's legs and calmly stretched them across his lap, as if that had been Ayden's intent all along. Ayden tensed but did not attempt, much to Freyrík's amusement, to pull away. Perhaps he'd rather bear the contact than betray his distress. Or perhaps he'd realized that pulling away meant suffering an indignant pose, or else relinquishing the sofa to Freyrík. And therein lay the beauty of the maneuver: Freyrík had gained a victory no matter the outcome.

Ayden seemed to realize as much, for he sighed and said, "If I ask you what this scroll is, will you move?"

Now Freyrík allowed himself a little grin. "Yes."

He waited, and waited, and waited some more.

Then, "What. Is. It."

"A gift," Freyrík said, altogether more pleased than he probably should be. *Carve away, Ayden. Here's your befanged stairway.* "Go on, have a look."

Though Freyrík kept his promise and stood, he was still treated to a sigh before Ayden deigned to sit up and unroll the parchment.

"What is this?" Ayden asked again, quite earnestly this time, though the edge of mistrust in his voice made clear his suspicion of the answer.

Freyrík's grin threatened to stretch right off his face. "Is it not self-evident?"

He watched as Ayden turned his eyes back to the scroll, staring hard, wonderment smoothing the lines from his eyes and slackening his jaw.

"'Tis a rendering of the bailey," Freyrík said nevertheless. "Every wall, every gate, every guard post, every bush and tree and fountain. I thought to spare you the trouble. You should enjoy your time outside, not squander it seeking ways to escape." He gave in and let his grin run wild. "That is what the evenings are for."

"But . . ." Ayden looked between Freyrík and the scroll, mouth agape like a grounded pond-fish. "How did you . . .?"

"Guess? I am no fool, Ayden, and neither are you. 'Tis what I would have done, if our positions were reversed."

"*We* don't keep slaves," the elf retorted, but it seemed mere unthinking reaction, half-hearted at best. He scrubbed a hand through his hair, scattering it to all points of the compass in a most endearing fashion, and Freyrík's urge to run his own hands through those black tufts was nearly irresistible. He managed to refrain, but only by concentrating on a future in which such gestures would be welcome.

"Why would you do this?" Ayden asked.

"Because trust must begin *somewhere*."

Unsurprisingly, his candor went amiss; Ayden narrowed his eyes and set his jaw in that mulish way of his. "Do not think to woo me so simply, Prince. 'Tis easy to trust when you pull all the strings, for the puppet can do only as you bid it."

Freyrík snorted and turned away. If it weren't for the shield of Ella's words round his heart, he suspected the barb would have struck deep and driven him off in a fury.

As it were, he paced but two tight circles before regaining control of his thoughts and modeling his voice after calm reason. "If my gift fails to please you, Ayden, I could take it back. You need only ask."

He held his hand out for the scroll, kept it outstretched as moment after moment passed, blessing the gods for his hours-long drills with the longsword. Ayden was watching his hand as if a darker viper, and the elf's fingers tightened and loosened round the scroll, tightened and loosened. Freyrík kept his mounting sense of triumph off his face with steely discipline.

Finally Ayden tucked the scroll by his side, and his eyes turned up to meet Freyrík's. "'Tis . . . not unthoughtful," he allowed.

Freyrík let his arm drop and nodded gravely, though he feared the elf could hear the full blast of his smugness, composed mask or no. Well, enough ground gained for the moment; pressing one's advantage was not always wise.

"'Tis time I take supper with my court again," he said. "I'll have something more substantial than a tea tray sent up for you." He inclined his head and made his exit, leaving behind a much befuddled elf.

One stair at a time.

Freyrík headed for the Great Hall with a small pang of guilt. 'Twas hard to believe the elf had come into his life only three days past, so long they seemed. But he'd not shown his face nearly enough these past days, and the gods knew his people needed a strong presence at the reins in these befanged times.

He endured an hour or two of the noise and the crowd, the prayer and the ceremony of a court supper, the subtle raunchiness of the merriment and the music and the free-flowing wine. His sharp hearing caught murmurs of the elves up and down the long tables perpendicular to his own, and his mood swung between amusement and irritation.

The food was superb as always, but the most pleasant aspect to the whole affair was the conversations with his sons, of whom he saw not nearly enough as prince-regent. They were doing well in the training arena, and he listened to them chatter about points scored and new maneuvers learned, and could they please fight in the coming Surge? He gently denied their pleas, and shivered inside when they vowed to be ready for battle soon.

Yet there were many other demands on his attention, not all of them present at the table. He'd grown quite skilled over the years at nodding and laughing in all the right places, entertaining lords and ladies alike with one half of his brain while the other fretted away over affairs of home and state, but this week's distractions were proving most formidable. His First Lady Consort, two moons pregnant with his seventh child (gods forgive him for hoping 'twas a girl), sat on the dais at his right, picking up his considerable slack throughout the evening with effortless charm and grace.

'Twas the thought of the dessert awaiting him in his rooms that spurred him to leave immediately after the main course, but Lady Drífa touched his elbow, leaned into his ear and whispered, "Lady Ádísa misses you, My Prince."

'Twas a conspiracy, no doubt, for at the same time Lady Ádísa glanced up at him through painted eyelashes, two seats down the dais table, across from two of his middle sons. He sighed and forced himself to smile, placed a kiss on Lady Drífa's cheek, and held his arm out to Lady Ádísa as he walked past. She'd gone five years without birthing him a living child, and he'd begun to wonder if his bloodline had any future in her womb. But he did not have the heart to cast her from his bed, grateful as he was for the two sons she'd given him early in their years together.

Their coupling was sweet and respectful as always, and Freyrík made a point to lie by her side until she drifted off to sleep, comforting her by his presence that she wasn't to blame for not bearing him more heirs. Then he untangled himself from the sheets, made hasty work of cleansing himself in her washroom, and headed back for the bed he truly wished to occupy. He'd already given Ayden two nights' respite to habituate; he would no longer be an exile from his own rooms.

The hour was approaching unseemly by the time he returned to his chambers, which seemed woefully empty in the light of a few scattered candelabras. A glance at the guards in his drawing room, however, reassured him that Ayden had not yet made good his escape. He crept into his bedroom and found the elf there, sleeping in the befanged corner again, cocooned up in Freyrík's bedclothes with only the faint glow round his hair peeking out.

The bed was stripped clean again.

Freyrík shook his head, but 'twas not irritation that moved him. True, Ayden was spiteful; but this particular defiance, this pitiful bundle of blankets and elf in the corner, smacked of fear more than hatred. But as Freyrík lived and breathed, had he not proven himself to Ayden already, at least on that account?

Well, he would prove himself again, if necessary.

A lantern flared within the groom's chamber by the washroom, and the man emerged, blinking and ruffled, to attend him. Yet for all their footsteps and candlelight, the elf remained asleep, and Freyrík couldn't help but wonder what mischief the creature had wrought to exhaust himself so.

"Has the evening been peaceful?" he said quietly, holding out his arms for his groom to peel off his doublet.

"Yes, Your Highness," the groom said, and after a pause that might have contained a glance at the sleeping elf, "After a fashion."

"He does carry a certain amount of turmoil with him," Freyrík said absently.

The soft conversation woken Ayden at last; one moment Freyrík's groom was agreeing with him, and the next, the nest of blankets in the corner erupted in a flurry, and Ayden was on his feet. Freyrík squinted as his elflight flared like a midnight sun.

"Oh, it's you," Ayden said after a moment, tension visibly draining out of him along with the worst of the glare.

Freyrík raised an eyebrow. "I do live here, you know." By the lantern's glow, he spotted a tome tangled in the discarded bedclothes, as if the elf had fallen asleep reading it. "I see you've helped yourself to my library."

Ayden glanced down, then back, and shrugged. "Your guards said they would—"

"Beat you if you touched my belongings?" Freyrík said, nudging his groom out of his petrified reverie. "Yes, they're consistent if nothing else."

He shrugged his shirt into his groom's hands, then turned to give the man better access to his belt buckle. He felt Ayden's eyes upon him, intent and intense and all but scorching his skin, and could not resist turning his head to meet them. The elf's stare brimmed with wary mistrust, certainly, but Freyrík dared hope 'twas not entirely without approval. Had he not admitted he found Freyrík pleasing?

"What are you doing?" Ayden asked, his voice half-choked.

"Undressing." Freyrík steadied himself on his kneeling groom's shoulder as he stepped out of his breeches. "'Twould be highly inconvenient to sleep in full regalia, do you not think?"

When Ayden remained silent, he added, "As it would be to sleep in that corner. Tonight, you and I shall both enjoy the comfort of my bed. Elf or not, I trust your backbone shall thank me in the morning."

He stepped out of his undergarment and turned to give Ayden a disarming smile, but faltered instead at the flash of panic he saw in the elf's eyes. Alas, with his groom at hand, he could offer only roundabout reassurance.

"Fetch my nightclothes," he instructed the man, ignoring the surprise that flashed across his features. "The blue silk." And with a secret nod at Ayden, "I'm quite sated for the night, and thoroughly tired."

At least 'twas only half a lie.

He left to the privacy of his washroom for his evening ablutions, and when he returned to the bedroom, he saw that attendants had re-made the bed, and Ayden was standing in the empty corner, timid as a new servant. Freyrík stepped forward and held out his hand, and Ayden took it reluctantly, letting Freyrík pull him over to the bed.

"I will not harm you," Freyrík whispered into his ear.

Ayden leaned in close and whispered back, "I will kill you in your sleep."

Startled, Freyrík studied the elf for a moment, taking his measure. A moment later, he was laughing so hard he could barely breathe. He truly hadn't meant to, but there was no help for it, and Ayden's affronted sniff only made matters worse. He was still chuckling under his breath as he climbed into bed, pulling a scowling Ayden in behind him, and closed the curtains on them both.

# Chapter Eight

*A*yden lay awake well into the night, watchful eyes upon his unwanted bedmate. The prince had gone under quickly and deeply, clearly confident in his safety. Foolishly confident, when 'twould be so easy for Ayden to do as he'd threatened, to roll over and wrap skilled fingers round the prince's throat, snuff him in silence and have the whole of the night to act with no one the wiser . . .

. . . And with a hundred guards or more between him and freedom, a whole garrison in the bailey, and fifty soldier-infested leagues to the elven border, all with Ella to protect—assuming he could even find her.

He huffed softly, careful not to wake the prince. Perhaps the man's confidence wasn't so foolish after all.

He meant to keep watch all night, lest the prince wake from some pleasure dream and choose to act upon it. Yet at some point he must have drifted, for here he was in a night terror, trapped inside his mind just as surely as his dream-self was trapped beneath the prince's rage; hands everywhere, squeezing his throat, tearing at his clothes and hair and striking him, striking him for teasing, for withholding, for daring to think his body his own. And then it wasn't his own anymore, the prince thrusting dry and vicious between his legs, and he knew that it was more than just a dream, that there were hands on him in the waking world as well, and he couldn't, *couldn't*, not like this, with broken promises and hatred—

He woke with a stifled scream in his throat, rolling and pinning the prince beneath him in the darkness. His right hand scrabbled for a knife at his belt, failed to find it, shot up to wrap round his attacker's throat instead. Hands fumbled at his wrists but then gripped them strong and steady. The prince's breathing was calm beneath him, measured, as if the man had not just—

*Oh.*

Ayden let go and tried to climb off, but the prince tightened his grip, holding him fast. His song was beyond Ayden's capacity to decipher, though its intensity was profoundly unsettling. So was the prince's erection, pressed hard like the hilt of a dagger beneath Ayden's left buttock. But then again, 'twas Ayden's own fault for straddling him.

He tried to jerk a hand free, but 'twas clear the prince wanted him where he was. "You shouldn't touch me while I'm sleeping," he growled.

"I wasn't aware I had," the prince said, strangely unruffled for a man who'd almost just been killed.

"You had an arm and a leg over me at least."

"Did I now?"

"Yes!" Ayden snapped, jerking his wrists back again, this time twisting them round to break the prince's hold. He flung himself away, found the headboard and pressed his back to it, put his knees to his chest and wrapped his arms round his shins. "'Tis your own fault you woke in a chokehold."

"My apologies." The prince's words floated up from the darkness, mercifully none the closer. "My Lady Consorts are rather fond of being cuddled; 'twas mere habit, I assure you. I did not mean to startle or impose upon you."

"I am *not* your Lady Consort."

"'Tis not what I meant—"

"And next you'll try to tell me your intentions are all noble?" Ayden couldn't feel the prince's erection anymore, or see it through the darkness, but he could almost *hear* the cracking thing straining against the prince's nightclothes.

"My heart beats, Ayden; you cannot fault it for wanting."

"Nor the beast in heat for rutting, I suppose."

The prince's song tripped a beat. "I deserved that."

Ayden squeezed his eyes shut. Fallen gods help him, was that a tingle of guilt he was feeling? "No," he said reluctantly. "You didn't. Don't make a bigger fool of yourself than you are. 'Tis just . . ." He shifted and pulled his knees in a little tighter. "When I woke to you atop me, I thought . . ."

Now sympathy wound into the prince's song, more grating upon Ayden's ear than the constant beat of arousal. He groped for a pillow and punched it into shape, shoved it behind his back. "You know what, never mind. I *didn't* think, 'twas just training taking over. You're lucky I was able to stop myself in time."

The prince made no reply, but neither did his song smooth down into slumber. His silence was, Ayden admitted after a time, unnerving.

He wished he could roll over and ignore it, but he had no intention of uncurling from his corner of the bed, much less turning his back on the prince.

Moments crawled by.

"Will you go to sleep already?" he finally snapped.

"I can't," the prince said, and before Ayden could berate him for his unquenchable lust, "You're glowing."

"I— what?"

A deep sigh, more self-conscious than weary. "I'm not used to sleeping with a light." Ayden only blinked at him, and the prince added, sheepish, "The gods know how you do it every night."

Ayden let his head thump back against the headboard. "It's not . . . really there, you do realize."

Confusion curled through the prince's song, and Ayden felt the man's stare upon him, as if he suspected Ayden were playing him for a fool. "But I can see it, clear as day."

This time, Ayden thumped his head on purpose. It was going to be a long, long night.

When Freyrík next woke, the hour was much more reasonable, and the method much more pleasant: the sound of the morning trumpet was familiar in his ears, the scent of the elf new and strong in his nostrils. He'd rolled over during the night, not quite touching Ayden but certainly crowding him, and a particularly demanding erection was now straining at his underclothes. He rolled back with much willpower, and offered Ayden a chagrined smile when the elf opened his eyes and glared at him.

"Good morrow," Freyrík said. "Did you manage some rest?"

"No. You snore."

"I do no such—"

"What's for breakfast?"

Freyrík would have snorted at Ayden's biting tone, relieved as he was to see the elf unaffected by their nocturnal incident—well, at least as caustic as ever—but he thought he heard an appalled gasp from beyond the bed curtains. His attendants would be in to prepare his morning ablutions, of course.

He shook his head at Ayden, then slapped his hand against his own thigh with an almighty crack, which luckily surprised the elf into gasping. "Watch your tongue, elf!"

He locked stares with Ayden until understanding blossomed in those green eyes.

"Apologies, Prince," Ayden murmured, five shades of sullen short of convincing.

Freyrík threw open the curtains and greeted his groom, nodded to the servant who was stirring the fire to life. "I'll break fast in the Great Hall today," he announced to both his staff and the elf. To the latter he added, "I'll have something sent up for you."

Ayden blinked and sat up. "You deny me your company?"

His tone was polite, almost earnest, but Freyrík felt the darts of his sarcasm strike home. The armor of Ella's words must be wearing thin, for he found himself growing irritated. "I miss my sons," he said shortly.

"You have *children*?" Ayden asked, almost outraged, as if Freyrík had suggested he'd birthed them himself.

"Six, actually. All boys."

"And you are how old?"

"Twenty-nine."

"Gods," Ayden spat, jumping out of bed as if he feared Freyrík might somehow infect him with his fertility. "You humans breed like field mice!"

"'Tis a duty to our people," Freyrík said, fighting mightily to keep his temper in check. "We must replace those who die. To speak true, I have fewer children than most noblemen of my years." When Ayden said nothing further, he asked, "And you? Do you have children?"

"No," Ayden said, and Freyrík was shocked at the depth of his own relief; he'd have hated to think he was keeping a father from his family.

Ayden sat down on the edge of the bed and picked at his shirt. "My clothes, can I have them back?"

The change of topic was so abrupt that it took Freyrík a moment to digest. "I'm afraid they're ruined," he said. "But I can have fresh clothes sent up from the seamstress, whatever you want."

"I want *my* clothes."

Freyrík tossed his hands, let them land with a smack against his thighs. "Must *everything* be a battle with you, Ayden?"

The elf bristled visibly. "I am trapped behind enemy lines, am I not?"

"So you remind me continuously. You would be much less hale and happy if *I* reminded you as often and with as much venom. Try to remember that I don't. And that I have no intention to."

Ayden's expression hardened, and Freyrík sighed again, cradled his forehead in one hand and shooed his attendants from the bedroom with the other.

"I see," he said. "You hate me for what I do. You hate me for what I don't do. You even hate me for my kindness, for it threatens to come between you and your hate, but you would hate me just as surely if I ordered you flogged. Nothing I do is or ever can be right."

"You can set us free," Ayden said. "That would be right."

Freyrík met his eyes, and he saw in them the truth of which Ella had spoken. "I cannot do that," he said. "You *know* I cannot do that."

A muscle jumped in Ayden's jaw. "I know you haven't *tried*."

'Twas all Freyrík could do not to shout his disbelief. "You would have me commit high treason against my own people, against King and Aegis, for a prisoner who's brought us nothing but grief and misfortune?"

Ayden glared but said nothing. Freyrík could well imagine his internal struggle, but he lacked elven perception and could hear no tell of which side of Ayden's mind and heart would win.

For both their sakes, he hoped it would be reason.

The prince readied himself to leave, ordering breakfast for Ayden before removing himself to the washroom. Ayden was glad to see him gone, for he could not bear to lay eyes on him just now, or to have those knowing eyes laid upon himself. Though it galled him to admit it, the human had a point.

And him . . . where did that leave him? Acting like a spoiled child, demanding favors with entitlement that even a friend would resent. He'd thought he'd been fighting for his pride, but in truth, he'd only been soiling it.

He sat heavily on the cedar chest at the foot of the bed, watching servants flit in and out of the room. Two approached to dress the prince's bed, giving Ayden wide berth and wary glances, as if expecting he'd pounce and savage them at the first opportunity. Crack it, he was *not* a beast!

Yet he was beginning to feel like one what with the chains and locked doors, the hostility and fear from the prince's staff, the obedience the prince demanded of him, the way he had to beg for every little thing. No wonder the servants thought him a dog, when a walk outside was a reward to dangle over his head! He all but shook with the wrongness of it. He wanted to run beneath the sun. He wanted his clothes back. Crack it, he wanted a bath. The fragrant steam wafting in from the washroom was a cruel taunt in his nostrils, but he'd resolved to demand no longer, and it would hardly occur to the prince to offer. Once more, where did that leave him?

Tired and aching and craving a hot soak.

Or perhaps not. He would not be the beast *or* the spoiled child; he would not beg, he would not demand. But he could *ask*, could he not? With plain dignity, as an equal, even though the prince refused to acknowledge him as such. Even though he was, in fact, much more than the human's mere equal.

Ayden stood from the cedar chest and strode toward the washroom door, but he took only two steps before the prince emerged, dressed for the day, hair damp and curling and face scraped smooth. Why he bothered to grow bristles every day, only to shave them off on the morrow, was beyond Ayden's ken.

Ayden cleared his throat and said, "Prince, may I . . ."

The prince drew to a halt and eyed him calmly, clearly waiting for him to complete his thought. Yet the words seemed stuck on his tongue, and he could not rattle them free.

A different tack, then: "It's just that I'm—" *filthy*, he thought, but that word got stuck as well, trapped behind the humiliating image of a pig in a sty.

Still the prince waited patiently, eyebrows arched, a soft smile on his face.

Crack it, he was no coward. And was it not a simple enough question, from one equal to another?

"Can I have a bath?"

The prince's smile brightened, and behind it Ayden heard surprise, pleasure, even relief. "Of course," he said. He nodded to two attendants hovering nearby and said, "See one drawn, just as you would mine."

The attendants bowed without hesitation and set to work, hiding their surprise much more deftly than Ayden did. Truly, all he had to do was ask? At best he'd hoped for some cold water and tallow soap—certainly not the prince's own finery. More likely, he'd expected a denial, condescending derision, another reason to hate the man.

He'd gotten what he wanted; why, then, was he disappointed?

Ayden dropped back upon the cedar chest as the prince took to a cushioned stool before a mercuried glass mirror. The prince's reflection smiled at him as a man rushed over with a comb to tame his mussed hair. Another came over with a heap of sapphire jewelry to match his eyes—brooch, wrist cuffs, rings, a collar of state worth more than Ayden would earn in a lifetime—and a third kneeled down to don and lace his boots.

"After your bath," the prince said, talking to Ayden as if no one else were in the room, as if there were nothing odd or ostentatious about a whole hive of worker-bees swarming over your person, "You may borrow some new clothes. The green tunic, I think," he said, turning to his groom, "the one my cousin brought back from Midr Province last year." The groom nodded and left, presumably to fetch said tunic. "And my personal seamstress shall attend you; she will fit you with a wardrobe of your own." He smiled at Ayden through the mirror again, as if to say, *Look how generous I am.* 'Twas all Ayden could do not to sing the glass broken in his face. "We have all the finest fabrics at our disposal, and surely she can duplicate your old clothes, if you wish it."

For a moment, Ayden was struck speechless. He could see in the mirror the beginnings of a wondering smile on his own lips, and the warmth pooling in his chest felt suspiciously like . . . Wait, gratitude? Ayden caught it short and wiped his face blank. Such kindness would be welcomed from a friend, but from the prince? From the prince it clearly aimed to provoke exactly this gratitude, to cast a fine chain round his neck, feather-light. And then another would surely follow, and another and another, and before he knew it he'd be bound tight at the prince's side, a mindless pet with no more will to fight. Oh, he could see the prince's stratagem clearly now.

Gods silence him forever, he would sooner die than let that happen.

He bared his teeth in a smile that lacked any trace of wonder and asked, "Would the elven fashions not offend your delicate tastes, human?"

The prince's song and shoulders tensed, and Ayden heard a cascade of anger, doubt, and hopefulness in rapid succession. Then the prince's shoulders untensed and he said, friendly as ever, "Don't be silly. I'm quite certain the seamstress would enjoy broadening her horizons."

"Indeed," Ayden said, feeling ever more confident as the battlefield between them grew ever more familiar. "If she doesn't run screaming away from me."

The prince swatted his worker-bees away and eyed him sharply through the mirror. "Has she reason to fear you?" he asked.

"You've been turning the hearts of your people against mine with lies for the last three centuries," Ayden replied, narrowing his eyes to hide the smugness he could feel lurking there. "What else could she do *but* fear me?"

Alas, his accusation bounced off the prince like arrows off an elf-steel shield. The man turned to look him in the eye directly, frustratingly calm. "Three centuries of lies did not kill sixteen of my soldiers this week. *You* did."

Well, crack him and his logic anyway.

The prince held his stare. "Have we a bargain, Ayden? A bath and new clothes for your word that you'll be naught but a gentleman with my seamstress."

And there the human sang his true song at last, as Ayden had suspected. He knew the question encompassed much more than baths and clothes, and for a moment, he longed to spit his refusal in the prince's placid face. But he also longed to soak his aching body, to be thoroughly clean again, to put on loose, practical clothes that he could run and climb and fight in when the time came . . .

He could have screamed in frustration. Surely there was a middle trail to walk between surrendering his soul and suffering the loss of every little right and pleasure in life?

Yes . . . yes there was. He would speak the words the prince wished to hear, but he would core them hollow, wrapping mock civility round pride and hatred.

"Ayden?" the prince asked. "Have we a bargain?"

Ayden leaned back, draped his arms atop the footboard. "Oh, I'm sure your guards will see to it that your precious seamstress goes unharmed."

"Your word, Ayden, or you'll spend the rest of your days here as bare as the gods made you."

Ayden narrowed his eyes. "A terrible hardship for you, I'm sure."

"You have no idea," the prince said. He gave his head a little shake, no doubt trying to dislodge the image of Ayden in the nude, and said, "Now, your word—I would have it."

"Fine," Ayden said, lightly enough to suggest he'd not heard the deeper meaning of the prince's demand. "I'll be nice."

The prince studied him as if trying to imagine such a thing and failing utterly. Ayden gave him a helpful smile; the prince winced.

"Your word," the prince repeated gravely.

Ayden shrugged. "Yes, yes, you have it."

But not me, human. Not one single piece of me.

Freyrík tapped a thumb against his knee beneath the long table in the Council Chamber, waiting for Lord General Vísi to finish speaking. 'Twas too hot in this windowless, closed-off room, especially as their session crawled toward its sixth hour.

At last General Vísi finished arguing that Tveir should be the village left to chance, and as he retook his seat, Freyrík stood to present his own plan. 'Twas his brother's way, and his father's before him, to speak last so as not to taint the ideas of those eager to climb into good graces. But oh, the waiting had never been so hard.

"My Lords," he began, accepting the pointer from Lord General Vísi with a thrill of excitement, as if taking up arms. He swept it in a precise arch over Eine, Tveir, and Háls, the three villages at the Myrkr foothills. "We are all agreed that the Surge is most likely to crest upon one of these?"

All round the table, graying heads nodded tiredly.

Freyrík bit back a fierce smile and stabbed the pointer at the grazing lands that sprawled between the villages and the forested slopes of the Myrkrs. "Then I propose we draw the line here, before they can spread to the border villages. Why choose our stand from among the three and risk choosing wrong, when instead we can check the fight at the border?"

His councilors seemed scandalized at his words, much as he'd felt at first. "We'll be slaughtered out in the open!" Duke Vesall cried, the others lending him their muttered support.

This time Freyrík allowed himself a smile, eager to visit Ayden's revelation upon them. "Hear me," he said with a raised hand, and silence fell round the table, however surly. "My plan begins with a trap: a box canyon. Ingress for the darkers, but no egress. Death from above by archers. The perfect battleground."

He waited as their stares roved over the map, seeking and failing to find this promised haven, for of course they were searching on the human side of the fissure. Duke Vesall alone was looking up at him, his countenance wary.

Freyrík swung the pointer and settled it with a sharp tap atop the box canyon that Ayden had chosen. "Right here, My Lords."

He waited for the storm of outrage and doubt that he himself had expressed only yesterday. His councilors did not disappoint.

"Gentlemen!" he called over the clamor, "Listen! I've not been afflicted with the Darker Fever, if that be your concern." Nervous laughter skittered round the table, compelled by his jest. "There is dark magic in these lands, true, but they are not haunted as some would claim. Our own scouts have set foot across the fissure and returned, have they not?"

From round the table came tentative murmurs of consent, but Duke Vesall was shaking his head emphatically.

Freyrík turned his attention on him. "I assure you, Your Grace, had the gods placed the perfect battlefield on our side of the border, I would sing their praises and never glance toward darker territory. But they have placed it across the border, and who are we to question their choice? 'Twould be folly to pass up this opportunity over wives' tales."

"With respect, Your Highness," Duke Vesall said, "our wives' only tales would be of our early demise if we do as you suggest."

"On the contrary, Your Grace. Our troops shall never fight a safer battle in their lives. We'll line the canyon walls with archers, far beyond the reach of any earthbound darker. At the canyon's mouth we shall lay a massive brush wall with but a few small passages. Soak the brush in oil, and when the last of the darkers has entered the canyon, set the blaze from above with arrows. Then they will be as beasts at the slaughter, trapped between fire and walls too steep to climb, ripe for our archers to pick off at leisure."

The duke was shaking his head even before Freyrík finished speaking. "All good and well, Your Highness, but for one small detail. Who but the dark elves or the gods themselves could herd the darkers to attack two leagues from the grounds where even you admit the Surge must crest?"

Freyrík waited out the restless mutters and headshakes prompted by the duke's question. Even Commander Hákon was wearing a troubled frown that bordered on disappointment. When quiet reigned again, he said, "The answer is bait, Your Grace." He flicked the pointer at Duke

Vesall as if saluting him by blade. "An entire battalion of our swiftest cavalry, more if we can commandeer the horses. You know the darkers cannot resist attacking at the sight of a human. They will chase the riders straight into the canyon, without pause."

Duke Vesall blinked, and blinked again. "You mean for our cavalry to ride into the canyon? And then what? Die a helpless death in the carnage you've so well described?"

"Ladders." This, much to Freyrík's surprise and delight, from Lord Commander Hákon, whose disappointment had transformed into guarded interest.

"Precisely," he said. "We shall anchor rope ladders along each wall of the canyon. Many darkers cannot climb or leap; a good number of our men shall reach safety. The archers will shoot down any darker who gains a ladder, and auxiliary infantry at the top of the ridge will help fend off those who do manage the climb or who attack on the wing. The horses, alas, must be sacrificed, though 'tis my hope that the darkers will ignore them as they've always been prone to do."

"A reasonable loss," Lord Hákon murmured.

Duke Vesall cast a brief, incredulous look round the table, as if entreating the others for help. "And if the Surge does not crest upon Tveir?" he demanded. "If the cavalry waits there in vain?"

Freyrík had expected the question; now came the last and best component of this threefold plan. "They shall have time aplenty to head off the darkers wherever the Surge crests, for we shall keep the beasts occupied with decoys."

"More bait?" This from Lord Audigr, who sounded vaguely horrified at the thought. Strange how he could be so ruthless leading the household staff and so squeamish about sending soldiers to battle.

"Not quite," Freyrík said, a slow smile curving his lips. He retook his seat, crossed his legs and laid the pointer across his lap.

"The infantry, then? Out in the open?" And this time Lord Audigr sounded *quite* horrified.

"Again, not quite," Freyrík said. "No; why sacrifice flesh and blood when we can call upon an army of false men?"

"Women?" someone asked, outraged, as another suggested, "Eunuchs from the midlands?"

Freyrík barked a laugh. "Mercy, My Lords, I'm not in jest." Though it was good to hear them reaching for solutions, however farfetched, instead of rejecting the notion out of hand. "Nay, we shall simply draft a battalion or two of scarecrows."

For once, no protests met his statement. It seemed he'd shocked his councilors beyond reply.

"Yes, scarecrows," he answered the question that Duke Vesall would have asked had he found his voice in time. "They need only distract the darkers long enough for the cavalry to arrive and claim their attention. We'll build them sturdy and dress them in well-used clothes, permeated with human scent. Spread a thousand of them or more all along the likely Surge areas. The darkers are incapable of learning; they'll tear into them with relish until nothing is left but slivers."

The faces round the table now were growing less doubtful, more intense, just as his own had as Ayden laid out the details. And he wasn't even finished.

"Of course," he continued with an unaffected air, rising to his feet once more, "we'll take care to arm them."

"Arm them?" The startled reply came from Commander Hákon, but his face was a mask of wonder now, as if waiting for Freyrík to produce the next miracle.

Freyrík grinned at him. "'Tis only fitting. Blades screwed into their frames, caltrops and wooden spikes at their feet, all coated with poison, as much as the apothecaries can brew 'twixt now and then. A single unlucky step and a darker lames, perhaps even dies.

"Our falconers will augment the scarecrow battalion, and fighting dogs will be at the ready to ride herd if needed. Do not mistake me, My Lords. We *will* lose flesh-and-blood troops and horses on the chase, but only a handful need reach the canyon for our trap to be sprung successfully. 'Tis nevertheless my sincerest hope and belief that many a life will be spared."

Now the murmurs of assent grew into open approval, all twelve of his council nodding. Well, eleven, at least; Duke Vesall, none to Freyrík's surprise, still looked tense and doubtful. Freyrík caught and held his gaze, awaiting the quieting of the others that he may speak.

At last the happy mutterings died out, and Duke Vesall stepped in. "And if the Herders see us laying the trap? What contingencies have you planned?"

Freyrík nodded his approval at the question and tapped the pointer a few times against the center of the darker territory. "'Tis not certain the

Herders will arrive," he said. "And even if they do, these dark elves have demonstrated no more capacity to learn than their servant beasts have; their strategy has gone unchanged for centuries. However, wisdom lies on your side, Your Grace, and preparations must be made. Fortunately this plan leaves free the bulk of our infantry. We will station them at the nearby Surge fortresses as a hedge against failure and to catch those few beasts who might slip through our trap. True, they will not suffice to stop a full Surge," he said, sweeping his stare round the table and meeting the eyes of each councilor in turn. "But neither will our entire army, as five hours of debate have proven today."

For a long while, no one spoke a word. Freyrík could all but hear their tactical worldviews shifting, sliding, thudding into place on a new landscape. Commander Hákon was grinning fit to split his face in two, a danger compounded by the rarity of his smiles. General Vísi was beaming at him like a proud father. Even Duke Vesall was staring at the box canyon on the map with wondering eyes, nodding thoughtfully.

"There are still a few details to work out," Freyrík told them, though in truth he and Ayden had discussed this plan to its minutiae. "But as for the skeleton of it, are we in agreement?"

Another moment of silence, during which Freyrík wondered what new opposition they might raise. But then Commander Hákon banged his open palm on the table in a slow, measured rhythm, and Lord Lini joined him, then General Vísi and Lord Audigr, standing up now as the beat gained in tempo and volume to a thundering chorus of applause.

Embarrassed, for the plan was not even half his, Freyrík waved them free of the meeting, and they filed out on a wave of bright chatter, in high spirits but for a few. It had not escaped him that some of the councilors had cheered with polite reserve, or that they would hold him responsible for the success or failure of this extreme plan, and the life or death of Farr with it. He accepted that; 'twas no burden he did not already shoulder on his own.

Lord General Vísi stayed behind to speak with him. "With your permission, My Prince, I shall see to the preparations. Carpenters, timber, old clothes . . ."

"All in your faithful hands," Freyrík said with a smile, and with one more nod and heel-click the general was gone.

Freyrík turned round at the sense of a presence at his back, and found Lord Lini awaiting his attention.

"Did you see their faces?" Freyrík asked. "Never have they been so hopeful this close to a Surge."

Lord Lini smiled, but his lined face belied concern.

Freyrík cocked his head. "Do you not approve of the plan? I would have trusted you to speak your mind, if such were the case."

"The plan is exquisite, Your Highness. You've saved many a life today."

Well, Ayden had, strictly speaking. He wondered if he could share that knowledge with his secretary; the man was more loyal to him than any, and not as devoted to prejudice as some. Before he could decide either way, though, Lord Lini spoke again.

"There is a second issue at hand," he said. "I have heard tell that the victims of the elf killings will seek blood retribution at the state funeral."

Freyrík felt his heart stumble within his chest. "'Heard tell,' Lord Lini?"

"Yes, My Prince."

"And who exactly is telling?"

Lord Lini took his ledger from under his arm and flipped through several pages too quickly to have read them. He still did not meet Freyrík's gaze when he said, "Soldiers, My Prince, and some servants. Perhaps just rumors."

"Well then, see them stopped. The elf is a soldier, not a criminal. There will be no more rumors, and no ritual at the funeral or elsewhere."

"But, Your Highness—"

"I said *no*, Lord Lini."

His secretary clamped his lips shut and bowed his head. 'Twas not the rousing "Yes, Your Highness" that Freyrík had expected, but he supposed that it would have to do.

# Chapter Nine

yden soon fell into a terse and uneasy routine, the prince going off each morning to do whatever it was that princes did, and Ayden remaining in the human's rooms, alone but for guards and servants who could have been statues for all that they ignored him.

Trapped indoors with nothing better to do, Ayden worked his way through the prince's library, reading up on human history, their so-called culture and art, their poetry and their stage plays. He jogged in place, walked whole days on his hands to amuse himself and unsettle the guards, hung from the canopy of the prince's bed and pulled his weight up over and over to stay fit for escape. He napped during the day to pass the time and to help keep vigilant at night. He stared out the window far too much.

Thus he saw when great wagon-trains of supplies began to flow into the outer wards of the bailey: commandeered nails and tools and old clothes, cord upon cord of lumber from the royal forests, and dozens of new horses each day from the gods knew where.

Soon caravans began pouring out west, laden with scarecrows and caltrops. He could hear the newly conscripted carpenters and blacksmiths at work from sunup 'til sundown, hundreds of them building the prince's fake battalions. He envied them all, for while they were in some ways slaves as much as he, at least they worked out in the open air, well occupied and laboring in defense of what they loved.

All Ayden could do was work subtly, carefully, toward his and Ella's freedom.

'Twas unusually cool this summer morn. Ayden had woken early and stolen all the bedcovers, and now he lay cocooned at the very edge of the bed, watching the prince toss and turn in the pre-dawn light.

When Ayden tired of that, he freed a leg from the covers and kicked the prince, then promptly pretended to sleep.

"Mmph," the prince said with the typical intelligence of his race. This was followed by a sleepy, "Why is it so cold in here?" and then, "Ah. Good morning, Ayden."

Ayden lay perfectly still and kept his eyes closed.

"I know you're awake," the prince said. His questing hand found the blankets and tugged. The other hand joined a moment later. "I'll not banish you from this bed, Ayden; your efforts are futile."

The prince threw his weight into the next tug, and Ayden found himself flipped over, off the blanket he'd trapped with his body.

"Can I see Ella today?" he asked into his pillow.

"I'm afraid not," the prince said, same as he had the last dozen times.

Then again, Ayden's questions remained constant, too: "Will you take me outside?"

The prince sighed. Surely the man was growing weary of this conversation, but Ayden meant to have it every day until he saw his sister and the sun again. How long had it been since his last trip outside? Four days? Five?

"I shall do my best," the prince said. "But you know I can make no promises, for—"

"—your time is not your own, I know. Nor, apparently, is *my* time *my* own. Bad enough that you claim it whole, yet you do not even use it!"

"You'll have plenty of fresh air and exercise when we march upon the Surge."

"You may march all you will, Prince. I'm staying with my sister."

"Ayden . . ."

"Do not bother to pretend you'll harm her just to force my hand. I know you better than that by now. Now if you'll excuse me, I've a long day of tedium to prepare for." And with that he rolled over, threw back the curtain, and stomped off to the privy.

When he returned, the prince was seated before his dressing table in a silk robe the color of dusk, watching servants fill his tub through the open washroom door. He did not look happy; Ayden took some respite in knowing he had caused that.

He felt the prince's eyes follow him round the room as he gathered up his new clothes, loose cut and tightly woven, the fabric much finer than his own had been. He changed quickly, pleased to feel no pain from his wounded arm but less pleased to feel the prince's eyes affixed to his bare skin.

When he went to fetch his boots from beside the dressing table, the prince stopped him with a gentle hand.

"I would take my morning meal with you," the prince said, his voice soft enough to turn the statement into a question.

"Fine," Ayden said, folding his arms across his chest. "If it pleases you." He realized as he said it that he preferred even the prince's company to being alone in these rooms again, and had to stifle a groan. Oh, how far he'd fallen.

The prince blinked at him, momentarily silenced by the reply. But then he smiled, bright as sunrise, and said, "Yes, it would please me very much."

Ayden smiled back with all the sincerity he could muster, and sat himself down on the footstool mere hand-spans from the prince. He leaned in close, feigning interest. "And perhaps afterwards we'll take a walk outside? Even for just a moment?"

The prince's smile wilted into a long-suffering grimace. "I'm afraid after breakfast I must grant audience to my people. 'Tis a vital duty, and one I've neglected since your arrival."

"I don't suppose you grant audience in the bailey?"

"Nay." The prince pursed his lips against a smile, gods crack him. "'Twould be rather inconvenient if it rained, don't you think? I grant audience in the Great Hall."

Ayden shoved aside memories of lying in a bloodied heap on cool marble tiles and focused instead on a hazy remembrance of vaulted ceilings and wall-spanning windows. 'Twas not quite the outside, but 'twould do well enough.

"Fine," he said, "I'll go with you."

"To the Great Hall? Whatever for?"

"For my sanity!" Ayden cried, shooting to his feet and throwing his arms out wide. "If I spend even one more day trapped inside these walls, I shall go mad!"

The prince had almost recoiled into the mirror, but unfortunately he'd regained his seat and his composure and was already shaking his head. "'Twould be no better there. I love my people dearly, but those who seek audience seek it mostly to air grievance." He smiled up at Ayden as if to say, *Well then, that's that.*

Ayden didn't smile back.

The prince sighed. "Look, you can barely comport yourself in private; in public you'd be a disaster."

"I can too, and I would not!" Ayden said, beyond caring that he sounded like some whiny elfling.

The prince snorted a laugh, but he was shaking his head again even before the sound had died away. "Nay, you don't understand—there's so many ways of the court you've not yet learned."

"Only because I've had no call! Here, let me guess." Ayden hooked the stool with his foot, dragged it over, and sat down again. "Do not speak out of turn. Do not insult or argue with anyone. Do not use my elfsong." He ticked the items off on his fingers as he spoke. "How am I doing so far?"

"Would that it were that simple," the prince said. "You fail to understand that we are not equals here. So far from it, in fact, that there is none lower in status than you, and only my king and the Aegis, may the gods bless them ever strong and wise, above me. When you address me in public, you cannot ever speak to me as you do in these rooms. In fact, you should not address me at all, nor anyone else, unless ordered to speak. Even then you must limit yourself, give all due respect and use proper titles: 'sir' or 'My Lord'—but no, you would not recognize the nobility. Better 'My Lord' to anyone but me, where 'tis 'Your Highness' or 'Master.'"

"Simple enough," Ayden said. He'd become quite the artist at saying one thing while letting his tone speak its opposite.

"And you must kneel at the foot of my throne, and hold perfectly still the entire time, and not look any of your betters in the eye."

Ayden reared back. "You cannot be seri—"

"I am."

He stood, paced a short line back and forth before the prince. 'Twas absurd: such debasement for a mere change of scenery! He did not know if he could endure it, or if the cost were even worth the reward.

"Never you mind, this is clearly a bad idea," the prince said. "You're a prideful man, Ayden—"

"*Elf.*"

"Beg pardon?"

"Elf. Prideful *elf.*"

The prince smiled wryly. "Yes, of course. You're a prideful *elf*, and rightfully so; this is clearly beyond your bearing. Best that you stay in the safety of my rooms. You're simply not ready for court."

Not *ready*? He was an elven ranger, by the fallen gods; had he not crouched motionless in ambush for hours at a time? Taken orders without question for centuries? He was perfectly capable of whatever manner of discipline a situation required. And if it meant getting out of these cracking rooms . . .

"I can do it," he said.

"I know, I know, 'tis too much to demand all at— Oh." The prince blinked up at him, brows creased to match the trill of doubt in his song. "Are you quite certain?"

Ayden dropped to one knee and ducked his head, half to prove himself and half to hide a grimace. "Yes, Your Highness." Confident he'd made his point, he plopped down on his arse and crossed his legs, met the prince's eyes again. "Can we go now?"

The prince took in his display with raised eyebrows, but all he said was, "Breakfast first. Then it would be wise if I dress . . . and if you tidy up."

Tidying up, it turned out, included two body servants tending to needs that Ayden had never even realized he had.

"Not that you need the help," the prince called from the washroom, "but you must look your best while on display; your appearance reflects upon the Crown."

Unaccustomed to being pampered or touched so intimately by strangers, Ayden squirmed through the whole of his grooming. The two servants rubbed scented oil into his skin, soaked and then buffed his nails, and attempted to lay his hair flat with grease despite his best glower. He glimpsed his reflection in the mercuried glass with horror, and was quite relieved when the prince returned from his bath shouting, "Wash that filth away!" and, with a half-smile at him, "'Tis part of his . . . exotic charm to have hair as stubborn as he is."

Ayden followed the servants to the washroom, where his head was dunked in the remains of the prince's bath water over his loud protests, scrubbed clean with soap, and left to settle into a hundred spiky tufts.

He was then brought before the prince for inspection. The prince cupped his chin in one hand and studied him as he might a stallion for breeding, his song belying his satisfaction long before he released Ayden's face. Then he pulled all the lacing and the sleeves from Ayden's shirt, leaving most of his chest exposed and his arms bared to the shoulders.

"Now he is ready," he said to the attendants, reaching out to ruffle Ayden's hair. It seemed less a gesture of affection than a curious exploration, and Ayden gritted his teeth and endured it for the sake of his pending quasi-freedom. At last the prince took his hand away and smiled. "I have wanted to do that since first I laid eyes upon that wild head of yours," he said.

Ayden canted said wild head toward the door. "Now you have. Can we go?"

The prince hesitated. "There is . . . one more thing." When he did not immediately continue, Ayden waved him on. "In the Aegean palace, the slaves wear chains of finely wrought gold and starfall, as beautiful and precious as they themselves. I'm afraid we have no such luxuries here, but I cannot let you walk unfettered. You must settle for shackles from the dungeon."

"Well gods be cursed," Ayden said. "However will I bear the shame."

'Twas a little more shame than Ayden had bargained for, as it happened. Once the shackles had been locked upon his ankles and wrists (with his arms round the front this time, at least), there was still one iron left over: a collar, heavy and chafing, attached to a chain for the prince to lead him by. He nearly balked at that, but the thought of another endless day in the prince's rooms, coupled with the memory of what he'd already endured to prepare for his outing, made turning back unbearable.

And so he walked two steps behind the prince, bracketed by the man's personal guard, head down as much to hide the humiliation that heated his cheeks as to obey the prince's rules.

The corridors were just as claustrophobic as the prince's rooms had become, but stepping into the Great Hall brought relief as profound as a northern breeze beneath a midday summer sun. The hall was packed full with people, yes, but the massive room dwarfed even the gathered crowd, its ceilings as tall as a proud oak, its many leaded windows opened upon a garden of flowers and fountains and fruit trees. It wasn't as pleasant as walking beneath the sun, but 'twas as close as one could come to it otherwise, and for a moment Ayden allowed himself to revel in the open air, to stop and close his eyes and let the garden songs wash over him.

Then the leash jerked and he stumbled forward, barely catching himself in time.

He realized that the room had gone quiet, and all the people in it were down on one knee, bowing to the prince.

Their party climbed three white marble stairs to the dais, and the prince settled himself upon a throne of exotic wood, smothered in jewels and gold. Ayden knelt beside it without being told, hating the cushion someone had placed there but making use of it all the same. At least all the room was still on one knee as well, heads down and unable to witness this particular ignominy. 'Twas easier to know he wasn't the only one kneeling.

Of course, he would be the only one not rising up.

The prince made a brief speech to the assembled masses, thanking them for making the journey and promising to listen with a fair and open ear. The resultant applause was so thunderous that Ayden couldn't help but wonder why the prince hated this all so much; his people clearly adored him, showered him with affection and praise. What more could he want?

One of the prince's men called, "You may rise," and Ayden felt a shift in the room as bodies straightened and eyes turned toward the dais, toward the prince, toward *him*. 'Twas a veritable symphony of distemper: notes of fear and curiosity, hatred and hunger, anger and lust twining round and round the open space. Atop this mental maelstrom rode physical murmurs, too soft and distant to decipher. The prince leaned in subtly and whispered out the side of his mouth, "See how they look at you? You captivate them."

Great. Just what he'd always wanted.

Ayden took care not to raise his eyes to all the stares clearly pointed his way, but there was no shielding his inner ear from the cacophony of emotions. He pushed back against it, just for a moment, just long enough to startle them all with a flash of aura only the humans could see. A flexing of sword-arms, of a sort, done and gone before the prince or the palace guards could chastise him for the anxiety now rippling through the room.

Satisfied, he settled on his haunches like a good little slave.

Paper rustled above his head and to the right, and the announcer summoned forth the first subjects to speak. The forest of boots and sandals and clogs below the dais—all that remained of Ayden's view of the crowd—parted down the middle, and two men stepped forth into his field of vision, prostrating themselves at the foot of the dais until their foreheads touched the bottom stair. Neighbors, it turned out. Apparently one had bedded the other's fourth wife, and neither was satisfied with the ruling of the local magistrate.

Ayden could all but hear the prince rolling his eyes. "Is she with child?" he asked of the husband. No, she wasn't. "Has she birthed you any sons?" No, she hadn't, the worthless whore, may the gods strike her forever barren. "Do you wish to keep her?" No, of course he didn't.

"Then she is your responsibility now," the prince said to the other man. "You will reimburse your neighbor twice her original dowry, you will take her as your wife, and you will treat her well, for if I hear otherwise, your lord's constable shall pay a visit to your household." A hint of vindictive pleasure curled into the prince's stern tone as he added, "And if ever again you steal another man's woman, I shall have my physicians remove the source of your urgings."

Beside him, Ayden couldn't help but cringe—not only at the thought of judicial castration, but also at the thought of this woman, of all human females, bought and traded for a flock of sheep and kept in fidelity to a single man. If ever Ayden needed reminder of the importance of the Ferals' work, 'twas laid out before him now.

The neighbors marked the first in a long and pathetic line of characters paraded before the prince, each decrying his petty human problems and begging His Highness for money or mercy or justice or miracles. Between requests, Ayden gathered intelligence as best he could, listening for the disciplined songs of the guards amongst the general hubbub and tracking the movements of leather boots branded with the royal crest. In the rare, precious moments when he felt no eyes upon him, he stole glances at the weapons decorating the walls and memorized their locations.

Yet some pleas were sufficiently amusing to draw his attention from his studies. Like the man currently prostrated before the prince, blathering on about his reserve duty and begging release from service after slicing off the tip of his boot (and three toes with it) in a training accident.

"Perhaps 'tis in everyone's interest that you lay down the sword," the prince said to him. "If we call upon your service again, 'twill likely be on a widow's harvest field rather than the battlefield. Now go, and do try not to lose any more bits of yourself on the way out."

Laughter all round the room drowned out the human's thanks. Finally the announcer—the prince's secretary, the one called Lini—called forth the next supplicant, whose story promised to be as pitiful as his predecessors': the man had but stolen some food.

Then Lini added, "From a Surge fortress," and the whole room went silent as death.

On the outside, anyway. Ayden's inner ear was bombarded by outrage and hate, crashing like great peals of thunder in his head.

He peered up as two guards dragged the thief down the runner and threw him to the floor by the dais. A well-dressed man stepped right overtop him and bowed deep.

"Your Highness," the man said. "This . . ." He glanced toward the thief, lip curled in disgust, and kicked him halfheartedly. "This *svíkja* has five years' reserve duty left, but we seek dispensation for his death."

*Death*? Truly? 'Twas hardly surprising that a people who executed horses for falling lame might execute one of their own for stealing, but that someone would begrudge this famine-struck man a handful of apples or wheat . . .

"There is no question of his guilt?" the prince asked.

"Nay, Sire. He was caught in the act, and confessed."

But surely the prince would not stoop so low. Surely he wouldn't—

"Remand him to the dungeons. He shall be executed at dusk tomorrow."

Ayden turned his eyes to the prince, hardly believing. "What are you—!"

A hard yank on his chain sent him slamming headfirst into the side of the throne, and he crumpled in a dazed heap on the dais, vexed by the prince's behavior. He'd not seen the man so cold or impersonal since their terrible first day together.

Yet when he picked himself up, fingers pressed gingerly to the bump forming above his ear, the prince laid a gentle hand upon him, stroked his hair and cupped his fingers round his neck. Before Ayden could shake him off, he leaned down over the arm of his throne and whispered, "I'm sorry I had to do that."

Ayden pressed his lips into a thin line and said nothing, pretending he hadn't heard the prince over the shouts and jeers of the crowd as the thief was led away.

"I know our ways may seem barbaric to you," the prince said, "but we are not beasts. We have but four capital crimes: murder, treason, desertion, and this. The Surge fortresses must be sacrosanct; an entire village may spend a week or more trapped within one. Stealing from them is stealing from the mouths of women and children, of soldiers who need their strength for battle."

Ayden discreetly eyed the crowded hall, the hundreds of people pressing noisily round the thief, hurling hatred like bolts of lightning and nearly stopping the guards from taking him away. Gods help him, why had he defied the prince's rules for the sake of a despicable human? He'd kill all these people himself, given the chance; why did it bother him to learn they used their laws to kill each other?

Principle, he decided. Killing in war was to be expected, as was Nature's purging of the human blight upon her lands. But to act as gods—to make the calm choice between death and life amongst your own kind—well . . . typical human arrogance.

And an easy trap to fall into, he supposed, when everywhere you looked, people were throwing themselves at your feet. Like this woman now, who rushed up to the dais even as the prince's secretary was announcing her, falling to her knees and pressing her forehead to the floor.

"A *woman*?" the prince asked.

Ayden heard the secretary shuffling pages, then, "Mrs. Bóndi Ekkja, Your Highness. Widowed, father deceased, no brothers, elder sons lost in battle, youngest son on active duty in the Drengr Infantry Division. She has no man to represent her."

"Very well," the prince said, leaning forward into Ayden's line of sight, notes of warmth and compassion playing round the edges of his song. "Speak, mother."

"I come to beg hardship release, Your Highness, for Nidr is the last surviving of my four babes and all I have left in the world. Please, Your Highness, won't you let him come home?"

Ayden heard clothes rustle beside him, then saw the prince's feet tread down the dais stairs, bringing his shins, then thighs, then waist into Ayden's view. He offered the woman his hand; she clasped it in both her own and pressed her lips to it, but even Ayden could tell that had not been the man's intent.

"Rise, mother," the prince said. "For you deserve all the respect I have to offer." He pulled her to her feet and added, "On behalf of the Crown and all the people of Farr and the Aegean Empire, I thank you for your sacrifice." He meant it too, Ayden could hear, listening beyond the words. "Now tell me, have you sister-wives?"

Sister-wives? Was that the pretty face these humans painted upon the ugliness of their female subjugation? 'Twas sickening, the way they traded and collected and bred women like so much livestock.

"Three, Your Highness. We're all of us too old to remarry; we work the patch of land our husband left our sons, may the gods reward him with the Warrior's Rest."

She touched her fingertips briefly to her forehead, and the prince did the same. "Your sister-wives," he said, "do you love them?"

"Of course, Your Highness. Like blood!"

"And do they have children?"

"Eight surviving between them, Your Highness."

"And you've raised them, loved them as your own?"

The woman nodded, eyes creased as if she couldn't even understand the nature of the question, it was so absurd. "Of course."

Nor, it seemed, could she understand where the prince's line of questions was leading, though 'twas tragically obvious to Ayden. He bit his lip against the protest that welled within him.

"Then you have much left in this world, mother, and House Farr and the Aegean Empire must ask you to risk one more sacrifice."

"Please, no!" the woman sobbed, throwing herself back at the prince's feet. Palace guards were there in an instant, reaching down to pull her away, but the prince must have stayed them, for hands and feet froze all apiece, then moved away.

The prince laid a hand upon the crown of the woman's head. "I shall make you a promise," he said. "Your son, if he wishes, may march with me in the coming Surge. I shall watch him as my own."

The woman sniffed, reached up to grasp the prince's wrist with both hands, then raised her head and kissed his palm, the side of his little finger, his knuckles. "You would do this, Your Highness?" she asked, nearly breathless with wonder and tears.

"I would," he said. "But I must warn you, I lead from no safe perch. If he fights with me, he *will* meet the darkers sword to fang, as we all must do. This is the most I can offer."

The woman bowed again, then stood and backed away amidst a flurry of tears and heartfelt thanks. 'Twas amazing to Ayden that she'd not gotten what she'd come for—far from it, in fact—yet still left so full of gratitude and consolation.

But so went the prince's power over people, it seemed. It would do to be careful of it from now on.

'Twas with much relief—and a touch of guilt at the sea of hopeful faces who'd come all this way and had yet to be heard—that Freyrík called an end to the day's session. His stomach was rumbling, his body sore from sitting so long in one attitude, his bladder uncomfortably full, and his mind benumbed by the litany of petty quarrels. And if *he* was sore and frazzled, surely Ayden was suffering threefold. They both needed a privy break, and lunch, and some exercise and fresh air.

Alas, there would be time only for the first two. He'd seen one of Lord Lini's assistants waiting patiently in the wings for perhaps fifteen minutes now, stack of dispatches in hand, and waved him and Lord Lini over as he stood from his brother's throne.

He looked to Ayden and found the elf glancing up at him with clear longing in his eyes, though not of any sort he dreamt each night to see there. "You may rise now," he said quietly.

Ayden stood with a grimace, hand on the side of the throne to stop himself from stumbling on what Freyrík presumed were numb feet. He tossed a warning look at Ayden's hand (promptly withdrawn), but paired it with a soothing smile. Ayden had done well, after all—much better than Freyrík had expected he would. "You pleased me today," he said.

Ayden closed his eyes—Freyrík imagined them rolling behind lowered lids—and muttered under his breath, "How *will* I contain my joy."

Freyrík snorted. "I gave you fair warning," he reminded the elf, but then had to turn from him as Lord Lini's assistant, Lord Sámr, approached with a sheaf of papers in his hands. "What news?"

Lord Sámr pressed his papers to his chest and bowed. "Outriders have come from the First Wife's party. She is to arrive tomorrow, Your Highness. His Majesty is most anxious to hear of her safe homecoming."

Freyrík nodded. "Send our best squad to meet up with her escort. The kingdom is in uproar between the Surge and the elven attacks, and I'll not take any chances with my brother's most prized possession."

"Of course, Your Highness." Lord Sámr rifled through his documents. "I also bring an update on the Surge preparations. Your carpentry master says just over twelve hundred scarecrows have been constructed as of this morning, and apothecaries all across the province are gathering herbs for their poisons apace. The chief smithy reports nearly three thousand caltrops, but can continue his work no more without a fresh supply of iron ore—unless you wish him to melt down tools?"

"Nay," said Freyrík, eyeing the remaining sheaf wearily, "'twill not be necessary. See to it the carpenters carve stakes, instead. Half as efficient, but they'll serve."

"Yes, Your Highness. The stable master reports that we've commandeered a sufficient number of horses, but training plow beasts for battle is proving difficult. He also sends word that scarce breeding stock remains for the upcoming spring. He humbly requests half an hour of Your Highness's time to review his arrangements and approve the necessary coin for his training and restocking plans."

"Very well." Though Freyrík sincerely hoped 'twould not be necessary to repurchase an entire kingdom's worth of horseflesh: he hoped not to lose them in the first place, but if it could not be avoided, he hoped the Aegis would see fit to replace what they lost in protection of the whole of the Empire.

He heard Ayden shifting behind him like a restless stallion, and hoped the elf was minding his manners. Still, best not to tempt fate any longer. "Is that all?"

"Nay, Your Highness. The Lord Keeper begs a word regarding recompense for the newly conscripted carpenters, and Lord General Vísi has news from a number of field commanders that he would not entrust with me."

"Yes, fine," Freyrík said, shutting his eyes for a moment and breathing in deep. "*Please* tell me that is all."

Lord Sámr gave an elegant bow and said, "Yes, Your Highness."

"The gods be thanked for small favors. I'll see Ayden back to my rooms—" the soft whine from behind him tugged at his heart, but he steeled himself to ignore it, "—fetch some lunch, then meet the stable master in the outer ward. See to it he is ready for my arrival; I wish to survey the new stock."

'Twas late evening by the time Freyrík returned to his rooms, weary as a soldier stumbled straight from the battlefield. It seemed no one remained in all the kingdom who did not require some slice of his time these days. So much for his plans to take Ayden outside as reward for his forbearance in public.

He was not surprised to find Ayden sleeping, but it saddened his heart to see him still nesting: curled up in the corner amongst Freyrík's blankets, asleep with his back to two walls. As if he still feared nothing more than Freyrík's bed.

Perhaps that were still true.

Freyrík indulged Ayden in many things, but this he could not allow. Appearances mattered. That he wished so very much to feel the heat of the elf by his side at night (and his skin, and his hair, and his scent, and his . . . gods, his *everything*) hardly even mattered in the face of how it would look for him to let his slave dictate the terms of their arrangement.

"Ayden," he called softly, feeling poorly for it even as he spoke, for the elf looked hopelessly weary all the time now, and Freyrík did not wish to disturb him. Assuming, of course, that he was still asleep. The elf's senses and instincts both were remarkably sharp when unimpaired by injury; he'd probably woken the moment Freyrík had entered the room.

And indeed, the elf cracked an eye open and grumbled, "What?"

"'Tis time for bed."

He tossed Freyrík what might generously have been called the evil eye.

"Come now," Freyrík said, pausing for a jaw-cracking yawn and then adding, "it could be worse. You could be lodged in the dungeons."

Ayden rose, dragging the bedcovers after him. "I'm not only because your people think I suffer more in your bed than amongst the mold and the rats. What exactly does that say about you, Prince?"

"That I'm a cruel and selfish lover, of course. Have you not heard that I beat my slaves bloody every night, bind them to the bedposts and rape them without oil? And when I'm finished, I let the guards and servants take their turns as well. It's all quite horrific."

Ayden made himself a new nest on the far edge of the bed as Freyrík spoke, but even in the dim light of the candelabra, Freyrík could see his humor besting the elf's tightly-pursed lips.

He chuckled and climbed into his own blanketless side of the bed, too tired even to call his groom for a change of clothes. He would sleep well tonight. And tomorrow . . . tomorrow he would reward his elf with the kiss of sunlight on his skin.

# Chapter Ten

Freyrík woke, as usual, to Ayden's watchful, moody stare. Less usual, the air within the gauzy curtains was hot and bright, and not for elflight; he'd overslept, and his staff had let him. Of course, he had no especially pressing obligations this morn, no meetings to attend, and no reason not to indulge himself, just this once, with some much-needed relaxation.

Just as soon as he looked in on a few things.

But afterward, he would take Ayden outside. The gods knew he'd neglected the poor elf terribly these last weeks, what with the Surge and Harvest Fest to plan for and Berendil still at High Court. And the elf's performance in the Great Hall had surely earned him a reward. He would put a smile on Ayden's face if it killed him.

And truly, given his plans, it well might at that.

He rolled onto his side, anxious to share his idea with Ayden, and smiled at the elf's customary scowl. "Before you go off moping for the day," he said, "I've happy news for you."

Ayden's eyes narrowed—so mistrustful he was!—and he asked, slow and careful, "Oh?"

"I shall join you after lunch."

"Happy indeed!" Ayden cried, rolling onto his back and crossing his arms. Freyrík's eyes were instantly drawn to the play of muscle and sinew beneath the glowing skin of Ayden's shoulders, and gods help him, how he wanted to touch—

No. He would not. He would *not*.

(But wouldn't it be delightful if he did?)

Ayden rolled his head toward Freyrík and snapped, "Stop it," as if he knew exactly what Freyrík was thinking.

"But hear me out," Freyrík said, pretending rather masterfully (if he did say so himself) that Ayden did not affect him, in *any* way. "For the truly happy part comes afterward: we shall spend the afternoon sparring."

Ayden's expression transformed instantly from belligerent to achingly hopeful. "Outside?" he asked.

"Indeed," Freyrík said, and the hope slid to cautious joy, then careful blankess, as if the elf feared to reveal anything at all. "We'll see where your proficiencies lie, determine how best to arm you when you march with us." He waited for the customary denial, but none came. "Would you like that?"

"Indeed I would," Ayden said, with a sly smile that both delighted and disconcerted Freyrík. "But I cannot promise the same for you."

Freyrík led Ayden to the eastern practice field by the smithy and the barracks, the one you had to walk past to reach the keep from the main gate. 'Twas mostly empty now, the cadets busy with their classroom studies through the worst heat of the day. But many a student and soldier, even some lords and ladies, were well within sight. Good—he wanted everyone to witness Ayden's battle prowess firsthand. And if that entailed their witnessing his own domination-by-elf, well, so be it; he would lose no respect from his men, many of whom had fallen to him in this very field. Word would spread of the elf who'd taken down the Crown Prince, and with it respect, no matter how grudging. 'Twould serve him well when they marched upon the Surge.

Against the near wall of the smithy stood rack upon rack of practice weapons: wooden short swords, wooden shields, dull-edged broadswords and longswords wrapped in felted wool, wooden pikes and quarterstaffs, tipless spears, wooden battle axes, bows and arrows, suits of battered armor. Freyrík gestured toward them all and said to Ayden, "Your choice. Pick your favorite weapon. I'll match you blade for blade."

He watched as Ayden examined the racks, hefting a short sword, fingering the armor. At one point he thought the elf would field himself with the quarterstaff, but after some deliberation Ayden moved on. At last he turned and said, "My weapon of choice is missing. Were you given my kit?"

"Your blowpipe, you mean? 'Tis not very effective in close combat."

Ayden waved his hand impatiently. "I meant my sticks."

"No, I'm afraid not."

Ayden tracked back to the short swords, grasped one in each hand and gave them an experimental twirl. "Never you mind," he said. He tossed the two swords at Freyrík, who caught them neatly but by the wooden blades, then picked up two more for himself. "These will do."

"No shield?" Freyrík asked, flipping each sword and catching it by the hilt.

Ayden's laugh was pure derision. "Shield?" he cried. "Shall I bring your mother's skirts for you as well?"

He walked out onto the practice field without waiting for a reply and took up a ready position, all loose limbs and easy confidence. Freyrík felt his body quickening with desire and battle fever as he followed him afield, though the sword in his left hand felt awkward. Whatever beneath the shadow of the gods was he to do with it?

He didn't have much time to consider his options before Ayden charged him in a whirling fury of arms and swords, grace and power and speed too great to discern one move from the next. All Freyrík could do was throw his hands up and trust to instinct.

'Twas a fine stratagem for perhaps four seconds, one strike blocked, then two, then three, the reverberation of clacking weapons numbing his fingers and ringing down his arms. But then Ayden's right-hand sword snuck through the space where Freyrík's shield would have been if he'd had one, and stopped, remarkably, a hair's width from crashing into the side of his neck. Freyrík froze, wide-eyed and panting. Such control!

Ayden chuckled and tapped him with the sword. "Dead!" he crowed, barely breathing hard at all. "Again?"

Determined to start on the offensive this time, Freyrík gave no answer but to step back and strike out. His first blow was hard enough to make Ayden grunt when it impacted his crossed swords, but rather than strain against the force, Ayden rode it to the ground. Then suddenly Freyrík was splayed face-down in the grass, his shins screaming so loudly that he feared he might vomit. He rolled onto his side, curled up tight, and clutched at his legs. But that hurt even worse, so he released them and flopped onto his back, thinking about beginning to contemplate a distant future in which he might somehow attempt to stand.

It came much sooner than expected, though, when he heard a "Hey!" and a pained shout from Ayden, then "We were just sparri—*Ow!*" followed by a thud.

His personal guard had clearly not taken well to Ayden's moves.

"Let him go," he called, forcing himself to his feet (*ow, ow, ow, and by the gods,* ow!) to prove he was intact, even if 'twere perjury. He limped over to where Ayden had become the unfortunate foundation of a four-guard obelisk, shooed them away and offered Ayden his hand. Ayden ignored it and stood on his own, one hand pressed to his ribs.

"Elbow," he said to Freyrík's questioning look, then glared at one of the guards, who took a step back in what struck Freyrík as an unconscious fear response. Freyrík moved to examine the sore spot but Ayden dodged with a muttered, "It's fine," then nodded toward Freyrík's shins and said, "And you, Prince?"

Freyrík tugged up the legs of his breeches, revealing a rapidly swelling red line across the center of both shins, the skin broken but not bleeding. "It's fine," he said, tucking the hem of his breeches back into his boots, all the while surveying from the corner of his eye the crowd of onlookers ringing the field. He straightened up, smiling fit to pretend he wasn't in agony, and dismissed his guards. "Again?"

"Are you serious?" Ayden asked, one eyebrow and both corners of his mouth twitching high. "This isn't sparring; this is beating a toothless dog on a chain."

*Oh, that little . . .* "Look," Freyrík said, nodding at Ayden's bruised ribs, "If your . . . wounds prevent you from resuming the match, I shall of course take pity upon you. You need only ask."

And as sure as a Surge follows the first darker scouts, Ayden ground out, "I'm fine," and stalked to the center of the training field, assuming position and raising his swords once more.

Freyrík endured two more deaths—one evisceration, one double-run through his back—before calling a halt to the abuse. "I think," he panted, rolling flat onto the grass, "that a change of weapons would benefit us both."

"Us?" Ayden asked, one sword canted jauntily over his shoulder, the other twirling in his left hand, and oh, what Freyrík would have done to the grin on Ayden's face if only he'd had any hope of reaching it before being knocked to the grass again.

He picked himself up to halfhearted cheers from a gathering crowd of cadets and gentlemen, who probably admired his tenacity if nothing else. Gods help him, Lord Commander Hákon was watching. And shaking his head.

Freyrík blocked the onlookers from his mind and turned back to Ayden. "Yes, well, this practice is unlikely to hone my skills, and I'm man enough to admit that I present little challenge. Besides, no matter how proficient you may be at routing a man with your sticks, they are but kindling to a darker bear. At most they would incite it to a greater rage."

Ayden shrugged, walked over to the weapons rack and laid down his swords. "As you wish, Prince," he said. "Your weapon of choice, then? Let me guess." He walked down the rack, skimming fingers over weapons as he went, until he reached the padded longswords. "These, yes?"

"How did you—?"

"I am built for speed, Prince. *You* are built for power, so 'twas either the longsword or the battle axe for you. But you also like to pretend at finesse, therefore the sword."

"*Pretend?*" Freyrík said, stepping beside Ayden and hefting a longsword with practiced ease. He took the field and paused for concentration, then ran through the first minute of the seventeenth advanced longsword form, which was, he might have admitted, rather showy.

Pretend indeed!

He ignored the clapping from the crowd, but was pleased to see Ayden looking suitably impressed.

"Well?" he called to the elf when Ayden still hadn't picked up his sword. "A change of heart?"

Ayden seized the hilt of the nearest longsword on the rack and pulled, stumbling slightly in a way that told Freyrík he'd not anticipated its weight. Freyrík couldn't help but bark out a laugh.

"How does that saying go?" he said as Ayden joined him on the field, lifting the sword in both hands as if 'twere a rug beater. "Ah, yes. Turnabout is fair play."

"Speak with your weapon, human!"

Freyrík smiled sharply and raised his sword, happy to oblige.

Ayden darted in close—too close, not utilizing the range of his weapon—while Freyrík parried and prowled in circles, waiting for an opening. It came after Ayden's third strike, an overextension, the weight of the longsword throwing his balance. Freyrík calmly brought his own sword down across Ayden's shoulder blades and sent him sprawling.

The elf lay unmoving in the grass, hands fisted and eyes squeezed tightly shut. Even with the padding, a clean hit from a longsword *hurt*, and Freyrík didn't have a tenth the control with his choice weapon that Ayden had with the short swords—the longsword was simply too heavy for that.

When Ayden still hadn't moved several seconds later, Freyrík crouched down to touch his shoulder and asked, "Are you well?"

And suddenly he was flat on his back, a sharp ache in his belly and Ayden crouching over him with a hand to his throat. The elf was laughing so hard there were tears in his eyes, and Freyrík knew then that he'd done right: this moment was worth all the pain the afternoon had and would inflict upon him.

"I can't believe you fell for *that*!" Ayden cried.

"Yes, well," Freyrík said, planting his feet and bucking his hips sideways to dislodge the elf—a maneuver that worked, he suspected, only because Ayden allowed it. "That's the last time I'll ever be concerned over *your* welfare."

Ayden had somehow rolled to his feet, and was now peering down at Freyrík with a smirk. "Again?"

Twice more Freyrík felled Ayden as he overbalanced, then a third time when he failed to recover fast enough from an attempted leg-swipe. Ayden was faster by orders of magnitude, but he was slight, and he wielded the longsword as if 'twere a single, overgrown fighting stick; he lacked the strength and weight it took to wield this particular weapon well, and the technique besides.

Freyrík knocked the elf down a fifth time, weaving behind him and slamming the padded blade into the backs of his knees. Ayden went down with a cry that made even Freyrík grimace, landing on hands and knees and staying there, head hanging low between his shoulders.

Cries of "Long live the prince!" and "That'll teach him, Your Highness!" rained on Freyrík's ears, souring the pleasure of his triumph.

He approached the elf cautiously, poked him in the shoulder with his sword lest he was faking again. Ayden lifted his head just enough to glare.

"Another change of weapons, I think," Freyrík said, for he knew the elf would never ask reprieve of his own accord.

He fully expected Ayden to refuse, to insist upon continuing the match until he scored a victory. But the elf only staggered upright with a groan and, leaning upon his sword, bent over to rub at the backs of his knees. "That might be for the best, yes."

"Pikes?" Freyrík suggested. "Long enough to fight outside the claw range of most darkers, light enough to take advantage of your speed."

"I've never used one," Ayden said, limping over to an equipment rack and pulling a battered pike from the stand.

"Balanced like a quarterstaff, only sharper. And heavier as well, but not by much."

Ayden gave it a twirl, swung it round his head and lunged hard at nothing. "Yes," he said, "this will do nicely."

And so it did, for their fight was more even this time, and by far the most enjoyable of the session. Freyrík would take a fair challenge over an easy win (or a hard loss) any day. They engaged and broke off and circled again and again, neither landing a strike. Ayden was lithe and elegant as a dancer, his bare arms glistening with sweat in the midday sun, his weapon as if a fifth appendage, controlled with all the precision of his hands and feet. The sheer beauty of it made Freyrík ache.

Then the weighted end of Ayden's pike slammed into his stomach, and he remembered what it felt like to ache for real.

"Dead!" Ayden sang, his cheer a balm to Freyrík's pain. Yet the moment passed quickly, and the elf turned quite serious as he added, "You were not paying attention. Focus, Prince, for I want my challenge."

"And here I thought you wanted to beat me bloody."

Ayden tucked his pike beneath one arm, eyes glinting. "One does not necessarily preclude the other."

Freyrík laughed, then winced and tightened his hold on his throbbing midriff. "Won't you call me Freyrík?" he asked, soft enough for Ayden's ears alone. "When none else might hear, at least."

"If you can beat me fair," the elf said, swinging his pike and jabbing its tip in Freyrík's direction.

At that, Freyrík straightened and took position again.

The next half hour passed in a relentless back-and-forth of clashing pikes and bashed knuckles, bruises and a split lip (not Ayden's fault; Freyrík had somehow stepped into that blow), the pleasure of hard exertion and more smiles than Freyrík had seen Ayden make in all their time together combined. Ayden had begun to keep score of their kills—"Only to know if you will earn your name," he said with such innocence that Freyrík almost, *almost* believed him—and it now stood at seven to five in Ayden's favor. Not an insurmountable lead, but Freyrík was growing tired and thirsty, and Ayden was not, if all his dodging and jumping and bouncing were any indication.

A woman's scream cut through Freyrík's concentration, and Ayden froze, mid-strike, as from somewhere behind Freyrík came a cry of "*Elf!*" and "Gods, why isn't anyone stopping him!"

Ayden's eyes grew wide; he tossed his pike away and dropped to his knees, throwing out his hands in placation or defense or both. Freyrík spun round and saw half a contingent of fully-armed soldiers, two with arrows nocked, two protecting the First Wife, and six bearing down upon him and Ayden. His own personal guard was fast approaching as well.

No wonder Ayden was anxious to make himself as non-threatening as possible.

"It's all right!" Freyrík called, signaling the charging soldiers to a halt. They seemed torn between his authority and the First Wife's panicked shouts of "Kill it!" and "Gods help us!" and the like. And surely, what a scene they must have made, Freyrík with his split lip and throbbing cheek and bloodied knuckles, attacked by an elf with a training weapon that could not be told from the real thing even a short distance away.

"It's all right," he said again, this time directly to Lady Kona. "We're only sparring."

"But he is . . . he's . . . he's . . . ." She wiggled all ten fingers in front of her lovely face in a gesture that meant the gods only knew what.

"An elf?" Freyrík tried.

"Glowing!" she shouted. "Unbound! They are savages all, and yet you arm him!"

Freyrík handed his weapon off to Ayden—tacit permission for him to stand and a clear order for the soldiers not to harm him—wiped his hands on his breeches, and approached the First Wife with open arms. As he'd hoped, her gaze swung to him, though her face screwed up in disgust at his dishevelment. She recoiled from his embrace but offered her hand as a reluctant consolation prize. Freyrík kissed it.

"Your smell offends, Your Highness," she said.

Freyrík laughed. "How good to see you too, my dear Lady Kona." He took a step back so as not to overwhelm her with his stench and said, "Listen. The elf is a trophy of war, and I vouch for his good behavior. I have trained him well." She looked dubiously between him and Ayden; he shuddered to think of how the elf was reacting to his words. Instead he said, "Am I a fool, Kona?"

"What?"

He repeated slowly, "Am I a fool?"

"Of course not, Your Highness!"

"And would anyone but a fool hand a weapon to a dangerous elf?"

She ducked her head and mumbled, "No."

"Then he cannot be dangerous, yes? And you've nothing to fear."

He waited for his logic to sink in but did not force her to repeat it—he felt poorly enough for what embarrassment he'd already caused her, or rather, she'd caused herself.

Yet she played the spectators masterfully, gazing between them and Ayden with a blushing smile and an affected laugh, then saying loudly enough for all, "'Tis hard to believe in any case that something so pretty could be dangerous."

Freyrík smiled back, though 'twas just as much a show. "He is rather, isn't he?" And then, because he didn't like the glint in her eyes, "Shame you're a woman married, Lady Kona."

She turned to him with mock outrage. "Bite your tongue, Prince Freyrík! For I am married to the king, and there is no shame in that. Now if you would, Your Highness, put your pet away and bathe off your battle, for I've important news to discuss with you."

He contemplated deferring her request, if only to make it clear how little he appreciated her forwardness—not to mention that neither he nor Ayden had been ready to adjourn their sparring. But she might bring news from Berendil or the Aegis, and they were both much dearer to him than pleasure or the balance of powers.

"Come to my drawing room within the hour," he said. He would only keep her waiting a little while.

She would *hate* it.

'Twas with no small disappointment that Ayden followed the prince back into the castle, holding his tongue 'til they reached the relative privacy of the mute stone corridor outside the human's rooms. Even then he said only, "Well, she was lovely," acutely aware of the prince's shadow guard.

"Indeed." The prince clasped his hands behind his back with a slight grimace that told Ayden his ribs still felt their sparring. "But she was not always so. I have known her since my youth; she cared well for me, like a sister. Especially after Mother died."

Ayden recalled the fear and hatred on her face, and how quickly it had melted into artful sweetness. 'Twas hard to imagine her motherly in any way. "What happened?" he asked.

"She is barren," the prince said quietly. "It has made her . . . bitter. And calculating, for her status is in jeopardy always without heirs." He shrugged, trailed his hand along a tapestry of some Feral hunt. "Or so she thinks. My brother loves her beyond reason. But I find it . . . more difficult now, to recall my fondness of her."

They arrived back in the prince's rooms, and Ayden delighted to hear the man order a bath drawn. But the prince seemed preoccupied. He deposited Ayden in the washroom and left, saying he'd be back shortly, "For I must see to the First Wife's proper welcome."

Ayden shrugged away the prince's concern and bathed in refreshingly cool water, scrubbing off sweat and dirt. He wandered back into the prince's bedroom to change into dry clothes, then grabbed an apple and the book he'd been reading and flopped down on the drawing room sofa. He was pleasantly tired, sore in the satisfied way of well-used muscles (and the not-so-satisfied way of having been destroyed by a longsword), and finally—if only for the moment—free of the cooped-up misery that had been building within him for so long.

He must have drifted off, for next he knew he was jerking awake to opening doors and a woman drawling, "Oh, it's *you*."

The First Wife. He sat up, glared at her. She was glaring right back, but beneath the façade of revulsion was a clear note of desire, sparking in her painted blue eyes and calling blood to her pale, high cheeks.

"Where is the prince?" she asked, taking her eyes from his face only to run them down his body and back again.

"Not here," he said, then turned his attention back to his reading with a great show of throat-clearing and cushion-settling and page-flipping.

A show it was, though, for he was no fool to disregard her, and while gazing at the page he listened to her song. Her frustration was building, as well as her indignity, or perhaps resentment.

"I can see that," she snapped.

He saw movement from the corner of his eye and looked up as she crossed her arms over her breasts, poorly restrained in a sky-blue dress top that seemed far too tight and revealing for her backwards culture. Besides, how could she breathe in such a thing? He decided he didn't care, turned his eyes back to the book again. Perhaps if he ignored her hard enough, she'd go away.

And perhaps not. He peeked up from his book to find her staring still, her gaze combing like greedy fingers through his hair, over his skin, across his mouth, which he flattened into a hard line. "Perhaps you'd care to frame me and hang me in the hall?"

The First Wife reared back, her face twisting with confusion and scorn. "Excuse me?"

"You're staring."

"I do no such thing!" Her meager song strained to lash out at him as she herself clearly wished to do, and off to his left, a guard came to attention and took a single step forward. "How dare you! I am the first wife of the king himself. Have you no manners?"

He allowed a slow smile to spread across his face, acerbic and cold, before returning his eyes to his book. "Of course I do," he said to the pages in his lap. "I've refrained from killing you, haven't I?"

The sound she made at that was pure outrage, and this time she did step forward and slap him—or tried to, anyway. He caught her wrist in a hard grip without even looking up from his book, considered and dismissed in a fraction of a second the idea of breaking it, and calmly turned a page with his free hand.

A heartbeat later, the guard at the wall spoiled his fun by slinging an arm round his throat. He could have flipped the brute right over him, but that would only have ended with more guards and more fighting—and truly, he'd had enough bruises for one day. So he let go of the First Wife's wrist and forced himself still within the guard's iron grip, even as she stepped forward and backhanded him. She didn't hit very hard or aim very well, but the rings she wore gouged lines into his cheek; he hissed and tensed, and the guard tensed in response, cutting off his air.

The guard seemed to be waiting for a signal from the First Wife to let Ayden go, but gods crack her, she only looked down at him with a tight smile. Ayden choked and flailed and finally grew too weak to keep struggling, his vision fading to a narrow black tunnel in a landscape of jagged music and chest-hitching pain.

When the guard released him, he somehow fell right off the sofa and onto the plush carpet below.

He was still there, coughing furiously on hands and knees, when the doors creaked open behind him. He heard the prince's tread and song, and saw from the corner of his eye the First Wife curtsey and the guard strike his right heel against the rug with a muffled thud.

"Would someone care to explain to me what is happening here?" the prince said, as calm as if asking, "How much is this bolt of cloth?"

Ayden tried to answer but only ended up coughing again. The prince crouched beside him, slapped him lightly on the back, then helped him stand with an arm round his waist.

He must have caught sight of the blood Ayden could feel dripping down his cheek, for he turned a glare upon the First Wife, much to Ayden's glee. "Kona," he said, drawing her name out in clear warning.

She flinched back hard enough to make Ayden wonder if she were accustomed to being struck, but she seemed to recover herself after a beat, cleared her throat and drew her lips into a sneer. "Your slave molested me," she said, thrusting her wrist before the prince's face. "See?"

Ayden peered too, but of course there was nothing to see; he hadn't bruised her. The smear of blood on her heavy middle ring, however, was hard to miss.

She snatched back her hand. "Thank the gods your guard was nearby, or there's no telling what this creature might have done to me. Trained indeed!" She crossed her arms across that full bosom again and *hmphed*.

Ayden bristled at the unfair accusation, but before he could speak out—as if he would touch that woman with a rod-long staff!—the prince had turned to him and cupped his chin in a gentle hand, tilting his head up and sideways to inspect his cheek. Ayden allowed it only because it clearly irritated the First Wife.

"No doubt you provoked him," the prince murmured, still studying Ayden's cheek.

The First Wife huffed. "He is a slave! 'Tis not his place to respond to provocation. And for your information, Freyrík—"

"Silence, woman," the prince said in that same disinterested soft tone.

Shockingly, the First Wife listened.

Ayden made a face at that—impressed, amused, and entirely put off by the misogyny all at once—then winced when the cuts on his cheek stung.

The prince took a handkerchief from his pocket and pressed it gently to the wounds. "He is *my* slave," he said to the First Wife, still not sparing her a glance, "and 'tis not *your* place to discipline him. You will respect my property. Are we clear?"

Ayden pulled another face, but once again he held his tongue; the words pained him, but they pained the First Wife much more. She pouted, though Ayden thought it an act; beneath her all-too-real humiliation, he heard anger and a trill of sharp intelligence at work. "'Twas not my intent to mar such a pretty face, Your High—"

"Are. We. Clear?"

"Yes, Your Highness," she said, ducking her head and curtseying.

"Good." The prince nodded once, took Ayden's wrist and lifted it to the handkerchief until Ayden held it in place himself. Then he sat down on the sofa, crossed his legs, and said, "Now, you have news from High Court?"

"Yes," she said, but then Ayden saw her eyes dart to him, to the palace guards, back to the prince, and he knew her what her next words would be. "'Tis . . . a *private* matter, Freyrík."

Back to his first name already? She was either much more brazen or much less intelligent than Ayden gave her credit for. And something told him she was no fool.

The prince scowled but shooed everyone away with a single wave. Ayden made for the bedroom, eager to leave any room that contained the First Wife, but the prince halted him with a gesture. So he lingered by the end of the sofa, unsure of what to do with himself, while the guards and attendants filed out into the hall and shut the doors behind them.

"Now," the prince said, "please sit, sister, and share your news."

Her gaze turned pointedly to Ayden again, and he met it with a raised eyebrow. "But—"

"*Sit*, sister, and tell me your news."

The prince gestured at the plush chair opposite the sofa, and she deposited herself in it without another word, taking several moments to arrange her full skirts despite them seeming perfectly well arranged already.

Ayden watched her fidget with great pleasure, even as he resented his use in this game of authority. Or perhaps the prince was merely making another show of trust, like the map of the bailey and the sparring session? Either way, he thought the decision unwise. The man would discover too late that Ayden had not and would not ever earn or deserve such trust.

The First Wife evidently thought it unwise as well, for she glared at him one last time before turning back to the prince. "You are needed at High Court, brother."

The prince leaned forward, propped his elbows on his knees. "Why? Is Berendil well? The Aegis?"

"The Aegis is fine, may the gods bless him ever strong and wise. But Berendil is . . ." She wrung her hands together, and Ayden needed no inner ear to sense her anxiety. "Berendil needs his brother."

"What's happened?" the prince demanded. "Is he ill?"

"No."

"Is all well with your sister-wife?"

"Yes, the gods be praised. She is, as always, hale and happy in her father's court."

Freyrík must have tired of guessing, for he straightened up and slapped his hands to his knees. "Just tell me, woman!"

The First Wife cringed from the outburst, looking suddenly near tears that Ayden thought not calculated at all. The prince cringed right back, stood up, paced in a tight line and then sat back down. "Where is the summons? Let me see it."

The First Wife shook her head and covered her mouth with the pads of her fingers, though Ayden could still see the tremble in her lips when she removed her hand. "There is no summons," she said. "'Tis but I who wish you to go. Please, Rík; your brother needs you. Your *king* needs you, for he is lost, and I fear he may do something dreadfully foolish."

"You speak in riddles, woman," the prince growled, scrubbing his hands across his face.

"I speak the truth," she said, leaning forward and laying a hand upon the prince's knee—a gesture so intimate and assuming that even Ayden was tempted to flinch away; he wondered how the prince stood it. "Freyrík, brother . . . I speak of brewing trouble. The princes and kings of the outer realms, they gather often in private now, talking late into the night, only to fall silent when a servant or wife or even a slave passes by. They've sent away many of their women; those they've kept I believe serve only to avoid suspicion. Why would they do that? Why would they need to?" She perched on the edge of her chair, clutched at both his hands with both of hers. "No good can come of this, Freyrík. He must return here. You must go there, break their hold over him and bring him back to me. Please!"

Unnoticed and perhaps even forgotten, Ayden looked back and forth between the two of them, the First Wife desperate and serious, the prince quiet and contemplative. He heard fear within the prince, sadness and worry, and two asynchronous backbeats that he recognized only belatedly as the sound of divided loyalties.

At last the prince shook his head. "I'm sorry, Kona. I cannot. For we march against the Surge in four days, and I must lead the army into battle."

The First Wife clutched so tightly at the prince's hands that his fingers turned white. "But . . ."

"No, sister. There is too much at stake; you know this."

"But your king—!"

"—would be most upset if he had no kingdom to return to," he said, exquisitely gentle. "You know this."

The First Wife nodded, sniffed once, a prim and delicate little sound. "Afterwards, then?" she asked, and now Ayden truly could hear the tears in her voice. "You will go afterwards?"

"Of course, Kona. The moment I can. I give you my word."

She sniffed again, nodded her acknowledgement. She was still clutching his hands. He pried one free, stroked his knuckles against her cheek. "Good. Is there anything else you wish to tell me?"

She shook her head. Ayden had only known her an afternoon, but already it shocked him to see her so silent.

"Then rest, sister. You've had a long journey, and it wears heavy upon you. Sleep now; tonight we feast in your honor."

Still she said nothing, but she stood, pulled the prince into a fierce hug. "I need him, Rík," Ayden heard her whisper, and for once, her song matched her words.

The prince nodded his head against her shoulder and whispered back, "I know. We all do, sister. We all do."

# Chapter Eleven

After Kona had left his rooms, Freyrík retired to the desk in his private study and shuffled through stacks of tithe records and army rosters, provision plans and the latest attack reports. His mind, however, was fixed firmly upon his brother, and soon he found himself pacing, unable to bear the confinement of his chair.

What trouble could Berendil possibly be finding to frighten Kona so? He could imagine nothing and everything all at once, a hundred horrid schemes, each less in line with Berendil's character than the one before.

He reached the wall and turned on his heel, nearly toppling a pile of books balanced on an end table. Perhaps Kona was mistaken. She was just a woman, after all, and knew naught of politics or war or the governing of kingdoms.

He reached his desk again, turned, paced back toward the pile of books.

"If you walk by me one more time," Ayden said, "I'll trip you."

The elf was watching him from the settee, eating from the nearby fruit bowl with obscene pleasure—always eating, that one, the gods knew how he stayed so lean—one eye on the book in his lap and the other on Freyrík. The cuts on his face were all but gone. So too, Freyrík suspected, were the bruises of their sparring. 'Twas absurd, but he found himself envying the elf, which did not help his temper. He growled and resumed his pacing.

"Perhaps some more exercise would burn your tensions?" Ayden said. "The bailey beckons."

"To you, perhaps. I've work to do."

"Ah, yes, and you're doing it so very well."

Freyrík wheeled round and thrust a finger at Ayden, but no words left his opened mouth. He closed it after too many empty seconds, stalked over to the settee, and dropped down beside Ayden. "I'm in no mood to be trifled with."

"How unfortunate," Ayden said, picking yet another apple from the bowl without taking his eyes from the book.

Freyrík turned an incredulous stare on him, then stole the apple right from his hand and bit into the fruit with a satisfying crunch. He winced when it reopened the cut on his lip.

"You're bleeding on my apple," Ayden said, snatching it back. His fingers brushed against Freyrík's in the process, and Freyrík's cock twitched despite his apprehension.

He moved away as much as the settee allowed before any more of his vital fluids left his big head for his little one. Alas, too late: his mind, eager for distraction, filled with thoughts of Ayden's touch, Ayden's heat, Ayden's spark and scent and skin. And befang the elf for simply sitting there, peering at him askance over the top of his book with those sparkling green eyes. Freyrík peered back at that chiseled face, at the tongue darting out every now and then to moisten lips that he longed to feel pressed against his own or stretched wide round his manhood . . .

And gods brace him but he was going to burst if he didn't, well, *burst*.

Ayden flattened his book on his lap and sighed, looking aggrieved.

Oh, befang it all, he should have stayed with Lord Jafri.

He cleared his throat uneasily and forced his thoughts to more practical matters. "Would you like to attend tonight's feast?"

"I would not. For I am as content today as any creature in bondage can be."

"'Twill be in the Great Hall," Freyrík tried.

Ayden's lips crooked into a sardonic grin. "My legs are quite well stretched from sparring, thank you. I've no need today of being walked by collar and leash." He opened his book again—Freyrík bristled at being so summarily dismissed—then glanced back up and added, "But dinner in your rooms would not go amiss."

Freyrík bristled tenfold at being ordered like a servant. Which made it easier to say, "Alas, the choice is gone from both our hands. The First Wife has requested your presence."

Ayden slammed his book shut and stood, tossing it aside. "Then why ask! I am not a child, Prince; you need not coat your demands in syrup for me to swallow them!"

"Of that I am well aware!" Painfully so, for no mere child could quicken his blood as Ayden did. And the thought of the elf swallowing *anything* coated in syrup . . . He shook his head, breathed deep. "Well, forgive me for hoping to avoid a fight."

Ayden snorted.

Freyrík pushed away from the settee and resumed his pacing, pausing to give the end table by the door a little kick. This time, the books balanced there did topple; he sighed, crossed the room, and threw himself down upon his desk chair before he could ruin anything else.

Befang this feast. Kona could hardly be faulted for her timing, but gods, could she not have arrived another day? He'd gotten Ayden to laugh before she'd come, actually laugh! And now . . .

"Truly, I must go?"

"I'm afraid so." Freyrík glanced up in time to catch unguarded misery curling Ayden's lips, forced himself to ignore it. "'Twould be unseemly of me—a slight to the First Wife, in fact—to arrive at her celebration without all the crown jewels. You are a prized piece in the collection."

The elf grimaced. "My childhood aspiration come true at last."

Freyrík allowed himself to chuckle at that, fairly certain 'twould not offend. Besides, he had sweet news with which to temper the bitter: "And your sister's as well, I hope, for she too will attend."

A grin lit Ayden's countenance, fair competing with his elflight. 'Twas a contagious thing; Freyrík grinned as well.

"And I shall see her?" Ayden asked, shooting to his feet in his excitement.

"Of course."

But then Ayden froze, his smile blinked away, and he dropped back to the settee as though his legs had been severed at the knees. "She will be in chains," he said.

Strange, how that had not occurred to Freyrík before. "Yes," he heard himself say. "I'm afraid so."

Ayden stared at his hands, lying limp and empty in his lap. His wrists bore no signs of the irons' last chafing, but Freyrík could still trace the heavy bonds in his mind's eye, and he had no doubt that Ayden was doing the same.

When Ayden raised his eyes again, his expression was desperate, fierce. "Then do not take her!"

He leapt to his feet, crossed over to Freyrík in two large strides and seized him by the shoulders. Freyrík stayed his guards with a wave; being pressed and crowded by Ayden was far from unsavory, at any rate.

"Spare her this shame and I will do anything at the feast, do you hear me? I will . . ." one hand left Freyrík's shoulder, tossed in the air as if seeking just the right words, the right promises. "I will dance for your guests, I will entertain them with elfsong—light the room with stardust. I will sit naked in chains at your feet and kiss the shoes of all who pass! But please, not her, not this!"

The groping hand landed on Freyrík's shoulder again, squeezed tight. 'Twas just enough pain to pull him back from the thought of Ayden bare as the gods had made him, on his hands and knees and pressing his lips to Freyrík's feet.

He cleared his throat and spoke, but all that came out was, "You can dance?"

Strangely, this seemed to cut through Ayden's panic; he released his grip and backed away. "I— yes, of course. You do learn a thing or two in eight hundred years, you know."

Freyrík could not help but wonder what other knowledge Ayden might have gained in the long span of his years. No wonder he cut such a fierce soldier. And his carnal skills, were they equally well-honed?

"Prince?"

"Fine," he said, for in truth, he hated the thought of Ella in chains just as much as Ayden did, and hated Ayden's distress even more. "She may abstain. But you must keep to your promise, no matter what."

"Yes, yes, of course!" Ayden's face slackened with relief, then slowly drew into a worrying frown. "Wait, which promise?"

Freyrík laughed, leaned forward and patted his arm. "Do not worry. I'll not have you kneeling naked before anyone but me." He'd meant it as a joke, but Ayden's expression went blank, stoic, so he hastened to add, "I *tease*, Ayden. 'Tis mere jest. You'll not be kissing feet or dancing for my guests' pleasure. Though your good manners would not go amiss."

Freyrík smiled, and Ayden tried mightily to smile back *politely*, but never had Freyrík seen a polite smile with quite so many teeth.

Ayden bore his grooming in silence, held out each arm and leg in turn for a servant to lock the shackles on, even walked two steps behind the prince and knelt beside the throne in the Great Hall without so much as pulling a face. He dared to think that would be the worst of it.

He was wrong.

Amidst all the entertainment—the minstrels, the dancers, the tumblers and jugglers and fire-breathers—he'd have thought the court would take no interest in his quiet self, perched unmoving upon a cushion and doing nothing more exciting than glowing faintly. Yet he felt hundreds of eyes upon him, and a great many hands as well, as the nobles and wealthy merchants and visiting dignitaries took turns greeting the prince and First Wife at the dais.

Everyone wished to touch him, to pet him, to examine his eyes and his hair and his skin and even his cracking teeth; it took every last drop of self-discipline not to bite off the first set of fingers that shoved past his lips, but he had help from the outside: the prince stared down at him in warning (and apology, and faint amusement, and even a little jealousy) as some merchant pried his jaw open and rambled on about the importance of good molars in breeding stock.

Lady Kona, "gracing" the dais on Ayden's other side, all but reverberated with gleeful song at his humiliation.

Food was brought out in several courses, held before the prince and the First Wife on silver trays, for they sat in the open for all to see. The servants remained as still and silent as Ayden did, their faces as blank, replacing one another in an endless stream of dishes and delicacies and flagons of wine. Ayden's stomach growled at the many scents that filled the air.

Halfway through the second course, he peered up at the prince, hoping the man might remember him. When that failed, he cleared his throat, then coughed, but both sounds were lost beneath the din of musicians and court chatter. The prince carried merrily on, talking and eating.

Hunger was bad enough, but even worse, he realized when the prince finally took notice of him, was to be hand-fed in public by a human.

Ayden clamped his mouth shut, shame flaming in his cheeks.

The glazed carrot in the prince's fingers kept nudging at his lips.

Crack the man, anyway. Ayden puffed air through his nose, then tilted his head toward the throne and hissed, "I'm not hungry."

He felt the slightest brush of air against his cheek as the prince leaned toward him and whispered, "It matters not. Eat."

Ayden turned his head away. Surprisingly, the prince's hand retreated.

And then returned with enough force to leave Ayden blinking on the dais floor, one hand pressed to his throbbing cheek.

"Shall I beat you pliant before my court?" the prince growled down at him. "They would quite enjoy the show."

Ayden crawled back atop his cushion, cheeks burning, chest heaving, struggling to compose the frantic storm of notes his song had become. He closed his eyes and silenced himself with such ruthless discipline that pain twanged in his temples. Yet it calmed him, and eased the risk that he might set the tables and tapestries burning all round them.

Then he opened his mouth like a cracking baby bird, took the prince's offering, and chewed.

. . . Just as long as the man understood that Ayden would kill him later.

Two courses and a cup of not-so-terrible wine later, the servants carted out the main course: a collection of whole hogs on massive beds of fruits and greens. The nobles *oohed* over the display and tapped the tables in polite applause. Ayden bit the inside of his cheek against his rising gorge.

The youngest hog was brought before the prince, and a servant with a knife that near rivaled a sword stood expectantly beside it. The prince rose to his feet, a towering presence in the corner of Ayden's view, to address the crowd.

"Today we celebrate the return of the First Wife from High Court. She honors us with her presence, as she has honored the Aegis Exalted these past two months. Today, House Farr reclaims one of its most exquisite jewels."

Ayden snorted, but the hall erupted with applause that rang sincere in his inner ear. He wondered if anyone had noticed the lack of sincerity in the prince's song, his words that were true but not true.

But the man's next words were pure:

"Let us all give thanks to the gods for her swift and safe journey, and pray they grant the same to her husband, His Majesty King Berendil of Farr, may the gods bless him ever strong and wise."

Throughout the hall, a hundred hands touched to a hundred bowed foreheads, and a murmur of prayer carried over the clatter of the serving staff. Ayden risked raising his head; he saw the prince flash a wide grin and gesture toward the throne before adding, "For my arse is not nearly grand enough to fill this chair for long!"

More applause and a wave of laughter, some of it distinctly uncomfortable to Ayden's inner ear but most of it loosed in good fun.

Another earnest prayer for their Aegis, the King of all Kings, another round of applause, and it seemed the time for speeches was over. The prince chose for himself the finest cut of meat, which the servant carved out with military precision. Throughout the hall, other servants followed suit.

No guests approached the dais for a while as the humans consumed their food. 'Twas a small but welcome respite, though Ayden fast grew weary without distraction. He let his head droop, his eyes close, his mind wander toward Vaenn . . .

And was pulled sharply back when the First Wife said, "I grow weary of these performers. Does it do any tricks?"

The "it," Ayden realized, was him.

"*He* is not an animal," the prince said.

Yes, well, Ayden might have appreciated his words a little more if they hadn't been spoken over his bowed head.

Skirts rustled, and the smell of the First Wife's perfume grew stronger; a small palm planted itself between his shoulder blades as she leaned over him toward the prince. "I know that, brother. But is he not a great and fearsome warrior? I hear he killed sixteen men with his bare hands!"

"A warrior's work is neither for show nor amusement, sister."

"But surely he must do *something* more than sit there all day looking pretty."

The prince paused, casual as a shrug. "He does walk on his hands," he said, "but 'tis hard to do in shackles, one presumes."

The First Wife *hmphed*, the weight on his back increasing as she leaned over farther. "Is he talented in . . ." a giggle, a trill of titillation in her song that shivered down Ayden's spine, and then a whispered, "well, you know."

What?

"Sister!" the prince cried. "That is hardly talk for polite company!"

What!

Her song chirped on steadily, unperturbed by the prince's chastisement. Her hand left Ayden's back, took hold of the unlaced v-neck of his shirt and pulled it from his chest. Ayden felt her stare creeping across his bared skin, sliming over him like an infestation of pear slugs. The prince, thank the gods, slapped her hand away.

"What?" she said, perfectly innocent. "The gods know why you bother to dress him at all. The Aegis doesn't cover up *his* slaves, you know."

"If he were naked all the time," the prince said, "I would never accomplish a single thing again."

Ayden rolled his eyes, but crack it if there wasn't a tendril of smugness in his resentment.

The First Wife said nothing more for a time, and the sounds of her supping renewed. But then she leaned over him again and asked, "And where is the female? Why is she not here?"

"She is not yet trained for public use."

Public *use*? Ayden's hands balled into fists and he bit his tongue hard enough to make his eyes water.

"Besides," the prince added, "I thought you didn't care for elves."

"Well, this one—" Ayden felt her fingers fist tightly in his hair, then, "—oh my, his hair is soft, isn't it!" She gave his head a few hard shakes that rattled his teeth. "This one is a wild beast. The female, at least, seems properly domesticated. Civilized, even. And did you see that red hair of hers? Gorgeous! Do you not just want to sit for hours and comb it?"

Ayden rather wanted to comb his knives down the First Wife's cracking *face*.

"I can't say the thought has occurred to me," the prince said, his spoken voice much more affable than the one only Ayden could hear. A pause, and then, "Perhaps you should let go of him, Kona. I think you're hurting him."

"Boys and their silly wars," she sighed, releasing Ayden's head but ruffling his hair again before withdrawing her hand. "You've no time left for the gentler passions—beauty, grooming, *family*—between all the fighting."

Even Ayden, who understood little of their relationship, recognized that blow for what it was. No wonder the prince was fuming beneath his polite façade.

"Yes, well," the man said, the words clipped as if spat, "the moment you're ready to live out your years in the stomach of a darker bear, do let me know, dear sister, and I shall stop fighting and start combing hair."

Ayden must have found the feast as unpleasant as Freyrík had, for he spent the next two days in unusually sullen silence. Freyrík did what he could to break him of it, but he simply had no time to spend with the elf amidst the last-minute preparations for war. And there was one preparation in particular that he had put off for far too long.

He crossed the bailey to the north tower and climbed the stairs to the second floor, stood outside the door to Ella's rooms and breathed deep. The urge to linger was strong, for this was no talk he wished to have, but the guards were looking-without-looking at him, and 'twould seem— 'twould *be*—cowardly of him to tarry. He raised his hand and knocked.

From the other side of the door came a lilting, "Welcome, Sir Prince."

He nodded at the guards to let him through. The cat darting in as the door opened caught him less by surprise this time.

Ella greeted him in her drawing room with a slow nod. He returned the gesture, taking in her new dress: moss green silk with white brocade, flowing floor-length skirts and tight bodice wrapped in satin ribbon, gossamer sleeves that revealed just a hint of the firm, glowing flesh beneath. 'Twas stunning fit to turn even a man such as he.

"Have you news of Ayden?" she asked, by all appearances oblivious to his attentions.

He cleared his throat and said, "He is . . . habituating. But I beg of you, do not ask if you may see him, for my heart would ache to deny you."

She frowned, but bowed her head in silence.

Yet more silence passed between them as Freyrík awaited Ella's invitation to sit, and Ella stood there, smiling blandly. Perhaps she did not know the manners of polite company.

Or perhaps she wished him gone.

He cleared his throat again, gestured toward her new dress. "A gift from my bond-sister?"

Ella gathered the skirts of her dress and curtsied. "Indeed. Does it please you?"

"Very much," he breathed, then found himself adding, "You . . . you should not wear such things before my men."

"I am not so defenseless as you may think, Prince. You need not fear for me."

"I . . . No," he said, nodding once, "of course not. And how do you find the Lady Kona? I hope you do not mind her attentions."

Ella's sudden smile crinkled her eyes, and Freyrík was seized by a memory of Kona some twenty-three years past, bundling him on her lap after the evening meal and reading his favorite story of the victory at Andlát Hill. She even let him flip the pages, though the book was very old and expensive.

Perhaps that was why it surprised Freyrík so little when Ella said, "She is . . . shy. Sweet. She asks many questions, seems eager for knowledge and listens as well as she speaks. She brings me much joy in this lonesome place, and no," she said, fingering the sleeve of her dress with clear fondness, "I've no objection to such lovely finery."

Oh, what her brother would think of all that!

Ella turned then and sat on the edge of her settee, inviting him to sit as well. "But you are not here to speak of the Lady Kona," she said as Freyrík settled into a nearby chair.

Ah, on to business—a subject with which he was entirely more comfortable. In some ways, at least. Maybe. "No," he said. "I am here to make you a promise. I do not know what news travels past these doors . . ."

"Much gossip, Sir Prince, for Lady Kona possesses a privileged ear, and your chambermaids seem to enjoy my company as much as I enjoy theirs. But news? Perhaps not so much."

"Have you heard we march upon the Surge in two days?" Ella nodded. "Do you know I shall be taking Ayden with me?"

Trussed up over my saddle, if he continues to argue.

"Surely not!" she cried, rising to her feet but then promptly retaking her seat, smoothing her skirts as if embarrassed by her outburst.

"'Tis true," he said, though he took care to withhold the reason. "But listen." He leaned forward in his chair, laid his hand atop hers where it rested on her knee. "I have come to promise your safekeeping in my absence. No harm shall come to you, and your every need shall be met, even if I do not return. This I swear."

She nodded but said nothing; he thought her teeth clenched, judging by the distress on her face. "And Ayden? Will no harm come to him as well?"

"That I cannot promise." She pulled her hand out from beneath his, inched back on the settee, out of his reach. "'Tis war, Ella; people fall. I cannot control that, only the gods."

"You can leave him here!"

Freyrík shook his head. "No, child. Every man must fight for his future. And believe me: Ayden will be safer on the march, by my side, than he would be here without me. I shall watch him as my brother, Ella. I can promise you no less and no more."

The prince, gods crack him, dragged Ayden to yet another feast—a pre-march celebration or some such—a mere two days after the first one.

'Twas yet another night of kneeling at the prince's feet, enduring a hand-feeding and a room full of hateful, lustful stares. He was as awful to the prince as he knew how to be, for he'd made no promise of good behavior this night, and the prince kept pressing his insistence that Ayden march with him come morrow. Well, he would learn otherwise soon enough.

At long last the merriment subsided, the servants cleared away the last of the meal, and the guests stopped one by one at the dais to give their goodbyes before retiring to their carriages or rooms. It felt quite late to Ayden, and he was very tired; 'twas with great relief that he heard the prince excuse himself and bid the remaining courtiers a good evening.

They exited through the side door behind the dais, the prince still leading Ayden by his chain. Halfway down the hall, someone called from behind, "Your Highness, I beg a moment of your time."

Ayden swallowed a groan as they turned to meet a vaguely familiar man, silver-haired and wrinkled but possessing of the bearing and carriage of youth. He spared Ayden only a glance, as if that were enough to take his measure. Ayden returned the favor. Two scars upon his left cheek, and at least five knives upon his person, concealed but not cleverly enough—an officer of the royal guard, he thought, and crack him for delaying Ayden's return to privacy and rest.

"Of course, Lord Commander," the prince said. He turned to Ayden and handed him his own leash. "Go straight to my rooms. Do not tarry, do not speak to or stop for anyone if it can be helped. I'll not be far behind. Do you understand?"

"No, for I am an idiot child who cannot follow simple instructions."

The prince glared pure murder at him, ripped the chain from Ayden's hand with a yank so fierce that Ayden stumbled to the floor. Next came a foot to his stomach, but surprisingly, it barely hurt; Ayden figured it for show, and curled up with a yelp lest the prince decide to follow through for real. Then he scurried to his knees and bowed his head. "Apologies, Your Highness. I understand."

A snort from the commander showed the man less than convinced, but he said only, "Shall I have a guard accompany it, Your Highness?"

"That . . . " The prince paused, as if the possibility had not occurred to him. "That would be wise, yes. Thank you, Commander."

The officer called someone over, and Ayden's chain was once again in human hands. The guard looked as displeased with the situation as he was, and made a point to shove Ayden ahead of him down the corridor, back toward his lavish prison.

And just when Ayden thought he'd endured the worst of the night's insults, they rounded a corner and he nearly bumped into the First Wife.

"Ho there!" she called, as if he were some horse she were riding.

The guard tugged him to a halt, moved up beside him, and bowed.

"I wish to speak with the elf," Kona said, holding her hand out, palm up, and waving her fingers until the guard handed her Ayden's leash. "*Alone*," she added, and glared at the man until he retreated.

Kona took one large step forward, nearly pressing herself flush to Ayden. He backed up and hit the wall; she followed. "Good evening, Pretty. Did you enjoy the feast?"

"Not at all," he said. "Now if you'll excuse me, I—"

"You are *not* excused." She leaned in closer yet, planted her hand against the exposed skin of his chest. She felt even colder than the prince, and this close she smelled like too much wine, sounded like honey and lust. "Come now," she breathed, and suddenly her lips joined her hand, brushing soft, dry kisses across his chest. "Surely you must hunger for a woman after all your days and nights with the prince."

"Not at all," he said again, as slow and clear as he could make it. He dared not shove her away, not with the guard so close and his behavior already so poor tonight, but he gave her forehead a gentle nudge, took her wrist in his hand and lifted it from his chest.

Her lips thinned into a hard line, and in her eyes he saw the intelligence that she'd so far kept at bay, hidden carefully from the men of this backwards empire. She peeled his hand from her wrist and gripped it hard, painted fingernails digging into his flesh.

"I understand how it is to be new to a place," she said, her voice gone low and cold as her expression, "so I will forgive your lack of manners this time. Be thankful I am gracious; I will educate you."

She pushed his wrist against the wall and leaned into him, reached up with her free hand to stroke his neck, the shell of his ear, stood on her toes to let her lips follow her fingers. Hot breath and moist tongue traced his earlobe, and he swallowed down a surge of nausea and shame and an even bigger surge of violence.

"Whatever you were before, elf," she whispered in his ear, "whatever mighty warrior or leader of your people, you are *nothing* now. Nothing but a slave, a plaything. You will do as you are told, or you will suffer great pains." She wedged her knee between his legs for emphasis, mashing his stones against the wall. He choked on a growl and somehow refrained from striking back, even as he gasped and sweated in her hold.

"But if you obey me," she purred, all pliant curves and sweetness again, her knee leaving his groin and sliding down his thigh, "I would give you such pleasures as you've never known, even in all your many years."

He shook his head, but daren't move anything else, not even to free his hand. "I thank you for the offer, Milady, but I must decline. For I belong to the prince, and only *he* may educate me." And for once, he was grateful for that. "And you belong to the king, who would have my head and more if I touched you."

Point made, he tried once more to nudge her off without inciting the guard, but she grabbed his other wrist and shoved him back into the wall, stood on her toes and crushed her lips to his. Though her tongue probed and her teeth bit, he kept his mouth firmly sealed, turned his head until she was kissing his cheek.

"Milady!" he cried, yanking one hand free to swipe at the dampness her painted lips had left upon his, "our masters—"

"Are not here," she said briskly, all traces of seduction gone as her hands tangled hard and painful in his hair, holding his head still. He heard a warsong rising within him and forced it down lest he burn her, made a noise of distress against her lips and turned his eyes to the guard in fruitless hope; the man had his gaze trained quite deliberately over their heads.

Well, fine. If she refused to see reason and the guard refused to mind them, then he need not be reasonable or mind the guard himself.

He pinched both her wrists between his fingers in a way that would leave no marks but cause great pain, smiling with grim satisfaction when she yelped and let go of his hair. Shoving her to the ground seemed an exceptionally bad idea, so he settled for spinning them round and shoving her into the wall, pinning her wrists as she'd done to him. Her song quickened for one hopeful moment—did she truly think he meant to kiss her?—then faded back to its earlier honeywine lust. Even when he squeezed her wrists harder, she refused to fear him.

But neither could he allow himself to fear her. He leaned in close and whispered in her ear, "You *will not* treat me so, or I shall cease to be polite. Do you catch my meaning, you filthy shrew?"

Both the threat and the insult ricocheted right off her; she laughed in his face, then pressed her lips to his cheek and licked his skin. "If that is how you wish to play it . . ."

He froze, trembling. Tried to pull away, but Kona freed a hand from under his slackened fingers and grabbed him by the ear.

And of course that was exactly when the prince came round the corner.

Ayden heard from him a moment of confusion, then livid anger; then all inner sounds were drowned by the First Wife's cry: "Rape!"

The guard at last jumped into action, punching Ayden in the kidney so hard his knees buckled. He fell in a gasping heap, clutching at pain he could not reach. No point in getting up, anyway; the guard would only knock him down again.

"Oh, *brother*!" the First Wife cried, throwing herself into the prince's arms, producing somehow a river of tears and a fake-panicked, stuttering babble of "The elf!" and "Oh *gods*!" and "He put his *tongue* in my mouth!" She clung to the prince as fiercely as she'd been clinging to Ayden moments ago, buried her face in the man's chest and sobbed.

From his miserable position on the floor, Ayden shook his head in denial. The prince, holding the First Wife tightly, spared him no glance, but he did turn to the guard and ask, "Is this true?"

Ayden could see the First Wife tense at the question, and silently thanked the prince for keeping his head.

Then pain exploded in his spine: a gift from the guard's booted foot. His howl almost drowned the guard's "Yes, Your Highness. Happened just as you arrived."

Gods, what cheap cover for having stood round doing nothing, you cracking deaf-eared sheep-fucker—

"You may leave us now," the prince said. His voice was soft and level, but fury spilled from his song, measure after roiling measure. Behind Ayden, a sharp click and retreating steps marked the guard's departure.

Ayden closed his eyes and resigned himself to whatever punishment the prince would inflict for Kona's honor, for his shameful display in front of the commander, for all his slights and insults and misdeeds these past three weeks. He should not have pushed so hard; he would never forgive himself if his actions brought harm upon Ella's head.

But the prince only looked at him, face tight and shuttered, and said, "You too. Wait in my rooms. Do try to follow my instructions this time."

"Yes, Your Highness," Ayden mumbled. For though 'twas surely too late to repair things now, he could at least not make them any worse. And that's exactly what he should have been doing all along, gods crack his stubborn pride.

Freyrík waited until Ayden was out of sight before releasing Kona. He desperately wished he could have reassured the elf before sending him off—'twas obvious just by looking at Ayden that he was steeling himself to be beaten or worse—but even as ghastly as Kona's behavior had been, he owed her more grace than a scolding in front of a slave.

The moment they were alone, though, he shoved her away, crossed his arms and glared at her until she had the decency to look ashamed.

"He is *mine*, Kona," he growled. "You cannot have him."

She mirrored his posture, crossing her arms and sneering. "Perhaps I should, for he is clearly clouding your judgment. Look at you! You're so busy with your pretty new fuck-toy that you can't even be bothered to go help your brother!"

The walls round him sheeted white with rage, and the next thing Freyrík knew, Kona was crying, her hand pressed to her mouth and cheek, Freyrík's own hand stinging with the force of his slap. She stared at him for a long moment, hurt and shock and shame written all across her face, then ducked her head and let her arm fall to her side. He'd split her lip.

"Apologize," he ground out, balling his hands into fists against the temptation to raise them again. "You *know* that's not true." He took a large step forward, menaced her right up to the wall. "Say it! Tell me you know!"

Her head bobbed in short, emphatic little bursts on her neck, but the words he wanted seemed trapped in her throat.

He turned on his heel, disgusted with both of them, and stomped down the corridor toward his rooms. Toward his elf.

"Ayden!" he called as he hurried through the doors to his drawing room, regretting his raised voice when he saw Ayden scramble off the sofa and to his knees with a wince. "No," Freyrík said, rushing over to him, grasping him by the shoulders and urging him to his feet. "No no no, I am not angry with you. I am *not*."

He drew Ayden into a quick, fierce hug, but the elf was board-stiff in his arms. He let him go, dropped down onto the sofa instead, and gestured for Ayden to join him.

"I know 'twas not your doing," he said. "Lady Kona was too forward. Did she . . . Are you . . . ?" He opened his mouth and closed it, but nothing more came out. He grasped Ayden's hands instead, but Ayden flinched away.

"Please," Ayden said, so soft 'twas nearly a whisper, staring down at his hands. "If you would, Prince . . . I do not wish to be touched."

"All right," Freyrík said, equally soft, drawing his hands back into his own lap.

"I am uninjured," Ayden said, his eyes still on his hands. "But I thought . . ." He turned his gaze, piercing and wounded, to Freyrík's face. "You did not even ask me what happened."

"How could I? The Prince Regent, the First Wife, a palace guard, and a slave? I could not even speak to the slave before such an audience." The hurt in Ayden's eyes deepened; Freyrík licked his lips and added, "Nor did I need to. The truth was clear as water to my eyes." He smiled, stifled the nearly overwhelming urge to touch Ayden again, to hold his hand, stroke his hair, his cheek. "Forgive me?"

Confusion creased Ayden's face, but he held Freyrík's gaze a moment longer, then nodded. "I understand."

And so, for what seemed the very first time, did Freyrík, who suddenly pictured himself in Ayden's boots, in Ayden's chains . . . in Ayden's impotent despair. He searched for words to make things right, or even just a little better, but of course there were none.

Finally, the elf stood and walked toward the bedroom.

"Ayden," Freyrík called, rising to go after him. He didn't know why; the elf clearly wished to be alone.

Ayden froze, peered over one tense shoulder. "I wish to bathe," he said, half statement, half question.

"Yes, of course."

Ayden looked at him with strange longing. "You—" He cut himself off, scrubbed a hand through his hair and left it there, fisted tight and tugging. "You're not . . . I mean, can I still go with you?"

"Where?" Freyrík asked, though what he really wanted to ask was *Tell me how to fix you*, or perhaps *What happened to the other Ayden, the one who insulted me in front of my Captain of the Guard?*

"To the Surge," Ayden said softly.

Freyrík felt his jaw drop, but this only made Ayden wilt further. The elf rushed back to him and dropped to one knee, grasping Freyrík's right hand in both his own. "If you'll still have me? Please . . . please do not leave me alone here!"

Freyrík knew not what to do with this sudden change of heart, with the great and crushing weight of Ayden's desperation. To think that after all the dark moments of Ayden's captivity, a mere *woman* had broken him . . . Though perhaps he should not be surprised. Had Kona not, in her own way, done the one thing Freyrík himself had considered too cruel?

He laid his free hand over Ayden's own, dared to stroke his thumb there in small, soothing circles. "Of course you can still come," he said. "I'd not— Look at me." He put two fingers to Ayden's chin, tipped his head up until he could look into the elf's eyes. Gods, were those *tears* threatening to spill? "I'd not have it any other way."

# Chapter Twelve

Freyrík lay awake long into the night before the march, twisting in his sheets and his doubts. So many things could go wrong, on the march and on the battlefield . . . not least of them involving a proud and spiteful elf amidst an army of elf-hating soldiers.

Said elf was lying atop the covers to his right, glowing in the stifling heat of the canopy bed. Probably awake, though he pretended otherwise. Freyrík had learned to tell the difference by the quality of his elflight: bright when awake, muted when he slumbered.

It was glaring now.

"You're glowing," Freyrík complained softly, if only to break the oppressive silence.

Ayden grunted irritation, but dulled his light.

"Get some sleep. We've a long day tomorrow."

'Twas a measure of Ayden's exhaustion that he offered no sharp retort. Freyrík thought back to what Ella had said of her brother trapped between two tall cliffs: this time the Surge on one side and the First Wife, perhaps, on the other?

Strange, but he was starting to feel the same himself, though his own cliffs he could not name.

None of that mattered tonight, though. He should clear his head, get some rest while he could. Tomorrow—

Tomorrow came with a loud trumpet call that startled him off the mattress.

*Finally.*

Freyrík rolled out of bed and headed to the washroom, sparing a brief nod for his still-yawning groom. His own sheen of tiredness he dunked in a basin of cold water, along with his head, then he quickly toweled dry. They had but two hours 'til dawn; then they'd march.

He left the washroom just as Ayden trudged in, black tufts sticking out every which way. The elf seemed groggy. Freyrík doubted 'twas only from lack of sleep, and wisely refrained from speaking.

His groom approached with an armful of clothes, and Freyrík stood by the mirror, with growing impatience, as the man dressed him. He was taking exceeding care, smoothing the cloth over Freyrík's chest and shoulders again and again, as if preparing him for audience before the Aegis himself.

At last Freyrík caught the man's hands and stilled them. "'Tis well enough, my dear Lord Vitr. Do not fret so; I shall return, gods willing."

Unmasked, the man smiled wanly and offered Freyrík his buff coat, which Freyrík brushed away.

"'Tis too hot for such attire. Pack it with the armor, and bring me my crest tunic instead."

His groom bowed and left, and kitchen servants entered, carrying breakfast trays. Ayden ate in lackluster silence, while Freyrík would have been fidgeting in his seat if not for his finer upbringing. But his excitement waned halfway through the meal, when the final item in their traveling ensemble arrived: a full set of irons.

Ayden glanced calmly at them between one bite of oatmeal and the next, but said nothing.

"I'm sorry," Freyrík said. "They are only temporary, I promise."

Ayden scraped the last of the oatmeal from his bowl and ate it.

"I'll remove them as soon as we're gone from the castle," Freyrík said.

The elf put down his spoon and picked up the shackles. He examined them for a moment, then bent down and fastened them to his ankles.

"I hope you're not . . ." *angry with me*, Freyrík meant to say, but when Ayden straightened up to lock the collar round his neck, his face was perfectly smooth, not a hint of anger to be found.

Ayden shrugged, held out the wrist cuffs and asked, "In front or behind?"

Freyrík shook his head. "What are you—?"

"When can we leave?"

*Oh.*

"Now," Freyrík said, though he hadn't yet finished his breakfast. He took the irons from Ayden's slack fingers and fastened them in front, then led Ayden from the table.

Ayden followed without a word.

Lord Commander Hákon and Lord Lini joined them in the Great Hall, and Freyrík led their small party outside, where lanterns vied with the early dawn to illuminate the bailey. Fog yet swirled on the ground, veiling the debris of the scarecrow construction and turning their trek to the stables into a challenge—particularly for Ayden, hobbled as he was.

The rest of the caravan was straggled all across the bailey's east ward: the last of the scarecrow crafters, and three contingents of officer-lords with their hundred-odd attendants. The men saluted as Freyrík passed by; he nodded in return and waved them back to work. And if there was a slight pause in their greetings, a caginess to their salutes, a beat in which their eyes slid from him and landed on the elf beside him . . .

He could not hear emotions as Ayden did, but the hostility that poured from every man they passed was tangible even to him. He tried to imagine being the target of such a barrage and shuddered. Yet Ayden walked blithely on.

The stables were bustling as they approached, young hands transporting horses back and forth to the long line of waiting attendants. The stable master himself had Freyrík's horse at the ready: a sleek black destrier named Spyrna, draped in the bright reds and purples of House Farr.

Freyrík heard a sharp intake of breath behind him, and turned to see Ayden staring at Spyrna with nearly reverent eyes. 'Twas quite the relief to see some animation return to the elf's too-passive features.

"Magnificent, isn't she?" Freyrík said.

Ayden's head bobbed up and down.

Freyrík reached for Spyrna's velvety muzzle, smiled when the horse puffed a welcome in his palm. "She's seen me safe through nine Surges now. Gods willing, this will make ten."

Behind them, well out of kicking distance, three stable hands were leading a dun destrier and two bay coursers, also draped in the colors of Farr. Lord Commander Hákon claimed his dun, and Lord Lini his courser. The other bay went to Ayden; the stable hand tossed him the reins and then bolted back into the stables.

Ayden looked to Freyrík, to the horse, and to Freyrík again, but made no move to mount. Gods help him, had the elf never sat a horse? He realized he'd never bothered to ask, had simply assumed that a warrior of Ayden's caliber would be a master equestrian.

Hoping 'twas an issue of permission rather than skill, he stepped into Spyrna's stirrup and hoisted himself into the saddle, then nodded at Ayden to do the same.

Ayden ran a shackled hand down the bay's withers, then looked pointedly at the irons binding his hands and feet. Freyrík could all but hear the insult burning on his tongue—*Shall I ride sidesaddle like a woman into battle, then?*—but Ayden wisely, and surprisingly, withheld it. Freyrík felt foolish enough as he pulled the key from a pocket and leaned down to offer it to the elf.

Spyrna chose that moment to sidle a step, and Ayden ended up grabbing Freyrík's wrist before managing to take the key from his fingers. The touch sent a tingle up Freyrík's arm and he grew aware, of a sudden, of how his crotch pressed against the saddle's pommel. He surged upright so quickly that Spyrna, picking up on his alarm, stepped back.

Only then did he remember their audience.

Lord Commander Hákon was frowning upon the scene from the high seat of his dun. He nudged his horse forward and said, "If I might suggest, Your Highness: I can put the elf in the wagons with the rest of the supplies."

All round them, attendants and hands turned to watch with open amusement. Freyrík's stare snapped to Ayden; the casual insult had obviously cut the elf to the quick, but he surprised Freyrík yet again by holding his tongue. Yet his hands, still shackled, clenched round his horse's reins, and he glared up at Freyrík as if *he* were the one treating him like *supplies*.

And perhaps Freyrík deserved that, for allowing that impression to stand uncorrected.

He spun his horse in a tight circle to face the bulk of the crowd and cried, "Hear me, soldiers of Farr!"

His call captured the attention of men from the stables all the way back to the practice field. With a sweeping gesture at Ayden, he said, "This elf is here to fight with us, not against us. Forget all that you know of him and his kind, and treat him as you would any man marching against the darker menace. Is that clear?"

His gaze swept round the crowd. The soldiers did not cheer for his order, but he accepted their grumbled replies in good faith. 'Twould hold, he hoped, until Ayden could prove himself in battle.

He looked back to the elf, drinking in the relief on his face like iced water in the summer heat. Ayden bent to free himself of his irons, then turned to examine his mount's saddle, checking the fit of the girth and adjusting the stirrups much higher than Freyrík thought proper. Apparently satisfied, he planted one hand on the pommel and vaulted into the saddle in a leap fit to put a show rider to shame. He slid his toes into the stirrups but ignored the reins, wrapping the ends round the pommel and leaving enough slack for the horse to do any befanged thing it pleased.

Apparently, it pleased the courser to bypass the hay stacked nearby in favor of high-stepping through a tight turn round Freyrík's mount and backing up to a halt beside it.

Master equestrian indeed!

Ayden looked at Freyrík and grinned like a child at play. Freyrík grinned back; 'twas the first real smile he could remember that did not involve Ayden beating him senseless.

He was on horseback, unchained, outside where the wind and every blade of grass sang out to him—if it weren't for the single thread of worry stretching back to Castle Farr and Ella, Ayden thought he would have been content. Even the caravan's turtle pace failed to dent his patience, and the poor company was mostly held in check by the presence of the prince.

Mostly.

Here came one of them now, a captain by the insignia on his sleeve. He rode up to the prince and reported, quite unnecessarily, that all was well with the men and the wagons, which the prince acknowledged with a scant nod. The captain reined in his horse, and Ayden hoped he would fall back, but no . . . He fell in beside Ayden, half a length behind the prince.

Great. Ayden debated asking his mount to take him to the prince's side, leaving the captain behind, but he quickly discarded the notion. He did not need a human's protection, even if it were an unusually decent human.

Instead he kept his face turned firmly forward, but even from the corner of his eye he saw the man looking him up and down. The human's smirk was lewd and contemptuous and covetous all at once, and when he realized Ayden was looking, he licked his lips and pursed them into a parody of a kiss.

Ayden turned to face him, smiled sweetly, and said, "Your horse has picked up a stone."

The human made a gesture with his hands that, if Ayden recalled correctly, was not meant for children or polite company. "I think I'd know if she had."

"Ah, but you do *not* think, human; 'tis a flaw endemic to your race."

The captain bared his teeth, but a glance ahead at the prince confined his ire to a quiet hiss. "Listen, you spawn of a—"

"'Twould serve you and she both to ask her, rather than assume the best," Ayden continued, still smiling. "Oh, wait—you *can't* ask her."

Yet the horse answered anyway, rearing suddenly, hard enough to throw the man.

Ayden almost wished he'd had a hand in it.

Especially when the man accused him of exactly that, and the prince seemed inclined to agree—at least until Ayden dismounted and went to the captain's mount, cupper her right front fetlock and turned up her hoof. There was the stone he'd warned of, wedged between the shoe and the cleft.

When they resumed riding, the captain fell back to the rear.

And so went Ayden's morning, one rider after another approaching the prince under pretence of a question or report. Invariably they would hover at Ayden's side, some glancing at him askance, others gawking openly. Oh, the humans checked their tongues lest the prince hear them wag, but Ayden made out many a hushed exchange about the royal bed-warmer or the too-pampered pet. Yet others spoke as if he were a woman of the finest order, a consort to be displayed with pride, a shining reflection of honor upon the Crown of Farr.

Regardless, one thing was clear: these men loved their prince as a brother, respected and obeyed him as a father, indulged and watched over him as a favored son. If he wanted to play with his "toy," nearly none among them would begrudge him that pleasure.

Ayden was more relieved than he wished to admit when, some hours later beneath a pounding midday sun, Commander Hákon announced a short stop for the afternoon meal. As the caravan line scattered, a lieutenant rode past Ayden and kicked him in the shin with a spurred heel hard enough to draw blood. The prince, of course, was engaged with his Captain of the Guard and his secretary. No matter: Ayden dismounted and walked the stiffness from his legs, keeping watch on the lieutenant throughout their meal. When the man retired to a far patch of roadside to water the grass, Ayden followed to do the same.

The lieutenant glared as Ayden unbuttoned his breeches and said, "It's a big road, *gróm*. Do your business elsewhere."

Ayden pasted on the same sweet smile he'd given the captain, then aimed himself discreetly and pissed all over the lieutenant's boots.

The lieutenant gave an outraged shout. No sooner had Ayden tucked himself away, the man was grabbing twin fistfuls of his shirt and snarling in his face. Ayden suffered it, counting slowly in his mind: *one . . . two . . . three . . .*

"What is the meaning of this?" the prince demanded, appearing as if summoned by elfsong.

"Your Highness!" the lieutenant cried, snatching his hands back and clicking his heel on the dirt road. His face flushed three shades deeper when he noticed he'd not yet re-sheathed his member.

Ayden snorted.

"Lieutenant?" the prince said.

"Begging forgiveness, Your Highness, but this *gró*— ah, your elf just watered my boots!"

The prince looked sharply at Ayden, who quickly buried his smirk and said with all the gravity he could muster, "What? 'Tis a sign of respect in my lands!"

The prince's lips quivered for a second before he covered them with his hand, eyes sparkling, and nodded with little more gravity than Ayden had managed.

The lieutenant's song cried murder.

When the prince wrested his humor back under control, he dropped his hand from his mouth and said, "Perhaps 'twould be best if you were a little less respectful in future. Come now," he added, giving Ayden's arm a little tug, "we must press on."

The lieutenant leaned in as Ayden passed him and whispered, "The dog is lucky his master arrived."

Ayden whispered right back, "Indeed you are, for I'd have broken every bone in your hands had you left them upon me a moment longer."

Grinning, he walked away.

They remounted and rode 'til early evening, across dirt and crushed gravel and even some paved roads, through endless acres of field and orchard and the outskirts of the occasional small town. They kept to a moderate pace for the horses' sake, and by the time they made camp, Ayden estimated they'd traveled no more than nine leagues.

He made no show of the stiffness he was feeling as he dismounted alongside the prince. Half a dozen soldiers were setting up a picket line, rounding up all the animals to be unsaddled and brushed down, watered and fed. Others were pitching tents, building fires, gathering wood and water, unloading the night's supplies from the wagons, scouting the surrounding area and posting guards. Everyone had a role and a task . . . except him. Even the prince was busy in discussion with two of his officers when Ayden went to ask where he could be put to use.

"Right here," the prince said, smiling and patting the chair beside him—and really, who brought *chairs* out on a combat march? "Keep me company, if you would."

Ayden rolled his eyes but took the vacant seat, listening in on the day's status reports from the front lines. When the prince's tent was pitched and stocked—"tent" being an unequal word for the massive partitioned structure, complete with luxury bedroom and traveling office—he followed the prince inside, along with General Vísi and Commander Hákon, where they continued their evening's work. Two soldiers stood watch outside the door.

"You're free to wander about," the prince said as General Vísi pulled a series of maps from a chest and laid them across a table. "As long as you water no more boots—" and there was that twitching almost-smile again—"the men will not harm you."

"Oh, I know they won't," Ayden said.

The prince did not bother to hide his grin this time. "I meant they won't try, Ayden. You are brothers in arms now. You should make their acquaintance. Break bread with them."

"I know about them all that I care to," Ayden said, sitting at the map table without invitation and plucking a peach from a bowl someone had set there.

"And they no doubt think the same of you," Commander Hákon said. He looked like he wanted to slap the fruit from Ayden's hand. At least, Ayden hoped he would be aiming for the fruit.

"Surely you wish to know the men who will be at your back in battle," the prince said, eminently reasonable.

Ayden flashed a feral smile. "Rest easy, Prince. I've no intention of turning my back to any of them—in battle or otherwise."

"Ayden . . ."

He shrugged and said, "I am tired, Prince. I wish only to sleep."

The prince nodded and pointed with his chin toward the bedroom on the other side of the canvas wall. "The bed is set, and there is water heated for washing. I'll be in shortly."

Ayden nodded, trying desperately to ignore the knowing look in Commander Hákon's eyes as he walked into the prince's bedroom, head held high.

In the lantern-lit dimness of the tent, the prince undressed himself and began to wash at his basin. Ayden lay in the prince's bed—an actual bed he'd seen fit to haul, frame and mattress and sheets and all—and watched him with idle eyes.

"Where is your groom?" he asked.

The prince whipped round, startled. "I thought you were asleep."

"Nay, prince. I did not wish to—"

He cut himself off; 'twas too intimate, too private to share how very much he longed for the chirp of the crickets, the rustle of the breeze through the leaves. And of course the *other* songs of the outdoors, the ones the humans couldn't hear. He didn't want to miss a single moment.

"I take no groom to war," the prince said. "But Lord Lini helps when I need it, and I've many an attendant at my disposal."

Ayden sat up in bed, acutely aware of a sudden that he was naked to the waist in the summer heat. "They all think you're bedding me right now."

The prince's hand, and the wash cloth he was clutching, stilled on his opposite shoulder. "So?" he said, a poor imitation of nonchalance.

"That is all they think me good for."

The wash cloth hit the basin with a splash, and the prince turned round to face Ayden. His broad chest glistened with tiny beads of water in the lantern light. "So?" he said again. "You and I know better."

"Do we really?"

The answering silence spoke volumes, though Ayden could not interpret its language.

At last the prince moved to the foot of the bed, sat gingerly upon the edge and asked, "What is this about, Ayden? You seemed . . . dare I say happy today?"

The prince placed a hand on Ayden's ankle through the sheet, but Ayden jerked his foot away and crossed his arms. "Happy to be free of those cracking castle walls. But clearly I cannot be free of *you*."

"No," the prince said, and Ayden both heard and *heard* the sadness in that word. "No, you can't. But you need not be what others make of you. And I will make nothing of you that you do not wish to be. You know that by now, I hope?"

"And yet here I am, warming your bed."

"Ah, yes," the prince said, his smile more lopsided than cheerful. "The heat of your surliness sets my heart aflame."

Ayden glared at him, but even he had to admit that there was truth in the prince's jest.

The prince patted his leg again, stood and returned to the wash basin. "Now still those stubborn lips of yours, Ayden, and sleep. For we've many a long day ahead."

Freyrík wished his warning had not been quite so accurate, but alas, their remaining days on the march proved long and numerous. They woke early and stopped late, eating and washing and falling into bed with little energy for anything in between.

He spent the better part of each day rethinking the Surge plan, shoring it up with provisions for every contingency. His mind, filled with decades of darker fights, supplied many a dire possibility for him to chew on.

As during the prior days, his officers rode up frequently—some for legitimate business, but most, it seemed, to hover near Ayden. He wished he could spare the elf their pestering, but if he denied them, their curiosity might fester into something much worse by the time they reached base camp, where he could not watch over Ayden every moment of the day. Besides, he doubted the elf would appreciate his meddling.

And Ayden seemed to handle them well enough on his own: he ignored most, scorned some, and occasionally, during breaks and night stops, took secret revenge that wasn't as secret as he believed. Freyrík allowed it, for Ayden never dragged him into untenable situations, and some of his men deserved a lesson or two.

And perhaps most importantly, Ayden seemed happy. Gone were his arguments and snapping retorts, and the lethal edge had worn off his humor. Oh, he was still dagger-sharp—Freyrík would have treated him for heat stroke had the elf become *nice*—but he smiled and laughed with growing ease, and thrice now had allowed Freyrík's touch upon his arm or shoulder.

Despite the looming battle, Freyrík thought he too might be happy.

The final day of the march began much like all the others. Freyrík discussed the day's route with Lord General Vísi over breakfast in his tent. Ayden refused all encouragement to break fast with the soldiers, and instead sat next to him—which Freyrík couldn't protest—and filched most of the food from his plate, which Freyrík knew better than to protest. Lord General Vísi looked on with customary disapproval, but Freyrík thought he detected a spark of humor in the older man's eyes.

Excitement gripped the caravan as they mounted and set out for the final time. Though they would yet spend days of waiting at base camp, the first tendrils of battle fever were creeping over the soldiers, and in part over Freyrík as well. Behind him, even Ayden seemed eager to reach their destination.

His officers chafed when he called for an early noon break to lunch and to water the horses, but he stood firm by his order, dismounting and passing his reins to a nearby attendant.

"Can't we press on?" Ayden asked with a charming little pout. "We must be nearly there now."

Freyrík swallowed his smile. "We must break by water. This stream," he gestured toward the one they'd been following since morn, "veers sharply south soon and will not rejoin our path until base camp."

Ayden shrugged. "I can make water, you know."

He cupped his hand before Freyrík's face—Freyrík almost flinched at the sudden movement—and a moment later, his palm brimmed with water, drops falling from his fingers.

"How did you . . .!" Freyrík breathed, even as the men round them cried "Sorcery!" and "Magic!"

Ayden raised an eyebrow, but then abandoned the haughty pretense and shrugged. "There's moisture in the air, Prince. I can call them apart, that's all."

As if 'twere that simple . . .

"Yes, well, enough for a man or two, perhaps," Freyrík said, tamping down his wonder. "But I've nearly two hundred men and half again as many horses. And besides," he said, tugging Ayden's wrist to his lips and pressing them to the side of the elf's palm, "I am the only one here who'd dare drink from your hand."

He tipped Ayden's palm and swallowed the trickle of fresh water, then licked his lips (and perhaps the elf's little finger) and released Ayden with a wink and a smile. The elf wiped his hand furiously on his breeches, but underneath his narrowed eyes, the corners of his mouth twitched up.

Freyrík cupped a hand round Ayden's elbow and led him to a pretty little spot on the bank of the stream, away from the noise and the eyes of the troops. It warmed his heart that Ayden allowed it with no more than a quizzical brow.

When they'd reached some semblance of privacy, Freyrík gently swung him round. "There are some things I must discuss with you before we reach camp."

Ayden's brow furrowed further. "Sounds serious," he said.

"'Tis indeed."

Freyrík fumbled in the pocket of his coat, squeezing his fingers round the true reason behind the stop. "Listen," he said. "When we reach base camp, you must ride right beside me, as close as you can, and half a length back. You must never pull even with me, and you must never leave my side, do you understand?"

Ayden nodded, his mouth twisting only a fraction over the possessive—and protective—nature of the gesture.

"And do try not to insult anyone," Freyrík added with a thin smile.

This earned him a roll of the eyes and a "Yes, mother."

Freyrík nodded, fingered the bundle in his pocket again. Then, with a deep breath, he pulled out the arm's length of rolled cloth, checkered in the colors of Farr, and offered it to Ayden. "I'd ask that you wear this round your neck."

The elf took it with a raised eyebrow, turned it in his hands. Freyrík could all but hear his questing thoughts. The cloth was sewn into a strip about an inch wide, and was just long enough to . . .

Ayden's eyes snapped up and narrowed to slits. "This is a collar," he said flatly.

"Nay!" Freyrík said. "'Tis . . ."

"A neck belt, perhaps? To hold my shirt up?"

"A cravat," Freyrík said firmly. "Very fashionable, I assure you."

He felt the elf's stare on his throat, unyielding as a choking hand. "Yet you do not wear one."

Freyrík looked down, then sighed and looked back at Ayden, dropping pretense in favor of earnest concern. "Please?" he said. "'Tis for your own safety. You may take it off soon enough."

Ayden studied him a moment longer, then shook his head . . . and tied the befanged thing round his neck.

Freyrík only hoped 'twould be protection enough for him, a single elf amongst eight thousand men and three hundred years of hatred.

# Chapter Thirteen

Ayden knew they were nearing base camp long before it came into view; he could *hear* it, a warning buzz like a massive hornets' swarm, thousands of humans each with their own feelings and fears. It came as mere vibrations at first, then swelled into whispered melodies, then shouted ones. Soon 'twas as if he were riding through the Stórr waterfall, an all-consuming crash of sound and sensation—

He clutched his hands to his temples and squeezed his eyes shut, scrabbling for equilibrium.

"What is it?"

Gods, another voice among the din. Louder than the others, clearer. Physical.

The prince.

"Ayden?"

"Huh?" He opened his eyes, focused them upon the handsome visage beside him.

"Are you well?" the prince asked.

Ayden nodded, swallowed, wrangled the background noise into submission by main force of will. He'd halted his horse, he realized, and so had the prince, and the entire caravan behind them.

"I'm fine," he said. "It's just . . . so many *people*. I've never . . ."

The prince peered round, even stood in his saddle to cast eyes to the distance, but of course he could not sense what Ayden sensed. "I don't understand," he said. "The camp is yet a fifth-league away."

"They are *noisy*," Ayden grumbled.

The prince barked a laugh, pointed at a nearby ridgeline. "If you think they're noisy now, wait until we crest that hill."

Ayden grimaced. He was *not* looking forward to meeting all those humans. Not only the noise, but the stares, the hatred, the desire, the contempt . . . all the things he'd endured since his capture, magnified a hundredfold.

Alas, the first of those humans were already on their way: a party of nine horsemen crested the hill in an arrowhead formation, their standard bearer riding point. Ayden recognized the colors of House Farr, but not the crest. He tensed, shaded his eyes with one hand and reached for a missing dagger with the other.

The prince leaned in his saddle and stayed him. "'Tis only the honor guard," he said. "They will escort us to camp."

"Whose flag is that?"

"Lord General Feitr's. One of my father's younger brothers, third in command of the Farr forces behind Berendil and myself. He oversees campaigns in our absence."

The prince talked on, but Ayden ignored the family history in favor of the approaching riders, bedecked in shining armor and the colors of Farr. When they arrived, all nine men promptly dismounted and fell to one knee in the grass.

"Your Highness," they said, so perfectly synchronized they'd surely rehearsed.

"You may remount," the prince said, and a moment later they were back on their horses.

It seemed everyone knew what to do here, for the prince began to ride again, and the honor guard fanned out to flank his procession, four on a side. Their standard bearer fell in behind the prince's own, who rode directly behind Ayden. Ayden himself rode half a length behind the prince, who'd taken the lead once more: a distinctly uncomfortable place, as far as Ayden was concerned. 'Twas bad enough that everyone would stare when he arrived, but to be out in front like this, exposed . . .

"It's all right," the prince said, turning round and pulling even to lay a hand upon Ayden's forearm. He called to one of the honor guard, who trotted up beside him and bowed in his saddle.

"Ride ahead; inform Lord General Feitr that I have brought along my elf and that he poses no threat. There must be no surprises when we arrive."

"Yes, Your Highness," the guardsman said, then bolted off toward camp as if fleeing the Ferals themselves.

Their procession crested the ridge shortly after, and the first sight of base camp struck Ayden like a punch to the gut. There before him lay a veritable canvas city, thousands of tents pitched in orderly rows across the valley floor, all flying pennants of Farr and Aegea and Feitr from their center poles. Within the encampment, Ayden knew, milled roughly eight thousand men, two thousand horses, half as many fighting dogs and birds of prey. He had, after all, helped to plan where each of those men and beasts would be posted. But 'twas one thing to read the registers, and quite another entirely to see them all gathered in one place.

The song that had battered his inner ear was now drowning beneath the physical noise: the clang of hammers on anvils, the saw and thud of trees being felled, the clacking of mallets on half-built scarecrows, shouted orders and the grunts of men at labor. He could smell them, too, so many beasts and humans in such close quarters.

Ayden wrinkled his nose and squeezed his eyes closed. 'Twas a shame he could not do the same with his ears.

At least the Hunter's Call had gone silent since last he'd neared Feral lands, as had all the songs of the forest-beasts; Nature, it seemed, had stripped this area bare. Yet though the camp was but a league or two from the border, no Feral song intruded on his hearing, either.

The prince began the short descent into the valley floor, and out of the mass below rose the fanfare of welcoming trumpets. At the sound, men left their work and rushed toward the wide-open street cutting through the encampment, cheering wildly as they went. The prince's train called out with equal enthusiasm, and the prince kicked his horse into a gallop; Ayden's mount, gripped by the excitement, nickered and followed suit.

"HAIL PRINCE FREYRÍK!" someone shouted from the throng, and others picked up the cry:

"HAIL PRINCE FREYRÍK!"

The great swarming mass, presumably by prearranged signal, split down the middle as the caravan neared. The prince reined in his mount just short of plunging into the crowds, then paraded at a high-step down the human aisle. Ayden leaned back in his saddle, and his own courser slowed to a walk.

Every soldier snapped his strange heel-clicking salute as the prince rode by, but every pair of eyes, it seemed, was on Ayden. Hundreds of them. *Thousands.* He felt deaf in the face of their curious-hostile-lustful-smug ruckus. Vulnerable. His throat moved against his so-called cravat as he swallowed, and suddenly he was glad for its presence.

By the time they neared the end of the passage, he felt close kinship with a prize buck in a human's snare.

At the end of the aisle stood an old man on a wooden platform, dressed in the sharpest, most medal-festooned field uniform Ayden had ever seen: the Lord General Feitr, presumably, judging by his insignia and the striking resemblance to the prince round the eyes and jaw.

The man clicked his heel sharply—he had taps on the soles of his shoes—and said, "Your Royal Highness, as ordered, I have held the field against your arrival. With your permission, I now turn command over to your eminently capable hands."

Ayden raised a hand to cover a snort.

Yet the prince took the formal greeting predictably well in stride. "'Tis my honor and my deepest pleasure to assume such fit command. House Farr thanks you, Lord General."

The man clicked his heel again and stepped back, but his rigid pose reflected the pride and vanity that hummed loud in Ayden's inner ear.

'Twas all he could observe of the general, though, for the prince spun his horse in a tight turn—taking Ayden's horse with it—to face the bulk of the crowd. The physical silence was staggering: how could so many men stand so silent amongst so much turmoil in their songs?

The prince handed his reins to a waiting soldier, and in a single fluid motion that impressed even Ayden, he stood upon his saddle where all could see him. The hush grew deeper still, until it shattered beneath the prince's cry:

"Warriors of Aegea! We stand upon the precipice of a momentous day!"

The prince paused, and eight thousand soldiers nodded silent agreement, their songs and faces set with grim determination, chinked with fear.

"You have all worked so very hard these last weeks, and you will work harder still in the days to come. Soon the Surge will crest, as it has crested upon these lands for generations, and soon we will fight the darkers, as we have fought them for generations."

Another pause, another round of nods, tense and expectant.

A cold smile crept up the prince's cheeks. "But this time, mighty warriors, we will *not fight fair*! Our wooden army will slay in our stead; our archers will butcher trapped beasts from afar; *we* will go home to our wives and our children with the taste of victory upon our lips untainted by the spill of human blood!"

The silence crumbled into thunderous cheers that Ayden both heard and sensed, a vibration through the ground, his horse, his seat, and with it a wash of anticipation so intense that it bordered upon fanatic. He felt dizzy with it, swept up upon its power; he clutched at his pommel in fear that he'd spill right from his saddle.

The prince sliced one fist through the air, as if thrusting a sword at a Feral, and shouted, "Victory to the Empire!"

"*SIGR!*" the crowd replied as one, their own fists slicing above their heads.

"Victory to House Farr!"

"*SIGR!*"

"Victory to every man who walks among us, in this life and the next!"

"*SIGR!*"

With one last wave, the prince dropped back into his saddle and spun his mount to the General again. Strange, how unaffected he seemed by his own words, his own show, as if the emotions buffeting the very air like the gods' striking fists made not a single mark upon him.

"Uncle," he said over the lessening din, "please see to my men, and meet me in my tent in one hour for a briefing."

The general saluted, then turned to a handful of men standing behind him—also wearing unusually clean and well-decorated uniforms—and barked out directions that would see the prince's order filled. His group dispersed then with one more salute, collecting men from the larger crowd as they went. In a matter of moments, it seemed, the whole of the impromptu swarm had returned from whence they'd come, and Ayden and the prince were left with a blessedly small handful of men ensconced in a blessedly calm silence. Ayden closed his eyes to it, let his head fall back on his neck and breathed deep, feeling his equilibrium return.

"Come now," the prince said, pulling him from his meditation, "we've work to do. You'll not stand idle tonight; you must learn to fit in, and the men must learn to accept you." He dismounted, passed his reins to a waiting soldier, then stretched his back by touching his toes, and his thighs by squatting on his heels.

Ayden thought that a fine idea and did the same. Still he felt eyes upon him, watchers beyond his counting, but nothing like when they'd first ridden in, nothing even like just a few moments ago.

The prince straightened up, called over some human from their own little train, and gestured between him and Ayden.

"Ayden, Corporal Ekkja. Corporal Ekkja, Ayden. You will partner tonight; go fetch firewood, and return to this exact spot when you're done."

"I do not need a *partner* to fetch wood," Ayden said, at the same time the human clicked his heel with a "Yes, Your Highness."

Not to mention 'twas surely idle work, for the prince would not otherwise concern himself with such trivial tasks.

"No man leaves camp alone," the prince said. "'Tis dangerous this close to darker territory."

"I am not a *man*," Ayden snapped. "The woods are no danger to *me*."

The prince sighed, rubbed his forehead with one hand. "Pardon," he said. "No *person* leaves camp alone."

Ayden sighed right back, but deigned to say, "Fine."

Then he took off toward the nearby woods at a fast run, not bothering to wait for a reply from the prince or his so-called partner. Let the human catch him if he could.

He could not, of course, but eventually Ayden had to stop running and start gathering wood, and shortly after, the human came to a panting stop beside him. Ayden tossed him a narrow-eyed glare and returned to collecting deadfall.

The human held up an armload of canvas and said, hesitantly, "I brought a tarp for hauling."

Ayden looked at the canvas, looked at the human—he seemed young, a boy yet, seeking even Ayden's approval—and had to admit that the tarp was a good idea. He'd been ready to use his shirt, accustomed as he was to gathering wood for much smaller parties.

"Thank you," he said, even if it was a bit grudging.

The boy smiled, also hesitant. The grin on his face looked quite familiar. "Do I know you?" Ayden asked.

"Nay, sir," the boy said, shaking his head as he spread out the tarp.

Ayden bent to stack his haul atop it, shrugging and mumbling, "You humans all look alike to me." Drab, lifeless, ugly little blinks in time.

Well, *mostly* ugly.

"Have you been about the castle, perhaps?"

"Nay, sir!" the boy said, eyes wide and wondrous. "Never had the honor. 'Twas the shock of my life, gods be praised, just to hear I were assigned to the prince's unit."

Ayden suddenly realized where he'd seen this boy—or rather, his mother, with whom he shared a remarkable resemblance. He was the last living child of the woman who had begged the prince for hardship release, the child to whom the prince had agreed to play nursemaid . . .

and whom, it seemed, Ayden was stuck with in the prince's stead. Great. Just great.

Well, at least the boy didn't seem to hate him.

By the time Ayden and Ekkja returned to camp with their load, the sun had nearly set behind the mountains to the west. They dragged their haul back to where the prince had instructed them to return, and two soldiers appeared as if from nowhere to relieve them of it.

A third soldier, carrying a lantern, gazed upon them both before saying, "That will be all, Corporal." His eyes returned to Ayden, but he seemed at a loss for a proper title, for he only jabbed his chin back whence he'd come and said, "This way, please."

Ayden was quite surprised at the politeness; it seemed the soldier's respect for the prince carried over to the prince's "pet." Why that same logic had not applied to the prince's own train, Ayden could not fathom. Perhaps logic had nothing to do with human politics.

Ekkja went off with a farewell nod, and Ayden followed the lantern-bearer toward the back end of the camp. A hike of a fifth-league or so took them high upon the eastern hillside. The ground there was paved with planks, the air free of the stench of unwashed bodies, and the tents much larger than the canvas city that sprawled at their feet. The officers' quarters, Ayden assumed.

"Here you are, then," the soldier said. He waved his lantern toward a small cluster of sumptuous tents, then abruptly left.

Ayden didn't see the prince nearby, but the prince's tent was unmistakable in its size and finery, even amongst its luxurious neighbors. He headed toward it, ignoring the occasional call or whistle from soldiers he passed along the way. 'Twas hard to ignore the two guards who stopped him at the entrance to the prince's tent, though, for when he tried to shoulder by them, they pushed him back hard enough to knock him to the boardwalk.

Ayden stood, anger carefully checked. "That is my tent too, you know."

The soldiers looked at each other and burst out laughing. The one on the left managed between chuckles, "The dog thinks it owns things!"

The one on the right feigned sympathy. "Aw, look how eager it is to warm its master's bed. Perhaps we should let it in?"

"Nay," said Left Soldier. "The dog is not allowed on the furniture without its master's say."

"And I say it," came a sharp call from inside the tent.

Both men startled, stood straight and rambled apologies as the prince pushed the tent flaps aside and held a hand out to Ayden.

Ayden took it for the sheer vindication of the act.

The prince glared at each of the soldiers in turn and added, "*He* will pass through these doors freely and without mockery. Is that clear?"

"Yes, Your Highness," they said as one.

Ayden shoved past them, making a point to knock into them both as he went.

Freyrík kept a firm grip on Ayden's hand as he led him through the office partition and into their little bedroom, then sat him down on the bed.

"Listen," he said. "This pettiness must stop."

"'Twas not even my doing!" Ayden protested, yanking his hand away and crossing his arms.

"This time," Freyrík said. "But what about last time, and the time before that, and the time before that? Did someone *else* piss on that lieutenant's boots?"

"I told you, that's a—"

"Sign of respect in your lands? Do you truly think me such a fool?"

"He drew my blood," Ayden growled.

"That was an—"

"Accident? His horse's fault? Do you truly think *me* such a fool?"

They glared at each other a long moment, until finally Freyrík chose to let his anger go—'twas too much of a challenge to hold it in the face of Ayden's boyish pout—and said by way of apology, "Are we done completing each other's sentences now?"

Ayden uncrossed his arms, let them fall to his sides with a sigh. "I suppose."

Freyrík smiled wryly, sat down beside Ayden and said, "Look, I know 'tis a lot to ask, but . . . I need you to be the better man."

"Better *elf*," Ayden said, all sulky petulance again. But then it disappeared beneath a mischievous smile as he said, "Elves are *always* better than men."

"Yes, yes. Then perhaps you can rise above the petty sniping and reach out to my soldiers. For one of you must rise first, and as you are so keen to point out, 'twill not be them."

"They think me a dog," Ayden said, arms crossing his chest again. "A spoilt pet."

Freyrík shrugged coyly. "In fairness, I do indulge you rather quite a lot."

"Get cracked," Ayden said, but his words held no venom.

"See?" Freyrík grinned. "You prove my point with every word that spills from your lovely lips."

Ayden twisted said lips into a scowl and said, "Fine, I will 'reach out.' Do not blame me if they fail to reach back."

At that, he stood and left the bedroom, dismissing Freyrík as if he were the slave instead of Ayden. From the sound of it, he was leaving the tent altogether.

Freyrík thought it prudent to follow.

The soldiers had taken advantage of their evening leisure time and the blazing firelight by constructing a makeshift wrestling ring: a circle ten paces across, roughed out with spare firewood. Two men were inside it now, having a rather athletic go at each other, grappling at clothes and limbs as they tumbled across the grass. Half the camp, it seemed, was gathered five and six deep round the ring, cheering them on—and, Freyrík suspected, betting on the outcome.

He caught sight of Ayden just as the elf nosed his way ringside, and made to follow. His own passage, of course, was much less challenging, and he soon settled beside the elf to watch the fight.

In the ring, one man caught the other in an arm lock, and after a brief but fruitless struggle, the trapped man yielded. The spectators erupted in applause, some more grudging than others, and the winner held out a hand to help the loser to his feet.

"Who's next?" the winner called.

Ayden stepped over the ring's log wall. "I am."

The crowd went silent.

Freyrík leaned in close and whispered sharply, "What are you doing?"

Ayden whispered back, "Reaching out, Prince, just as you asked."

Before he could say that he'd meant no such thing, Ayden strode to the center of the ring. The winner of the prior match looked at Ayden, then at Freyrík, then back at the elf, a sneer pulling at his features. Then he strode out of the ring. Freyrík suspected he hadn't spat at Ayden's feet only for fear of offending his prince.

Yet Ayden seemed undeterred. "Well?" he shouted, spinning in a slow circle to face the assembled men. "Surely someone can offer me a challenge!"

The elf stopped spinning, pointed at someone. "You, perhaps?"

Freyrík followed the elf's finger until his stare fell upon a familiar man: the lieutenant whose boots Ayden had pissed on. He groaned, braced himself to interfere—

The lieutenant stepped into the ring, opened both arms to the crowd and laughed. "What is this?" he cried. "I'll not fight His Highness's *pet*."

"Oh?" Ayden said, arms crossed loosely and a familiar smirk fixed upon his face. "Does your cowardice still your hands, human?"

"To the contrary, elf. 'Tis *respect* that stills my hands, for I would do the Crown a great disservice to break such a pretty face. A man as grand and honorable as His Highness Prince Freyrík should not be made to display a ruined elf."

The lieutenant smirked and thrust his chest forward. Around him, soldiers laughed and cheered.

Ayden called overtop the noise, "'Tis not *my* face you should fear for, human."

As the cheers turned into "oooh"s and chants to fight, Freyrík stepped into the ring and yelled, "Gentlemen!"

The crowd quieted, and all eyes turned to him.

He turned his own eyes back to the lieutenant and said, "Do you forget so quickly what I said about the elf?"

The lieutenant stepped forward, clicked his heel and shook his head. "No, Your Highness!"

Freyrík swept a hand out toward the crowd. "Then tell your fellows in arms, if you would, for they have not yet had the opportunity to hear it. Speak up, now."

"Yes, Your Highness," he called, in a voice fit to carry over half the camp. Yet the confidence in his tone did not quite hide the embarrassment coloring his cheeks. Good. "Your Highness said that the elf fights with us, not against us."

"Indeed," Freyrík said. "And what else?"

"That we treat him as any other on the march against our enemy, Your Highness."

"Correct. So please," he said, sweeping his arm at the ring, "spar with him. Strike as carefully as you would against your countrymen. And do not fear for his face . . ." he turned, winked at Ayden, "for elves heal quickly, I hear. Isn't that so, Ayden?"

A slow, sly smile spread across Ayden's lips. "Indeed, Prince," he said. "You speak true."

Freyrík nodded and backed out of the ring, clearing the way for their match and feeling rather sorry for the unsuspecting lieutenant. Well, the fool would no doubt be sorry too, the moment he put his face anywhere *near* Ayden.

'Twas a thing of beauty, watching Ayden in the ring, and quite the relief not to be on the receiving end of it. Freyrík could not rip his eyes from the elf: his casual stance and sharp gaze, lean limbs loose and striking with all the care and speed of a snake. The soldiers round the ring were watching in silence, breaths held and eyes locked upon their champion and the "prince's pet."

Ayden had not yet put the lieutenant down, though Freyrík had no doubt he could have. He was toying with him, circling him, grinning like a predator and picking his moment just as surely. The lieutenant, by contrast, struck and struck again, not pulling his punches at all, his confidence fading with every miss.

At last it seemed Ayden grew tired of the game: he used the lieutenant's own momentum to sweep his legs out and send him face-first into the grass. Ayden landed hard atop him, one of the lieutenant's legs still trapped between both of his own. The lieutenant screamed, tapped out immediately and frantically, clutched at his shin with both hands the moment Ayden released him.

Befang that reckless elf; he'd broken the lieutenant's leg!

Ayden bounced triumphantly to his feet and called, "Who's next?"

But 'twas Freyrík himself who rushed into the ring, before the rest of them might do so all at once, seeking revenge.

"What have you done?" he demanded through clenched teeth, all the while scanning the crowd for a physician. None stood round the ring, so he pointed to a man at random and sent him to fetch one.

Ayden glared him with narrowed eyes and set jaw, though his posture screamed defense. "I was merely trying to fit in, as *you* said I should."

Freyrík felt his hands curling into fists at his sides. "'Reaching out' does not involve breaking that which you touch!"

"'Twas an accident!" Ayden cried. He pointed to the fallen soldier, who was still clutching at his leg. "He fought with full force. I took my cue from him, for I know not the rules to your games."

Freyrík scrubbed a hand across his eyes, cupped it at his chin and left it there. "Fine," he said through his fingers, loudly enough for all assembled to hear. "You're right, 'twas clearly an accident." More quietly he added, "But 'tis enough reaching out for one day. Go to my tent. You can take your supper there." He turned back to the crowd, found two faces he recognized, and said to them, "See him back safely or suffer as he does, is that clear?"

The two men saluted and stepped into the ring, near Ayden's side but out of arm's reach. Ayden clenched his jaw but said nothing more, offered Freyrík a single curt nod, and left with his escorts.

Freyrík watched him go. For the first time, he realized, every man at camp gave Ayden a *very* wide berth.

When Freyrík returned to the tent, 'twas to find Ayden tilted back in a chair, feet on the map table and supper plate in his lap. He'd been ready to scold Ayden, but one look at the elf's face—part petulance, part frustration—stole the venom from Freyrík's bite. Ayden looked miserable, lost. Maybe he really had been trying to do as Freyrík asked . . . even if he had gotten carried away.

Ayden looked up at him, sighed, put his fork and his feet down, and finally said, "You're right. It wasn't an accident."

He even sounded contrite about it.

"You *know* I need every able hand for this fight, Ayden."

"You still *have* every able hand," the elf returned.

Freyrík sighed. "Was it not enough to ruin his boots?"

Ayden chuffed, twisted his lips into a scowl. "They all think they're so much better than me. That I am good for nothing but *easing your tension.*" Freyrík's laugh at that caught even him by surprise. "I think they have the 'easing' part backwards. Besides," he said, relieved to see that Ayden was smiling now, however hesitantly, "I think it safe to say you have shown them wrong. But you must promise me 'tis enough. Put your pride aside now, Ayden; you have served it well, but it no longer serves you. Do you understand?"

Ayden said nothing, though Freyrík saw his scant good humor fleeing before resentment and could well imagine a new challenge spilling from his lips.

He cut it off before Ayden could voice it. "Look, it does not matter what these soldiers think of you, for the Surge will be over soon and you'll be done and gone from them all. I've every confidence that you can bear their judgment in the meanwhile; you have borne much more even in our short time together, and you are far above letting others dictate your mindset toward yourself."

Ayden looked up at him with wide eyes that slowly narrowed, chewed on his bottom lip, and finally nodded his head. "You know what?" he said, and frankly, Freyrík wasn't certain he *did* want to know.

Which is why Ayden's next words came as such a surprise.

"You're absolutely right."

# Chapter Fourteen

Ayden woke at first light in fine spirits, and not just because he'd snapped a tormentor's leg like a dry twig last night. In truth, he'd found a freedom in the prince's words after the fight, in the prince's fierce protection, in his deep well of patience and his almost elflike capacity to look at Ayden and simply *know*. At peace on his back in the prince's bed, hands folded beneath his head, Ayden couldn't imagine why he'd ever let the soldiers bother him so much in the first place.

He did not even mind the prince's hand upon his person, resting lightly at his hip. Its coolness seeped through his thin summer nightclothes, affectionate and not altogether unwelcome. The prince had shown a penchant for reaching out to him in sleep since the first, he remembered. Back then, he hadn't quite appreciated how agreeable the man's strong hands could be—

—And where in the purview of all the fallen gods had *that* thought come from?

Ayden rolled out of bed before any more could join it.

The motion woke the prince, who stretched and yawned and grunted like a bear debating another week's hibernation and then mumbled a sleepy "Good morning" at him.

Ayden returned the greeting, then padded quietly through the office partition, where Lord Lini still slept, and out the tent in search of the field privy. The idea of the chamber pot was simply too foul given other options.

When he returned, the prince was leaning back in a padded chair, still half asleep, a steaming cloth wrapped round his face to soften his stubble. Lord Lini was up and attending him, heating his wash water and laying out clothes. Ayden had never seen the prince's secretary concern himself with such menial chores before, but the man didn't seem to mind.

Ayden nodded at him and said, "Good morning, Lord Lini."

The secretary nodded back, but the prince startled upright, displacing the cloth from his face. He seemed entirely awake now; his eyes were huge.

"What?" Ayden said with a shrug.

"You . . . You—"

"I do have manners, you know."

The prince waved aside the new cloth Lord Lini offered him. "I know," he said to Ayden. "Only I've never actually seen you use them."

He shrugged again, and Lord Lini saved him from replying by claiming the prince's attention once more.

"Your head, please, Your Highness," the secretary said, unfurling a shaving kit on a nearby dresser.

Ayden lounged on the bed, watching Lord Lini tilt the prince's head back and draw the razor across the underside of his jaw. Such trust he simply could not comprehend. 'Twould be so easy for Lord Lini to slip, to slit his throat or maim his face. Whether an accident or an act of purpose, the result would be the same. And why bother with it anyway? Was there some meaning to this human ritual that he did not understand?

"What is it, Ayden?"

The prince's words, slurred through carefully unmoving lips, startled him from his thoughts.

"Hmm?"

"You're staring. Did you wish to ask me something?"

Ayden had the distinct impression that the prince would be smiling if there weren't a razor on his face.

"I was merely wondering . . . why do you bother to grow your beard, only to go to the trouble of scraping it off every morning? It seems so bothersome."

This time the prince did smile, then pushed Lini's hand away and let out a laugh. "Indeed it is," he said. "But there is no choice to it. I cannot merely wish it away like you can; humans have no control over such functions."

"Oh," Ayden said, scratching idly at one smooth cheek. Being human seemed worse and worse to him with each passing day. He nearly found himself feeling sorry for the prince's misfortune.

Nearly.

Ayden's first full day at the border encampment felt much like the march to get there had: wake early, ride long in generally poor company, and never leave the prince's side. They wove their way from one end of the sprawling camp to the other, meeting with advisors and leaders and field commanders, making brief appearances with the conscripts, watching them train and ready for the battle to come.

They passed thousands of men at work that seemed strange for soldiers: building and clothing yet more scarecrows, cutting and hauling wood for construction and smithy fires, distilling poisonous sap from thousands of wolfsbane plants picked all across the empire, crafting the caltrops and blades and spikes upon which the poison would be smeared, working with the newly-acquired horses not yet trained in the art of war . . . the list of tasks went on and on, and the prince, with assistance from his many lieutenants, somehow managed to oversee it all. 'Twas quite impressive, he had to admit.

As was the scarecrow field, more than a thousand figures staked in widely spaced rows over a league wide and a third-league deep. He couldn't help but wonder how much of the empire's wealth had gone into their creation. Some of them could likely be re-used, if the plan worked. Many might not survive the day, let alone the week; small parties of Feral beasts had already ripped several apart—nearly two hundred, according to the commander minding the field—and more needed replacing each day as the Ferals came and went.

Yet amidst and beyond the scarecrow army lay the evidence of its power: dead Ferals with wounded paws and hooves and muzzles and heads, small marks of no real consequence . . . until the poison felled them. Several contingents of infantrymen worked to retrieve the bodies, carting them away to be burned. Ayden felt poorly for those innocent creatures, twisted and used against their will and dying long before fulfilling their purpose. That was his doing, his fault.

At least the poison was swift, though, and their suffering was over now.

The sun was low in the sky by the time the prince had finished the day's rounds, and by then they were both hungry and tired and in need of a good wash. They returned to the prince's tent just long enough to wolf down a snack. Then the prince turned to Lord Lini, whose head was bent over a mass of scrolls, and said, "We're going for a swim."

They were?

"Yes, Your Highness," Lord Lini said, glancing up from his papers just long enough to show proper respect.

"Alone," the prince added.

"Very good, Your Highness. I'll see to it. Where will you be, if I may ask?"

"Just upstream of the Tveir dam."

"Of course, Your Highness. I'll warm your evening meal upon your return."

"Thank you." The prince turned to Ayden with a grin then, grabbed his hand, and said, "Come now; you'll love this, upon my word."

Ayden raised an eyebrow at the prince's hand wrapped round his own, but followed him readily enough. The prince led them south through the edge of the camp, round the foothills between which it was perched, and into a wide, flat plain a tenth-league off. No man stood guard here, but they were still within sight and sound of the encampment, and in the near distance lay the outskirts of Tveir, a wide expanse of potato, corn, and lettuce fields irrigated by a clever series of channels and locks. The dam, a stack of masonry blocks and mortar, bisected the narrow river and formed a pool behind it. The waterfall plunging over the dam spun the wheel of a grist mill perched upon the bank.

'Twas a stunningly pastoral scene, idyllic and inviting, and he meant to take advantage while he could. He bolted out ahead of the prince, stripping down to his underclothes as he went, and with a whoop of joy leapt out into the water.

The surface was sun-warmed but the depths crisply cool—delicious relief after the grinding heat and stench of the encampment. He sank deep, kicking toward the surface only when his lungs began to ache, reveling in weightlessness and the sense of freedom that came with it.

The prince was standing by the bank when Ayden broke the surface. He was topless and shoeless, halfway through unbuttoning his breeches, and smiling with the same childish pleasure that Ayden felt upon his own face.

When he caught sight of Ayden, his gaze froze, as did his fingers. The tip of his tongue poked out and made its slow way across his bottom lip.

"What?" Ayden demanded, though he knew cracking well. He dropped his head back into the water to push his hair from his face, suddenly and acutely aware of his near-nakedness before the prince, of the heat of the blood rising to his cheeks. At least the water hid him well.

"Nothing," the prince said, still smiling. He pushed his breeches and underclothes down without a hint of self-consciousness, stepped out of them, and walked into the water as naked as the gods had made him.

The gods, as it happened, had made him very well indeed.

For a human, at least.

"What?" the prince asked, mirroring Ayden's tone, smiling smugly as he dallied ankle-deep near the bank.

Ayden realized he'd been staring, and there was that cracking heat in his cheeks again. And somewhere lower, too.

"Nothing," he snapped, suddenly nervous. "Those scars . . ." He lifted one hand from the water and pointed to four parallel lines raking from the prince's left chest to the bottom of his right ribcage. They looked vicious, lethal. "How did you get them?"

"Dark cougar." The prince lifted one foot from the water, swished his toe across the surface. "I was sixteen, 'twas my first real battle. Over a hundred sutures and half a cycle in bed. Nearly a year before I could convince Berendil to let me on the field again."

"Oh," Ayden said, treading in place, unable to think of anything better.

"I killed it, though," the prince said, running absent fingers along his scars.

Ayden caught himself imagining what that pale, raised flesh might feel like. Simple curiosity, surely; he had no scars of his own. "What?"

"The dark cougar." The prince smiled, fierce and proud. "I killed it."

Ayden grimaced at the thought of that poor cat, twisted and used and then slaughtered for its trouble. He ducked his head to hide his expression, but suspected he need not have bothered; when he came up, the prince was still just standing there, staring at him if not through him, fingers brushing across the scars. Ayden dropped his gaze from them, but it landed rather unfortunately upon the reddish-brown thatch of hair between the prince's legs. He hastily dropped it lower still. Calves. Yes, those were safe.

And a conversation piece as well, apparently, for he saw there yet another scar, a bite mark no larger than a circle made by thumb and forefinger, imprinted upon the side of the prince's right calf.

"And that one?" he asked, once again lifting his hand from the water to point at it.

The prince followed Ayden's finger with his eyes, blushed from head to toe, and promptly stepped knee-deep into the water.

Huh.

"It, uh ..." the prince said, dropping his eyes to the water and rubbing one hand across the nape of his neck.

Ayden cocked his eyebrows, drummed his fingers against the surface of the river.

"Itwasasquirrel," the prince mumbled, flushing even redder than before.

"*What*?" Ayden spluttered, forgetting for a moment to tread; his head dropped below the surface, and he swam back up, laughing and spewing water.

"Yes, you heard me: a squirrel! It *was* a darker, you know! Fast and big—" the prince shaped an oval from the air with his hands "—bigger even than a housecat, with huge, sharp teeth!"

His fingers, still miming the squirrel, curled into hooks—presumably squirrel teeth—and that was it for Ayden; he disappeared beneath the water in a roar of bubbling mirth.

"... not funny!" he heard the prince shout as he broke the surface, still snickering, and then a wall of water crashed onto his head and the prince was diving toward him, red-faced and laughing himself, splashing and clutching and finally latching hands round Ayden's shoulders and pushing him under.

Ayden planted an elbow in the prince's middle, twisted round, and broke the surface by pushing off the prince's back and driving him down. The prince kicked him away and popped up a length distant, gasping for air but grinning still.

"You've done it now!" the man cried, trying and failing to hold a scowl. "Nobody sinks the Crown Prince of Farr and lives to see the moon rise!"

Then he was gone beneath the water again, every bit the fish that Ayden was, and a moment later a weight slammed into Ayden's thighs and carried him back beneath the surface in a tangle of arms and legs and unrestrained laughter.

Already worn from the exertions of the day, they fast grew weary of wrestling in the river and broke apart, panting, to float on their backs beneath the late afternoon sun. Ayden had managed to forget for a while that the prince was naked, but he certainly remembered now, and took care to avoid casting his eyes upon all that muscled flesh.

Instead he watched the sun crawl across the sky, partly hidden by a gentle cloud cover, and listened to the songs of the fish darting in the water below. "Freyrík, look," he said, calling up one of them: a multi-hued sunfish the length of his forearm.

The prince rolled onto his stomach and paddled over, a wondrous smile brightening his face. "How did you—" But then he stopped, wide-eyed, and shook his head as if he'd gotten water in his ears.

"You called me Freyrík," he whispered.

Ayden's eyes snapped to him in surprise. "No, I didn't."

He startled as *the prince* flicked water into his face and said, entirely too pleased, "Yes. Yes, you did."

The splashing had startled the fish away, or perhaps 'twas Ayden's movement. Either way, he glared at the prince. "Perhaps I should call you 'idiot,' instead."

But the prince only smiled like a hunter who'd snared a prize.

Well, crack him anyway. Ayden splashed him wholly—no mere flick of water—and then swam for the shore.

"Dinner awaits, *Prince*," he called, "and my belly will have no more delay."

"Wait!"

The prince swam toward the bank and rushed out after him. Ayden turned round, forgetting again that the prince was nude, and caught an eyeful of dripping flesh that made more than just his cheeks flush with heat.

The prince, at last seeming to recall the modesty with which his kind was perpetually afflicted, blushed as well, bent down to retrieve his undergarments and hastily pulled them on.

"I've an idea," he said as he dressed. "A gesture of goodwill toward my men."

"I've no more interest in—"

"I know," the prince said, "but look, you must learn to live side by side, and you must fight together. Your . . . demonstration last night surely engendered respect, but it also stoked their fears. And you and I both know there is no small resentment toward you. So, hear me out: a gesture of friendship?"

"Fine," Ayden said, because the prince spoke truer than he cared to admit. "Tell me your idea."

And so it was that Freyrík found himself watching a most remarkable display of elven sorcery: Ayden weaving a net from the branches of the willow trees that grew beside the river. Or rather, the branches were weaving themselves, for he laid no hand or finger upon them.

"Shall I fetch a proper net from camp?" Freyrík asked.

"Nay, Prince, this will be faster," Ayden said, eyes closed and head cocked toward two trees as they reached out to each other, branches shedding leaves as they twined like fingers.

Freyrík was most decidedly not gawking at the elf as he worked.

Nor had he the time to, for it took Ayden but moments to form a net two paces square, as supple as any rope creation and just as secure.

"Remind me again why I'm doing this?" Ayden asked as he waded back into the river with his net.

"To build trust. Take comfort in the knowledge that you alone possessed the fortitude to make such an overture."

"And, apparently, the fortitude to lead innocent creatures to their slaughter."

Strange—Freyrík hadn't expected such bitterness. "Do the elves not hunt so always?" he asked.

"'Tis one thing in the lean months," Ayden said, splashing waist-deep into the water. "But to call creatures to their deaths in the height of summer's bounty? Never. So tell me true, Prince: do you believe this trust you speak of holds more value than the willows whose branches I stripped and the fish whose lives I am to forfeit?"

Freyrík settled himself against one of the willows in question and nodded. "The trees will suffer no ill, and the fish will breed anew. Cooperation between our two peoples, however, is a rare and precious thing. Hold no ill conscience for engendering it."

Ayden kept silent a long moment, then tossed his net into the water and said, "'Tis not cooperation when one side is forced against its will."

Yet his words lacked their customary venom, and Freyrík felt fondness, rather than exasperation, upon hearing them. "I think you're not happy unless you are fighting," he said.

"Perhaps," Ayden replied, the tiniest of smiles playing upon his lips. "Perhaps."

He fell silent again, and the light round him gathered and grew, contracting for a moment before bursting like the sun itself unleashed—a blinding, heatless flash so bright that Freyrík threw his hands up and jerked away, smacking his head against the tree trunk.

Cautiously, he peeled his fingers from his closed eyes, clamped them back when the light hurt even through his lids. He checked again a minute later, and another minute after that, and then gave up, propping his elbows on his knees and waiting, face cradled in his hands and mind turning toward the source of the light.

Ayden had called him by name.

Those full lips, so adept at spouting vitriol and sarcasm, had puckered together to form the whoosh of an *F*, then two lilting *R*s, strangely at odds with the brisk, clipped *K* of his northlands cadence.

Freyrík. He'd finally called him Freyrík.

Never mind that he denied it now.

No, Freyrík knew well what he'd heard, and only one question remained in his mind: What would it take to make Ayden speak his name again?

"You can look now," Ayden said, rousing him. The elf was panting hard, like he'd been racing. Freyrík peered through his fingers, saw naught but faint sunlight, and dropped his hands, blinking his eyes open.

Ayden was standing in the stream near the bank, holding the net's four corners in his fists, gathered round a catch of fish so big it could barely contain them.

Freyrík realized his mouth was hanging open, and closed it. Ayden held the net out to him, looking decidedly . . . sheepish? And tired, as well; Freyrík leapt to his feet and waded ankle-deep into the stream to relieve Ayden of the haul. The weight of it surprised him when he lifted it from the water: 'twas like hefting a full-grown man.

"Amazing," he murmured as he dragged the net onto the grassy bank.

Ayden moved to follow, took two steps, and stumbled hard.

Freyrík dropped the net—fish flopped everywhere but got nowhere—and rushed forward, grabbing Ayden under the arms and hauling him onto the bank.

"Are you well?" he asked, unable to quash the note of panic in his voice.

Ayden nodded and let Freyrík lower him to the grass. "I need a moment," he said. He gestured toward the fish, slowing now in their useless thrashing. "'Tis tiring work to sing so loud for so long."

No doubt. And indeed, the color was already returning to Ayden's cheeks. Still, Freyrík sat close beside him in case he toppled again, watching for some moments as the elf caught his breath.

When 'twas clear that Ayden would recover, Freyrík grinned and bumped his shoulder. "Do not think this gets you out of carrying them."

Ayden bumped him back and returned the grin. "The gods forbid the Crown Prince of Farr smell like fish."

"'Twould be completely inappropriate," Freyrík said with an almost-straight face. "But I also think it wise that the men see *you* bringing them their supper, rather than me."

Ayden's eyes narrowed, then softened, and his lips parted slightly. Freyrík knew that look well by now, and grinned wide in the face of it: he'd caught Ayden by surprise.

But the elf picked up the net in silence. Gods forbid he should ever admit to finding wisdom in Freyrík's words.

Ayden thought he'd hauled a cracking good catch, but the prince pointed out 'twould not feed eight thousand men, and suggested they share the bounty with the officers and his own unit. After all, Ayden would be fighting alongside those men directly, and where the opinions of the officers went, so went the opinions of their subordinates.

Ayden didn't even mind carrying the catch back, despite it weighing at least half as much as he did, for the thought of some peace between himself and these humans was strangely appealing. Since he couldn't kill the lot of them, it might prove easier to fit in than to spend each day battling their hatred and his own. And if that felt a little like giving up, well, he tried to remind himself that he—unlike the humans—had many a long year ahead, and he had a duty to survive until such time as he could return home, even if that meant gritting his teeth and playing the part of the pet they all thought him to be.

They reentered the encampment through the officers' quarters and instantly attracted a crowd. He'd thought the prince might address the men, make some small speech about his gesture, but none was forthcoming. Indeed, the prince was looking at him expectantly, as were the hundred-odd officers.

With a mental sigh, Ayden slung the net off his back and said, "A gift. For you all. I thought perhaps . . ." Thought what? He had no idea how to finish that sentence, but the men were waiting, so he filled in the silence with the only words that came to mind: ". . . perhaps you would enjoy it."

Gods, oration was not nearly so easy as the prince had made it seem. Besides, he'd spent far too many years in the solitude of border patrol to remember how to speak to people.

Fortunately, the prince saw fit to rescue him, stepping forward and saying, "Ayden felt terrible for the accident in the sparring ring last night."

Terrible? That was going a bit far, was it not?

"He wished to express his apologies and extend the hand of friendship to you all with this humble offering of fish, caught by his own hand. Even the net is of his creation. Here." The prince scooped the net from the ground with envious ease, passed it to a man Ayden didn't recognize, and said, "Take them. Clean them, eat them; they're yours. See to it my unit and all the officers present can share in the bounty. We'll join you shortly."

They retreated then to the prince's tent—or rather, the prince left, and Ayden had little choice but to follow.

When they were at last alone but for Lord Lini in the next room, Ayden whirled on the prince and said, "You made me sound like some sniveling beast with its tail between its legs!"

"I made you sound," the prince said, calm but firm as if scolding a particularly foolish child, "like any other human being with a bridge to mend and a serious intent to mend it."

"But I am not—"

"Human, yes, I know." The prince turned his back, poured water from a pitcher into a bowl and washed his hands. "But the men will never be comfortable thinking of you otherwise. You may not see it now, but I swear to you, Ayden, I have done you a kindness."

He wiped his hands on a towel, held it out to Ayden and waved toward the soap and water. Ayden snatched the towel and washed his hands with entirely too much vigor, and though he said nothing more, he could not help but think that the prince was right. *Again.*

"Now come," the prince said, "and let us enjoy your catch and the company of our fellow warriors."

Ayden's rumbling belly made the prospect sound at least somewhat better than sitting in the tent all night and sulking . . . though not, perhaps, by very much.

The men had made fast work of the fish, gutting and deboning them and throwing them over the fire. Someone handed the prince a loaded plate the moment he was spotted; no such kindness was shown toward Ayden, despite him being the source of their fine meal. The prince, however, passed his own plate to Ayden without comment, as if 'twere the most natural thing in the world to feed your slave before yourself, and of course a new plate was pushed immediately into his hands.

Despite the slight, a few soldiers did offer their grudging thanks as Ayden passed by to take a seat by the fire. The officer sitting on the log which Ayden occupied did not get up and move; he supposed that was a little victory, too. Or perhaps the man daren't leave, for the prince had settled on Ayden's other side. At least he partook in the bounty, even if he did keep staring at Ayden askance.

The same could not be said of the handful of men on the opposite end of the fire pit. Their hands were conspicuously empty as they cast their sideways glances at him and spoke quietly amongst themselves.

Ayden focused all his senses upon them and heard one say, "'Tis bespelled, all of it."

The other man nodded. "That *gróm* is no different from the rest. He's dangerous, and if the prince thinks he's tamed him, he's a fool. More so if he believes what happened to Lieutenant Hrani last night was an accident."

"Had me fooled up 'til then," the first man replied, "but I know better now."

A third man scolded his neighbor, who was eating quite heartily of Ayden's catch: "Don't eat that, fool! You'll fall under the *gróm*'s spell, just as happened to the prince, may the gods bless him stronger and wiser than he is now."

Ayden frowned at his plate and picked at the roasted fish. Were these men truly foolish enough to speak so openly against their prince? Or was the prince too soft—as permissive with his men as he was with Ayden? Crack the fool, he'd get them all killed if he continued to allow this. And crack those so-called soldiers; their disrespect was a stain upon all their kind.

The men blathered on, yet still the prince said nothing. Ayden turned to him, but the man's expression was neutral as he ate his fish, no indication in his face or song that he'd heard the soldiers across the pit. Maybe he truly hadn't; most humans possessed senses no more developed than their closed-off little minds.

Appetite gone, Ayden cast his plate aside and licked his fingers clean, refocusing his senses upon the danger brewing cross the fire. It seemed he would have to do the watching and listening himself, then—for the prince's sake and for his own.

# Chapter Fifteen

orning brought Freyrík a fresh day laden with familiar challenges: despite Ayden's overture the night before, his men seemed no more inclined toward friendliness at the morning meal, and Ayden wasn't exactly wooing them, either.

Freyrík disdained running from one's problems, but he also recognized the wisdom of the occasional strategic retreat: 'twas time to inspect the box canyon in Ayden's company, with perhaps a handful of trusted men. The trap need be at utmost readiness, after all, for tomorrow marked a full cycle from the first darker sighting: come morning, the Surge might crest at any time.

Ayden wished to time the ride from the scarecrow field to the canyon, so they made a race of it: the two of them, Lord Lini, and Freyrík's shadow guard. All but the elf rode in full armor—Ayden still refused to wear it—so it came as no surprise that he and his courser beat the rest of them to the brush wall by at least fifty paces. Lord Lini drew up the rear, and upon his arrival, Ayden turned to him with a smile full of teeth and said, "Whatever will the prince do if you get eaten?"

"I'm quite unappetizing, I assure you," Lord Lini said primly, gesturing to himself. "No meat on these old bones."

"I hope so," said Freyrík. "For without you, the kingdom would crumble round my ears."

He dismounted, and Ayden and Lord Lini followed suit. The guards remained on horseback; with a wave he sent them spreading out on watch.

He turned to the brush wall then, a formidable barrier over thrice his height that blocked the mouth of the canyon but for half a dozen small passages.

"How does it look to you, Ayden?" he said.

The elf paced, poked, paced some more, then waved him over. "Might I borrow you, Prince?"

Freyrík went, but suspected he might regret it a moment later when Ayden grabbed hold of his breastplate and spun him round 'til his back was to the brush wall.

"This might hurt," Ayden said, his toothy smile returning, and before Freyrík could protest or even ask what "this" was, Ayden shoved him with all his considerable strength.

Freyrík cried out in surprise as he went flying back, arms spinning madly for balance until he slammed into the barrier. Equally surprising, it did not hurt—his armor saw to that. Neither did he fall. The tangle of briars and brush, it seemed, had been woven dense and sturdy. His men had done well.

He pushed back against the brush to regain his footing, ready to give Ayden an earful about his testing methods. Even Lord Lini, ever staid, looked near to violence now, shock and outrage stamped all across his face.

Ayden, on the other hand, had a fist pressed to his lips, trying so hard not to laugh that even the tips of his ears had turned pink.

"I think," Ayden said, then stopped; he snorted once, shoulders shaking with silent laughter. "I think 'tis built very well, Prince."

Freyrík straightened up, flicked a twig from his hair with princely dignity, walked up to Ayden and clasped his shoulders in both hands.

"*I* think it needs another test," he said, spinning Ayden round by the shoulders.

Ayden barely had time to shout, "No, wait! I'm not wearing any—" before Freyrík released him with a tap on the chest that hardly made him wobble.

The look of surprise on the elf's face was priceless, and Freyrík gave in to his laughter. Ayden joined in a moment later, punching Freyrík sloppily on the upper arm.

Lord Lini looked at them both as if they'd gone utterly daft.

When Ayden could breathe again, he cleared his throat and said, "We should walk the line."

Freyrík nodded, setting out north along the brush line. "Mind you," he said, "next time you wish to test the wall, use my secretary instead."

They both burst out laughing again. Even the primness on his secretary's face cracked into a grin.

*Gods*, but it was good to see Ayden happy.

They paced the wall from end to end, testing it often with a hard push, paying particular attention to the passages cut for the riders and darkers.

"Do you think we've enough openings?" Freyrík asked as they passed by the sixth and final one.

"Hard to say. A blockage here would be deadly, but any more breaches in the wall and it might not hold against a stampede. You also risk the Ferals running back the way they came if the fire cannot span the gaps. As it stands, two riders can pass abreast through each door; it should be enough."

"A thousand riders," Freyrík muttered, pacing slowly back toward their mounts, "passing twelve at a time . . ."

"A thousand will *begin* the chase," Ayden said. "But . . ."

"Not all will make it."

"I still think hardly *any* will." The elf paused, kicked absently at the wall. "A hundred, maybe two, if you insist upon riding in armor. Twice as many, perhaps, if you ride light."

They had reached the first passage again, and Freyrík paused there, fingered the edge of the opening, a thousand oil-soaked branches filed smooth lest they cut a passing horse or rider. "How many more would die in the canyon if trapped there without armor?"

"That," Ayden said, "is a choice I am grateful I do not have to make."

Freyrík would have given much to be able to say the same.

They remounted and toured the interior of the canyon, searching for debris that might trip a horse or catch fire, scanning the sheer walls for protrusions that could snag or chafe the rope ladders. They found nothing to concern them; here, too, the soldiers had done an admirable job.

Done with the canyon floor, they began the walk to the top via half a league of deer path round the whole of the low mountain from which the canyon had been carved. At the last fork, Freyrík chose the path that would take them to the north ledge, where they dismounted and approached the precipice. A waist-high wall of timber and packed earth separated them from the sheer drop some forty paces to the canyon floor.

Ayden stepped back from the edge and held out a hand toward one of Freyrík's guards. "Give me your bow," he said.

The guard pulled a face that made it clear he took no orders from an *elf*, but Freyrík met his eyes and nodded toward Ayden. Not that he had any idea what Ayden wanted with the weapon.

The guard sighed and passed over his bow and quiver.

"Thank you," Ayden said mildly, no hint of the triumph Freyrík had expected. The elf slung the quiver over his shoulder, nocked an arrow, muttered, "Third opening, center," and loosed it home into the brush wall, right where he'd announced.

"How many archers to ignite the wall?" he asked.

"I've assigned a whole contingent to the task, ten on each side of the canyon. Do you think it sufficient?"

Ayden nodded. "The brush will go up quickly, and the shot is not so difficult. My concern is how exposed these men are; they must hold the line long enough to loose their arrows."

"We'll have five hundred infantrymen forming lines behind the archers on all three sides. Falconers and fighting dogs too, and men whose only job is to attend the ladders."

Ayden spun in a slow circle, and Freyrík followed his gaze round the flat, rocky expanse, wondering what he was seeking, whether he approved. The soldiers had cut the tree-line fifty paces back on the north and east sides, twenty on the south side, to clear the way for the fight. Twenty man-sized gaps studded the earth wall: eight on each long side and four along the back. Massive iron spikes, anchors for the ladders to come, had been driven into each.

"Just as you'd imagined it?" Freyrík asked.

Ayden nodded, one idle finger on his bottom lip as he gazed off into the distance.

"And yet?" Freyrík asked, because clearly something yet weighed upon the elf's thoughts.

Ayden shrugged, took another slow look round the canyon.

"Truly, Ayden, we've prepared for every potential concern we could foresee."

"Ah," said Ayden, "But it's the ones you *don't* foresee that always end up killing you."

Ayden had to admit: he was quite impressed with how thoroughly the humans had implemented his plan. They would do well when the time came.

Not that he actually cared.

Their little group remounted and began the climb back down the mountain. They'd traveled but halfway to the canyon floor when a warning bell went off, followed closely by eight short horn blasts, two long ones, one short one, and two more long ones. The humans kicked their mounts into a gallop as one, and Ayden followed course, pulling up beside the prince and shouting, "What was that?"

"Darkers!" the prince yelled back. "Pack of eight. Two leagues out, west-northwest. We might be able to head them off."

"Just the seven of us?" Ayden yelled.

The prince grinned at him, nearly feral himself.

The Ferals beat them to the scarecrow field, as had two contingents of mounted archers. Ayden summed up the field in a glance: Seven Ferals, two humans, and half a dozen scarecrows lay dead on the ground. Three more humans had fallen back, clutching bleeding wounds.

And one Feral eagle, its wingspan twice as long as Ayden was tall, was circling above.

As the prince's party joined the soldiers, the eagle dived, screaming, into the scarecrow field, then rose up again with great talons full of horsehair from a scarecrow's head. Half a dozen arrows shot up after it . . .

And missed.

"Falconer!" someone shouted. A moment later, two trained hawks climbed into the sky, racing after the Feral bird. They collided mid-air in a great screeching flurry of wings and talons and snapping beaks, but the Feral, more than thrice the hawks' size, dispatched them both in moments. They dropped from the sky like limp rags.

Enraged, the Feral folded its wings and dived again, this time ripping an entire scarecrow from its base. Another round of arrows sailed past it as it banked and soared with its prize. Ayden chuffed; were it not for the poor dead hawks, the humans' ineptitude would have been comic.

The eagle released its wooden victim, and two mounted archers scurried out from under its shadow.

Ayden reined in beside them, then glanced back. Lord Lini and the shadow guard were holding the prince back from the battle, but not for long, if he read the man's expression true.

"Falconer!" the same voice barked again. "Launch the whole befanged mews, I don't care—just see that thing dead!"

Ayden's attention snapped forward again. "Wait!" he shouted, dismounting and running toward the falconer.

Every human head in the field turned toward him, mouths open in various states of shock and fury. But before anyone could say or do a thing, the prince came riding up beside him.

"Hear him out," he commanded, reining in so sharply that his horse reared.

Ayden felt warmth flood his heart even as he jumped aside, dodging the deadly hooves. He nodded up at the prince; the significance—and risk—of the man's intervention did not escape him.

The prince nodded back.

Ayden turned back to the falconer and said, "I'll kill it."

In the silence that followed, the eagle's cry rent the sky.

Then the falconer laughed. *Everyone* laughed. The prince looked outraged, ready to intercede once more, but Ayden signaled him back and faced the falconer again.

"Spare your birds," he said. "It's not their cracking war."

As if cued by the mention of war, the Feral eagle folded its wings and launched into another dive. Everyone held perfectly still for a moment, hoping to escape its notice, but for Ayden, who jabbed his chin at the falconer in encouragement. Alas, the eagle tangled with a scarecrow again and flew off with its head.

"Give him your bow," the prince said to one of the archers, startling everyone.

But Ayden waved off the archer and said, "Wrong weapon."

Instead he unlaced one sleeve from his shirt, shook it off his arm, and hooked his index finger into a short leather loop at the shoulder-end. He gathered the cord woven into the wrist-end with his other fingers, making a cradle of the cloth, the slitted leather elbow patch forming a cup at its center. Then he plucked a palm-sized stone from the ground and fitted it into the cup.

'Twas fortunate for them all that the prince's seamstress had been so competent in her workings.

He began to swing the whole thing in circles like the sling it had become, tracking the Feral's flight path with narrowed eyes.

Just as the Feral eagle tucked its wings back for another dive, Ayden gave the sling a single hard swing and unleashed the stone. Unable to maneuver in its dive, the Feral rammed headlong into Ayden's projectile. A shower of feathers and a whoosh of displaced air, and the eagle canted sideways and crashed to the earth.

There followed a stunned silence, then awed whispers, and then—much to his surprise—a smattering of applause.

Ayden ignored it all in favor of the Feral, which he approached with care even though its strident song had ceased. 'Twas an ugly thing up close, muscled where it should not be, talons and beak grown huge and serrated. He crouched beside it and laid a hand upon its chest. Its heart no longer beat.

"I am sorry," he said—softly, for the eagle alone. "Your work is done now. But take heart, brave one, for you have served Nature well."

Talk of Ayden's feat had reached the main encampment by the time he and the prince returned for the evening meal. He couldn't understand what all the fuss was about; all he'd done was hit a target the size of a barn with a toy any half-grown child could wield. But once again they looked at him differently, and not just because the prince had armed him after the Feral run-in.

The man next to him eyed the daggers at his belt as he sat, then inched ever so subtly further down the log.

Ayden possessed enough ego to prefer fear to mockery, but this change could not bode well for the prince. His sensitive ears, inner and physical, had already intercepted subtle changes: it seemed whatever esteem he'd garnered came out of the respect owed the prince. In quiet corners, at odd hours, he heard murmurs that the prince was a "trusting fool," an "elf lover" (this said with particular venom, as if 'twere the worst possible insult), too besotted with or spelled by "that filthy *gróm*."

At dinner, Ayden picked at his food, wondering why it bothered him so to hear these things. Wondering if he should tell the prince, though surely the man already knew; he commanded too well to remain unaware of the tempers of his men. Besides, if he alerted Freyrík, would the man still treat Ayden with the same respect and camaraderie? If not . . . Ayden didn't think he could abide it, not now, when things were finally . . .

Finally what, exactly?

That did not abide considering, either.

He returned to his food, and the prince leaned up against him, solid and cool in the day's fading heat, and asked, "Are you well, Ayden?"

Ayden nodded, poked at his stew with his spoon. These humans ate far too much meat. 'Twas disgusting, all that killing for nothing.

"Perhaps some music would cheer you," the prince said.

"Oh?" Ayden eyed him sideways. "Did you really drag your poor minstrels all this way?" He winced the instant the words left his mouth; the prince did not deserve his sarcasm tonight.

'Twas fortunate, then, that the man did not seem to notice it. "Nay," he said, "even better. Wait here, I'll be back in a moment."

The prince stood, and so did everyone else. Ayden rose belatedly, forgetting as he always did this particular bit of decorum.

Everyone rose again when the prince returned a few minutes later. He was carrying a wooden instrument case, polished to a high shine and inlaid with gold—not your typical battlefield fare.

"Truly?" Ayden asked, cocking an eyebrow toward the case as the prince sat down beside him.

The prince smiled almost shyly. "'Tis a small thing, no trouble at all to carry along. Besides," he added, unlatching the case and pulling from its velvet interior the loveliest violin and bow that Ayden had ever seen, "a touch of civility never goes amiss, especially in a place such as this."

He put his instrument to his chin and plucked at each of the four strings in turn, adjusting the tuning pegs to some internal measure that Ayden had never before known a human to possess.

Then he raised his bow and launched into a jaunty tune that soon had the officers clapping hands and stomping feet and indulging in all manner of merriment. Two men linked arms and danced, their fellows cheering them along.

Even Ayden found himself smiling when the music changed and the men broke into song.

The prince's repertoire was vast and flawless, his energy never waning as one song segued into the next. Ayden recognized some: generations-old war ballads and minstrel music he'd heard while their two peoples had been at peace, and even an elven dance tune typically played at new moon celebrations. It reminded him of home, of that one new moon when amorous boys had plied Ella with wine until she'd cleared away the clouds with but a fleeting thought and danced, giggling and twirling in the starlight.

Gods, how he missed home.

"Ayden?"

The music had stopped. When had the music stopped?

The prince was on his feet, holding a hand out to Ayden. The low firelight flared in his hair like a red-gold halo.

"Yes?" Ayden said, squinting up.

"It's getting late."

Freyrík's hand was still extended, open, waiting. All round them, men were cleaning up their dishes, banking the fire, retiring to their tents.

Ayden took the prince's hand and allowed himself be helped to his feet.

"You're very talented," he said as they headed for their own tent.

The prince smiled, and even in the dim light of glowing embers and stars, Ayden saw the blush in his cheeks.

"And yet," the prince said, "it seems I've failed to cheer you."

They walked a moment in silence, but then Ayden shook his head and said, "'twas not the case, Fr—" He cut himself off so suddenly it sounded like a sneeze, then said mildly, "for it reminded me of home. I liked it very much."

"Then I would play again tonight," the prince said, blessedly deaf.

Ayden stopped and turned to view the fire ring they'd left behind. 'Twas almost empty now, only a few stray men minding chores or keeping late company. "But your audience has retired."

He found himself gripped by the shoulders and spun round to meet the prince's eyes.

"You misunderstand me," Freyrík said, and 'twas a strange thing, Ayden thought, how indecipherable the man's gaze *and* song had suddenly become. "I would play for *you*."

"Oh." Ayden wondered what to make of the prince's offer, wondered if he even wanted to know. Yet his lips did not wait on his thoughts, saying for him, "I would like that."

He followed the prince to the tent, to their shared bedroom, where the man sat him on the bed and pulled up a stool for himself. Then he laid his violin case next to Ayden, retrieved his instrument, cradled it to his chin and shut his eyes. He lifted his bow and arced it gently across the strings.

Ayden's world fractured into a million points of color and light.

Behind closed eyes he saw a long-ago vista, a memory faded by the passage of centuries. There in the long slow caress of bowstrings against the fretted D lay the Meiri Sea, slate blue beneath the high sun. The vibrato—a perfect semitone—rolled like wave upon wave in endless turns upon the rocky shore; restless, dissonant, mournful: awaiting resolution that would never come.

The tempo slowed, warm sweeping notes like sand beneath his bare feet. The music *ached*, fragile and yearning. Gulls circled on a soaring crescendo, a moist breeze blowing from waters whose salt he could taste upon his tongue . . .

He opened his eyes with a gasp, fingers skimming lips damp with tears. Freyrík played on, his body swaying to some internal beat, held enrapt by a melody that dipped and curved, soared and sank and rose again in tones as pure and perfect as a cloudless summer sky.

Ayden stared at Freyrík's fingers: so capable of ending a creature's song forever, now coaxing a thousand new ones into being.

He knew not how long he sat there, how long the prince wove whole new worlds into existence note by note as if a god himself, granted the power to create.

He knew only how bereft he felt when it ended.

Freyrík lowered his instrument, the dreamy smile on his face now joined with a hint of bashfulness. He placed the violin back in its case with all the care and fondness of a parent laying a baby in its crib, then turned to Ayden.

Slowly, so slowly, one of Freyrík's hands reached out toward him and then stopped, hovering between them. Ayden could not help himself; he clasped it in both his own, pulled it close, turned it palm-up and stared at the gentle curve of the fingers, the band of the signet ring, the calluses on the palm and fingertips and joint of the thumb. He smoothed his own weapons-rough fingers across the prince's, cool and strong and dotted with little nicks and scars. How was it that these hands, these *human hands*, had sung of a place he'd not seen since the birth of the Ferals? How was it that *these hands*—hands that had struck him, bound him, brought him grievous harm—now moved him to tears with their beauty, their hunger and their pain?

He seized the other hand, reading it as he'd read the first, but nowhere in its countless lines or whorls or creases lay any hinting of its power. He wondered what else these hands might show him. How else they might surprise him.

Gifted fingers closed gently round his own, and Freyrík lifted Ayden's hand to his lips and brushed a chaste kiss across it. His breath puffed hot and fast on Ayden's knuckles.

Ayden's own breath, he realized, was coming just as hard.

Freyrík's free hand reached once more into the space between them—and when had that space grown so very small? There it stayed, fingers outstretched, a question mark hanging in the silence. He swallowed, licked his lips, inhaled as if to speak. Ayden could see his fingers shaking.

They were still holding hands.

Ayden met the man's eyes, now but a thin rim of blue round big black centers, and silently urged him to ask what he would.

"May I—?" Freyrík said, his hovering hand inching closer.

Ayden wasn't certain what permission the prince was seeking, but it mattered not. "Yes," he whispered, and when that caught in his throat, he swallowed and said it again: "Yes."

Freyrík's fingers—those magical, world-weaving fingers—brushed across the exposed skin of Ayden's chest, as feather-light as the kiss upon his hand. Ayden felt his eyes close, his head tilt back, his chest moving like a bellows beneath the prince's hand. The prince's fingers skimmed up to the hollow of his throat, moving with it as he swallowed, then slid inside the neck of his shirt. There they settled, pressing flat atop his heart.

Ayden heard the ocean.

He felt the sea breeze (*Freyrík's breath*) on his face, the sun (*Freyrík's rising heat*) shining warm on his skin. Heard a song not his own but so very much like it, and opened his eyes to see . . .

. . . The prince, his face mere inches from Ayden's and moving closer. Just the prince: hungry, hopeful, flush with desire. There was no ocean here, no breeze, no sun, and just what in the name of the fallen gods did Ayden think he was doing?

He jerked back, pulled his feet up on the bed and fumbled away.

The prince opened his eyes.

"I . . . " Ayden found the room very dry all of a sudden; he swallowed, cleared his throat. "I am . . ."

The prince looked on, expectant, disappointed. Perhaps even angry, though Ayden did not sense that in his song; he only knew how he might feel if their roles were reversed.

"Apologies, Prince. I am very tired. I . . . I should like to sleep now."

"Yes." The prince nodded and cleared his throat too, his eyes darting round the room in a manner that suggested a hundred things easier to look upon than Ayden. "Yes, of course. It has been a . . ."

His eyes set to roving again, as if the end to that sentence were hidden somewhere in the shadowed corners of the tent.

Finally he settled on, ". . . a long day."

He gestured at the bed, still not looking at Ayden. "Please, sleep. I think I'd like a walk."

He stood, ran his fingers over the case of his violin. Ayden wondered if he was imagining caressing something—some*one*—else, and to whose tent he might be going to ease the ache that Ayden had caused. He wondered why the thought of that bothered him.

The prince walked through the partition flaps but held them open behind him, pausing in the doorway to say, "I'll take care not to wake you when I return."

'Twas too dangerous to leave the camp alone at night, so Freyrík settled for circling its outskirts, ghosting along tents and banked fires and lookout towers and night patrols with only a lantern for company. He yearned for solitude, but such was never within a regent's purview. At least the camp was fairly quiet at night.

Yet the silence held dangers all its own, for within it, reflection took sturdy root, and all that he'd hoped to escape turned over and over in his mind. He no longer knew what to make of the elf now lying in his bed, the untamed creature who had scratched and bitten for so long, and now suddenly . . .

Freyrík was a patient man; though pushed to the limits of forbearance and beyond, never once after their first night had he tried to claim what was rightfully his. Self-denial he could endure, but not this . . . this *teasing*, this temptation, as if Ayden were but some blushing virgin, wanting-but-not-wanting, titillated but terrified.

An *eight-hundred-year-old* virgin. Freyrík chuffed.

He had even grown to *like* the elf, and certainly to admire him: that clever mind, that sharp tongue and droll wit. His love for Ella, manifested in sacrifice and secret smiles; his sense of honor and duty; his pride in the face of unceasing subjugation. His joy of nature, his respect for all things living, his skill with . . . well, *everything*.

*Gods*, Freyrík could still taste the not-quite-kiss on his tongue, smell it in his nostrils. Forest loam and autumn leaves and, yes, desire—he was certain of it.

"Your Highness."

Freyrík startled at the greeting, looked up to see the guards at his tent flaps bowing their heads. How had he gotten back here? He peered up at the night sky; the stars had crawled a good twenty degrees since last he'd looked. He'd been walking for over an hour.

He crept into the tent, careful to not wake Lord Lini, who was snoring lightly on the bed in the office. In the bedroom he saw Ayden lying on his back, covers thrown off in the humid air, dressed only in those loose, light breeches he so favored and glowing fit to make the lantern obsolete. 'Twas a sure sign he was awake, but his eyes were closed and he was holding very still; he clearly did not wish to speak. Freyrík didn't know what to say to him anyway, so he let the elf pretend.

He stripped down to his underclothes, washed his hands and face and then rubbed the wet wash cloth over his chest and arms. The cold water felt good. Ayden would be smoldering; Freyrík knew he'd feel the heat of him even across the bed. And that would feel good too, despite the stifling air, because it came from *him*.

Gods, he was *hopeless*: some poor, lovesick pup chasing after—

Freyrík's hand stilled over the basin. *Love*sick? Truly?

He tossed the wash cloth down and strode over to the bed. Befang it all, 'twas far too late for such nonsense. The Surge might crest at any time, and he needed to rest, not pine and tarry like some woman. His men were right in their murmurs; he was besotted. 'Twas a dangerous thing for a prince.

Yet as he crawled into bed, he could not resist stealing a touch: a gentle caress of fingertips across a cheekbone, a brow, a hand skimming through that wild hair. The urge to follow fingers with lips was nearly beyond bearing, but Ayden lay unmoving, still pretending at sleep: allowing this to happen but inviting nothing, and Freyrík daren't take more than Ayden offered. Especially not now, when he could feel the barriers between them weakening by the day.

He threw himself away from the elf, lay down on his back and clasped his fingers tightly across his belly. Waited for sleep to come. He'd hoped to tire himself with his walk, to quiet his mind, but all he could think about was Ayden: his eyes, his lips, the expression they'd formed as he'd played for him; the way he'd leaned in, enrapt, for a kiss before losing his nerve . . .

Freyrík sighed, shifted to ease the ache between his legs. Rolled onto his side. His back. His side again. Tried rolling onto his belly but could not even begin to consider sleep with his erection pressing into the mattress. Once more onto his back, hands fisted at his sides, eyes focused resolutely on the canvas above him, washed nearly silver with elflight.

His gaze crept back to Ayden, topless, perfectly still, and his hand crept of its own volition down his belly, to his manhood, which had been standing at full arms for so long now that it *hurt*, and befang it all but if he stayed in this bed for even one more moment he would not be responsible for what happened next.

He threw back the covers and lurched out of bed. The pattern of Ayden's breathing shifted subtly, but whether from relief or disappointment, Freyrík knew not. He was certain only that Ayden knew exactly what had just occurred, exactly what had *almost* occurred. Part of him hoped the elf felt guilty. But most of him was concerned now with only one thing: finding somewhere private to satisfy—or at least to subdue—this befanged arousal. And as for tomorrow, and the day after that, and the day after that . . . well, he had suffered through worse. He would, as always, find a way to endure.

# Chapter Sixteen

*M*orning came far too early—for both of them, it seemed. Ayden shot up in bed at a warning bell and the horn blasts that followed, and the prince sat up beside him, blinking and bleary-eyed, groping for his sword.

"They are not here," Ayden said, falling back against the sheets. He'd learned the horn code quickly; this attack was but a skirmish of six beasts, closing in on the scarecrow army. "Others will manage it. Go back to sleep."

"Nay," the prince said through a jaw-cracking yawn. "I am awake now."

He certainly didn't *sound* awake. Ayden wondered if Freyrík had gotten as little sleep as he had, how long the man had lain awake after satisfying his needs gods-knew-where. He himself had tossed the night away, thinking again and again, *I did that to him.* And sometimes, in a voice he kept shoving ruthlessly back from whence it came, *He did that to me.*

'Twas still dark out, judging by the near-blackness inside the tent, so Ayden forced his eyes closed and focused on the monotony of Lord Lini's sleepsong from the next partition, hoping to find dreams again himself. The prince, despite his earlier proclamation, did not leap up for his morning ablutions; in moments his breathing had slowed and deepened. In and out, in and out, and Ayden thought of the ocean, waves rolling onto the shore and back, soothing and steady and eternal.

The prince rolled over in sleep and nestled to Ayden's side, draped a hand across his bare chest and hooked one knee over his leg.

Against all better judgment, Ayden curled his hand round Freyrík's where it lay near his heart, closed his eyes, and dreamed of what new worlds those fingers might weave if only he'd let them.

The warning bell rang twice more by breakfast (though not to herald the final Surge), and the whole of the camp was on edge, the horses included. Freyrík listened to the stable master's report with pursed lips. Many of the mounts had begun the season as plow or cart horses and knew not how to bear armor with grace, let alone obey a rider while fleeing from a darker horde.

"Is there aught you can do?" he asked Ayden, who was idling nearby, stroking a horse's muzzle through the corral fence.

Ayden lifted his chin at the horse, and it calmly leaned out over the top rail to rest its head on the elf's shoulder.

*Huh.* Freyrík supposed that was answer enough.

And so he spent the morning perched upon that same fence, watching Ayden work his magic. The elf would lay hands upon each horse in turn, close his eyes and cock his head as if exchanging whispered secrets. Perhaps he was explaining the situation to the beasts; perhaps he was simply convincing them to trust him. All Freyrík knew was that every time, the horse would follow Ayden like an obedient son and allow itself to be armored.

"Are you not tired?" he asked the elf round noon.

"I'm enjoying the company," Ayden said with a nod at the horses. "Thirsty, though."

Freyrík signaled an attendant to fetch a water skin. They did not lack for cups, but the thought of Ayden tilting his head back to drink from the skin, his long neck flexing with every swallow . . .

"Your soldiers distrust me still," Ayden said, ambling over to the fence and propping his foot on the bottom rail. "They say the *gróm* has spelled the horses to run towards the Ferals, not away."

Freyrík reined himself in, hoping Ayden hadn't heard . . . well, *heard* . . . his wandering thoughts. "I know. But 'tis only the men of the northern climes, no doubt raised on stories of elves snatching unruly children."

Ayden chuffed at that. "What will you do?"

"Nothing, for now." Freyrík sighed, kicked the middle railing with his heel. "Only one thing will sway them: victory against the Surge, with you at the forefront."

"And until then?"

"We'll endure. I'm their Prince Regent, after all. They may gripe, but they'll indulge me, or turn a blind eye at worst. And I'll allow no harm to come to you." Freyrík laid his hand over Ayden's where it rested upon the top rail. "You have my word."

Ayden raised his eyebrows, a little mocking, a lot something else, frustratingly unreadable.

The attendant returned with the water then, which Freyrík silently passed to Ayden.

"Thank you," Ayden said. Then, with a hint of a smirk, he lifted the skin and drank just as Freyrík had pictured he would.

An hour later, Ayden was leading a chestnut mare without rope or halter to be armored, when he froze mid-step and cocked his head.

"What's wrong?" Freyrík asked, jumping down from the fence.

Ayden ignored him, his stare snapping instead to a nearby row of tents. His body slowly pivoted to follow, one hand clutching at a sheathed dagger. Freyrík reached for his own sword, but merely rested his hand upon the pommel; he could see nothing wrong with those tents.

"What is it?" he tried again, growing aware of the crowd they were attracting.

Ayden held up a hand and continued to stare at the tents.

Freyrík clenched the hilt of his sword and stifled a growl at being shushed. Enough was enough. "Look, I need answers right this mo—"

"Ferals," Ayden said, his eyes still glued to the tents.

"What? Where?"

Ayden shook his head.

Freyrík scanned the nearby tents, the air, the ground, and so did the stable hands and soldiers round him; the mention of "Ferals," as the elves called them, was enough to set everyone on edge.

"Surely the lookouts would have sounded the horn," Freyrík said, but Ayden shook his head again.

"Nay. They are small. They have come through unnoticed."

Amongst disbelieving snorts from the nearby soldiers, Freyrík voiced the question they surely all shared: "But *you* have noticed them?"

Ayden glanced at him askance, lips twisting. "I can hear them," he said. "There." He pointed toward the nearby tents, still as innocent-looking as any other. "Close. Be vigilant."

More snorts and murmurs from the men, who began to disperse. Ayden spared them a glare, and Freyrík debated ordering them back—the elf had no call to lie, and his magic was a powerful thing—but Ayden chose that moment to shrug and return his attention to the chestnut mare.

"Gone?" Freyrík asked.

"No." Ayden ran a glowing hand down the horse's neck. "Do not expect me to weep when you die."

"I'll post sentries near those tents," Freyrík said by way of compromise, but Ayden only shrugged again.

Then the screaming began.

Everyone startled and froze but for Ayden, who gave a soft vindictive huff, and for Freyrík, who unsheathed his sword and ran toward the tents.

"Assemble!" he called, whirling his sword overhead in a gathering circle, "Soldiers, assemble!"

He sensed more than saw the men rush after him. Up ahead, a tent pitched over in a flurry of human thrashing, and then another. It took him a moment to realize why.

Field mice, two dozen at least, each the size of a dungeon rat. Scurrying up people's legs and tearing out hunks of flesh as they went. The bitten men screamed in agony and tried to rip the beasts off, while their tent-mates stood helpless, swords drawn but too dangerous to use in such close quarters.

"Get them on the ground!" Freyrík shouted, falling to his knees to skewer a darker mouse making for his legs. The thing squealed and writhed, tried to bite him even after speared through. Grimacing, Freyrík snatched the dagger from his belt and slit the creature's throat.

All round him, people were slashing at the ground, but the befanged creatures were faster than the men.

"Fire spitters!" Freyrík roared.

The next minutes were a horror of prying darker mice from writhing soldiers and tossing them to the ground, where wide-sweeping fire spitters torched grass and tent and rodent alike.

When all was done, three soldiers were lying dead in the grass, their throats torn; another was clutching at his knee, where his leg ended—an unfortunate sword slice, Freyrík assumed—and too many others nursed various wounds, mangled hands and missing fingers.

He preferred darker cougars any day of the week.

The fallen tents were of course burnt to cinders, but a nearby tent, still standing, had caught fire as well. Soldiers were already ferrying water from the horse troughs to put it out, but the fire threatened to spread before they could douse it.

"Hurry up!" Freyrík barked. "Move, move!"

He spun round and saw Ayden, casual as could be, lounging against the corral fence beside the chestnut mare. Freyrík stormed towards him, but before he could get far or even work up the breath to scream *Do something, befang it!*, Ayden sighed and pushed off the fence and glowed like the fucking *sun*, and a gust of wet wind spun round and round the burning tent and blew the fire dead.

Freyrík blinked, rubbed his eyes. In the sudden stunned silence, punctuated only by a cough or a moan, everyone stared at Ayden.

Ayden stared back as if to challenge them all, and one by one, their gazes fell away.

But Freyrík's gaze he met last, and in the end, 'twas the elf who averted his eyes.

The elf was exhausted in the wake of his magical feat—and perhaps for other reasons as well, for Freyrík suspected that Ayden had slept as poorly as he himself had—so Freyrík saw him to their tent, ordered food for him, and left to oversee the aftermath of the darker attack.

The three dead were the least of his troubles; the dark rodents had disabled another eight men who might nevermore clutch a sword in their mutilated hands. The soldier who'd lost his leg—his friend had tried to strike a dark mouse off his calf—was lying motionless and ashen.

"Does he yet live?" Freyrík asked the physician.

The physician followed his gaze and his face darkened. "Oh, he lives, that one." And at Freyrík's raised eyebrow, "I believe he saw to his pain quite thoroughly; an entire pouch of anodyne powder's gone missing from my stores this afternoon."

Freyrík tried to imagine losing a leg and shuddered. "I don't blame him."

He no longer blamed Ayden, either, by the time he returned to their tent. 'Twas hard to comprehend that the elf seemed to like him personally yet still despised mankind in force, but there it was. Watching your sworn enemy die was hardly reason to engage in battle, he supposed. And Freyrík had believed him when he'd said, with wounded sincerity, that the Ferals were deaf to all but the Hunter's Call; not even he could have swayed them.

Freyrík found Ayden still sleeping, and woke him with a gentle nudge. The elf rolled over, stretched bodily like a cat (*gods*, how quickly Freyrík's manhood came to arms at that!), and grumbled something distinctly unseemly about being disturbed.

"They're serving dinner now at the fire pits," Freyrík said.

Ayden was out the door before he'd even finished speaking.

His officers were in heated conversation as he and Ayden approached the fires. Ayden stopped a ways back, in the shadow of a tent, and held up a hand for Freyrík to do the same. Freyrík's hearing was not as sharp, but listening with intent, he could hear the talk that tongues would dare not speak in his presence:

"It was spelling the horses today," someone said.

"And lifted not a finger to slay the dark mice," said another.

"It controls the beasts," said a third. "Did it not charm the fish? Did it not bespell the horses? I bet you a year's pay it was controlling those dark mice, too."

A chorus of agreements, and an angry, wounded exclamation: "It corrupted the horses all morning, and His Highness just sat there and watched! The *gróm* will betray us all beneath his very nose!"

Freyrík lurched forward, but Ayden stilled him with a hand to the chest.

"Nay, Prince," he said softly. "What would you do?"

"Have them flogged," Freyrík growled.

Ayden shook his head. "'Twould only nurture their suspicions. Besides, do you not need every able hand? Flog them after the Surge, if you must."

He was right, of course. But oh, how it *rankled*, this lack of trust, this... this *presumption*. He was their *prince*, not some ignorant schoolboy being led round by the cock, befang it!

"Peace," Ayden whispered. "I would speak of betrayal, if that is what they wish to hear. I would tell a story."

He looked to Freyrík, seeking permission, and Freyrík nodded. Ayden nodded back, and they resumed their walk toward the fires.

"Your Highness!" someone cried—no doubt as much a warning to the others as a proper sign of respect—and all round the fires men went abruptly silent and rose to their feet to salute.

Freyrík sat, struggling mightily at nonchalance. Ayden perched on the log beside him. Someone pressed a plate of food into Freyrík's hands.

"The elf too," he said, for this time he sensed that passing Ayden his own plate would fan too dark a fire.

Someone pushed a dish into Ayden's hands, and men and elf alike ate for a while in silence. But soon Ayden broke it, saying in a voice made to carry round the open space, "I would speak to you all."

Heads turned toward Freyrík, but he made no reply. Whatever this moment was, it was Ayden's.

"I would tell you a story," the elf said. "Of betrayal. Of the beginning of all things ugly and violent between our peoples."

He handed his plate to Freyrík and hopped onto the log seat, where he stood a head above the crowd.

"Perhaps you have heard it, passed down from father to son. Waxing in grandeur and self-flattery with each passing year, and waning in truth. But I was there. I lived it. And I remember it all."

By the gods, when had Ayden learned to speak so? Freyrík looked round the fire and saw every eye upon the elf, the men leaning subtly toward him—with interest, yes, but also with violence barely restrained. The silence had shifted, grown dark and cold.

"Elvenkind has long been Nature's favored children—"

The officers broke their silence for jeers, but Ayden merely raised his voice. "For never have we pushed or imposed our will upon her. Yet men . . . you strive to shape the earth in your image, forgetting that the gods have already shaped it in theirs."

The grumbling grew louder, and from somewhere across the fire came a perfectly eloquent, "Fuck you, *gróm!*"

Freyrík said nothing—merely held up his hand. The men fell silent.

Gods, he hoped Ayden knew what he was doing.

The elf continued, unperturbed. "And yet our two races lived side by side for many hundreds of years, for when the very first Aegis united your warring tribes, we saw great potential in you, the builders and inventors of this world. We saw an opportunity to exchange knowledge.

We welcomed your scholars into our homes, allowed them to study our magic, to seek why we possess it and you do not. You claimed friendship, a strengthening of ties. We believed your good intentions. Yet in this, we were fools."

Ayden paused, stare sweeping over the fire pit with languid purpose. Freyrík used the interlude to do the same. The silence remained thick and warning, broken only by the pop and crackle of the fire. Surely Ayden heard the tension here, the danger. And yet he pressed on.

"Our people grew close, came to love one another. Yes, love. We were fools in this as well, for we trusted the only child of our Grand Elder Gallin to your Lord Naemr, Aegea's chief scholar. Perhaps he truly sought to love her. Or perhaps he sought only her secrets, for he believed that humans had once possessed magic as we do, and your Council of Eight conspired with him to reclaim it. But of course you could not reclaim that which you'd never possessed—that for which the gods at creation had deemed you unfit."

Across the fire, Freyrík heard a plate clatter to the ground and a grunt of disgust, saw a man stand and stomp away. A second man joined him, then a third. For a moment he feared—hoped?—the whole of Ayden's audience would do the same, but no one else moved, and Ayden kept talking.

"Your Council could not bear this truth; their jealousy drove them mad. And so they lured our three most beloved leaders—elders beyond time itself—deep into the Myrkr Mountains. And there they slaughtered them."

"Shame they didn't get the lot of you!" someone called.

Freyrík's head whipped toward the sound, but he could not see the speaker, and even if he had, what could he have done?

Ayden spoke on as if he hadn't even heard the slur. "The whole of elvenkind felt this Great Betrayal like a ripping of soul from body. The very earth split wide and wept molten fire for her lost children. I shall never forget that moment—the agony of our sorrow like a physical blow that would not fade—for death is no near neighbor to my people. I held my sister as she wept, inconsolable, for nearly one whole cycle of the moon.

"And then Nature, in her agony, turned upon you. She raised the Hunter's Call, the unquenchable drive for retribution upon your people. She summoned her children, great and small, imbued them with new strength and hurled them like thunder into your lands.

"You blamed us for this scourge, of course. Dark elves, you called us, and concocted deceitful stories of our hand in your destruction. But in truth, we only entered Nature's war to avenge a wrong so despicable that you could not admit it even to yourselves."

Freyrík listened, mesmerized, as a tale he knew as well as his own heartbeat unfurled before him in strange, dark shapes. If this truly was how elves recalled the Great Betrayal, 'twas no wonder their two peoples hated each other so. He shuddered in the momentary silence, which seemed to breathe and seethe with the fury of lost centuries.

Ayden let the silence build, grow, feed upon itself 'til 'twas ripe near to bursting—

And then rent it right through, a spear to the chest:

"Now you die while we live on, and you've no one to blame but yourselves. So do not speak of betrayal behind my back, humans. For the Great Betrayal is *your* shame, not mine."

He stepped off the log while his words still battered ears, took his plate from Freyrík's slack hands, and stalked away.

Freyrík thought it for the best, for if Ayden had waited round 'til the shock wore from his men, blood would have spilled for certain.

Yet long after the elf had gone, the silence persisted, queer and hostile in his absence. Freyrík yearned to go after him, but he knew he must show solidarity with his men. He picked up his stew, cold now, and took a bite. All round him, others did the same.

"It seems," he said after another bite of stew, "that history is not carved in stone."

Stares and blinks, some significantly more hostile than others, pointed his way. For a moment he regretted breaking the silence.

He clutched his plate until it dug into his palms. "I mean only that our tale of the Great Betrayal is very different from theirs. Perhaps the truth lies somewhere between."

More stares.

"No matter," he said, feeling sweat begin to pool between his shoulder blades. "For whatever the cause, the outcome is the same: we've a Surge to fight, and we *will* strike it back, as always. And you will note," he added, thanking the gods that Ayden was not there to hear him, "just who is enslaved to whom, and which of our two peoples ran to the cold north with piss streaking down their legs when they could no longer stomach the war."

That seemed to do the trick, for some men smiled, and others laughed, and many gave a sword thrust and a short cheer. The typical evening-meal chatter began afresh, and Freyrík wolfed down his food, near desperate to return to Ayden.

He found the elf not in their tent but several paces behind it—up a tree, of all places, perched with his back to the trunk, one leg dangling and the other propped on a branch. Were it not for his elflight, Freyrík would never have spotted him.

With a sigh, he heaved himself up to the first branch, stood upon it and propped his arms near Ayden's feet. Ayden eyed him coolly.

"You weave a fine tale," Freyrík said.

"'Tis no tale. I was there, remember?"

"Oh? Were you there in the Myrkyrs with the Council of Eight when they killed your elders, as you claim?"

Ayden narrowed his eyes, crossed his arms. "No. But I felt it. I knew."

"You felt their *murders*, or their deaths?" When Ayden made no reply, Freyrík added, "I would tell you another story, if you'd come back to the tent with me."

Ayden shook his head.

"Will you sleep the night here, then?"

The elf shrugged.

"It does not seem very comfortable," Freyrík said.

Silence, strained and heavy.

Freyrík tried on a smile and asked, "Might I bribe you with apples and honey?"

He held out his hand, waited. Ayden glared at it for a long while, then slowly uncrossed his arms.

"You have honey?"

Freyrík chuckled, and when Ayden glared afresh, he laughed so hard he nearly fell from the tree. If only he'd known two months ago how easy it was to get Ayden to listen: all he had to do, it seemed, was feed him.

Back in their tent, Freyrík fished a pot of honey and a plate from a supply box and plucked two apples from the fruit bowl in the office. He found a fresh flagon of wine and poured two glasses, left the rest for Lord Lini to enjoy. He and Ayden carried their snack into the bedroom, settled at the tea table, and used their daggers to cut the fruit.

Ayden dipped a slice into the honey, bit into it almost daintily, and made a noise that went straight to Freyrík's groin. "*Gods,*" he said, his eyes fluttering closed as he dipped the remainder of the slice and popped it into his mouth. "I've not tasted honey in years . . . I'd forgotten how good this is."

"Yes, well," Freyrík cleared his throat, took a large sip of wine, and hooked his feet behind the legs of his chair lest he launch himself over the table and steal the sweetness straight from Ayden's mouth with his tongue. "There are *some* advantages to being a prince."

Ayden licked a drop of honey off his finger, and Freyrík balled his fists into his thighs and spelled the names of all sixteen Aegean trade ministers backwards in his head until he no longer feared to pop the buttons on his breeches.

"So, you have a story to tell me?" Ayden asked, eschewing the apple and dipping his index finger straight into the honey pot. He sucked it clean with relish, took a drink. The wine stained his lips a dark red.

"Huh?" Freyrík asked, but his voice cracked, so he cleared his throat, tried again. "What?"

"Story?" Ayden said, taking another swallow and grimacing slightly. The honey must have rendered it bitter. "The Great Betrayal?"

"Oh," Freyrík said, taking an apple slice for himself. "Yes. But listen . . ." He put his hand on Ayden's wrist, caught his eye. Ayden gazed back, calm and open. "You must promise me we'll not fight over this. I do not wish to argue."

"Nor I," Ayden said, then chuckled when Freyrík reared back in feigned shock.

"Good, because my tale runs quite contrary to yours. We are taught that your people, ever envious of man's mastery of science, sought to destroy us when we united beneath the Aegis, for you saw our union as a threat."

"Come now, we never—"

"Your elders lured our ruling council into the Myrkrs with promises of secrets revealed, and there sought to murder them all with the very magic you'd sworn to share. Yet two escaped to warn us, and we were able to prepare for the true danger: the dark race you then created."

Ayden had dropped his apple to the table, and though his jaw was hanging in outrage, Freyrík pressed on:

"But we proved far greater foes than you'd expected, you see. We could not be ended so easily, not even when you took up arms beside your servant beasts. Your losses grew too great and your women bred too slowly; you retreated to the north, and with time on your side, left the darkers to finish the war in your stead. *That* is what we are taught."

"And do you believe that?" Ayden asked. He spoke softly, but his upper lip twitched in a snarl, his eyes hard, his body tense. His long-forgotten apple slice oozed honey onto the table near his fist.

"I did . . ." Freyrík pursed his lips, sighed through his nose. "Now I don't know what to believe."

Ayden snorted. "Typical."

"Perhaps . . ." Freyrík laid his hand atop the table, tapped its surface with his thumb. "I think perhaps it no longer matters. For we are not the same people we were three centuries past. And I have learned—" he cut himself off, pointed at Ayden, "*you* have taught me—that we need not hate as our fathers did."

# Chapter Seventeen

Ayden woke up fighting. He did not recall falling asleep, knew not what time it was or even *where* he was, only that 'twas dark and a human loomed above him with ill intent. He had no weapons within reach, but the dagger currently sailing toward his head would do nicely; he deflected the blow with crossed arms, rolled to the side and planted a foot in his attacker's belly while grabbing the man's forearm and snapping it in two. The man screamed, and the dagger fell to the bed.

Ayden seized the weapon and whipped to his feet as a second man charged forward, swinging and missing in the darkness of the tent—*tent* . . . Freyrík's bedroom! The human overbalanced and Ayden stepped round behind him and buried the borrowed dagger between his shoulder blades. The human collapsed to the bed without a sound.

Ayden whirled back on the first attacker, now pulling himself toward Freyrík with his one good arm, hand fisted tight round a second knife. Ayden lunged for his ankle and tugged. The man shouted, fell, and Ayden dragged him away from the prince, rolled him over and pummeled his head 'til he stopped moving.

Ayden thought to end the human right then and there, but no . . . best to keep him alive; the prince would have questions.

He searched the man for hidden weapons, found none. Tassels from a nearby cushion made fine rope for binding his hands and feet together behind his back. He would not be going anywhere.

Ayden sucked in a steadying breath, scrubbed his hands on his breeches, and stood to check on the prince. His hands shook a little as he lit a lantern, but 'twas only natural—the battle rush had not yet drained away.

Finally the wick caught, light flared, and he saw the prince sleeping soundly in bed, chest rising and falling—apparently unharmed, thank the fallen gods. Ayden sat beside him and shook him by the shoulder. Shook him again. Then searched him frantically for injuries, for he could not wake him, and Freyrík would never sleep through such commotion. Unless . . .

*The wine.* The cracking bitter wine. He should have known it'd been dosed the moment he'd tasted it, but he'd been so involved with Freyrík's tale. His carelessness had nearly killed them both. Crack it, his mere *existence* had nearly killed them both, for the ill feelings toward Freyrík stemmed from the man's staunch defense of Ayden.

Ayden tore a hand through his hair and punched the tent wall. 'Twas entirely unsatisfying, and anyway, there was work to be done before he could indulge his guilt.

He went to check on Lord Lini, who, like the prince, was sleeping deeply within thrall of the wine. Content that all was safe within the tent, he silenced his song and exited, stepping over two unconscious guards on his way out. He expected to find nothing as he paced round the exterior, for he'd heard no other songs while in the tent. He was not disappointed.

Tasks complete, he returned to the bedroom, shoved the dead man off the bed, and sat down, a dagger in each hand, to wait for Freyrík to wake. Strange, that he could think of no better way to pass the time than to watch the man sleep. Especially since each time he looked upon him, his mind conjured an image of that handsome face pale in death, blood pouring from slack lips that cried *You killed me,* and *You were too late,* and—worst of all—*I regret nothing.*

Freyrík slept another hour, then woke abruptly, as if from a night terror, and asked, "What's that smell?"

"Blood," Ayden said softly.

The prince sat up and moaned. "I think," he said, rubbing his eyes and then pressing his fingers to his temples, "that I overindulged last night, though I must confess I cannot recall it."

"'Twas not your fault," Ayden said. "Is your mind yet clear?"

Freyrík grunted, then eyed him sharply of a sudden, though his hands still cradled his head. "I'm sorry, did you say *blood*?"

Ayden's prisoner picked that moment to let out a groan.

"Ayden . . .?"

"'Twas not my fault either," Ayden said.

He watched as Freyrík stood from the bed, swayed once, and stumbled his way round it. There his gaze fell upon the two assassins.

"What happened here?"

It did not escape Ayden's notice that he didn't ask, *What have you done?*

"Two of your men crept in under cover of drugged wine and darkness to kill us."

"Oh."

Freyrík sat heavily on the bed, realized he'd landed in a puddle of blood, pulled a face and moved over.

"Us?" He squeezed his eyes shut, pinched the bridge of his nose. "Wait, drugged wine?"

If the situation were any less serious, Ayden probably would have teased Freyrík for his muddled repetition. Instead he merely said, "You almost died because of me; of that I am indeed quite certain."

"Nay," Freyrík said. "None would dare it, and even those who think me spelled into treason would also think me released once you were dead."

Ayden shrugged, for on this he sensed Freyrík would not hear him, no matter how clearly he spoke. Besides, the man would learn the truth from his prisoner soon enough.

Freyrík laid a hand on Ayden's knee, looked him in the eye and said, "I thank the gods they did not succeed."

Then his eyes squeezed closed again, and his hand tightened on Ayden's leg.

"Do you feel as poorly as you appear?" Ayden asked.

Freyrík nodded, but seemed to regret it. "The chief physician reported a theft of anodyne powder yesterday. I suspect we drank it with our wine, though 'tis cruel irony that I feel so much the worse for it."

"Too much will do that," Ayden said. He leaned forward, gripped Freyrík's shoulders with both hands. "Clearly you are not yet yourself, or you'd have asked after your secretary."

Freyrík startled at that, and Ayden quickly added, "He is fine, merely sleeping as you were. There were but two attackers; I suspect no accomplices. This one," he pointed his chin at the man lying bound by the foot of the bed, "remains alive for you to discover what truths you may. But if your mind is not yet sharp—"

Freyrík pushed at Ayden and rose to his feet. "I am ready now. If any others would dare harm you, I must know it without delay."

"*Us*, Prince," Ayden said, cupping a hand beneath the man's elbow to help steady him. "They came for you and I both. Do not be false in your security; you must promise me."

Freyrík's lips quirked into a tiny smile, though whether in pleasure over Ayden's concern or in patronage of it, Ayden could not tell. "Fret not, Ayden. I'll be fine."

Freyrík squatted down beside the prisoner, lifted his head by the hair. It seemed that he recognized the man, judging by the betrayal on his face. It also seemed that his head was beginning to clear, for his stare sharpened upon the would-be assassin and his song's tempo increased.

He poked at the unnatural bend in the prisoner's forearm, turned to Ayden and shook his head. "Must you break *every* human you touch?"

Before Ayden could open his mouth, Freyrík smiled grimly and said, "I jest, Ayden. You acted in self-defense, I know. And truth be told, you have made my task easier, for I must question him now, and I would have answers." He paused, looked to the prisoner and back to Ayden again. "I would have privacy, too, if you please."

Ayden hesitated, loath to leave the prince alone. What if the attacker broke free and tried to harm him again? Or if others of his ilk were yet unapprehended, awaiting the perfect moment?

"Please," Freyrík said, the word stripped of all command by anxiety and longing. And Ayden understood: he did not wish to be seen in his necessary cruelty. Perhaps he feared to remind Ayden of his own interrogation. Or perhaps he believed that Ayden would despise him for what he must do as much as he would despise himself.

He was a fool on both counts.

Nevertheless, Ayden nodded and stood, clasping the prince's shoulder on his way out.

Though Freyrík would not have approved, Ayden went to eat his morning meal round the pit fires with the other officers. If any would be surprised to see him alive and walking, let them show it. He trusted none of them; from whence two assassins came, more could follow.

Alas, he felt naught but the typical hostility and contempt, mixed as always with a touch of curiosity and a nauseating splash of lewdness. He ate in silence, one ear cocked toward the officers and the other toward Freyrík's tent. He kept waiting for the screaming to begin.

It never did.

He tarried as long as he dared, then put a plate together for Freyrík and returned to their tent. New guards had been posted at the entrance.

He heard only two songs inside: one in the low, slow drone of slumber, the other buzzing with conflicting melodies too tangled to sort through. It seemed the traitor had been removed.

As he walked through the office partition and pushed aside the flap that served as a bedroom door, he called out to Freyrík, lest he startle him: "I brought you breakfa—"

Freyrík met him at the door, grabbed him by the shoulders and kissed him.

'Twas desperate and fierce, clenching hands and hard lips and Freyrík's morning stubble rasping across his chin. 'Twas also over nearly before it began, before Ayden's grunt of surprise had even faded from his throat.

Freyrík stepped back, hands still gripping Ayden's shoulders, licked his lips and said, "You saved my life."

Ayden blinked. His mind felt suddenly as stuck as his tongue, and all he could think to say was, "I do believe I mentioned that earlier."

Freyrík laughed, but 'twas an uneasy sound. "Apologies, I . . ." He ducked his eyes, took the plate from Ayden's hands and placed it on a chest of drawers. "Am I too forward?"

Was he? Or was he merely finishing what Ayden had begun earlier, after the music and the ocean had faded and Ayden had ruined everything by thinking too much?

He thought now of his vision of this grand weaver of worlds: face pale in death, dried blood upon lips that would nevermore speak his name. 'Twas unfathomable how very much would have died with Freyrík had the assassins succeeded—so much hope slain, so many songs never to be sung.

And all because of *him*. He knew not why that upset him so—only that it did. He thought of Freyrík's words, so much wisdom from a life so short: *We are not the same people we were three centuries past . . . We need not hate as our fathers did.*

And though to part of him it felt like giving up, giving in, he had to admit that he was not the same elf he'd been even three months past, three *weeks* past, and he *wanted* this.

He stepped forward, closing what little space remained between them, and took Freyrík's hands in his own. Lifted Freyrík's left palm to his lips and whispered, "Play for me," against the roughened skin.

Freyrík shuddered in body and breath as his fingers stretched to caress Ayden's lips and cheek. 'Twas sunshine and cool wind, green grass tickling Ayden's skin, and he closed his eyes with a shaky sigh, leaning into the touch.

But 'twas gone all too soon; Ayden opened his eyes to see Freyrík reaching for the violin case propped against a chest.

"Nay," he said, curling his hand round Freyrík's arm and pulling him close again. "That is not what I meant."

Freyrík looked at him quizzically.

Ayden kissed him.

'Twas softer this time, but no less intense, Freyrík's song pure and sweet with gratitude and longing: a susurration of waves upon the shore and a moist brush of ocean breeze across Ayden's skin. He sighed into Freyrík's parted lips and slid his hands up Freyrík's arms, neck, tangled them in his hair.

"I am so sorry," Ayden whispered, pressing his lips to Freyrík's cheek, jaw, earlobe. He caught the soft flesh between his teeth, suckled and soothed it with his tongue. "You stood for me before all your men and nearly paid for it with your life."

"Nay." Freyrík tilted his head back and wrapped his arms round Ayden's waist, pressing them close. "For you did not let it happen. I took you from your people, from your sister; I hurt you, I threatened you, I displayed you like an animal in a cage and yet *still* you chose to protect me."

Ayden hummed against Freyrík's neck, nuzzled his throat, tasting salt and feeling fleeting life beat beneath his lips.

Freyrík gasped, cupped Ayden's face in both hands and steered them back into a kiss. "I was a fool," he said against Ayden's lips, teeth nipping soft as a whisper. "I did not believe you. But I know better now. Those men were cowards; I did not even have to touch him to make him speak."

"Shhh." Ayden wove his fingers through Freyrík's hair, tugged him closer yet and kissed him quiet. "I would not hear of such things now." He freed his hands just long enough to pull his shirt over his head, claimed another kiss even as his fingers worked the buttons on Freyrík's doublet.

"Buttons," he growled against the man's lips when his fingers encountered not one row but two, impossibly long.

Freyrík shoved his hands away with a murmured, "Let me," unbuttoning thrice as fast. Yet still 'twas not fast enough, for if Ayden didn't soon feel the press of skin against skin, he was quite certain he'd go mad.

Freyrík's hands busy at task, Ayden yanked down his own breeches and kicked them off with his boots. The prince at last tore off the doublet and the shirt beneath, and Ayden wasted no time shoving him toward the bed.

"You are *too slow*, human," he growled as Freyrík overbalanced and fell to the mattress.

Before Ayden could climb atop him, socked feet hooked round his hips and tossed him bodily onto the bed.

"What I lack in speed I make up for in strength," Freyrík said, rolling atop Ayden and finally—*finally!*—pressing skin to skin, chest to chest, cool flesh and coarse hair and thrashing human heartbeat against his ribs.

Pinned by his wrists, Ayden twisted and pulled and arched, but Freyrík, immovable, only lowered his head and claimed a hard kiss, grinding their lips and hips together. A jolt, a storming cloudsong; Ayden bucked as Freyrík's breeches roughed across his cock, sucking the center of his being to that single aching place. He used the momentum to roll them and straddle the man, one hand resting at Freyrík's throat and the other squeezing the bulge in his breeches.

"What I lack in strength I make up for in *skill*," he said, licking his lips like a wolf at the kill, tasting faint traces of Freyrík. "Now remove those breeches before I remove them for you."

"I would like to see you try," Freyrík growled, grinning mischievous as he reached out to tweak Ayden's nipples.

More stormsong, a flash of heat straight to his cock; Ayden yelped, somehow ended up beneath Freyrík again. Freyrík's lips and teeth were at his neck, his collarbone, nipping and lapping, painting small circles of warmth and moisture that set Ayden's flesh abuzz. When Freyrík's stubbled cheek scraped across his chest, he felt each bristle as if a whetstone, sharpening nerve endings to a razor's edge. He made no struggle beneath the onslaught—was not even certain he could have—for it took all his rapidly fading concentration merely to unbuckle Freyrík's belt.

He was halfway to the buttons of Freyrík's breeches when Freyrík's lips closed round his right nipple and suckled as if he could draw the whole of Ayden's song right up through it. Ayden's heart stuttered and his fingers stilled, powerless.

"You are *too slow*, elf," Freyrík mumbled against the sensitized flesh, the bass hum of his words twinging straight through Ayden's chest and stealing his breath. Teeth followed, and Ayden squirmed anew, the whole of his world contained within and bursting from that frenzied, ravished nub.

Freyrík's lips left his nipple with a wet slurp, coaxing a moan from Ayden's throat. Sensation ebbed and thought flowed in its place, and he realized how utterly Freyrík had taken advantage of his distraction: he was trapped, one wrist wedged beneath the point of Freyrík's knee, the other pressed to the mattress by a hand half again as large and twice as powerful as his.

Yet 'twas all pointless, when Freyrík's stare alone could have pinned him in place.

"Have you any idea," Freyrík said, shifting round atop Ayden to wiggle out of his breeches, "how long I have dreamed to touch you so? To pleasure you? To hear you cry my name?"

'Twas Ayden's turn to make use of distraction; he worked a knee beneath Freyrík's hip, planted his foot on the bed and flipped them over, straddling Freyrík and pinning his wrists on either side of his waist before the man could recover.

"Well," Freyrík added through a smirk, as if their roles had not just been so vigorously reversed, "To hear you say my name *again*."

Ayden leaned in to ply Freyrík's nipple—half revenge, half curiosity to taste, half desire to feel that hard-muscled body writhe and strain beneath him—no matter that it made three halves—and growled, "I said no such thing."

"*Yes*, you—"

A nip, a gasp, the body beneath him arching-twisting-bucking as if seeking nearness and escape all at once. Ayden thrilled at his power, bucking his hips in sympathy. "You dreamed it, Freyrík."

"I did no— There!" Freyrík jerked his head up off the mattress, and Ayden jerked his own back lest they end the night with bloody noses. "See? You said it again!"

Ayden dipped his head to Freyrík's ear, nuzzled his lips against its shell to hide his smile, and whispered, "I'm not deaf, Prince; I heard."

"Say it again."

Ayden rose up just enough to look Freyrík in the eye. "No."

He smirked as Freyrík struggled within his grasp, sweat-slick thighs and belly and—*gods*—cock sliding against his own but finding no leverage or purchase. He held the man's stare in silent challenge, breath coming hard and hot and mingling with Freyrík's in the narrow space between them.

'Twas Freyrík who gave in first, falling still and grinning fit to split his face in two. Yet still he demanded, *demanded!*, trapped and helpless though he was, "Say it again!"

Ayden leaned in oh-so-close, nipped at moist, parted lips with his front teeth, and whispered, "Make me, human."

Nearly nose to nose, he still held the man's stare. Freyrík licked his lips in a manner positively indecent and said, "Come a little closer, and I shall make you indeed."

Ayden shook his head; he would follow no orders this morn, tempting though they might be. Instead he pushed himself up from Freyrík's chest, spun round to straddle the man backwards, hunched over his lap and swallowed his cock down whole.

"*Gods!*" Freyrík cried, hips bucking up beneath Ayden and fingers digging almost painfully into the raised cheeks of his arse.

Ayden's lips, already well and truly stretched round a cock as large and powerful as befit its owner, pulled further yet into a grin round the heated flesh. Gods, but it had been too long since he'd tasted this—the bitter-salty-sweet of arousal and need, lovesong twining like tendrils of sunlight round his own ardent call, sheltering like staunch arms. *Human* arms—who'd ever have guessed?—yet not so different from his elven lovers, and certainly not a single jot the lesser.

Ayden cupped Freyrík's stones in one hand, rolling them 'twixt his fingers and into his palm. The man's skin was tight, firm, cooler than Ayden's but blazing with kindled song. Ayden clenched his hand the tiniest bit, and felt the powerful body below him go rigid and still.

'Twould be a greater pleasure to break such stillness than it had been to cause it.

He slid his hand down past Freyrík's stones and brushed his little finger across the tight ring of muscle behind them, pressing without breaching. Freyrík bucked so hard that Ayden had no choice but to swallow round the cock driving down his throat, taking him in deeper. Which made Freyrík buck all the harder; Ayden sat firmly upon his chest to hold him steady as he writhed, moaning and panting like a man run through.

Hands clutched bruisingly tight round his hips, and Freyrík rasped out, "Gods! Is there *anything* you do poorly?"

Ayden pulled up, chuckling. "Not really, no," he mumbled against Freyrík's engorged flesh, then licked a long stripe up the front of the man's cock with the flat of his tongue. *Gods*, the taste! "Perhaps the prince would care for a lesson?"

"None required," Freyrík said, "I assure you. Now come here."

A sharp tug had Ayden up on all fours, his groin above Freyrík's face, his cock bumping Freyrík's chin. He could have broken away, but no matter; when moist lips wrapped round his cock, he lost all recall of why obeying commands had seemed a poor idea.

They moaned in unison round each other, vibrations sending shockwaves from lips to hips to toes and back as their melodies quickened, aligned, matched note for note and beat for beat.

Freyrík's tongue swiped along the underside of Ayden's cockhead and nearly made his knees buckle; Ayden did the same, and felt the quiver in Freyrík's thighs, the jerk of his hips. Freyrík's cock bumped the back of Ayden's throat, and Ayden hollowed his cheeks, hummed round it as he swallowed. Freyrík mirrored—a moist, tight heatwave surged round and through him. His flesh felt like the head of a snare drum round his frame, stretched taut near to breaking beneath this musician's skilled hands.

A moistened fingertip stroked round behind his stones, then plunged inside him. Ayden's pleasure broke like a tidal wave, hurtling down upon the shore; with a loud cry and a sounding of horns and a great crash of cymbals that shook the very room, he burst into Freyrík's mouth, Freyrík nursing him through his ecstasy 'til he was naught but a quivering, twitching ball of nerve endings singing their pleasure to all who would hear.

When at last Ayden stilled, sights and sounds inching back into focus alongside taste and smell and feeling—*gods, what feeling!*—Freyrík's lips pursed tight and dragged down the length of Ayden's softening cock as his head dropped back to the mattress. His satisfaction rumbled through Ayden's mind-ear like a purring cat, and when Ayden turned and curled up beside him, Freyrík smiled shyly and asked, "Did I please you?"

Was he quite *serious*?

Ayden bit him on the shoulder, soothed it with smiling lips. "Did I say your name?"

Freyrík cupped Ayden's face in both hands, pressed soft little kisses to his forehead, his nose, his lips. Freyrík's own lips were swollen with use and arousal, moist with the taste of Ayden's seed. "You did indeed."

"I shall have to trust you," Ayden said, "for my mind was quite occupied with other matters at the time. And," he said, sitting up and urging Freyrík to do the same, "I would have it occupied so once more."

He guided Freyrík against the headboard with pushy hands and nipping teeth, then knelt down and gripped the base of Freyrík's straining cock, sucking the head into his mouth.

Freyrík threw his head back with a gasp, Ayden's name on his lips as he tangled both fists in Ayden's hair. Ayden watched him through his lashes, lathing him with his tongue while pumping his cock with one hand and stroking his stones with the other.

He was moving in earnest now, in tempo with Freyrík's frantic song, seeking out the peaks of his ecstasy and chasing them with more of the same: there, his tongue against the vein on the left side, a blast of pleasure like a smithy fire flaring with air; and there, the slightest scrape of teeth along the front edge of the head, whole measures of grace notes tripping and stumbling overtop one another in their haste. He glanced up again and saw the bottom of Freyrík's stubbled chin, his head lolled back on his neck, his shoulders taut with strain. Small moans—*Yes* and *Gods!* and *Just like that* and *Oh, Ayden!*—spilled from his parted lips on every rapid exhale.

Ayden sped his mouth and his hands as Freyrík's pleasure swelled through its final crescendo, as his fingers tightened in Ayden's hair, and Ayden let Freyrík hold his head and thrust into his mouth until he burst in a spray of heat and salt and passion, collapsing back against the pillows with a shout that rang in Ayden's ears and reverberated inside his head.

In the silence that followed, there were but two songs playing as one, soft and slow and sated. Ayden laid his head on Freyrík's belly, wrapped his arms round the man's waist, and fell asleep to the rhythmic stroking of song to song and fingers through his hair.

# Chapter Eighteen

Freyrík awoke to Ayden's head pillowed on his chest, a blanket draped loosely across their naked bodies, and a tray of food and drink set on the bedside table. He did not wish to wake Ayden, but neither could he resist the urge to touch him now that his touch was welcome; he lifted the hand curled round Ayden's shoulder and brushed it across wild hair, then dropped his head to follow his fingers with a kiss.

Ayden sighed softly.

'Twas a heady thing to imagine their days together now: no more squabbles or bitterness, only pleasures shared: the best of all he had to give. To think that he could wake each morning like this, Ayden in his arms, and fall asleep the same—to think of all the joys in between . . .

The mere thought of it set his blood to racing, and he pressed his lips to Ayden's hair again, breathed deep of his woodland scent.

Ayden stirred beneath him. "So sentimental, human," he mumbled into Freyrík's chest. "Do I smell food?"

Freyrík barked out a laugh. Of course, *of course* those would be the first words from his mouth after all they'd endured and shared this night. "Yes, you do. It seems Lord Lini slept off his sedation at last."

Ayden climbed over Freyrík to reach the tray, then settled atop him, elbow in his ribs, and jammed a handful of grapes into his mouth.

"Do you mind?" Freyrík asked, though he couldn't quite manage to summon the outrage the situation clearly called for.

"Not at all," Ayden said through a mouthful of grapes with a smirk that Freyrík could hear.

He snatched the bunch from Ayden's hand and plucked one between his teeth. "Well, it is . . . comforting to know that some things never change," he said round the grape, his free hand wandering to Ayden's bare arse and squeezing firmly. "But I feel it only fair to caution you that if you remain atop me, I shall have to—"

Warning bells. Freyrík's pulse quickened at the trumpet blasts that followed: no mere accounting of a raiding party.

The Surge was cresting.

"They're coming," he said, nudging Ayden off him and bolting from the bed just as Lord Lini rushed in, Freyrík's buff coat and armor in hand. Close on his heels was Lord General Vísi, who walked in two steps and turned aside sharply, shielding his eyes.

A naked man and elf could do that to people, Freyrík supposed.

"The men rally, Your Highness," General Vísi said into his hand. "The signal came from the northwest lookouts, two leagues across the border."

Freyrík let Lord Lini handle his breeches while he himself tugged on his thick leather buff coat. Behind him, Ayden was already lacing his boots.

"How long before they reach the scarecrow field?" Freyrík asked.

"We estimate thirty minutes. Riders are scattering the caltrops now, and all units will be in position with time to spare."

Freyrík bent to strap on his shin guards. "Thank you, Lord General. Dismissed; see to your duties."

General Vísi saluted and strode from the tent with the unhurried confidence of a man who'd led armies through Surges beyond counting. Freyrík envied him; he'd commanded nine such charges in his years, marched in fourteen more, and still his heart was thrashing in his chest, his lungs heavy, his mouth rank with the taste of fear.

"Your Highness?"

Freyrík turned to see Lord Lini holding his armor.

"Nay," Freyrík said, recalling how much quicker Ayden's horse had been without such encumbrances. "Just the breastplate and helmet, and a vambrace for my sword-arm."

By the time they'd finished dressing and arming, stable hands were waiting outside the tent with their horses, armored only behind the saddle for protection from the rear.

They rode to the muster point behind the hill that would hide them from the scarecrow field, where cavalrymen were assembling in neat blocks and rows, ready to charge forth into victory or death.

"Remember," the prince said, leaning in his saddle to close the distance between them, "no matter what happens, stay by my side."

Ayden nodded. He meant to protect Freyrík in any case, but of course Freyrík also meant to protect him. Not from the Ferals, but from his own men, who might seek to use the chaos of the battlefield to sink a blade into Ayden's back.

And the gods knew there were enough men at his back right now.

But 'twas not the men that set his mind so on edge. Rather 'twas the convergence of all that he and Freyrík had planned: the cavalry arrayed at the base of a hill; the scarecrow field on the other side, a barrier between them and the forest; and the Ferals racing toward them through the woods in a great, hungry wave, afroth with screaming fury. Their songs raked as razors over glass, as a league-long swarm of locusts through a field of ripened wheat. He gritted his teeth and clenched his fists round the hilts of his borrowed short swords to keep them from clutching his temples.

The second horn signaled that the Ferals had reached the scarecrow army. From beyond the hillock came the roars of countless creatures large and small, the crack of wood, the thud and crash of falling decoys and beasts alike.

The carpenters had built the scarecrows, and the apothecaries had distilled the poison, but 'twas Ayden who'd concocted this massacre in a strategy session so far removed from its consequences. And for what? To out-show the prince?

*I'm sorry*, he thought, smoothing his thumb across the hilt of a short sword. *You came for a holy battle, and I have stood in your way. I only hope the death I deal will put swift end to your misery.*

Behind him, men shifted restlessly in their saddles, and mounts pawed in skittish fear.

"Steady," murmured Freyrík. "Steady . . ."

They must reveal themselves in the right moment: too early, and the last of the Ferals would find the field abandoned and rush ahead to the soft villages beyond; too late, and the Ferals would decimate the scarecrows and surge past them.

"Steady . . ." Freyrík repeated at his side.

The third horn rang loud and clear above the ruckus, announcing that the better part of the Feral surge had cleared the forest and come afield.

"Now!" Freyrík roared, kicking his horse into a gallop. "Charge!"

Swept up in his excitement, Ayden leaned forward and sent his courser racing beside the prince. Behind them, a rumbling roll of thunder swelled and spread and shook the ground as the great mass of cavalrymen spurred into motion.

They crested the hill in a jagged line and reined in again. Ayden saw the Surge for the first time, and nearly fell off his horse. Never had he witnessed so many Ferals, so many beasts of any kind (but for humans) in one place. He felt very small of a sudden, exposed and framed against the sky.

Already the orderly scarecrow rows were so much rubble, torn clothes and carved limbs strewn all about the field. Amongst them lay hundreds of Feral corpses, oddly bloodless in their poisoned deaths. From the living beasts churned wave upon wave of shining hatred, slashing claws and snapping fangs, ramming horns and trampling hooves.

The fourth horn blast, and a great noise went up from the humans. Standard bearers waved their flags, and every soldier shouted, cursed, or whistled. The crash of sound threatened to punch through Ayden's ears, even as he clamped his hands to them.

Of course, it also got the Ferals' attention.

The fifth horn, and the chase began.

He and Freyrík peeled off due west, and the whole of the cavalry fell in behind them. For a moment, Ayden felt as if he were fleeing the humans, not the Ferals. But a quick glance back showed the beasts had taken the bait; they were running *en masse* at an angle to the column, as if hoping to cut off its tail. The noise was deafening—calls and cries from thousands of men and beasts, countless hooves pounding upon the earth, churning up clods of dirt and a massive cloud of dust.

"It's working!" he shouted to Freyrík.

The prince grinned back at him, then drummed his horse's flanks for more speed.

The horse, it seemed, did not need to be asked twice.

Birds shrieked overhead, and Ayden dared a look up and back, trusting his mount to keep her footing. 'Twas like the fight with the eagle in the scarecrow field, magnified by hundreds, wings and arrow clouds blotting out the sun. A screech, a dive, a rider ripped from his saddle and thrown to the ground, trampled beneath the stampede.

A second screech, closer, *too* close, and Ayden whipped back to warn—

Freyrík lurched to the left with a startled cry as a Feral raven raked talons across his right shoulder. His right foot pulled free of its stirrup and he began to topple sideways; Ayden locked legs round his horse and lunged, grabbing hold of Freyrík's ankle with one hand before the man pitched clear from his saddle.

"Are you all right—" they called together.

They both nodded, then both grinned.

Up ahead and to their left, the forest receded into rocky foothills and the Crack came into view, a foot-wide rent in the earth amidst a beach-like expanse of magma and glassrock. They raced toward it at a sharp angle, horseshoes clacking hard against barren earth. Nearby, a horse lost its footing on the treacherous terrain and went skidding to the ground, taking three more with it as they tripped and tangled in a bloody heap. Ayden grimaced; 'twas impossible to ignore their dying screams.

The cloud of winged Ferals rode low over their heads. More birds swept in, the smaller beasts ripping armor or hunks of flesh or hair, the larger ones ripping men right from their saddles.

Ayden cared not for the others, but he feared deeply for the prince. 'Twas with thanks to the fallen gods, then, that they fast approached the hillock behind which a hundred fresh riders—and ten contingents of animal handlers—were waiting.

Their train cleared the Crack and the barren land beyond it, then stormed past the hill, and fresh cavalry came spilling out, closing in to stop the Ferals from flanking the main line through the forest. Dogs barked furiously, running herd alongside them, and cries from hundreds of trained hawks rent the skies as they assaulted from behind, colliding mid-air with the Feral birds and diving into the mass below. The shadows fell away as winged Ferals were forced into battle with the humans' puppets, and Ayden all but heard the cavalry's collective sigh of relief at the slowing of the aerial barrage.

Yet another glance behind revealed how very short-lived their relief would be: The back of the line was crumbling, sucked whole into the Ferals' open jaws. The line had shortened, and each passing second carried death some paces closer. There went another, and another: five, ten at a time, horses and men alike screaming their last as they sank into the dust.

Ayden turned round and begged his horse and the prince's to give more speed. For they were racing up a rope whose end was burning, and he feared the fire would catch them long before they reached the top.

But at last the box canyon came into view. Freyrík veered off to the side of the line, slowing to a trot and letting dozens of riders fly past. Ayden followed. He thought he heard Lord Lini cry, "Your Highness, you mustn't!," but he couldn't be certain over the thunder of hoof beats and voices. Whatever the case, Freyrík took no notice, and Ayden knew—as

Lord Lini did as well, no doubt—that if any riders remained outside the canyon, Freyrík would be among them.

Not nearly far enough behind them, the frothing mass of Ferals and dust split down the middle, flanking them on both sides, creeping up round the cavalry line like a massive set of jaws. Ahead, riders were already crowding the openings in the brush wall, their horses wild, some fighting to push through, others veering right past the canyon and into the hills beyond.

If they didn't get everyone inside soon, they'd end up with a full-on ground war outside the canyon. They'd end up with a rout. A month ago he'd not have cared, but now . . .

He sang out to the horses, as long and as loud as he could: *Peace, friends. Safety lies beyond the brush.*

It did not seem to help.

Freyrík clearly saw the same, for he reined to a stop, turned his horse in a sharp half-circle and yelled, "BEHIND ME, FORM UP!"

Criers passed the order rapidly back, and the hundred-odd riders left behind him turned and clustered in formation. Mounted swordsmen and pikemen formed a tight front line, and to the rear, archers locked knees in their oddly long-legged stirrups and loosed one hail of arrows after the next.

'Twas impressive, Ayden had to admit; surely these men knew they'd die to the last, yet there they stood, facing their ends with honor to buy time for those ahead.

Ayden drew his blades, and so did Freyrík. From the brush wall behind them he heard shouts of "Go go go!" and "Move your arses!" and "Come on, ladies, hoof it!"

Then General Vísi raced past them, grabbing hold of Freyrík's reins on the way. The black destrier squealed in surprise, but peeled off toward the brush wall. Ayden raced after.

"Apologies, Your Highness!" the general shouted atop Freyrík's vocal protests. "These men must have their prince!"

Ayden rather agreed, and he sang a path ahead through the clustered mounts, so loudly it hurt his own head. Horses cleared before them, and moments later, Freyrík and Vísi crossed into the canyon abreast, Ayden and Lord Lini close on their heels.

They rode head-on into chaos.

Several dozen Ferals had already breached the wall—foxes, coyotes, rabbits, hawks: the small and quick, the birds of prey. Bare-saddled horses milled round in a frenzy, the lucky riders safe atop the canyon, the others climbing ladders or dead. Or waiting; soldiers crowded round ladders that could only hold so much weight—two, Ayden saw, had already snapped—fighting their best against the agile Ferals, where every fall spelled death by hoof or claw.

Freyrík wrenched his reins free of General Vísi's grip and pulled his mount to a hard stop.

"Order!" he shouted, but 'twas unlikely that many could hear him.

He looked round wildly, then waved at a soldier. A trumpeter, Ayden realized, as the man struggled to ride through the chaos.

"Give the tenth!" Freyrík shouted at him.

The soldier lifted his instrument to his lips and blew a lively fanfare that told Ayden nothing.

It got Freyrík the attention he'd wanted, though.

"To the walls!" he roared, standing in his stirrups and circling his sword round his head. "Form up! To the walls!"

"To the walls!" the order echoed from man to man.

Soldiers queued ten deep at the ladders turned round, raced forward, and formed into rough lines facing out—rows of men wielding fire spitters or sword and shield backed by a row of pikemen—just as the Ferals began to outnumber them. Freyrík, Ayden, Lini, and Vísi backed themselves up to a line near the far wall and drew their weapons.

Even through his saddle, Ayden could feel the ground trembling as the main body of the Ferals surged into the canyon—a massive, churning wave that drowned the soldiers' screams and crashed upon their ordered lines. 'Twas a strangely quiet fight for all the noise: no clashing of steel on steel, just grunts of effort and shrieks of pain and the sick, dull thud of blade and claw ripping through flesh.

The Ferals flowed right past Ayden, never attacking despite his alliance with their human foes. He struck them as they went by, felling beast after beast with his swords. Yet more came to replace them, hundreds, thousands, while the humans' numbers dropped by the moment through death or escape.

The brush wall erupted into sudden flames. Horses nearby screamed their terror and backed deeper into the canyon despite the desperate orders of their riders.

In the new chaos came the archers' trumpet blasts and shouts of "LOOSE!" from atop the canyon. Humans all round the canyon floor huddled tight to the walls and crouched beneath their shields as five hundred arrows rained down upon the Ferals. Another round came but seconds later, and then another, and another, and more after that, and in mere moments, the Ferals ceased to outnumber the humans quite so much, even as more and more soldiers climbed to safety.

Ayden's own party had almost reached safety themselves, just four men ahead of them on the ladder, when Freyrík kicked his horse toward a pack of Feral wolves twenty paces afar. The black destrier balked; the prince dismounted, sword swinging, and charged into the fray.

"What are you doing!" Ayden shouted, dismounting to race after him, then ducking as a wolf lunged right over his head and landed on something soft and screaming.

"Help them!" Freyrík yelled. He swung at a wolf, missed, recovered just in time to throw his shield up as a massive paw slammed into its curved metal surface. Freyrík went sprawling, and the wolf lunged again.

*NO!* Ayden sang—screamed—at the wolf. He'd not expected it to work, but his contingency plan, a thrown dagger, drew the beast's attention to himself.

Freyrík took advantage of the respite by popping to his feet. "Help them!" he yelled again, pointing with his sword to a group of men—small and getting smaller by the moment—surrounded by the wolf pack.

No wonder Freyrík had raced forward so urgently: in the center of the mess stood Corporal Ekkja, bloodied and limping, shield lost and sword gripped in two mangled hands.

There was no cracking way they were going to save him.

Still, Ayden ran in, swords swinging, cringed when he missed the neck of a moving target and chopped off half a foreleg instead. The wolf fell with a whimper, but stayed down only a moment before struggling back to three feet and tearing at the nearest human belly with its teeth. It lunged without thinking, and Ayden slipped a blade between its ribs and dropped it clean.

Freyrík had fought his way to Ekkja, and Ayden had almost fought his way to Freyrík when Freyrík screamed and dropped his sword, staggered back with his arm pressed to his chest. He hunched behind his shield just as a swipe that would have killed him knocked him on his arse instead.

Fallen gods!

"*Hey!*" Ayden shouted, this time adding his physical voice to his inner song. "To me, wolf! To me!"

The Feral turned its head, eyes narrowed and lips pulled back from an enormous mouthful of teeth, but it didn't charge. No need, though; Ayden threw a dagger straight through its left eye, dropping it where it stood and buying Freyrík enough time to reclaim his sword and his feet.

Alas, Ekkja had not been so lucky. Ayden saw him the same moment Freyrík did, dead on the ground with his throat torn out. He almost—almost—felt a pang of regret at the boy's death. Or maybe 'twas Freyrík's feelings painting his own, guilt and sorrow pouring from the man's chest as if blood from a fatal wound.

Freyrík stood over the boy for a long moment—far too long in the midst of battle—then raised his sword two-handed and charged the two remaining wolves. His anger was understandable, but this was cracking foolish.

Ayden sighed and raced after him.

The prince severed the head of the lead wolf just as Ayden reached him. That left but one: good odds with two fighters as skilled as they, pressed shoulder to shoulder with weapons bared . . .

Until half a dozen Feral squirrels and a cougar rushed into the fray.

"Watch the befanged squirrels," Freyrík said, catching one with a well-timed lunge and slicing it in half. "They're fast."

"Crack the squirrels—find the ladder!"

He backed into Freyrík, pushed him bodily toward the wall, but the prince stopped after a single step.

"Too many horses! We have to fight!"

Crack it, all the soldiers had gone from this corner of the canyon, and the archers would not loose arrows with the Ferals so near to the prince. They were alone, and Freyrík would be dead in moments if Ayden didn't stop this.

Ayden cursed, caught a squirrel midair as it leapt for Freyrík, and snapped its neck. "Mind the cougar!" he shouted, then turned to deal with the horses.

They were running and bucking with white-eyed panic, streaking sweat and foam. *Peace,* he sang to them, giving his all to create a small pocket of harmony in the strident chaos. *You'll not be harmed. Peace.*

Behind him, Freyrík was shouting, "I told you, it's the squir— Gah!"

Ayden turned in time to see Freyrík thrown to the ground by the wolf, who landed atop him, jaws to his neck—

Only it wasn't his neck; Freyrík had slipped an arm between teeth and veins, and his vambrace dented but didn't break, not yet—

Ayden tackled the wolf and dragged it to the ground, flailing and snarling. He clutched at the hilt of his last dagger, seeking a worthwhile place to thrust it in . . .

The wolf tried to roll off him to lunge at Freyrík again, and Ayden found his opening, plunging the dagger into the wolf's flank at just the angle to its heart. The wolf dropped atop him without a sound, a hot slippery mass of fur and deadweight. It took three tries to heave the body away.

Once free, he wrenched his dagger back, scrambled to his feet, and turned to find Freyrík. Where— *oh, gods*, the man was fighting the cougar, blade to claw and tooth, and three squirrels were scurrying across his person, though they at least seemed mostly stumped by his buff coat.

Ayden shouted a warning, then plunged between Freyrík and the cougar, lashing out with a short sword. He'd lost the other somewhere, but still had a dagger, at least. The cougar tried to skirt him from the right, then the left; he got in its way each time.

"Ladder!" he reminded Freyrík, and this time the man went, cursing and grunting, as Ayden held off the cougar.

The cat made a temporary retreat, and Ayden risked a moment's glance toward Freyrík. He found the man rodent-free, stripped of his chest plate, still near the base of the ladder. He was climbing slowly, one-handed; his right arm hung useless beside him, blood dripping from his fingers.

"Hurry!" Ayden shouted, backing away as the cougar stalked forward once more, keeping himself between it and the ladder.

He lunged, managed to wound the feline's paw but not lop it off as he'd intended. The cougar screamed like a gale and knocked him aside, hard enough to jar his ribs. He looked down, bracing himself to see his insides out—but no, the cougar had sheathed its claws. It did not want him dead, it wanted—

Freyrík.

The cougar was gathering itself to leap at the ladder. It crouched low, but just then a barrage of arrows struck it from above and it lurched sideways, screaming, and backed away.

*Finally*, the archers had caught on.

But they couldn't hit the agile rodents that now climbed after Freyrík. The man was hanging by his good hand and kicking them down as best he could, but even from the ground, Ayden could see he was weakening. He ran toward the ladder, thinking quickly: The canyon walls were sheer—too sheer for the Feral squirrels. If it weren't for the ladder . . .

He ran to it, climbed until one of Freyrík's kicks almost caught him in the head, and slashed off the ladder beneath Freyrík feet. 'Twas a short fall for him, full of rope and rodents, and he rolled and rose smoothly to his feet. The squirrels scrabbled at the wall but gained no height.

Ha.

From above, thank the fallen gods, the soldiers began to help Freyrík along, hauling up the ladder hand over hand.

Of course, that left Ayden stranded where he was, didn't it.

*Curse them all, the bloody beasts.* And no, he did not mean the Ferals.

But then his world darkened as a huge shadow passed overtop him. He heard Freyrík scream and looked up sharply.

The cougar had taken advantage of his distraction and leapt clear over him, latching onto one of Freyrík's legs. Its hind paws were gouging ruts into the rock face for purchase, but its front paws hugged to Freyrík's calf in a blood-dripping grip.

The soldiers above dropped the ladder under the sudden weight, and both Feral and Freyrík came plummeting down. Freyrík slammed into the canyon wall and lost his grip on the ladder; he screamed, slipped from one rung to the next, hand grappling at nothing—

Until he caught himself on the second-to-last rung, his free leg kicking wildly, his injured hand grasping and slipping and grasping again as a cat nearly thrice his weight fought to drag him down.

Ayden swung his swords at the cat's dangling rear paws. This time he cut one clean off, but he could reach nothing more, and the Feral took little notice of its own pain. He daren't risk killing it with lightning while its claws were buried in Freyrík's leg, nor could he throw his short sword or dagger; one was not balanced, the other too small to matter, and if he missed . . .

Ayden heard a *fwip!*, then another and another and another, and the Feral cougar fell dead to the canyon floor with a dozen new arrows jutting from its back and chest.

Cheers from above, and a cry of distress—or perhaps relief?—from Freyrík, who sought traction with new vigor but still failed to haul himself up. Ayden sheathed his weapons and raced up the rock face as fast as he could, for though Freyrík was a mere five paces aboveground, a fall might well kill him in his current state.

"Hold on!" he shouted, even as men atop the canyon walls shouted the same. He thought to say something else—*You just won me; 'twould be a shame to lose me now*, or *What would happen to me and Ella if you died*, or *Your people need you!*—but they were mere platitudes, and unnecessary besides. Freyrík would hold on because he wished to live and he was too strong to give in. 'Twas as simple as that.

Ayden's right toehold crumbled and he nearly fell, cursing the canyon walls for being so cracking sheer (nevermind that he'd praised that very trait when they'd planned this battle), himself for cutting so much off the bottom of the ladder (nevermind that he'd done that to keep the Feral squirrels from attacking Freyrík), and the human archers for not having shot the cougar before it pounced.

"Ayden . . .!" Freyrík panted, a little panicked, a lot pained, and the words he hadn't spoken—*Hurry, I'm slipping*—spurred Ayden all the more. He reached Freyrík only moments after, heart hammering from any number of causes he did not wish to consider, hooked one arm round the third rung and his legs round Freyrík's waist, and hauled them both bodily up the ladder.

Alas, he lacked the frame for prolonged feats of strength, and he gained but two rungs before he could haul them no more. "Pull your feet up!" he shouted, watching Freyrík's one good hand clenching round a rung and praying, praying that the cougar hadn't left a foot impotent as well. He dared to remove one leg from Freyrík, bent it to snag the bottom rung. A few deft twists and he'd anchored the rope round his ankle, used it as leverage to haul them up further.

He was trembling so hard he thought for sure he'd slip, sweat blurring his vision and fatigue threatening to spill them both, but at last, thank the fallen gods, Freyrík managed to bring a knee up and prop it on a rung. His other knee followed seconds after, and he clung there, half to Ayden, half to the ladder, bleeding all over everything, panting and shaking with relief.

'Twas safe now for the ladder team to heave them up, and they let the men above do the real work while they dangled there, clutching to the ladder and each other.

Once at the top, several pairs of hands pried Freyrík from Ayden's grasp and hauled him over the edge, where he flopped onto his back like a beached fish. Nobody helped Ayden. He seemed in fact such an afterthought that he'd just barely secured a handhold on the canyon rim when they let the gathered rungs fall back toward the canyon floor. He heaved himself up with a growl and lay down beside Freyrík, trying to convince his heart to settle, his fingers to unclench. He was safe now, after all.

More or less.

The crowd round them thinned as a man with wide red bands on both sleeves shoved his way forward and fell to his knees at Freyrík's side.

"Where are you hurt, Your Highness?"

"'Tis nothing serious," Freyrík ground out.

Did he not realize how very much his tone contradicted his words?

"Begging Your Highness's pardon," the man said, reaching for Freyrík's right hand, "but I'd be most grateful if you'd allow me to see for myself."

Freyrík gave in without a fight, letting the man cut away the sleeve of his buff coat. "Where is Lord Lini?" he asked. "And the Lord General Vísi? Have they made it?"

"Here, Your Highness," Lord Lini said, pushing through the crowd as the physician *tsked* and pressed a bandage to Freyrík's arm. "General Vísi is tending what remains of the killing field. He took no serious wounds."

"The gods be thanked," Freyrík breathed. "Has someone seen to Ayden?"

Ayden leaned into Freyrík's line of sight and shook his head. "Nay, Prince. But I am unharmed."

Freyrík eyed him hard. "I saw that cougar throw you."

"And I landed on my feet." *Sort of.* "Its claws were sheathed; it did not wound me."

He heard a shift in mood at that admission: confusion, tension, suspicion, amazement, in varying degrees from those gathered round. All eyes turned to him, perhaps to confirm his words for themselves, perhaps to be ready if he attacked.

He looked back at the physician and snapped, "Tend your patient."

The physician glared at him, but then returned his attention to Freyrík, wrapping a thick bandage round his left calf.

"Can you ride, Your Highness? I would not mend your wounds here if it can be helped; 'tis not clean."

Freyrík sat up, tensed and closed his eyes—dizzy, Ayden suspected, if all the blood the man had left on the canyon floor was any indication—but then nodded his head.

"We've some carts on the way . . ." the physician said.

"Nay. Surely others need them more than I do. I can ride."

Ayden helped Freyrík to his feet as a soldier led a horse over, handed Freyrík the reins, and dropped to his hands and knees at the creature's side. Freyrík seemed a touch uncomfortable at the prospect of using the man as a mounting block, but he did so nonetheless, and a good thing for it: he looked quite unsteady in the saddle. 'Twas foolish, and probably dangerous, for Freyrík to ride now. Yet Ayden understood the importance of the gesture, of not being carted away before all his men.

It seemed, then, that a compromise was in order.

"Perhaps," Ayden said, "I should ride with you." He did not wait for a reply before mounting up behind Freyrík, wrapping his arms round Freyrík's waist and taking the reins from his hand.

Freyrík leaned back into Ayden's chest, sighing tiredly. "Someone find Lord General Feitr," he said as Ayden began to lead their mount across a ground littered with dead Feral fliers and climbers and a smattering of humans.

"Right away, Your Highness," Lord Lini said, pacing their horse on foot.

"If he lives, have him meet me in my tent at his earliest convenience. If he does not, send Lord General Vísi. There's much work yet to be done."

"Of course, Your Highness," Lord Lini said in a tone that made clear his belief that Freyrík should be resting, not working. Still, he went off to do as he'd been bid.

*Don't worry,* Ayden thought to Lord Lini's retreating form. *I'll see to him myself.*

# Chapter Nineteen

Ayden held no love for the royal physician, nor for the barbarity he called healing, and the man's dressing of Freyrík's wounds did naught to improve his view. Ayden kept firm hands on Freyrík's shoulders as Freyrík grunted and moaned and squirmed through the physician's brutish ministrations, praying 'twould be over soon and thanking the fallen gods that Freyrík's armor had seen no cuts too deep.

Alas, the physician explained as he took needle and thread to Freyrík's calf as if his prince were but sock or breeches, Feral wounds were known to fester if not treated with the utmost care.

Ayden scoffed; *this* was the man's idea of "utmost care"?

At last, the physician smoothed the final poultice on Freyrík's leg, and when he withdrew his touch, all the tension flowed from the muscles beneath Ayden's grip.

The physician stood to wash his hands in a nearby basin, saying, "All should be well, Your Highness, may the gods bless you ever strong and wise. You will have new scars, but nothing more."

His assistant started pulling jars from a leather satchel. 'Twas unexpected relief to see them promptly intercepted by two newly-acquired tasters.

"The white powder is for pain," the physician said. "One teaspoon thrice daily will dull the worst without clouding your mind; two teaspoons will see you slumber. The brown powder will smother infection: two teaspoons in water with each meal."

Freyrík nodded, and thanked the man with altogether more grace than Ayden could have mustered.

"Now with your permission, Your Highness, I'd take a short leave to assist my fellow physicians, for we are desperately in need of skilled hands this day."

Freyrík nodded again, and the physician left, taking his assistant with him.

When the tasters finished with the powders, Freyrík wasted no time in reaching for them, but he measured not even a full teaspoon of the anodyne into his watered wine.

"I must keep my wits about me now," he said to Ayden's sidelong glance. "I shall wallow later, I promise."

Ayden smiled softly, ran a hand across Freyrík's hip to his groin. "I would relieve your suffering another way, if Your Highness would permit."

"Stop that," Freyrík said, slapping Ayden's hand away with a grin. "For I fear the sky is falling when I hear the words 'Your Highness' spilling from your lips."

Ayden laughed, pleased to have taken Freyrík's mind from his pain, if only for a moment.

"But," Freyrík added, cupping his good hand over Ayden's and squeezing gently, "I would that your offer still stand when our work here is done."

Ayden leaned in to place a less-than-chaste kiss upon Freyrík's lips and whisper in his ear, "Far be it from me to deny Your Highness anything he desires." He let his tongue trail his words, felt Freyrík shiver as he pulled away.

Freyrík sighed and squeezed Ayden's hand again, this time a little too hard. "You are a cruel, cruel elf, my friend. Now make yourself useful, if you would, and let Lord General Feitr know that I would see him now."

General Feitr listened to Ayden politely, then followed him back to the prince's tent without complaint. Ayden was almost disappointed; he'd been eager to see the prince's order carried out no matter what.

Back in the tent, he discovered that Freyrík had hoisted himself off the bed and into a nearby chair, crack the stubborn man. 'Twas also the only chair, so Ayden plunked down onto the empty bed.

The general clicked a salute, stood at attention. "Your Highness."

"Lord General Feitr," Freyrík said. "'Tis good to see you alive."

"And you, Prince Freyrík," the general replied with a nod of his head, a small non-military smile.

"What news?"

The general had news aplenty; Ayden lost interest and track within moments. The bottom line, which the general seemed determined to overlabor, was that less than six hundred men had died (plus a thousand or so wounded)—not only counting those on the chase, but also the footmen and archers who had manned the cliffs and the nearby villages, and the men who patrolled the area for the odd loose Feral.

They'd done well.

"Have you searched the canyon floor for survivors?" Freyrík was asking.

"Not until the brush wall burns out, Your Highness."

Ayden snorted, and Freyrík must have felt alike, for he said, "Take men down the ladders. Volunteers, if you can."

"Yes, Your Highness."

"I'll go," Ayden chimed in, hopping off the bed.

Two sets of eyes turned to spear him, one angry, one curious. He focused on the curious ones; he liked them better, anyway.

"I'm afraid I'm not fit for such adventures now," Freyrík said.

"Which is why I said *I'd* go, not *we*."

"Why, exactly, does he wish to go?" General Feitr said to the prince.

Ayden caught and held Freyrík's gaze. He debated giving reason the humans could agree upon—the horses would need calming, after all—but nay; he owed Freyrík truth. "Because someone must see to the Ferals. Give them a clean end, if they're but wounded."

After a long moment, Freyrík nodded, despite a muffled noise from the general. Ayden smiled.

Freyrík turned back to the general. His mouth opened, but no words came out. A trill of longing and something else—chagrin, perhaps?—flashed throughout his song. Interesting.

Finally Freyrík cleared his throat and said, carefully, "See what horses you can save from the canyon, will you, Uncle? We'll need all the stock we can get for next year."

Ayden looked at him with narrowed eyes, then caught on: Spyrna. The man was missing his warhorse but uncomfortable to ask for her while humans still lay wounded.

He resolved to find and deliver the black destrier, even if he had to sing her out of the canyon through a wall of flame.

The Lord General had scraped together some thirty men to climb down into the massacre grounds. The stench of blood and burnt flesh and

excrement made Ayden gag, and he quickly unlaced his sleeve, wrapped it round his mouth and nose. The other soldiers wordlessly followed his example, many snatching bandages from the physicians' kits for the task.

The canyon floor was littered with bodies and corpses, Ferals and soldiers and horses all tangled atop one another. He could hear the odd whimper; he could *hear* faint songs of anguish and hate and despair. The distress of stray horses bayed now and then on the air.

He hugged to the wall, picking his way through dead flesh toward a nearby stuttering song: a Feral wolf, whimpering softly, though it bared its teeth with faint purpose as Ayden approached. It was pierced through the chest with half a dozen arrows and a sword wound, lying beside a not-quite-dead human who, by the look of things, had been the one to run it through.

Ayden stepped over the man and crouched down beside the wolf, smoothed his hand across the soft tufts of fur between its ears, and whispered the prayer of passing. Then he unsheathed a dagger and ended its suffering. He did not bother to retrieve the arrows as Lord General Feitr had ordered; let someone else scavenge the dead.

He straightened up from the Feral wolf, only to fall sprawling atop it from a shove to the back.

"What the fuck is wrong with you, *gróm*!"

Ayden stood, wiping blood and grit from his palms, and turned to face his attacker: a tall, lean corporal smeared in blood and soot and looking every bit as tired as Ayden felt. The man's fists were balled, and though 'twas tempting to teach him a lesson, Freyrík had made perfectly clear he needed every able body for the Surge.

Of course, 'twas more or less over now, so perhaps he wouldn't mind . . .

Ayden sighed. Of course he would.

"Are you deaf, *gróm*?" Ha! "I said, what the fuck is wrong with you?"

"Aside from the fact that I'm sharing air with a cracking human, you mean?"

The corporal stepped forward and shifted his weight—he might as well have shouted his intention from the hilltops—then kicked at Ayden's groin. Ayden caught his foot and held it in the crook of his arm, but for Freyrík's sake resisted breaking it or even knocking the fool on his arse.

From the corner of his eye he caught movement: one human, two, three, creeping up round them. Their songs spoke of anticipation, excitement, disgust. Vultures gathering for blood. He hoped General Feitr would stop them before they made him spill it.

"Let go of me, *gróm*!" cried the human whose foot he was clutching.

Ayden bent the man's knee sideways, pressing the limits of its natural motion. The man groaned, eyes dilating with fear.

Ayden bared his teeth. "Not until you speak your piece, human. What is wrong with *you*?"

The human must have realized his place in the order of things, for he stopped struggling and pointed to the unconscious man lying near the now-dead wolf.

"That!" he cried. "You step over our fellow soldiers like so much garbage that you may soothe your darker friends!"

Ayden felt the hairs on his nape stand on end; from behind him came noises of assent, drawing too close.

"I knew not the man still breathed," he lied, releasing the corporal's leg. "And the darkers are dangerous, are they not? Even more so in the rage of pain. Would you prefer I let them live that they might savage you as you pass them by?"

The corporal turned his head and spat—not quite in Ayden's direction, Ayden noticed with some satisfaction.

Ayden began to walk away when another soldier called, "You do not fool us, *gróm!* We saw the darkers refused to harm you even when you made a show of striking them. We know you're in league!"

He took a deep breath, and another, and another. Freyrík had been so pleased with the death count not long ago; it would certainly . . . un-cheer him to add thirty more to the toll.

He went on in search of more wounded Ferals, keeping an eye out for a certain black warhorse.

Freyrík woke from the indulgence of a midday sleep to the sound of Ayden washing and dressing. He caught a brief and glorious glimpse of a damp, naked backside before Ayden pulled his breeches up and asked, without turning round, "How fare you, Freyrík?"

"I fared better a moment ago," he said, eyes still glued to the curve of Ayden's back, the play of muscle in his shoulders as he fastened his breeches, the wild hair, wet from washing, scattered as if by electric charge.

Ayden turned with a grin, came to his side and leaned in for a long, lazy kiss. Freyrík moaned his pleasure, then shifted wrong and moaned his pain instead.

Ayden pulled up sharply. "Did I hurt you?"

"Nay," Freyrík said. "My own foolishness did. How went the search?"

Ayden shrugged, lips pursed; surely the task had been unpleasant for him. "We rescued nineteen wounded," he said. "One of them . . ."

"Yes?" Freyrík prompted when the elf said no more. "One of them what?"

Another shrug, but this time, Freyrík felt fair certain the elf was pursing his lips against a smile. "One of them sends you her regards, though she feared you'd abandoned her in the heat of battle."

*She?* He couldn't mean . . . Could he?

"Spyrna?" he asked, the longing in his voice stark even to his own ears.

And yes, there was the elf's smile, thoroughly unrestrained now as he nodded. "I believe that's ten Surges and counting?"

Freyrík nodded, then bolted upright to seize Ayden in a hug.

Ow.

Ayden pressed him back to the bed with a gentle admonishment. "But enough about horses," he said, "for unlike you, she is well. I should like to remedy that if I could, for it . . . displeases me to see you suffer."

Freyrík held back the urge to laugh. "'Displeases' you? Do not be so passionate, Ayden—you might break a rib."

Ayden laughed for the both of them, smacked Freyrík lightly on the shoulder. But he sobered quickly, intent in his eyes. He pulled a chair to the bed, then sat and put his ear to Freyrík's injured arm.

Ayden's eyes closed and his face took on the slightly strained, deeply studious look he'd worn while Freyrík had played the violin.

"What ar—"

"Shhh!"

Freyrík dropped his voice to a whisper and asked, "Can you heal it?" For he recognized this action, had seen Ella do the same before performing a miracle upon her half-dead brother.

Ayden sat up and shrugged with one shoulder, made a face that seemed to say *Sure, why not?* or perhaps simply *We'll see.*

"I'm afraid I don't possess my sister's talents," he said, "but it cannot hurt to try, can it?"

"I don't know. Can it?"

"Perhaps a little," Ayden admitted. "Shall I?"

Freyrík gestured in welcome, and Ayden placed his hands just above the bulky bandage on Freyrík's arm.

Freyrík felt a spark of heat deep in his muscles and sucked in a breath, perhaps a bit nervous, as the heat grew and grew until it— "*Ow!*"

He jerked his arm away, which burned now as though touched to a live ember.

"Sorry!" Ayden bit his lip and drew his brows in an expression best befitting a scolded child. "As I said, 'tis not my strength." A pause, then, "Did it mend, though? It sounds . . . clearer to me."

Now that the burn had faded, the wound indeed felt better. Not completely whole, but a week's worth of healing at least, done and gone in moments. "Yes," he said, flexing his fingers in demonstration. "Thank you."

Ayden gave the same treatment to his leg, sparked the same burning pain but finished with the same dramatic result. He seemed weary when it was over, sitting hard and heavy in the chair beside the bed and propping his chin on his hand.

"Come," Freyrík said, giving his arm a tug, "Come lie down, and let me thank you proper."

Ayden slid into bed, fitting snug beside Freyrík, and wrapped an arm round his belly. Freyrík wrapped his own arm round Ayden's shoulder and let Ayden pillow his head on his chest. He felt hot lips pressing to his collarbone, his neck; soft hair tickling his chest and cheek. He pressed a kiss to the top of Ayden's messy head, skimmed a hand down the firm planes of his belly and dipped his fingers beneath the waist of Ayden's breeches, but Ayden made no move or sound. The poor thing had worn himself straight to sleep.

But that was all right. Freyrík was content merely to hold him, and to be held, and to watch his lover sleeping in his arms.

# Chapter Twenty

Though eager to return to the comforts of home and those affairs of state that the Surge had so thoroughly interrupted, Freyrík found himself delaying their departure time and again. First he wished to remain until the brush wall had burned down and the horses could be retrieved from the canyon. He wished to see all his men retrieved as well, pressing his commanders until they'd accounted for every last soldier. Then he couldn't possibly depart until he'd said a prayer over the dead and lit the pyres to usher them to the Warrior's Rest; and after such sobering business, he thought it best to stay through a victory feast for the living.

It took nearly three days to manage these things, at which point he felt comfortable returning command to his uncle for what tasks remained. Yet doubt remained, even as the last of their wagons were loaded, even as he mounted his steed to lead his little train back home.

One look at Ayden showed the same reluctance, but why, he could not fathom; Ayden held no attachments to Farr's soldiers or their purpose. Perhaps he feared for Freyrík's health on the long march home. Or perhaps he merely dreaded return the stuffy confines of the castle.

Freyrík swore to himself to do all within his power to make that life less oppressive for Ayden, now that such trust between them had been reached.

The march back to the castle always felt longer to Freyrík than the march out. This one was no different—worse, in fact, than usual—for here they were but a day on the road, and already he'd grown weary of the saddle, anxious for the comforts—and privacy—of a home shared with Ayden.

"You should not ride beside me," Ayden said of a sudden, breaking an hours-long stretch of companionable silence.

Freyrík turned his head and said, rather intelligently, "Huh?"

Ayden's worry-creased features melted into fondness, but 'twas gone in moments, replaced by the furrowed brow. "Your men. They do not trust me."

"I know," Freyrík sighed.

"They do not trust *you*."

He paused a moment, not wishing to admit it, but finally said, "I know. Even this grand victory is tainted by a vocal few who sow seeds of doubt amongst the rest."

Ayden nodded, fell silent, his eyes closing and his elflight flashing brighter. Freyrík wondered what he was focusing upon with such intent. But then Ayden scowled, elflight fading once more, and asked, "What will you do?"

Freyrík shrugged. "You killed more darkers than any, and you saved my life at great risk to your own. If that does not convince them of your lack of complicity with the beasts, nothing will. I'll not punish you for their prejudice and fear."

Ayden nodded, but said, "Ignorance has unseated greater men than you."

"Perhaps, Ayden. Perhaps. But not today."

The afternoon's conversation weighed heavily on Ayden's mind, even as he spent the night with Freyrík in carnal embrace. Perhaps it haunted the prince as well, for their coupling was strangely quiet: muffled sighs and bitten fists, passion murmured against firm flesh, stolen cries of pleasure sealed between their joined mouths.

Yet they set out in the morning riding side by side, for whenever Ayden tried to fall back, Freyrík's glowering displeasure saw him returned as surely as if by collar and leash.

Ayden respected the man's determination, his unbreakable will—a lesser being would surely have pandered to his soldiers' fears—but he worried that the man's pride might spark an uprising. Freyrík would emerge victorious, of course, but Ayden knew how much it would cost the prince to take arms against his own men, and he had no wish to be responsible for such pain.

The least he could do, then, was play his part well: address Freyrík properly, hold his tongue in public, give no challenge to the soldiers.

After all, he need only pretend for a few more days. And at night, in the privacy of their tent, he could shed the false cloak for the naked truth beneath and just *be*.

"I would thank you," Freyrík said as they crested the hill rising up to Vegr City and the outer ring of palace walls came into distant view.

"Whatever for?"

"For taking such care not to provoke the men these last days. I know it could not have been easy."

Ayden shrugged. "'Twas for your protection. You'd have done the same." He paused, corrected himself: "You *have* done the same."

"Nevertheless, I would show you my gratitude this night."

Ayden smiled slyly, leaned in his saddle to bump Freyrík's shoulder. "You show me your gratitude *every* night, and most mornings as well."

"That is not what I meant," Freyrík laughed. "Not that I would complain, mind you, but I thought perhaps you'd wish to see Ella first."

*Gods,* yes. Ayden felt a huge smile break across his face, and despite the promise he'd made to himself, he could not help but lean over Freyrík's saddle and plant a long and zealous kiss upon the man's lips.

They marched through the crowded city streets to great fanfare, peasants throwing flowers and clamoring to gift fruit and wine to the soldiers as they passed. The soldiers had collected an astonishing number of teeth and claws from the Ferals—miniature trophies of their victory for all the land to share—and they tossed them to passers-by or traded them for sweets. Ayden watched, disgusted, as men and children fought for the prizes, but he had to admit to the cleverness of such tools of statesmanship—he was his father's son, after all.

'Twas interesting, though, that what few grown women were out on the streets made no attempts to chase the items the soldiers threw, or to approach them with gifts; that was men's work alone, it seemed.

'Twas also, it seemed, men's work to foist their young daughters upon the soldiers. He cringed at the sight of girl after girl pressed forward toward the train, their virtues extolled by male relatives: their skills as homemakers and potential wives, the dowries they carried, the sons they could birth. The girls held wooden tokens the size of a fist, and every few moments, a soldier would reach out to take one.

Ayden leaned in close to Freyrík and asked, "What are those?"

"Address markers. So the men will know where to locate those women they find pleasing. The soldiers use their battle rewards to buy new wives; there are always a great many marriages after a Surge."

Ayden fought to hide his grimace, but he must have failed, for Freyrík added, "This is our way, Ayden. Do not judge these men so harshly; they wish only for children, and some happiness in their fallow years."

Ayden thought of Ella, wooden tokens in a trembling hand, and said nothing.

Despite the promise of seeing Ella that evening, the sight of the palace walls unsettled Ayden. As they rode under their shadow, he felt the whole great weight of them settling upon his soul.

They arrived just before the afternoon meal, and Freyrík was promptly intercepted by a messenger. He took the carrier scroll aside; even with his sharp sight, Ayden could not read it, but he could well read the expression on Freyrík's face, a mixture of anger and dismay which he quickly smoothed over as he rejoined their party.

"Is the price of cocoa on the rise?" Ayden prompted gently.

That won him a bark of laughter, however hollow, and then Freyrík pressed the letter into his hands.

*Dear Rík,* the letter began, *I am chafing for news from the west. Any villages lost? Enough men left to fight next year? This madness must stop before we're too exhausted ever to raise arms again.*

*Forgive me, I am troubled. I'll pretend that word of your victory and survival is en route already.*

*Grave news, little brother: I cannot come home for the Fest. Much is happening here, and I am needed. I promise when I return we'll drink the Council under the table.*

*Keep them strong for me. Love, Berendil.*

It seemed an ordinary letter to Ayden, and Freyrík refused to explain it, but his internal fretting carried over the songs of all the nearby soldiers.

Freyrík was still distracted, perhaps even distraught, when they reached his rooms. His groom, perhaps sensing the man's unease, welcomed his master's safe return effusively but quickly, then set about unpacking Freyrík's trunks.

Ayden wandered toward the bed, fingering its posts and cushions. Strange . . . was that fondness he was feeling? Nay; 'twas merely his body speaking, imaging how 'twould be to lay with Freyrík amongst such pristine comfort.

Freyrík came up behind him and wrapped arms round his waist, leaning in as if he'd fall without Ayden's support.

Ayden laid both hands atop Freyrík's and turned his head in attempt to meet the man's eyes. "Will you not tell me what disturbs you so?" he asked.

"Berendil has *never* missed Harvest Fest."

Ayden waited for more, but that was all that Freyrík would say. Still he clung to Ayden, so Ayden turned round to embrace him proper. "Would you like me to stay a while?" he asked, for though he missed Ella desperately, another quarter hour would matter little to her, and might matter much to Freyrík.

"Thank you, but I'm fine," Freyrík said with a softness that belied his words. Then he disentangled from Ayden's arms and sent Ayden off to bathe away the stench of the road.

Ayden was standing before Freyrík's mirror, cinching the last lace on a new pair of boots, when Freyrík approached, seeming himself again, and said, "Give Ella my respects, if you would."

Ayden froze, one foot still propped on a stool, and eyed Freyrík suspiciously. "You're not coming with me?"

"Nay. I've much work to attend, especially given my brother's absence. Besides, my court expects a speech from me tonight." He turned to one of his personal guard, standing at attention by the door. "Lieutenant. See Ayden to the north tower. You will treat him with every respect, and await his pleasure to return. Understood?"

The guard saluted sharply and said, "Yes, Your Highness."

Freyrík turned back to Ayden. "I'll be back in about three hours; I'd thank you personally if you've returned by then as well, but I'd certainly understand if you haven't."

Ayden bit his lip, simultaneously wishing to thank Freyrík for the leave and rail against him for falling back so quickly into his old role of master. But he understood the need for it—truly, he did—and he proved it to them both with an unhurried kiss before following the guard to Ella's rooms.

The soldier in him took careful note of every twist and turn: out the door to the right, down the servants' passage to the stairs at the end of the hall, out into a little covered courtyard and then back inside, to the kitchens, never stepping out into public view.

The kitchens were a hive of activity, aproned women and children sweating in the heat of a massive row of brick ovens and open fires, scrubbing the pots and dishes of the court's evening feast, heaping food upon great platters, rolling dough for the morning's bread. Accustomed as he was to the northern climes, the temperature here was a stifling misery, and he felt sorry for the poor creatures—human or no—who were forced to work there. In comparison, his life seemed quite the luxury.

'Twas with great relief the guard led him clear of the heat-choked rooms, passing through a door outside and crossing the bailey northward. At last they reached the turret, and entered through the curtain by an orchard.

His guard conversed briefly with the guard outside Ella's rooms, then grumbled something about waiting for him in the hall. Ella's guard opened her door without a word, and his sister's song washed over him in a rush of familiar comfort long denied, so loving and eager that tears pricked his eyes.

The door had barely closed behind him when he heard Ella squeal, "Ayden!"

She raced through the drawing room and tackled him straight to the floor, where he landed with an *oomph!*, laughter bubbling from his throat as he wrapped his arms round her shoulders and hugged her 'til she squealed again.

"Pleased to see me, little whelp?"

She kissed both his temples, then wiggled from his embrace and stood. "Pleased to see you alive, I suppose." She crossed her arms, the very picture of aloofness, but her façade cracked moments later in a snort of laughter and she raced forward to give him another hug.

Done squeezing the life from him, she stepped back and held him at arm's length, giving him a critical once-over. "You look well, brother."

"And you," he said. He pointed at her dress, all flowing white silk and lace and matching satin slippers. "What's this you're wearing?"

She twirled round once, layered skirts spread in her hands. "Humans make such lovely dresses, don't you think? Kona brings me a new one every time she visits. Come, sit."

She grabbed his hand and tugged him to the settee before he could ask if she meant *the* Kona, the crack-mouthed shrew who'd brought him such grief, and then she trotted into the back room with a quick "Wait here."

He took the opportunity to look round, surprised to see the room nearly as well appointed as the prince's, at least to Ayden's untrained eye: 'twas all plush carpets and carved furniture and gilded trinkets. Even the drab stone walls lay nearly hidden behind rich tapestries, bright silk and wool weavings of woodlands and waterfalls and victories of yore.

Of course, she'd made it very much her own, in a way the prince could not, by bringing the outdoors in. Butterflies flitted round the ceiling, and cats lay sleeping in the narrow sunbeams along the covered floors. Potted plants and flowers graced every flat surface, and creeping ivy wended its way in through the windows. From somewhere he heard crickets chirping, and a squirrel was perched warily atop a curtain rod, watching him on its hind legs.

It made him think of Freyrík, and he shook his head with a chuckle.

Ella returned with a silver tray piled high with fruit and cheese and a flagon of wine.

"So," she said without preamble, handing Ayden a golden goblet, "I hear you're in love with a handsome prince."

Ayden sputtered and nearly dropped his drink. "And where, pray tell, did you hear such nonsense!"

She reached out and rapped her knuckles against his forehead.

*Oh.* And also *ow.*

"We are . . ." He rubbed his forehead, popped a cube of cheese into his mouth, chewed for a long moment, swallowed, and finally settled on, ". . . finding common ground."

"Oh, is that what you call it?" Ella asked, playing at innocence she'd not possessed for at least a century now. "I knew not you'd chosen to follow in our father's diplomatic footsteps."

He felt a blush creeping up his cheeks—he would *not* discuss such intimacies with his *sister*—and blurted, "And what is this you say about Kona?"

Gods, but he was bad at this.

Ella grinned, but indulged him. "Women are treated so poorly here," she said. She must have caught sound of his anger and alarm, for she quickly added, "I don't mean *here* in this house, only ... Aegea in general."

"Oh," Ayden said, thinking back to those girls with the wooden tokens. "Yes."

"Truly, the prince's people have been nothing but kind to me. Kona especially. She visits often, brings me gifts." Ella took a sip of wine, ate a strawberry. "Truth be told, I cannot help but feel pity for her—a woman so vital, blessed with such wit, expected only to keep silent and look pretty on her husband's arm. I think she fancies me so because I am not a 'proper Aegean woman,' as she says: I do not hold my tongue before men that they might speak in my place."

Ayden barked out a laugh. "You do not hold your tongue before *anybody*."

Ella punctuated his statement by pointing said tongue in his direction. "Yes, well," she said once she'd returned it to its proper place. "Even the First Wife of Farr does not have such freedoms. I would that you remember that next time you see her."

"She *belittles* me," Ayden spat.

"Perhaps because you are the only male she can. Or perhaps because you wounded her so when you scorned her affections."

*Affections?* Ayden spluttered, put his goblet down a little harder than necessary. "What would you have me do, then? Bed the creature?"

"Nay, brother, don't be absurd." Ella smiled her soothing smile, laid her hand atop his own. "Just ... think of her as you would me, as a person with feelings and dreams and—at least for now—no way in which to indulge them."

That last bit sobered him quickly; he heard the trill of Ella's sadness at the edge of her words. "You are trapped here while I traipse about playing soldier," he said, but she was shaking her head before he'd finished his sentence.

"Bear no guilt for me, Ayden. 'Tis my fault we're here, no one else's. Besides, I come and go as I please. I must merely take an escort."

*You shouldn't* need *an escort*, he thought. And then, with surprising bitterness, *Nor should I.*

"I do miss home though." She sighed, fiddling with the stem of a strawberry. "I wonder who tends my sheep now."

Ayden knew not what to say to that, so he held his tongue.

"Mother must be terribly worried."

"Ella . . ."

He reached out to hug her, but she nudged him away. "No," she said. "No, it's all right. I'm being silly; you were gone eighteen years on your *Foldfara*; we've been here but two months."

Yes, except on his *Foldfara*, he went where he wished to go, seeing new nations, new faces, new oceans with each passing year, never tarrying long in any one place and *certainly* never against his will.

"Now come," Ella said with forced brightness, taking his hand in both her own. "Tell me all about this handsome prince of yours lest I be forced to hear my gossip from the servants."

They spent the afternoon at talk and watched the sun set. By then, exhaustion weighed Ayden's limbs and forced a yawn from his jaws. With a last hug (and another one), he took his leave, for if his body insisted he sleep somewhere, 'twas better to be pressed against Freyrík's firm chest than sprawled across Ella's settee. Besides, if he stayed with her, wherever would all those cats sleep?

They parted with promises to meet in the bailey come morrow, and he left her rooms in strange spirits; seeing her again had soothed an ache long festered, but it sparked several more in its place. There was too much scorn and hatred in this place. Too many stone walls and not enough sunlight. And *far* too many guards and locked doors and cracking *escorts*.

He followed his escort out to the bailey beneath a stunning night sky, a quarter moon and more stars than even he could name glittering above. He wondered, sometimes, how they might sound if ever he climbed close enough to hear, what music of the heavens had graced the gods' ears. Beauty beyond bearing, he liked to think. Perhaps that's why the gods had left the skies to walk upon worlds so many millennia past.

The kitchens were just as hot and bustling as they had been some hours earlier. Passing through them only served to amplify his mood, for it reminded him that Freyrík had taken pains to hide Ayden's freedom from judging eyes.

Pretending, always more pretending. When, he wondered, would it end?

"We must talk," Ayden announced the moment the doors to Freyrík's drawing room had closed behind him. "For I cannot—" He stopped, taking in the silence and the darkness at last. Freyrík was nowhere in sight: sleeping, most like. Ayden sighed noisily, filled to the brim with righteous anger and no way to disperse it.

Crack it, he was waking the man.

Well, he supposed he could at least do it gently. He tiptoed into the bedroom, stripped off his clothes (Freyrík's groom, appearing as if from nowhere, snatched up each garment from the floor as Ayden dropped it), and slid naked beneath the covers, wrapping himself round Freyrík like a blanket. Freyrík stirred, made a happy little sigh in the back of his throat and burrowed deeper into Ayden's embrace.

"Morning already?" he slurred, pulling Ayden's arm tight round his chest.

"No," Ayden said, and before he could press on, Freyrík mumbled, "Then stop glowing, 'm trying to sleep."

Ayden had to bite his lip against a smile; he was supposed to be angry, not fond, and crack the man for making that so hard. "Nay," he said. "I would you'd wake. We must talk."

Freyrík's song picked up tempo, but he was clearly still more sleepy than worried. "Can't it wait 'til morning?" he asked.

"It can," Ayden said, "if you would have me lie here upset with you all night long."

That got Freyrík's attention: a sharp thread of concern wove through his song as he rolled to face Ayden, rubbed his eyes and asked through a jaw-cracking yawn, "What's wrong?"

Ayden sang the bedside candles alight that he might look Freyrík square in the eye. "You sent me through the kitchens tonight."

Freyrík blinked at him, blinked again. Finally said, "'twas the safest route."

"As may be. But for me or for you?"

Another blink. Then another. Then Freyrík let out an explosive sigh and rolled onto his back. "Ayden," he said, but nothing else followed.

His name—and the tone in which it was spoken—hung there between them, heavy in the silence.

"Do you remember," Ayden said, "on the march, when I held my tongue before your men? When I played at the good little slave that they might still *their* tongues and speak no more ill of you?"

"Of course!" Freyrík rolled to face him again, laid a hand across Ayden's wrist where it lay on the mattress between them. "And did I not show my gratitude?"

"You did. But that is not the point. The point is that I told myself 'twas no concern to act thus, for it was precisely that: an act. And like all acts it had an end: returning to the castle." He paused, let that sink in, then added, "At least I thought it had. Yet here I am again, with armed escort, slinking along the back stairs! I pray you tell me, Freyrík—when does it stop?"

Freyrík lay silent a long moment, though his song fair bellowed his sorrow. At last he said, "I hope you know I do my best, and that your pain is my pain, for I— I care very deeply for you. But I am as new at this as you are, and bound to make mistakes. I beg your patience, Ayden, and in return, I swear to find a way to make you happy."

Now 'twas Ayden's turn to lay silent. Had Freyrík almost said what Ayden thought he'd said? And did it matter? For despite—or perhaps because of—the man's position in his kingdom, Ayden could see no way for them ever to move beyond master and slave outside these rooms. And he knew from weeks past that these rooms, rich and spacious though they were, would fast become a cage of intolerable cruelty if he were forced to remain within them.

Still, he trusted Freyrík . . .

(And when, precisely, had *that* happened?)

"All right," he said, curling an arm and a leg round Freyrík and placing a kiss on his bare chest. He heard the man's relief fluttering in time to his heartbeat, felt Freyrík's pent-up breath puff through his hair and his arm curl tight round his shoulder. "All right."

Because truly, some things in life were worth the wait.

One day passed, then two, then five, and despite Freyrík's promise, life inside these walls went on almost as it always had. Ayden spent the majority of his days trapped in Freyrík's rooms as Freyrík attended to his endless list of tasks: preparation for the Harvest Fest, redistribution of surviving livestock and supplies commandeered for the Surge, compensation for items—and men—that could not be returned, and all the other day-to-day minutiae of running the kingdom. If this was the life of a prince, then Ayden was quite glad to have been born into common stock, for not all the riches in the world could make up for such demands on his person.

In his absence, Freyrík assigned Ayden a guard to see him round the castle as he pleased, but there was only so much he could do within these walls, and he discovered quickly that "as you please" more accurately meant "where nobody can see you."

Without Freyrík, he could travel only through the servants' halls, the back stairs, the empty courtyards. The bailey was almost completely inaccessible to him, for large and maze-like as it was, no ward within it ever stood empty for long, especially with the Fest preparations underway.

This meant that Ella was also almost completely inaccessible to him, for his guard adamantly refused to cross the open bailey to the north tower lest a lord or lady—or even some carpenters building a festival pavilion—might spot Ayden without his master.

Each night, Freyrík would return to his rooms late and overtired, seeking to embrace and caress and not understanding why Ayden would not bed him. Yet it pained Ayden to wound Freyrík's feelings, and he struggled daily with doubts about the source of his grief—their strange situation, or Freyrík himself? So he soothed his rejections as best he could with chaste kisses and hugs, and let Freyrík fall asleep in his arms. He himself would lie awake long into the night, staring at the canopy above and wondering, wondering if things would ever change.

And so it was he found himself wiling away yet another afternoon's seclusion perched on Freyrík's sofa, trying to stop his guard's heart with song. Of course he had no hope of conducting such a complex arrangement; better musicians than he spent millennia perfecting this particular trick, and he'd not yet even managed to single out the heartsong from the rest of the guard's body. Still, he craved the exercise and the challenge, and took no small pleasure from the nervousness that creased the human's forehead every time he looked the man's way.

Lord Lini broke his concentration by bustling through the drawing room doors and announcing, "Your presence is required in the Great Hall."

Ayden turned his stare from the guard to Lord Lini, swiped the sweat from his brow, and said, "Is it, now."

Lord Lini held out a familiar set of shackles. "Kindly put these on."

Ayden ground his teeth together and fought very, very hard not to punch the man as Lord Lini crossed the room to the sofa, two guards at his heels, and gently placed the chains in Ayden's lap. Ayden glared at them for a moment, then stood and let them clank to the floor. "He said I did not need to come today. Can you not see I am otherwise occupied?"

Lord Lini took a long, slow look round the room, rather pointedly eyeing the lack of distraction or task—not even a book or a quill in Ayden's hands. But then his expression softened, and he bent down to pick up the chains and held them out to Ayden again.

"He did not seek to deceive you, Ayden. But men await his audience who seek grievance against you, so you must be there. If 'tis any consolation, His Highness asked that I express his regret for the inconvenience."

Inconvenience? *Inconvenience?* Crack his regret, and crack his *inconvenience.*

The guards behind Lord Lini tensed, hands moving to their sword hilts, but Lord Lini kept his calm and once more proffered the chains.

"I would that you'd not force my hand," he said, and somehow from his lips those words seemed not a threat but a sorrow. "For my master is very fond of you, and 'twould grieve us both to see you come to the slightest harm."

No choice, then. Always no cracking choice.

Ayden clenched his jaw against foolish words and thrust his fisted hands at Lord Lini, forcing himself still as the man chained him.

Yet all the long walk to the Great Hall, a single dark thought preyed upon his mind: *Thus fares the promise of a human.*

# Chapter Twenty-One

hen Freyrík saw the afternoon's docket of men awaiting audience, a great heaviness gathered round his heart. He'd promised to treat Ayden with all the fairness he deserved, and yet once again, circumstance had taken the choice from his hands and made of him a liar.

Men had come to air grievance of the elf, no doubt to argue entitlement for ritual bloodshed, and Freyrík could make no excuse for Ayden's absence that would not sound just that—an excuse. His people already doubted his judgment toward Ayden far too much; he could give them no reason to doubt it further.

A rippling murmur through the crowd marked Ayden's entrance into the Great Hall as he followed Lord Lini in from the dais curtain. Freyrík cringed at the sight of the chains on his wrists and ankles, at the collar round his neck. Lord Lini bowed and handed him Ayden's leash; the elf's scowl burned holes into Freyrík as he wordlessly directed Ayden to kneel beside the throne, sans cushion.

Ayden obeyed in body without pause, but his anger was a palpable thing, seasoned with the poison of betrayal, and it lay bitter upon Freyrík's tongue. Freyrík swallowed against it to no avail, laying a gentle hand upon Ayden's neck and trying with all his might to beg understanding through the touch. With the tiniest of motions, Ayden shrugged him off.

Once Ayden was settled, Lord Lini took his customary place beside the runner to announce each attendant who'd lost loved ones or livelihood in the Akrar attack. Freyrík hadn't realized quite how many there were until they began to step forward and kneel, one by one, eyes locked upon Ayden and burning with hatred.

Twenty-four men were kneeling in orderly rows before him when at last Lord Lini fell silent. And this was just the group from Akrar itself.

Freyrík stood and laid his hand upon the shoulder of the man in the lead—a boy really, likely not old enough to fight. The boy folded beneath the touch, clasped Freyrík's ankles and pressed a kiss to his boot.

"Your Highness," he said, in a voice still pitched with youth. Yet the words that came next from his lips were quite grown. "You honor us with your ear."

Freyrík waved him to his feet. "Rise, and speak your piece."

The boy scrambled to his feet, bowing again as he went. Then he cleared his throat, lifted his chin, and said, "As brother to two victims in the Akrar massacre, I come to claim my right to *Blód Sekt*."

Freyrík drew a long breath, taking in the seriousness of the boy's intent, the loathing that creased his features as he looked upon Ayden. There was no question of this boy's conviction, nor of the others with him—not all children those, but many a hardened man who knew well what the boy demanded. He wondered how he would sway them.

"The elf is not a criminal," Freyrík said, "and should not be punished as one. He killed only in battle. He serves now as a prisoner of war, as has always been the fate of fallen soldiers."

"But he trespassed upon your lands, Sire! There'd have been no battle if he'd not broken the law."

Befang it, the boy had a point. Clever little thing, he was; he left Freyrík groping for another excuse.

"That's as may be. But perhaps we should be glad of it, for he saved my life and the lives of many others this last Surge. Would you still see him punished so, knowing that your prince stands before you today only because the elf fought for me?"

The boy fell to his knees again, bowed his head. "Begging your pardon, Your Highness, for your life is indeed more precious than mine or any others lost that day, but . . ." His voice was shaking. So was the rest of him. He stopped, swallowed, but Freyrík knew perfectly well what he was too afraid to say.

Fortunately for the boy, there existed braver men amongst the group. One rose, stepped forward, dropped back to his knees, and said, "We would, Your Highness. We all would." He paused to make way for a chorus of agreement. "The *gróm* killed both the boy's brothers in that fight, Your Highness. Only fourteen he is, and saddled now with their three wives. The *gróm* also burned down my orchard and home—my livelihood, all gone to ashes!"

Freyrík felt his insides chill as if by sudden frost. "You were compensated for your losses, were you not? And the fallen soldiers honored, their wives and children seen to?"

"Yes, Your Highness, but—"

"And it does not satisfy your honor to see the elf subjugated so, shackled and kneeling at my feet and yours?"

The man hesitated, and now he too began to tremble. Still, like any soldier worth his salt, he held his ground. "'Tis a sure fine start, Your Highness, but—"

Freyrík cut him off, not wishing to hear another word, not in front of all these people who would surely agree.

Yet no matter his own dread, he owed it to these men to let them all speak. He turned with a sigh to the next man in the row and asked, "And you? What is your grievance against the elf?"

"His fire burned the corner of my tool shed, Sire."

Freyrík raised an eyebrow; the man had traveled fifty leagues for *that*? Such did not merit his attention, so he turned to the next man. "And you?"

The man crawled forward to kiss Freyrík's boots. He left a smudge of dirt behind. "The *gróm* spelled my swine, Your Highness: sent them running to four corners and beyond. I spent near half a day rounding them up!"

Freyrík turned sharply and took the throne again, barely refraining from asking, *Are you* quite *serious?* He did not suffer fools or hangers-on in the best of circumstances, which these most assuredly were not.

'Twas with considerable irritation that he turned to the fifth man and asked, "And you? Did he startle your chickens into laying bad eggs?"

Nervous chuckles broke out through the hall, but he knew well the sound of obeisance when he heard it, and it failed utterly to conceal the wary resentment building beneath.

Which was why it seemed such remarkably good timing when a woman shoved through the crowd and tore down the runner, screaming his name.

He stood from the throne as his guards moved to intercept her, holding a warning hand out to Ayden who, even in his anger, was rising to his feet to protect him.

As if he needed protecting from an old woman.

"Prince Freyrík!" the woman shouted above the clamor of the crowd as the guards descended upon her. "No, let me go!" She tugged one arm free, then the other as the first was recaptured, and in between caught Freyrík's eye.

Freyrík stumbled back a step from the venom on her face. Where had he seen her before?

"You promised!" she hissed in a whisper so harsh that it carried down the aisle, over all the anxious voices in the hall. "You lying pool of darker piss, you promised!"

A guard punched her clean across the face and she fell like a rock, one hand pressed to her jaw and the other pointing straight at Freyrík. The crowd cheered.

"Is this how you let my son die?" she screamed. "You sat on your fancy chair while your men did your leading for you? Did you, Prince? *Did you*?"

Another guard drew his foot back to kick her quiet, but Freyrík stayed him with a shaking hand. He remembered this woman now. And he deserved every last poisoned word she jammed down his throat.

But gods, was it ever painful.

His eyes closed against her onslaught, but all he saw behind them was Corporal Ekkja, practically a boy still, the look of terror on his face as the wolves closed in, the sword he could barely hold in mauled hands, the blood—*gods,* the blood!—when he'd fallen dead at last, throat ripped out by a darker's teeth.

". . . did you take him from me!" Mrs. Ekkja was shouting, weeping, and Freyrík walked down the dais stairs, down the runner, his feet moving of their own accord until he crouched where she had fallen, reached out and touched her shoulder. He made no attempt to speak to her; what could he possibly say?

She smacked his hand away and a collective gasp ran through the crowd, murmurs of shock and fear, but Freyrík barely heard them; all his mind was focused upon the fury spewing from Mrs. Ekkja's lips. He touched her again, and this time she sprang to her feet, into his chest, kicking and hitting and screaming and blaming him for taking the last of her babies, for breaking his promise, for stealing her hope, her future, her child's life. He stood still and let her rail, barely feeling her blows over the agony of her truths.

At last she seemed to exhaust herself, and she fell silent and still but for the occasional sniffle. Freyrík enveloped her in an embrace and nuzzled his chin atop her head, tightened his grip when she swooned. He realized how quiet the whole of the Great Hall had become, how surreal it seemed to be surrounded by hundreds of people and hear naught but the sad, spent mourning of a mother with no more children.

At last a guard dared to break the silence, stepping forward and laying a blessedly gentle hand upon the woman's trembling shoulders. "To the dungeon, Your Highness?" he asked.

The question was so preposterous that Freyrík could hardly parse it. This woman had spoken truth, not treason.

Freyrík shook his head. "Fetch a carriage. See her home. Take a cook and a maid, for she cannot care for herself while she mourns so."

"If I may, Sire—"

"Do as I say!" he roared, startling even himself with his vehemence. He breathed in deeply through his nose, held it, let it out slowly, preparing himself to lay yet more poison upon his tongue: "This poor woman is clearly ill," he said to no one and everyone at once. "For her grief has left her vulnerable to darker spirits. House Farr does not condemn its ill; we nurse them to health."

The crowd erupted with applause, even as Mrs. Ekkja glared daggers at him. He turned away, pacing toward the throne to hide his face from the hall, for now along with the shame of failure heating his cheeks, he felt also the shame of cruel deceit.

When at last he turned back round, feeling as if he could speak again without crumbling to pieces, he waved over his secretary and said, "Lord Lini, see to my commands. And get these people out of here."

His secretary nodded, stepped forward and gently pried the weeping woman from a guard's arms. Thus freed, Freyrík fled the hall, stopping only long enough to take a hold of Ayden's leash on his way out.

Ayden had heard much in his years on earth, and little held the power to surprise him anymore. Yet here he was, voluntarily shackled, sitting in a human's bed with his arms wrapped round said human as if round a child, petting and shushing and consoling the man as he cried into Ayden's shoulder.

Even more surprising was how ready he'd been to cut the man asunder with hateful words, and how quickly and easily he'd laid that hurt aside to tend to Freyrík's. 'Twas impossible to rail against the man when he was wounded so, and suddenly so easy to remember that Freyrík's burdens were a great deal heavier than Ayden's own. 'Twas a stark reminder of why Ayden admired and liked—

No, that's not the truth of it anymore, is it . . .

—admired and *loved* the man, to see him mourn so over a boy he hardly even knew, to see the love he held for his people and his willingness, always, to sacrifice the whole of himself for their future.

So Ayden held Freyrík, stroked his hair and said, "'twas not your fault," and, "You did all you could," and, "You did what you had to do."

The gods knew they were both all too familiar with the truth of that.

Freyrík locked himself in his study for the remainder of the day, still clearly so upset that Ayden forgot to be angry with him until he came to bed. Even then he had no stomach for it, for Freyrík slipped beneath the covers without a word and pressed up tight, clutching at him like a child to a doll. Ayden pressed his lips to Freyrík's forehead and left them there a long moment, tasting the cool skin beneath him.

"'Tis not healthy to brood so," he said, as gently as he knew how.

But Freyrík merely shrugged and murmured, "Good night, Ayden."

Ayden thought to let it drop then, but something else had been bothering him the whole of the evening, and he suspected 'twas bothering Freyrík too.

"Freyrík?" he said, and when Freyrík hummed back at him, "What's the *Blód Sekt*?"

He felt Freyrík's answering sigh deep in his bones.

"Barbarism," Freyrík spat into his chest.

When the man said nothing more, Ayden prompted, "Care to be more specific?"

Another long sigh, and then, "No."

"It frightened you. I heard it." He laid his hand atop Freyrík's heart and added, "I hear it still. What would those men see done to me that scares you so?"

Freyrík sighed a third time and rolled onto his back, pillowing his head on Ayden's outstretched arm. "They would see you flogged near to death, your blood spilled by your victims' kin, and then leave you on the posts to die."

Gods, barbaric indeed! How long, he wondered, would it take to succumb to such wounds? How many days would he hang there, begging gods he no longer even believed in to end his agony?

"Do not judge us," Freyrík said into the silence, but his tone belied his protest. "You must understand: Only the Crown may punish a man for his crimes, but 'twas not always so. Once the people of Farr were many tribes, each meting out justice as they saw fit. When they united beneath Farr's banner, the *Blód Sekt* was made law to give families of victims their due."

Ayden supposed that made sense enough, despite the horror of the act. 'Twas not as if his own people could claim innocence in all manner of violence, after all. "The victims' kin take turns at the whip, then?"

Freyrík shook his head. "Women are not permitted to wield weapons with purpose. A soldier is chosen for the task. The kin participate only after; they shed blood to the dirt from the criminal's wounds. When he dies, they take the soil and spread it upon their crops. 'Tis blood for blood, and life from death." A pause, and then, "All very *poetic*, you understand."

Poetic indeed.

"You'd see the ritual ended, then?"

"Of course I would! There is enough gruesome death in this world already. What business have we adding to it?"

Ayden nodded, though Freyrík was still staring at the canopy and could not see it. But he didn't need to, Ayden thought; they understood each other well enough without.

Ayden had hoped that their talk last night, dark though it became, would release Freyrík from his gloomy isolation. Alas, Freyrík spoke little during breakfast, and threw himself into work promptly after.

Ayden followed him into the study and read on the settee, walking over occasionally to kiss the back of Freyrík's bent head or rub his shoulders. Freyrík returned the gestures with wan smiles and affectionate—if absentminded—pats of the hand, but otherwise ignored Ayden and everyone else who came and went through his doors.

Some hours after the midday meal, Ayden must have inflicted one supportive touch too many, for Freyrík turned to him with a strained smile and said, "It seems a lovely afternoon outside. Would it not be more pleasant to spend it with your sister than cooped up in here with me?"

Ayden took advantage of Freyrík at last unburying his head from his scrolls by kissing him on the lips. "I couldn't possibly enjoy myself knowing that you wither away in your study," he said.

Freyrík gave him a little nudge and a littler smile, though at least 'twas genuine this time. "Go," he said. "I promise I shall cease my wallowing soon enough; I'll even take my evening meal in the Great Hall. I just . . . The crown weighs heavy on my head of late, and I must allow myself to feel weary on occasion lest I go mad."

His lips curled up at the corners again, and he grasped Ayden's hands in each of his own. "But I thank you for your care. Truly. It means much to me." He flashed another almost-smile, bigger than the last. "Even if I am casting you out."

He tugged Ayden down by the hands to claim another kiss, and then sent him on his way.

Ayden's guard fell in step before him and, as per the prince's suggestion, led him through the bailey to the north tower, despite the lords and ladies milling about to spot them.

Sometime between the outraged stares from a trio of gentlemen chatting by a fountain and Ella greeting him as usual with a tackle-hug that nearly knocked him to the floor, he decided that maybe, just this once, he could be forgiving of Freyrík's recent offenses against his dignity.

He respected Freyrík's desire for privacy for as long as he could bear to, visiting at length with Ella, who seemed sweetly unbothered that he spent most of said visit speaking of Freyrík. The gods knew he could sympathize with the need to be alone, but after a pleasant evening meal in Ella's rooms, he decided 'twas long past time to make sure that Freyrík had kept his promise of supping in the Great Hall.

He kissed his sister farewell and left her apartment, crossing the bailey with his guard in tow and entering the castle keep through the kitchens. Halfway along the servants' passage behind the Great Hall, he slowed at the sounds of shouting from up the stairs. 'Twas a voice he well remembered, and he winced at its shrillness, pity welling inside him for whomever was enduring it up close.

". . . many times do I have to explain? Gah, stupid girl!"

"Begging your pardon, Milady!" he heard someone say. "I'll not do it again, I swear!"

Ayden paused with his foot on the bottom stair. Perhaps he should just wait; Kona would move on when she was done berating whatever poor servant-girl had offended her, and he could sneak away without being seen.

*Or...* he could do as Ella had implored last week, offer Kona a smile and a kind word, and perhaps reach a kind of peace, if not actual pleasure, in each other's company.

Crack it all, he'd not be reduced to cowardice by some pitiable harpy. He took one fortifying breath, then another... then another, then wrapped his hand round the banister and pulled himself up the stairs.

He was halfway down the hall toward Freyrík's apartment before he caught up with Kona. When he'd closed the distance between them, he stopped and said, "Good evening, Milady," to her back.

She turned round, midway through an acknowledging nod before she realized who he was. Then her eyes narrowed, and her lips pulled back in a disgusted sneer.

He tried on a smile and a bow, hoping to diffuse the tension—*gods, what I do for Ella!*—and she smiled back. But 'twas cold, predatory, completely devoid of pleasantry. Ayden didn't like the look of it at all.

Then Kona screamed.

"Chain it!" she shouted as two guards came barreling down the hall and knocked him to the floor. Then every last guard in the castle—or so it felt, at least—piled atop them.

"Oh, gods protect us!" he heard Kona wail as the men wrenched his arms behind his back and fastened shackles round his ankles and wrists. Through the heap of guards he caught sight of his own escort, standing off to one side, looking torn but doing nothing.

"He'll kill us all!"

Someone kicked him in the stomach, someone else in the thigh, Kona screeching all the while in the background; and crack it all but he was growing awfully weary of being beaten every cracking time he dared to walk ten paces from Freyrík's side.

He heard pounding footsteps, a whole group of running men, and then, "What is it, Milady? What's happened?"

'Twas Lord Lini, though Ayden could barely see him beyond the mass of human flesh pressing him to the floor. His hopes rose nonetheless, for if Lord Lini were here, then Freyrík might not be far behind.

"That, that . . . *creature!*" she cried, pointing his way. "Did you know he was prowling the halls without an e— Your Highness," she said suddenly, bowing deep.

The guards stood away from him and saluted, and Ayden took the opportunity to peel himself off the floor.

"Why do you molest my property?"

Though Freyrík had spoken to no one in particular, it was of course Kona who stepped forward to answer.

"Your *property,*" she spat, "was sneaking through the servants' passage without an escort!"

What? Had she failed to notice the guard trailing no more than two paces behind him? Or had she *chosen* not to?

"He was no doubt prying into the affairs of the kingdom," she continued. "The gods only know what secrets he might have uncovered if I'd not been there to stop him."

"Indeed," Freyrík said. "Thank the gods you were here to safeguard our kitchen gossip from elvenkind."

She narrowed her eyes and spat, "You do not take me seriously."

Freyrík dismissed the guards with a nod, saying nothing until they'd all melted back from whence they'd come. When the hall had cleared, he stepped forward and said simply, "Kona . . ."

To Ayden's ears the word was part exasperation, part warning, and part desire to put things to rights between them. Kona must have heard the same, for she dared to push far beyond her station.

"You do not take *him* seriously," she said, thrusting a finger at him. "You are deceived into confiding with the enemy by a pretty face and fair form!"

"Enough, woman—"

"He undoes you, brother. Your own soldiers lose faith in their prince, and your guards speak ill of you behind your back. How long do you think it will be before all the people of Farr know you for an elf-lover? Before word spreads to the rest of the Empire that you have been addled, spelled by the enemy?"

The lack of surprise on the prince's face was telling, but all he said was, "'Tis not so simple, sister."

"Isn't it?" she demanded. "I would remind you, brother, that you're home from the Surge a week, and yet still you are here with your little pet while your *king* needs you by his side!"

Ayden fully expected Freyrík to strike her—was shocked, in fact, that he'd let her prattle on for as long as she had. But when he separated the shrill notes of their anger from their argument's song, he heard the reason for it: Freyrík's melody had gone deeply contemplative, tinged with chords of resignation and flitting trills of disgust.

He wouldn't.

. . . Would he?

Freyrík nodded, head down, and said softly, "You're right, Kona; my men talk."

Kona's eyes widened, the surprise on her face outdone only by her vindication. She was breathing very fast, her chest heaving in her low-cut bodice.

"But they are fools," Freyrík continued, "and talk of that which they do not know. *You* talk of that which you do not know."

"Your Highness—"

Freyrík silenced her with a raised hand. "Nevertheless, they *talk*. No doubt you encourage them. But perhaps . . ." He glanced over to Ayden, eyes brimming with reluctance and sorrow, shame and apology. "But perhaps I encourage them as well. Ayden . . ."

"Freyrík," Ayden replied, terse and challenging. He was fair certain he did not wish to hear the prince's next words, for already he could sense Freyrík's desperate longing to be pardoned.

Freyrík wouldn't even look at him when he said, "Go to my rooms. Stay to the servants' halls. Wait for me."

Ayden glared at him, at her, at him again, daring Freyrík to look him in the eye, to face him like the warrior he claimed to be as he cast his own lover aside. But he did not; he stared resolutely at his feet instead, his face and even his song held carefully in check.

Ayden lifted his head high, brushing Freyrík's side as he hobbled toward their—toward *Freyrík's*—rooms.

"*Coward*," he whispered as he passed the man by.

Freyrík hadn't even possessed the nerve to unshackle him before casting him away.

# Chapter Twenty-Two

For the first time in nearly two months, Ayden gave serious thought to escape. He knew where Ella was now, after all, and how to get to her. He knew she could come and go as she pleased, as long as she took an escort. He knew that he could overpower that escort, even with his hands and feet chained, and steal the man's weapons. He knew his way round the bailey, knew where the horses were kept . . .

Of course, he also knew that Freyrík's men would hunt them down like animals. Perhaps slaughter them like animals too, when they found them, for find them they would; he could not cross fifty-odd leagues while hiding from an entire nation.

He stomped down the servants' hall to Freyrík's rooms, ignoring the looks from the guards when they saw him bound.

"The prince ordered me to wait here for him," he forced himself to say. The words scraped like glass in his throat, and he could not meet the men's eyes as they opened the doors to let him pass.

Gods, what a *fool* he'd been! Letting himself believe, even for a moment, that they might be equals, that Freyrík might see him as more than just some pet, some bed slave to be pampered and used as fit his whims. He'd believed because he'd *wanted* to believe, because the thought of years immeasurable spent as a prisoner, ogled and chained and raped while his sister rotted in some castle hold, was entirely beyond bearing. So too was the thought of whoring himself by choice, even for his sister's safety. So he'd invented . . . what? Affection? Desire? . . . Love?

It served him right for ever letting his guard down in the first place, for believing in some silly fantasy. He'd told himself he'd just been taking advantage of the human's weakness, plying the man for a chance to escape, but it seemed 'twas actually the other way round. Oh, he'd pretended at first, of course, but at the end . . . 'twas only the human pretending at the end, and Ayden deserved every last drop of hurt that now filled his heart.

He kicked the door as it closed behind him. Or tried to, anyway; the chain caught and his ankle jerked so hard against the cuff that he nearly toppled. He shouted wordlessly, then slumped down where he stood and tipped his head back, letting it bang against the drawing room doors. His eyes felt hot and his throat swollen, and he sniffed once, twice, then banged his head against the doors again and clenched his jaw against another shout.

He smelled smoke and turned his eyes toward it; gods, he'd set the cracking rug on fire.

For a moment he thought to let it burn, but he was stuck in here, after all, and he took no particular joy in destroying things to which Freyrík seemed scant attached. He put it out with a sigh, squeezed his prickling eyes closed (smoke-stung, nothing more). When his eyes cleared, he wiggled his cuffed wrists round his arse and legs 'til his hands were chained in front of him, then pushed himself from the floor.

Gods, he was tired. All he wanted to do was sleep.

'Twas with no small trepidation that Freyrík approached his rooms that night, despite the happy news he carried. He'd seen the betrayal on Ayden's face, and perhaps 'twas true he was a coward, for he could hardly bear to endure such a look again, no matter how short-lived it would be. Well, he was near certain 'twould be; Ayden's stubbornness might yet come between them.

His heart broke afresh when he crossed into his bedroom and found Ayden nesting, as he had in their first days together: all the sheets and blankets stripped from the bed and piled in the far corner of the room. Ayden lay curled in the middle of it all, unmoving, eyes closed, but no doubt he'd woken the moment he'd heard Freyrík's footsteps in the drawing room.

Freyrík dismissed his attendants and guards and approached Ayden slowly, the key to his shackles gripped between thumb and forefinger.

"Do not touch me," Ayden said flatly as Freyrík crouched down before him. He'd not moved an inch, not even opened his eyes. Did he mean to shut Freyrík out so completely?

"I thought . . ." Freyrík realized he wasn't sure how to finish that sentence. Or rather, there were so many things he wished to say that he hardly knew where to begin.

And here he was, choosing cowardice again, picking the one ending with no meaning: "I thought I might unchain you."

"Why?" Ayden said, and this time his eyes opened, but only to glare. "What difference would it make?"

Once more, Freyrík knew not where to begin. This time he said nothing. He reached out for Ayden's cuffed hands instead, but Ayden recoiled from his touch, shoved off from the wall and to his feet.

"Look at you," Ayden said, lips twitching in a snarl. "So quick to take away what liberties you have given! Do not look so wounded when I do the same in return."

"But you are mistaken!" Freyrík cried. "Nothing has changed between you and I, I swear it, and if you'd just let me exp—!"

"You can't possibly be that stupid!" Ayden thrust his shackled hands out between them. "Or did you fail to notice somehow that I am your slave again?"

"Please, Ayden, I beg you listen!" Freyrík crouched down to place the key upon the carpet, took three large steps back and watched, hopeful, as Ayden pounced upon it. "In the corridor tonight with Lady Kona, I realized—"

"I was there, remember?" Ayden spat, thrusting the key into the lock on his left wrist, then the right, then throwing the shackles to the carpet hard enough to dent the wood beneath. "I know what you *realized*."

Freyrík grimaced. 'Twas clear Ayden would not let him speak without first draining his vitriol.

"Tell me, then," he said softly, "what thoughts were in my head."

"Cowardice! I'd dared to think you a better man than the rest, that you were like *my* people, but no . . . you think only as the rest of your petty, dying race." Ayden's lip curled in disgust and he leaned forward to spit on the rug. "Kona made you fear for all you might lose: your power, your crown, your respect amongst creatures who deserve no such consideration—and you succumbed to your fears. You cast me aside to save your own skin."

Gods, but those words held such power to hurt! Yet this was not about him, and he had no right to lament his own suffering in the face of that which he'd caused. He squared his shoulders and said, "You have the right of one thing—"

Ayden turned the lock on his collar and ripped it away, hurling it at Freyrík's feet.

"—but not the one you think. Kona made me face the truth that our lives in this place are as oil and water." No, that wasn't quite right . . . "Oil and fire, more like. They may seem together a grand passion, but the truth is that one by necessity consumes the other, and they create of each a danger where none existed before."

He paused, but Ayden made neither reply nor reaction, merely bent down to unshackle his ankles. Was he even listening?

It mattered not. Freyrík had no doubt his next words would pierce even shielded ears:

"I did not wish to believe this, but I realized in that corridor tonight that nothing we do can change the truth: You cannot stay here; I cannot leave. So you must go alone."

Ayden's head jerked up, jaw slack, eyes wide as wagon wheels.

"What?" he said at last, hesitantly, as if afraid of the answer he might receive.

Freyrík dared a single step forward, then another when Ayden made no protest, closing half the distance between them. He locked eyes with the elf and said, "I am setting you free."

"What—"

Freyrík's eyes were drawn to Ayden's throat as he swallowed, swallowed again, clearly in the thrall of shock, his mind unable to leap so quickly from the deepest depths of betrayal to . . . well, to wherever it was this news had brought him.

Freyrík tried not to think about the too-near future when he'd not be able to see such things again, when Ayden would no longer be standing before him.

"What manner of teasing is this?" Ayden whispered.

"'Tis no tease." Freyrík felt a wistful smile tugging at his lips; this might be the last time they'd ever exchange those words, but they worked as he'd intended them to. Ayden's face slackened with . . . relief? Euphoria?

No, 'twas belief, Freyrík decided. Ayden believed him.

"Come," he said. He held his arms open, and Ayden, still enrapt, stepped into them without hesitation, pressed his chest to Freyrík's chest and laid his chin upon Freyrík's shoulder.

"You would do this for me," he asked-but-not-asked.

"Yes. You and Ella both, just as soon as I determine how to manage it safely." Freyrík paused, smiled in the face of Ayden's continuing shock. "I'd rather hoped you could assist me with that part. Though I could not resist the opportunity that Kona shoved in my path, to give air of surrender and avoid further suspicion."

Ayden shifted his head upon Freyrík's shoulder, his breath ghosting along Freyrík's neck.

"Do you forgive me now?" Freyrík asked.

He felt Ayden's head rubbing back and forth against his shoulder, a wordless nod. The elf's arms tightened round his waist.

"You are pleased?" he asked.

Another nod, more vigorous than the last. It wounded him, this reply, for a part of him had dreamed, *hoped*, that Ayden would wish to stay here, no matter the cost. Yet he knew 'twas unfair, knew how much joy this news would have brought him if their roles were reversed.

All he could do now was make the best of what little time remained between them; he cupped Ayden's neck with one hand, stroked his back with the other, inhaled deep of his woodland scent and pressed closer, chest to chest and cheek to cheek, feeling the heat of Ayden's body soak through to his very bones.

They embraced for moments beyond counting, clinging to each other in the middle of his bedroom. Ayden persisted in his silence, but Freyrík imagined he could hear all the wondrous things that Ayden took so for granted: happiness, gratitude, trust—the music of love. He wondered if Ayden was hearing now his sadness, longing, regret—the music of sacrifice.

At last he could stand the silence no longer. He stepped out of the embrace, gripped Ayden by the shoulders and stared him in the eye. "Say something?" he begged.

Ayden seized him by the head and kissed him.

But no, "kissed" wasn't right, didn't do *justice* to Ayden's fervor. The elf was clutching him by the ears, mashing together lips and teeth and tongue, breathing hard through his nose as he backed Freyrík toward the bed in a long and stumbling rush.

There they collapsed, tearing at each other's clothes, popping buttons and laces and ties with abandon until at last he felt skin pressed to skin, hard muscle beneath his fingers. It took the edge off their hunger, and they banked the fires of their passion as one, teasing it red hot with roaming hands and panting breaths, leisurely kisses and soft moans. For once there was no contest, no competition to best the other or to make one cry the other's name first.

They arranged themselves side by side upon the bed, face to face in each other's arms, and their next kiss was savory, slow, a mapping of features with gentle lips and fingertips, a sweet exchange of air. Ayden's hand slid down Freyrík's ribs, the curve of his arse, up and over his hip, brushed oh-so-teasingly along the tip of his member and then continued on down his thigh, the back of his knee, his calf.

Freyrík knew Ayden's intent, even if Ayden did not—his own hands, in fact, were doing the same: Drawing out the moments, painting portraits, crafting memories of each other to cling to on that day when such treasures were forever gone from their grasps.

# Chapter Twenty-Three

Ayden dreamed of home. Yet when he woke in Freyrík's arms this morn, the ache in his chest was not for Vaenn. The day had begun to dawn, but Freyrík slept on, and Ayden took advantage by studying those rugged features, that incongruently soft-as-silk hair. And his music, of course: the notes that sang of love and duty and strength, even in sleep; the gifted musician's heart that beat at the center of it all. He would *miss* this man.

He wondered if, a hundred years from now, Freyrík's memory would evoke such fondness and pain as his father's did.

Yet Freyrík was right; Ayden could not remain here. Not even this ... whatever it was they had . . . could rise above the shadow Castle Farr cast upon them. And even if he could find it bearable, there was Ella to consider. Poor Ella, practically a girl still ... Her days should be filled with family and friends, meaningful work, music and courtship and love. He owed it to her to see her home at any cost.

Yet he'd never have believed that the cost could be so high.

He bit his lips, freed his hand from where it lay wedged between their chests and brushed his fingertips across Freyrík's eyebrow, cheek, traced the shell of his ear, the line of his jaw. Freyrík moaned ever-so-softly, still half asleep, and when Ayden's fingers found their way to Freyrík's lips, Freyrík pursed them into a kiss. Then his lips curled into a smile, and blue eyes blinked open just inches from Ayden's own.

"Peace," Ayden whispered. "Be still."

He wanted to remember this.

Freyrík obeyed, smiling softly, and Ayden propped his head on one hand and stared and stared, tracing the hard planes of Freyrík's body with his fingertips. Freyrík's hands took to wandering as well, and though the touches did excite, they failed to incite; both of them, it seemed, were too preoccupied with the future to throw themselves into the now.

Inevitably Ayden's mind turned to said future, and to the puzzle of seeing it done. He understood that Freyrík could not simply let them go, so how then to free them of this place?

As if hearing his thoughts—and true, perhaps, that they were playing out clear upon his face for all who knew to read them—Freyrík captured Ayden's wandering hand in his own and said, "We should talk."

"I know," Ayden said.

But he said no more.

Freyrík tossed back the bedcovers and sat up, still holding Ayden's hand. "Lord Vitr," he called.

His groom materialized by the bedside as if from nowhere, bowed deep, and said, "A good morning to you, Your Highness. Shall I start your bath?"

Freyrík shook his head. "Bring me my blue robe, and one for Ayden, and then kindly see the rooms cleared. We should like breakfast in bed this morn, but I would that you'd knock before you enter."

If that didn't sound like a long morning of indulgent coupling, Ayden didn't know what did. For a moment, he was almost sorry 'twas but a ruse.

The groom bowed again. "As you wish, Your Highness. Will that be all?"

Freyrík nodded, and his groom scurried off to fetch their robes. When Ayden threw Freyrík a questioning glance, Freyrík said simply, "'Tis hard to strategize while you're naked, for my mind inevitably wanders along with my eyes."

Ayden chuckled. He could sympathize.

The groom brought over their robes, then shooed everyone into the hall and shut the doors behind him.

"I have been thinking," Ayden said as he stood to slip the green silk over his shoulders. "Can you not simply pretend to sell us?"

"And then what?" Freyrík asked, shrugging into his own robe.

Ayden climbed back into bed and propped his back against the headboard. "We would sneak away. Or perhaps travel with someone you trust to see us to the border."

Freyrík tucked back in beside him, draped a hand on Ayden's thigh and shook his head. "I thought the same at first. But Berendil would wish to see the funds. You alone are worth more coin than I am capable of raising discreetly, and of course there is Ella to consider."

"Then sell us for real. We could escape in transit."

Freyrík shook his head again. "An elf cannot be sold without first being bound by the Aegis. And even if we were to do so . . . No doubt word of my fondness for you has reached even the Aegis's ears. If you escaped on the way to High Court, 'twould seem deeply suspicious. And not even a prince or king is above an accusation of treason." His hand moved from Ayden's thigh to Ayden's palm, and he turned to face Ayden, gripping tight. "But I promise you, if there is no other way . . ."

"No," Ayden said. "There is always another way." He'd not be able to live with himself, forever wondering if Freyrík had died to set him free.

"Perhaps it can be made to work in any case: If you can bear it, we'll wait a month or two, and use that time to cultivate the appearance of bad blood between us."

Ayden nodded. 'Twould be no hardship, none at all, to have a little more time with the man. Plus, "The more cruelty you show me now, the less suspicion there will be later of your complicity in our escape."

"Precisely."

"That leaves only the question of the escape itself. Who would take us?"

"Lord Lini," came Freyrík's decisive reply. "His family has served mine for thirteen generations. He tutored me as a child. I trust him with my life and with yours."

Ayden nodded. If Freyrík himself could not take them—and of course he could not—then Lord Lini stood alone on the list of humans he could bear to trust in stead.

"He cannot be seen near the border with you, of course. He would drive you east by wagon for a time; under nightfall you'd switch to horseback and don the uniform of a scout. The three of you would ride into darker territory and head north toward Vaenn that way. You'd not be able to set foot on human lands again once you crossed the fissure; 'twould be too dangerous."

Ayden nodded. "'Tis all right; we do not fear the Ferals as you do." And then, lest Freyrík think that an insult, he added, "For we have no call to. But Lord Lini . . . he would do that for us?"

"He would do it for me."

"And how would he explain having lost us?"

Despite the seriousness of their talk, a mischievous smile quirked upon Freyrík's lips. "Perhaps 'twould be best if you beat him senseless before you—"

A knock on the drawing room door startled them both.

"Yes, yes, come in," Freyrík called. 'Twas, as expected, two servants from the kitchens with trays. Less expected was the presence of Freyrík's secretary behind them, as if conjured by their words.

"Your Highness," Lord Lini said. "Forgive the intrusion, but I'd heard you'd woken and I must speak with you at once—"

Freyrík waved him silent with one hand, reached for the tray a servant had settled across his lap with the other. "'Tis all right, Lord Lini. As it happens, we were just speaking of you. Please, sit."

Lord Lini snatched up a chair and carried it over to the bedside, then forced himself into it. But his song was fretful, frenetic, and Ayden suspected he'd rather be pacing. His eyes darted between Freyrík and the servants as if willing them to hurry up and leave; yet the man's nervous gaze did not, Ayden noticed, land upon him at all.

The moment the rooms were clear again, Lord Lini said, "Your Highness, those men seeking audience from Akrar . . ."

Freyrík's gaze snapped sharply to Lord Lini, and the poor man nearly fidgeted clear off his chair. "What of them?"

"They are not alone."

"Your point, Lord Lini?"

He sat up a little straighter, cleared his throat. "I have received, as of this morning, forty-seven letters with over six hundred signatures from friends and family of the dead, all demanding their right to *Blód Sekt*. Nearly two thousand subjects have gathered already for Harvest Fest, and they speak of little else."

Freyrík pushed the tray off his lap and rose to his feet, pacing a single line down the bed and back.

"I do not answer to the people," he said, but the words sounded hollow, even to Ayden's physical ears. Of course he answered to the people, and never had Ayden known or heard of a regent more aware of that fact, or more respectful of it.

Lord Lini seemed to think the same, for he bowed his head and said, "I never thought to hear myself say this, but I fear an uprising if you do not give them what they want."

Ayden tensed against the headboard, even as Freyrík vehemently shook his head. "Nay, Lord Lini, you exaggerate."

"Wouldst that it were so. By week's end, half the kingdom will be camped inside our outer wall. With respect, Your Highness, hope is rare enough already; how will your soldiers feel if they must loose arrows upon their women and children, fathers and brothers to protect the creature who slaughtered their fellows-in-arms?"

He turned guilty eyes to Ayden and added quickly, "No offense intended. You know where I stand on this matter personally."

Ayden nodded; he did know, and he bore no ill will against the messenger of this news. Not that it came as any surprise to him. The question, then, was what to do about it. How could Freyrík rule without his people's respect? And what would his brother do when at last he returned from High Court? Would he see Freyrík's denial as treason against the Empire?

Freyrík was pacing again. "I'll not let it happen," he said, pointing an accusing finger at Lord Lini, as if this were all somehow his fault. "I'll *not.*"

Lord Lini held his ground. "The ritual need not end in death, Your Highness; the people know the value of the elf. Killing him would be foolish, even they can see that. But they'll not be satisfied without—"

"I said *no!*" Freyrík roared, so loud that both Ayden and Lord Lini flinched away, so loud they'd likely heard him all the way in the kitchens. "No! 'Tis not my duty or Ayden's to satisfy the bloodlust of fools!"

Freyrík tore his hands through his hair and then tossed them, disgusted, to his sides. This time when he turned to pace, he went all the way into the drawing room. Something crashed. Then another something. Lord Lini looked to Ayden, brown eyes wide and worrying, mouth agape but lost for words. From the drawing room came a third crash, and Lord Lini rose to his feet, but Ayden shook his head, reached for his arm and pulled him back into the chair. This was his fault. He would be the one to face Freyrík.

But before he could even rise, the man came storming back into the bedroom. He threw another accusing finger at Lord Lini and snapped, "Get out."

Lord Lini rushed to his feet, but Freyrík waved him back down. He pinched the bridge of his nose and shook his head in his hand. "No, I'm sorry," he said, "I did not mean to shout."

His secretary sat heavily, and Ayden heard him gathering courage for one last attempt to convince Freyrík to save himself from the mob, from an uprising, from accusations of treason, from the gods even knew what else this might cost him.

Ayden decided to save the man the trouble.

He swallowed hard, looked Freyrík in the eye, and said, "I'll do it."

"No." Freyrík gripped Ayden hard by the shoulders and pushed him back onto the bed. He wanted to shake the elf until his teeth rattled from his skull. "No, I won't allow it!"

Ayden peeled Freyrík's hands from his shoulders and held them with tenderness, even as he tried to glare Freyrík down. "You do not get to make that decision," he said.

Of course I do, I'm the befanged Crown Prince of Farr!

But before Freyrík could utter those words, the elf added, "You spent the whole morn scheming to sacrifice for me. How can you deny me the same?"

Freyrík tore his hands from Ayden's and shouted, "Because it's *not* the same!"

"That's right," Ayden replied, so calm that Freyrík wanted to shake him all over again. The elf rose to his feet, stepped close enough that Freyrík thought he might kiss him. "It's *not* the same. *You* spoke of risking your name, your crown, your very life. *I* speak of nothing but a moment's pain."

"A *moment's* pain? Have you ever *been* flogged?"

The muscles in Ayden's jaw twitched, and when he sat down on the bed again without replying, Freyrík dared to hope he'd won.

But then Ayden nodded and said, nearly too soft to hear, "Yes, actually."

Truly? Ayden had no scars, Freyrík was sure of it—he'd seen every inch of the elf. Whatever Ayden thought to call a flogging couldn't possibly have been serious. And yet . . . this elf was a hardened soldier, had suffered pains before Freyrík's very eyes that would have broken a lesser man. Surely the tremor in his reply held import.

Freyrík stepped forward, knee to knee, and looked down upon the elf's untidy hair. "And?"

"And *I lived*," Ayden said, grinding out the words as if a millstone crushed his tongue.

In the silence that followed, Freyrík guessed, "You wished you hadn't."

Ayden tilted his head up, green eyes meeting his in challenge. But then the elf shrugged, ducked his head again. Freyrík thought he saw Ayden's cheeks color before they were hidden from view. "For a day or two, perhaps. But the humans held me only three days, and my rescuers healed me, and it was over."

Well, Freyrík supposed that Ella could heal him too after the—

*No.* "I will *not* permit this."

"This ritual of yours will be not even three hours, and it may determine the whole of your future! How can you lift suspicion if you will not let it happen?"

Befang it all, but he had a point. A very, very sharp point.

And clearly Ayden knew it, for he gave a curt nod and said, "But Ella must be sent away as soon as possible. Certainly before the ritual. I'll not let her see it. I do not even wish her to know of it. Besides, if I were to—" He stopped, and his bottom lip caught between his teeth, slid slowly free. "I must know she is safe, no matter what happens to me."

Freyrík meant to say no again, *no* to all this foolishness, this barbarism, yet he found himself nodding his head, speaking words that lay unwelcome upon his tongue. "If she leaves," he said, "who will heal you this time?"

Ayden schooled his features, but not quite fast enough; Freyrík saw well the fear that flashed across his face. "Elves heal quickly," he said, though 'twas cruel irony how sick he sounded as he said it. Then he looked up at Freyrík and added quite pointedly, "Decapitated princes do not."

Freyrík paced a single tight circle, then dropped down on the bed beside Ayden, cradling his head in his hands. He could hardly believe he was going to allow this. How could he possibly allow this? Besides . . .

"We are left with the same trouble," he mumbled into his fingers, "of how to see Ella safely away on such short notice."

He felt Ayden lean into his side, warm and solid and so frighteningly comforting, even now. "Claim you've sold her as punishment to me. Word of her may not yet have reached your brother or the Aegis, and even most of your subjects do not seem to realize she exists."

Freyrík shook his head; if only 'twere so easy. "'Tis the same problem as claiming to sell you. My brother would know of her eventually, even if he does not now. He would ask after the coin she fetched. What would I tell him?"

Lord Lini cleared his throat, and Freyrík startled at the sound. The man was sitting but two paces away; how had he forgotten he was there? "If I may, Your Highness?"

"Please."

"Claim she died of wretchedness," Lord Lini said. "Have not many elven slaves been known to will themselves into such release from servitude?"

"Yes . . . " Freyrík felt his despair lift ever so slightly. "Yes, mayhap 'twould be a better lie than the first. But what of the body?" Befang it, could *nothing* be simple? "What if they wish to see the body?"

For a moment, the silence of thought prevailed, but then Ayden's brows rose and he said, "Immolation. Claim she set herself alight with magic. 'Tis how you humans bury your dead in any case, so it may not be so hard to believe."

"Yes," Freyrík said again, the first familiar stirrings of anticipation fluttering in his chest. "Yes, that could work. We'll gather up bones from a pyre to present as evidence. And you must act as if grieved, and angry; rage against those who took her from you." Just as he had for real at the beginning. It should not be difficult for him to pretend.

A sister thought pierced his mind like a sword through flesh. "We can do the same for you," he said to Ayden, and when the elf shook his head, "No, listen: surely you'd despair more over your sister's death than she would over the *Blód Sekt*. It makes perfect sense."

Yet still the elf was shaking his head. "You know I put little faith in the wits of your race, and gods know I'd avoid such torment if I could, yet even *I* do not believe that your people would swallow such a story. Ella they do not know, and would not care if she died. But me? They would have your blood in my stead."

Befang it all; did the elf *never* grow weary of being right?

Yet even knowing this, 'twas with deep reluctance that Freyrík nodded his agreement. He turned eyes to Lord Lini and said, "I would entrust you with this task, old friend. You will see her safely home."

Lord Lini dipped his head. "Of course, Your Highness. I shall keep your secret to the grave and beyond, even on pain of torture."

Freyrík stood, clapped him on the shoulder. "I know. And you have my sincerest love and gratitude. But listen: Before you take her home, you must arrange for the *Blód Sekt*. If it truly is the tale on every tongue, then let us start the Fest with the ritual. But 'twill be *symbolic*, do you understand?"

Lord Lini nodded, but he spoke to the contrary even so. "He must endure at least one lash for each surviving next of kin or we'll lack the opportunity to read all their names."

Damn this befanged, barbaric tradition! "Fine," Freyrík growled. "One—*one* lash apiece." Except . . . "Wait, how many is that?"

Lord Lini had the answer in his head; of course he did. Yet 'twas with stone-faced hesitation that he muttered, "Two hundred and three."

By the gods, so *many*? Freyrík nearly missed Ayden's breath of shock over the noise of his own.

When he turned round, Ayden was pale—well, paler than usual—eyes wide and lips parted slightly. He looked desperate to take back his offer, and Freyrík meant to give him the chance.

"Ayden—"

"No." The elf shook his head, adamant despite his obvious dread. "I am doing this."

Well, damn him too for not backing out while he still could.

Freyrík turned back to Lord Lini; he couldn't bring himself to lay eyes upon Ayden again, not yet, not with thoughts of martyrdom racing through his head. "All right," he said, barely audible, the words sticking to his tongue like molasses. "See it done. But bring me the soldiers who might wield the whip. I would choose the man, and I would have words with him."

Lord Lini stood, bowed quickly, then did something so unexpected that Freyrík hardly knew what to make of it: he pulled Freyrík into a hug.

"All will be well, Rík," Lini said into his ear, and only then did Freyrík's mind catch up to the fact that it would be polite to hug the man back. He wrapped his arms round his secretary, his friend, and said simply, "I hope you're right."

They broke apart a moment later, and Lord Lini's old mask fell back into place. "I can arrange to transport Ella tomorrow morning," he said, "and I'll have soldiers sent to speak with you about the *Blód Sekt* by evening meal. If there is anything else you need . . .?"

Freyrík nodded. "Return after noon to speak with Ayden about Ella's transport. We've been forming a plan, but he knows the borderlands better than I, so 'tis best to work out the details with him. In the meanwhile, see my schedule cleared, and make my apologies to whomever I shall miss. I think . . ." He looked to Ayden, silent and resolute, and then back to Lord Lini. "I think we should like to be alone now."

Lord Lini bowed once more and hastened away.

When he was gone, Freyrík rushed to Ayden's side, fell to his knees at the elf's feet and clutched at both his hands. He burrowed his head into Ayden's lap and said, with much vehemence but no venom, "Damn you for a fool."

Ayden tugged a hand free and stroked it through his hair. "Come," he said. "Breakfast is getting cold."

# *Chapter Twenty~Four*

They passed the day in a tense and sullen silence. Freyrík paced, and worked (and broke four quills in rapid succession), slammed a lot of doors and drawers, and pressed up to Ayden in between it all, clinging as if to life.

Ayden could hardly be blamed, then, for fair pouncing upon Lord Lini when the man returned to plan Ella's escape. Yet once the task was done and the human gone, the rooms fell as solemn and quiet as they'd been before. 'Twas as if someone were already dead.

Not that he planned to die, of course. But 'twould be all the same to Freyrík, he supposed, once he was gone. Surely they'd never see each other again, though he at least would have Ella's comfort in that loss. Who would comfort Freyrík?

Freyrík pulled him from dark musings with a kiss to the top of the head, then sat down on the sofa beside him and propped his elbows on his knees.

"Are you scared?" Freyrík asked, staring out as if at nothing. 'Twas easier, perhaps, than looking at Ayden.

"Of course."

Freyrík's head snapped round and his eyes locked with Ayden's, brimming with the same surprise Ayden heard in his song. He thought it not for his fear, but for his honesty; had the prince hoped that Ayden would lie to him?

Nay, they were beyond that now, and these words, once prompted, demanded hearing:

"I fear for Ella's safe passage home," Ayden said. "I fear for pain I cannot bear. And I fear . . ." He bit his lip, gripped Freyrík's knee and squeezed hard. "I fear I shall never see you again."

Freyrík nodded his understanding, and they both went back to staring at the drawing room wall. "You, uh . . ." From the corner of his eye, Ayden saw Freyrík lick his lips, felt him pat the hand still resting on his knee. "You should see Ella now. But speak softly, for the walls have ears."

"Will you not come to say goodbye?"

Freyrík shook his head, and low notes of sadness scratched across Ayden's inner ear. "I do not think it wise."

Ayden nodded; there was truth to that on many levels.

"But I pray you bid her farewell and safe journey for me. Tell her . . . tell her that she has been a dear and true friend. And be certain that she understands the route to the tunnel."

Ayden gave Freyrík's knee another squeeze, turned to kiss him on the cheek and pressed his lips there a long moment, relishing in the scratch of stubbled skin. "I will," he said softly.

"And remind her to rage against the *Blód Sekt*; the guards must hear her," Freyrík added, though they'd been over this a hundred times already. Ayden didn't mind; he understood Freyrík's fear.

"I know," he murmured against Freyrík's cheek.

"And the cats . . ." He was truly grasping at straws, Ayden thought, to worry over Ella's furry companions. "Be sure they're gone before the fire."

He placed a kiss against Freyrík's jaw and said, "Peace, Freyrík. 'Tis under control."

Freyrík tipped his head, as if chasing Ayden's lips as they pulled away. "I must chain you now," he said, his head still tilted sideways.

"I know. It's all right."

"Fight the guards as much as you dare; I have given them leave to use small force."

"A wise choice."

Freyrík lifted his head, but still he did not face Ayden. Ayden understood why when Freyrík said, in the same soft monotone as the rest, "I love you."

Ayden squeezed Freyrík's knee one last time, then stood to fetch his chains.

Freyrík shut himself in his study and paced. 'Twas already well and truly dark outside; what was taking Ayden so long?

*He is saying goodbye, you fool. Be patient.*

Yet patience was far beyond reach. He'd not felt this nervous since his very first command of a Surge campaign. How long could Lord Lini tarry at the stables, pretending to wait for a High Court dispatch, before someone grew suspicious?

Freyrík left the study mere minutes after he'd entered it and paced over to a bedroom window. If he squinted, he could see the lantern lighting the stables across the bailey. Nobody moved over the grounds. The evening meal was long done; the court was sleeping.

He pried himself from the window, pasted on an appearance of calm, and invited his groom to a game of chess. 'Twould help to pass the time.

He was well on his way to losing when four guards shoved Ayden through the drawing room doors. Freyrík stood, turned round to face them. Ayden's nose was bleeding, his lip split. He looked positively murderous.

"What is this?" Freyrík demanded. "What happened?"

A sergeant stepped forward, dragging Ayden along with an iron grip on his bicep, and saluted sharply. "He didn't want to leave the female, Your Highness," the guard said. "She was screaming something fierce; heard her straight through the doors. Finally had to go in and shut her up."

Freyrík grimaced, praying the dimness of the candlelight would hide it, or at least that the guards would mistake it for disgust. He forced his voice into disinterested calm and asked, "Did you harm her?"

"Nay, Sire. But this one—" the sergeant gave Ayden a hard shake, forced him the ground with a vicious kick behind the knees, "—fought like a darker."

Freyrík glared daggers at Ayden, and Ayden glared back. *Well done*, he thought, certain that Ayden could hear it, or at least the nub of it. The elf had played his part better than Freyrík could ever have hoped.

He turned his attention back to the guards and said, "Thank you Sergeant, you did well. Dismissed."

The guards saluted again and backed out of the room, closing the doors behind them. That left just Ayden, still on his knees at Freyrík's feet; his groom; and a handful of servants. "All of you," he said, "dismissed." Then to his groom, "You may go to your rooms. I'll not have need of you 'til morrow."

The instant they were gone, Freyrík seized Ayden's shoulders, pulled him onto the sofa, and asked, "Is it done?"

Ayden nodded, held his hands out to be unchained when Freyrík took the key from his pocket.

"What did you tell her?"

"Only to trust me, and that I would follow as soon as I am able without raising talk of treason. She knows it will take time to erase the memory of the favor you've shown me."

"And Kona made no mention to her of the *Blód Sekt*?"

"I think not," Ayden said, rubbing his wrists, "for she surely would have fought me if she knew."

"And the guards did not question the package?"

"They thought it was a gift from you. They did not touch it. But enough questions; I must know she'll be safe. Is Lord Lini in place?"

Freyrík stood up, offered his hand to Ayden. "He's at the stables with two horses at the ready. Come, we'll watch from the bedroom."

Ayden offered a small smile as Freyrík pulled him to his feet, then hissed when it reopened his split lip. Freyrík cupped his cheek, brushed a thumb across the cut, wiping the blood away.

"Are you certain you're well?" he said quietly. "You look as if you set about your distraction with far too much enthusiasm."

"I'm fine." Ayden captured Freyrík's hand in his own and pulled it from his face, pulled Freyrík toward the bedroom. "I was rather busy singing the key bent; I had no time to defend myself. 'Twill all be healed by morn, though."

"Did you manage? Are you sure they could not lock her door?"

"*Yes,* Mother," Ayden said, and risked reopening his split lip once more.

Freyrík nodded, and they moved to the casement overlooking the bailey. He did not need Ayden's ears to sense the tension crackling round them.

"The stables are there," he said, pointing for Ayden. "Lord Lini should be there by now."

"I have eyes, human," the elf growled at his side.

Which was hardly fair, for night had fallen over the bailey, and the buildings were hard to discern.

They stood there together, watching, waiting. Naked in their apprehension. Ayden leaned heavily upon him after a time, clearly in more pain than he wished to admit; Freyrík wrapped his arm round the elf's shoulder and tucked him against his side.

"And you're quite certain she can spell the guards to sleep, even through the door?" Freyrík asked.

Ayden nodded against his chest. "The door is only wood, not stone. Besides, she's a much more gifted musician than I, even without proper training. She's probably already hiding in the tool shed."

Another moment went by.

"What if she couldn't set her rooms on fire," Freyrík said, gripping the window sill. "Perhaps the fire died, and she had to sneak back and was caught—"

Alarm bells disproved him with a teeth-rattling clangor.

"She did it," Ayden whispered, still tucked against him, staring out into the night.

Shouts rang down the hall, across the bailey: for water, buckets, men. A light flashed thrice from the stables, innocent enough to unknowing eyes. But somewhere in the chaos, Freyrík knew, Ella was running there now, disguised in the cloak and helmet that Ayden had brought her. The guards at the gates wouldn't dare to question Lord Lini or his shrouded companion. They would be in the clear soon.

Now remained only the last stage of the plan.

Freyrík cupped Ayden's head in his hands, placed a gentle kiss upon the blackening eye the elf had earned for his part in the escape. "They will be here soon," he said. "Are you ready?"

Ayden nodded. "Tears will not be hard to conjure."

And no wonder, Freyrík reflected—the gods knew Ayden had more than enough pain, past and future, to draw upon for inspiration.

They waited long and anxious minutes as his men fought the fire in the north tower. When at last a group came to inform him, 'twas led by Kona, who didn't even knock before barging in and flinging herself into Freyrík's arms. Not that he'd had no warning; her wails of grief could surely be heard the next kingdom over.

"She's *dead!*" Kona cried into his chest, and Ayden, playing his part to perfection, snapped round in a panic and said, "Who's dead?"

Freyrík echoed the question just as his guards came rushing in behind Commander Hákon. Kona's grief rendered her speechless, but Lord Hákon stepped forward to answer.

"The female elf, Sire."

"*What?*" he and Ayden demanded as one.

Freyrík freed an arm from Kona's shoulders to slap Ayden across the mouth, barked a sharp, "Silence, elf!" and turned back to Lord Hákon. "Speak, Commander. Tell me exactly what happened."

"There was a fire, Your Highness. After the male left her, my men heard her weeping; shortly thereafter, they smelled smoke. When they opened the door . . ." He paused, grimaced. "It seems she lit herself aflame with magic, Sire. There was nothing left of her bedchamber but ashes and bone."

Kona let loose a mighty sob. Freyrík held her tighter, stroked her hair. Her pain was upsetting, even to him, even now. He saw Ayden collapse to his knees, face pale as death, but he ignored him, thanking the gods 'twas just a show.

"Her grief at news of the *Blód Sekt* must have been terrible," Freyrík murmured. "But to take her own life . . ."

"No . . ." Ayden whispered from the floor, shaking his head.

"And so gruesomely at that, Sire," Lord Hákon added.

"*No.*" Ayden's elflight flared, and all eyes turned upon him as he shook with feigned shock, his whispered denials rising in force and volume until he was screaming, "*NO, NO, NO, NO, NO!*"

Then his elflight flashed so bright that even Kona, face buried in Freyrík's chest, threw her hands up to cover her eyes, and as Ayden's screams transformed into a wordless roar of agony and grief, the very floor beneath them began to shake. "*MURDERERS!*" he wailed. "YOU KILLED HER! YOU *KILLED HER!*"

A heartbeat later he was on his feet, launching straight at Kona and Freyrík, and Captain Hákon rushed in to shield them with his body, even as the guards gathered their wits and struck Ayden down in a flurry of pikes and fists and feet.

Ayden went down hard, not struggling after the first few blows—as if succumbing to his grief rather than the attack—his cries of pain quickly devolving into whimpers and then sobs.

"Enough!" Freyrík shouted. The guards froze mid-strike, backed away, leaving Ayden curled in a tight, trembling huddle on the floor, his ragged tears cutting through the sudden silence. "'Tis bad enough we've lost one prize tonight; I'll not lose the other. Besides, he must stand for the *Blód Sekt.*"

Freyrík pried Kona from his arms, stepped forward, and nudged Ayden onto his back with his foot, jaw clenched against his rising gorge. Ayden flopped bonelessly, still sobbing, his arms curled round his head.

"He merely grieves," Freyrík said, "and rightfully so. He'll cause me no more trouble, isn't that right, elf?"

When Ayden made no reply, Freyrík gritted his teeth and kicked him in the side. He'd not struck very hard, but he must have hit something very painful, for Ayden cried out and curled round it, and Freyrík doubted the reaction fake. "I *said*, isn't that right, elf?"

Ayden sniffled, hiccupped, sniffled again, and at last stemmed his tears enough to stutter, "Y—y—yes, Your Hi—Highness."

Freyrík nodded and turned back to Kona, who stood forlornly, hugging herself tight with one hand and wiping at tears with the palm of the other. He opened his arms to her again, but she merely glared at him and said, "*You* caused this, Freyrík. This is *your* fault."

He let his arms fall to his sides and shook his head. "Your grief seizes your tongue, Lady Kona. I understand that. But *do not* forget yourself again."

Her glare faded, and she nodded short and fast, lower lip trembling under threat of fresh tears.

Good enough. He turned back to Lord Hákon and said, "Lord Commander, please escort the First Wife to her rooms, or to the temple if she wishes to pray. See to it her ladies attend her well in her time of grief."

"Of course, Sire."

"Is the fire out?"

"Yes, Sire. Damage was minimal; near every hand on the grounds set to containing it."

And likely the rest to gaping at it—just as they'd planned.

"Well done, Lord Commander. Dismissed."

More salutes all round, and then the Lord Commander left, taking his guards with him. Freyrík had no doubt that four or five would remain in the hall lest Ayden make more trouble, but that was fine; they'd not overhear a word through his thick wooden doors.

Once again, Freyrík found himself rushing to Ayden the moment those doors closed, much more worried this time than the last. They'd beaten him hard enough to make Freyrík wonder if his tears were still but an act.

"How bad is it?" he asked, kneeling down beside him where he lay, still curled up tight, on the drawing room floor.

"Nothing broken, I don't think."

Not particularly encouraged by that, Freyrík touched a hand to Ayden's shoulder, meaning to see for himself.

Ayden flinched and scrunched his eyes closed. "Gods," he groaned, flopping onto his stomach and dragging himself to his hands and knees. He groaned again, pressed one hand to his stomach and nearly fell flat on his face. Freyrík rushed in to support him, settling on the floor with his back to the sofa and pulling Ayden to sit between his legs.

Ayden leaned back with a grunt and let his head roll against Freyrík's shoulder. "I think," he said, swallowing hard, "that pretending to attack you was not the wisest thing I have ever done."

Freyrík barked a startled laugh and pressed a kiss to a spot on Ayden's head that seemed unharmed. "Mayhap not. But 'twas surely convincing. My heart ached watching you weep, even knowing 'twas pretend."

"Perhaps I should change vocations," Ayden panted, rearranged himself a little in Freyrík's arms. "I hear acting is much less painful than soldiering, by and large."

Once again, against all circumstance, Freyrík found himself laughing. "Clearly you have never been jeered off a stage."

"And you have?" Ayden asked, incredulity coloring his tone.

"Of course not. I am the Crown Prince of Farr; who would dare?"

"Boooooooh," Ayden whispered, and Freyrík laughed yet again. "Now get me off this cracking floor and medicate me into blackness, if you please. I would that I'd not feel again 'til morn."

Freyrík nodded; that was one command he could happily obey.

# Chapter Twenty-Five

Freyrík lay awake all the night, watching Ayden twist in his drugged sleep and wishing that a darker might eat the sun and stop it from rising.

But of course 'twas not to be. The elf woke well before dawn, anyway, clearly anxious and in pain. How he'd risen up through the physician's elixir, Freyrík couldn't figure, though 'twas true he'd been the first by far to shake the effects of the assassins' drug, and he certainly ate as if his body's furnace burned thrice the fuel of a human's.

Freyrík lit the candle on his bedside table and asked, "Shall I summon the physician?"

Ayden eyed him through the dimness, bleary and hostile in his long silence, and finally said, "I'm fine."

Freyrík had to admit that answer pained him. Had they not yet moved beyond lies? Did they not confide in one another now?

But he knew not how to ask those questions without upsetting Ayden further. He had no experience with such complexities between lovers.

Instead he hazarded a touch, inching close and sliding his hand across Ayden's hip. "I would make you feel better if you'd let me," he said, fingers stroking a gentle invitation through Ayden's silk nightclothes.

Ayden nudged his hand away and rolled over to face the opposite curtain.

"Ayden?"

No reply.

"I beg you speak your troubles! Let me help you."

Still no reply. He thought to confess his love again, but could not bear to hear it go unanswered a second time. Besides, he was fair certain that such would be no balm to Ayden's pain ... If anything, it might cause all the more.

Befang it all, they were supposed to be *happy* now.

Freyrík sighed, pressed a kiss to his fingertips and brushed them across Ayden's cheek. "She is safe, I promise you," he whispered.

Ayden said nothing, but the tension in the line of his back told Freyrík he'd hit the mark. He rubbed at one bunched shoulder, the back of Ayden's neck, then patted his arm and said, "Go back to sleep, Ayden. I am here if you need me."

*Or even*, he thought, *if you do not.*

Three days hence, Ayden yet skulked in silence about Freyrík's rooms. He knew 'twas not fair to Freyrík, but he was unaccustomed to sharing his fears, to facing his pain by someone's side. Perhaps he'd forgotten how.

'Twas a truth more pleasant, at least, than admitting he was a coward.

Oh, he would face the *Blód Sekt* tomorrow without pause. He would not struggle or beg, despite his fear. But matters of the flesh were naught compared to matters of the heart, and therein lay his failure.

He'd learned these past three days, spent testing the thought of a world without Ella, just how weak he truly was. 'Twas the pain of his father's death all over again, for all that she likely lived. And soon he would have to face the reality, not the thought, of losing Freyrík forever . . . He would *not* suffer this a third time.

And Freyrík . . . poor, sweet Freyrík. Busy as he was now with the Harvest Fest tomorrow and some fifteen thousand subjects camped inside his outer wall, he yet made time to fret over Ayden, to eat with him, to speak with him—one-sided though those conversations had been— and to hug and hold him when Ayden allowed it.

Such moments were a balm to Ayden's heart, and surely as soothing to Freyrík. 'Twas selfish of him, to hold back like he was doing. After all, 'twas not he alone who faced the loss of a loved one.

But he had enough to worry about, walking willingly into such torture as he was while Ella's fate remained a mystery. He could not worry about Freyrík too.

He yawned, stalked into the drawing room and sprawled across the sofa, plucking a book at random from the stack Freyrík's groom kept fresh for him on the tea table. *History of the Aegean Empire through 600 AE.* Sure, why not. 'Twas better than sleeping. Better than dreaming of Ella recaptured, ravished, killed before she could make it home.

He was halfway through the book when Freyrík returned from wherever he'd spent his day.

"Ayden!" Freyrík shouted as he bustled into the room, pausing only to kick the doors shut.

Ayden spotted a little tin carrier tube in Freyrík's fist, and he put his book down, heart tripping in his chest. He ruthlessly sang it calm. The news could be bad, after all.

He swallowed hard and took the tube from Freyrík's outstretched hand.

"Did you open it?" he asked. 'Twould be easier to hear the news from Freyrík than to force his fingers to unroll the little scroll, his eyes to read its secrets.

But Freyrík shook his head. "Nay. 'Tis not mine to read."

Ayden took a quick, sharp breath that seemed to stab at his throat. The tube shook in his hand.

Freyrík's hand covered his, stilling its tremors. "But I could, if you wish it."

Ayden bit his lip, shook his head, and set his trembling fingers to opening the tube.

There were no words on the paper inside. Just a simple ink sketch of their mother's home, where Ella had lived since they'd come to Vaenn three centuries past, rendered with all the talent that mother and daughter shared.

The drawing blurred through a film of tears, and he swallowed hard against the burn in his throat, clutching the paper to his chest.

She was safe. Fallen gods be praised, she was *safe*.

"Well?" Freyrík asked, clearly hesitant to intrude upon the moment.

Ayden swallowed again but could not dislodge the happiness swelling in his chest, so he settled for nodding yes, *yes*, held the paper up to Freyrík but then stood and threw himself into the man's arms instead. He hugged him so hard that Freyrík stumbled back a step, then he grabbed Freyrík's head in both hands and kissed him square on the lips, pouring every last drop of his love and relief and gratitude into the gesture.

Startled at first, Freyrík froze, but then his hands came up round Ayden's shoulders and he kissed back just as fervently, laughing into Ayden's mouth and saying, "She's home? She's home!" Then they were both laughing, hugging, kissing, and Ayden knew he could spend forever like this and be happy—

Until he remembered that he couldn't. Humans didn't have forever. And even if they did, 'twould not be possible with *this* human.

He pulled away and wiped at his mouth with the back of his hand.

Freyrík was still gripping him by the shoulders, not pulling him close but not letting him go, either. "What? What's wrong?"

Ayden knew not how to answer him, just shrugged beneath Freyrík's powerful hands and shook his head.

But Freyrík seemed to understand: "Oh," he said, and, "It's all right," he said. His hands still rested on Ayden's shoulders.

"I, uh . . ." Gods, Ayden was tired. When had last he slept for more than an hour or two, before the worry and the night terrors ripped him awake? "I think I'll go to bed now," he said.

He didn't know whether to dread or pray that Freyrík would follow.

Ayden dreamed of home.

'Twas different this time though, for Ella was there, happy and safe in her freedom. And then so was he, both of them together, swimming in the dammed up pond behind Vaenn's gristmill.

Ella's laughter bubbled up fresh as air from the water below.

"It is good to have you home," she said when she broke the surface, splashing him as she always did when he treaded nearby.

"It is good to *be* home," he replied. No more locked doors, no more guards, no more begging permission for the simplest things. Just familiar faces, familiar places, familiar things. And freedom. Blessed freedom. He rolled onto his back, closed his eyes and floated beneath the shining sun, sighing his contentment.

"What will you do now?" Ella asked.

Ayden shrugged. He hadn't really thought about it. "Go back to patrols, I suppose."

"But everything's changed now, hasn't it."

"Yes," he said, "I suppose it has."

He heard Ella splash nearby, cutting a flip through the water. "I'm sorry I got you into this," she said.

And before he could even think how to answer that, his mouth replied for him: "I'm not."

'Twas true, he realized, now that Ella was safe. He'd suffered, yes, but look what it had brought him. Look what he'd found.

And then lost.

"Stop it," Ella chided, splashing him again. He splashed her back without opening his eyes, but as always, she'd made him smile.

Something brushed across his calf, then another something, than dozens of them, and he jerked up in a hurry, opening his eyes and ears to a school of sunfish and Ella's summoning song. One nipped at him, so he swam away. They followed.

Ella giggled.

"Why you little . . ." he growled, swimming now straight for her, the fish fast on his heels, Ella fleeing with a scream of glee but unable to escape his longer reach and stronger stroke.

He grabbed onto her ankle, smiling wickedly, dragged her back and submerged her for a second. She came up sputtering and laughing, climbed right up on his shoulders and sank him in return. The fish were everywhere now, drawn by their playful happiness, rainbow blurs beneath the water.

He'd played like this with Freyrík, in a gristmill pond outside of Tveir, surrounded by sunfish then too.

Gods, he missed him so much it hurt.

He broke the surface of water and sleep simultaneously and sat up gasping, a smile dying on his lips and the afterimage of sunfish bright against the darkness.

The castle. Freyrík's room.

Freyrík.

He ran a hand through his hair, half expecting to find it wet. The joy had been so real.

So had the pain.

And it would be, he realized, no matter what he did now. In a month's time, a year's, ten years', a hundred, he'd be wishing Freyrík there, thinking back and remembering. The question was, would he remember with pleasure or with regret?

'Twas true that Freyrík didn't have forever, but he—they—did have now. And crack it, he'd be a fool—had *been* a fool—not to make the most of it while he still could.

"Freyrík," he whispered, lying back down and rolling to face the man. "Freyrík."

Freyrík made no reply but a sleepy little snort.

"Freyrík," he said a little louder, tapping him gently on the arm splayed atop the covers. Freyrík mumbled and tucked his arm beneath the sheets.

Crack it, he'd just have to play dirty.

He tucked his own hand under the sheets, then his head, felt round for the waist of Freyrík's nightclothes and reached inside. He found what he was looking for, and had it in his mouth a moment later.

That certainly seemed to do the trick.

Freyrík moaned, and his hands fumbled round, finding Ayden's head and clutching there as Ayden licked and sucked him to attention. One hand left his head and the covers were tossed away, releasing a wave of trapped heat.

"Ayden," Freyrík panted. "Wait."

Ayden paused, looked up in the darkness with Freyrík's cock still firmly between his lips, then sang the candles on both bedside tables alight. The light flickered through the gauzy curtains and revealed a slack mouth and furrowed brow to match the hum of confusion weaving round Freyrík's head.

Freyrík sat up, propped his back against the headboard; his cock slid from Ayden's mouth.

"Are you all right?" Freyrík asked.

"Yes." Ayden nodded, nodded again, closed his teeth round the crest of Freyrík's hipbone and bit down gently. "Better than all right. You?"

Freyrík shrugged, smiled philosophically. "I can certainly think of worse ways to be woken."

Ayden kissed his navel, but Freyrík's hand touched to his head again, stilling him.

"But are you . . . I mean . . ."

Freyrík's hand stroked through Ayden's hair, down the line of his jaw. Ayden's skin fair vibrated beneath the touch; he closed his eyes and leaned into it, humming his pleasure.

Freyrík cupped his chin and lifted his head, and as much as Ayden didn't want to let the man's worry intrude, he opened his eyes to Freyrík's fixed blue gaze.

"You don't have to do this," Freyrík said.

Ayden nodded, his chin still cradled in Freyrík's slack fingers. "I know."

Freyrík's thumb brushed across his lips, as if it couldn't help itself. Ayden grinned and sucked it into his mouth. Rough and salty and *gods*, he'd missed this, this partaking of Freyrík with all of his senses.

"It's just that I thought you didn't want to—"

Ayden bit his thumb. "Freyrík?" he mumbled round the digit.

"Hmm?"

"Shut up."

For a moment, Freyrík stared, dumbstruck. But then a slow smile spread across his lips, and he ducked his head and said, "Yes, Your Highness."

Next Ayden knew, strong hands hooked under his armpits and tugged him up, pulling him to Freyrík's lips.

Freyrík's mouth was moist and eager, and Ayden hummed against it, hungry to taste and be tasted, to feel the rasp of Freyrík's stubble against his chin.

Freyrík broke for air, and thought returned to Ayden—if but for a moment. He tore himself away and said, "No, not like this."

He sat up, yanked his clothes off so quickly he felt a seam give in his breeches, and then straddled himself, naked, across Freyrík's thighs.

"Like this," he said, bending forward to tongue one nipple, then the other, his fingers tickling down the smooth expanse of Freyrík's sides.

Freyrík's song shivered along with his flesh, and Ayden bit down ever-so-gently on his left nipple, flicking and then soothing until Freyrík was naught but a quivering mass of tense muscle and trembling skin, clean sweat and desperate moans, writhing and bucking beneath him.

"Please . . ." Freyrík panted, eyes closed, head thrown back to expose the long, glistening line of his neck. He groped blindly along Ayden's body, face, chest, his fingers trailing shivers like ice.

'Twould have been so easy to lose himself in that, in the taste and scent and sight of the man, the feel of his own cock sliding back and forth against the silk of Freyrík's nightclothes, the heady force of rendering this powerful man—this leader of men—insensate at his touch.

But no, not yet. Now was for Freyrík, and whatever the man was asking for, Ayden meant to let him have it. All of it—all of *him*.

"Yes?" he asked, one nipple still between his teeth, his fingertips still dancing up and down Freyrík's sides.

"I . . . I . . ."

"Say it, Rík," he whispered, brushing his lips across Freyrík's sternum, down his stomach, rubbing his cheek against the little trail of reddish-brown hair sprouting just below his navel. His skin smelled like the honeysuckle used to scent his soap, like salt and musk and *need*. "Tell me what you want."

But it seemed he'd rendered the man speechless, for Freyrík merely plowed his hands through Ayden's hair again, gripping tight and nudging him south.

Ayden grinned and licked his lips, remembering the feel of that firm flesh against his tongue, the salty-bitter sweetness of it, the heat that pooled and coiled there as blood rushed just beneath the taut skin and pulsed against his lips.

He tugged impatiently at Freyrík's breeches. Freyrík lifted his hips, then his heels so Ayden could toss them away, leaving Ayden with a glorious view of muscled thigh and fat erection, straining toward his lips as if by mind of its own.

Hungry as he was for that, he bent in only to tease, gripping Freyrík's cock at the base and blowing hot air on it, flicking his tongue across the head with but the tiniest pressure. The sound and scent of Freyrík were as intoxicating as he remembered, the taste and feel even more so, but it wasn't enough. He wanted *more*, wanted . . .

He sat up abruptly, and Freyrík's hips made chase, the man's moan of denial echoing in his ears.

"Shhh," he said, balancing over Freyrík's hips with one hand, stroking the firm planes of his belly with the other. "This is better, I promise."

He spat into his hand, seized Freyrík's erection and stroked to coat it, then poised himself above it, breathing deep.

"Ayden . . ." Freyrík said, his eyes wide with realization, his hands reaching out to steady or perhaps to stop him. "You don't—"

"I said *shut up*, Rík."

And with a deep breath, eyes closed in concentration, he sank onto Freyrík's cock.

Ayden barely heard the man's gasp over the heat of their joining, so intense he couldn't breathe. 'Twas not quite pain, but certainly not yet pleasant; he'd not done this in almost two hundred years, and he hadn't exactly gone about it properly now.

Yet he couldn't wait any longer, not after so much time wasted, not after all he'd kept from Freyrík for so long.

A hand wrapped round his cock as if the hilt of a sword and stroked, and the not-quite-pain fled beneath an onslaught of bliss that nearly tipped him past the edge right then and there. Freyrík must have sensed this, for his hand stilled, rough and heavy against Ayden's heated flesh, and squeezed round the base of his cock.

Ayden's head tipped back and he moaned, desperate for the heat of the ember in his belly, now banked; Freyrík's touch could easily fan it to conflagration, if he could only get enough friction ...

He clutched at Freyrík's hips and rocked atop him, filled near to bursting, relishing every sound, every sensation: the harmonic buzz of lovesong in his ears, the drip of sweat like tickling fingers down his thighs and back, even the burn lurking there beneath the tightness in his stones, the fullness in his arse, the quivering pressure of Freyrík's hand on his cock.

Freyrík's knees came up behind him, rocking him forward so they pressed chest to chest. He thrust up beneath Ayden, strong, fast, frenetic, rutting like a beast in heat, his rhythm as irregular as their songs had become.

Ayden gripped the headboard for balance and leaned in to kiss Freyrík, swiping his tongue along the man's lower lip, claiming his open mouth just as Freyrík claimed his body.

Freyrík's hand swirled over the head of his cock, gathering moisture as it went, and Ayden swore he saw stars fall from the sky behind tightly-clenched eyes. For a moment he lost all sense of place, of focus, forgot how to work his lips and clacked his teeth together with Freyrík's. They laughed, the both of them, but did not slow, and he buried his face in Freyrík's neck and breathed deep, bit down on the nearest flesh to hand and moaned, "Oh gods, Rík, *yes!*" as music swelled all round him, waves crashing and crashing upon the shore.

With the one shred of consciousness he'd somehow retained, he wondered whyever by the fallen gods he'd waited so long to let this happen again.

His climax barreled into him unseen. One moment he was tracing the cords of Rík's neck with his tongue, the next he was bolting upright with a cry, his buttocks clenching tight and rhythmic round Freyrík's cock as he burst into the man's hand, up his stomach and chest and all the way to his cracking chin. Time slowed, stopped, his quivering muscles failing him utterly, and next he knew the world was spinning ...

... For real, it seemed, for suddenly he was beneath Freyrík, all but folded in two, legs hooked over the man's shoulders as Freyrík plowed into his still-quivering flesh, and he didn't mind at all, wasn't afraid, never wanted it to end. Freyrík was thrusting toward climax with battle-hardened focus, the bed rocking beneath them with the force of it, banging into the wall.

Yet still Ayden wanted more. He grabbed Freyrík's head and pulled him down, ignoring the stretch in his thighs and the burning heat pooling between them, and mashed their lips together once more, letting Freyrík's tongue thrust into his mouth in time with his cock and twining Freyrík's song round his own. Freyrík grunted, moaned, hips bucking faster yet—

Freyrík froze flush against him, and Ayden devoured both his shout and his seed with eager greed, holding him tight as he collapsed, panting, atop Ayden's chest.

Ayden freed his legs as Freyrík lay insensate, sucking air like a frothing horse. Freyrík made to roll off, but Ayden tightened his arms and pulled him close.

"No," he whispered. "Stay."

Freyrík smiled and leaned in for another kiss, slow and sweet now, sated as they both were. When they broke apart to breathe, Ayden took gentle hold of Freyrík's head in both his hands, turned it 'til his lips brushed the shell of the man's ear, and whispered the words he should have said four days past, when cowardice had seized his tongue:

"Freyrík Farr—I love you."

# Chapter Twenty-Six

The morning trumpet startled Freyrík from sleep. He squinted against the early light and threw an arm across his eyes; never in all his life had he wanted less to rise from his bed. Not even his first Surge battle had been so fraught with dread as this *Blód Sekt*.

Alas, such were not his choices to make, and 'twas not his turn to be weak now besides. Ayden would surely need him.

He rolled toward his bedmate, pressing his chest tight to Ayden's back, tucking his knees into the hollow behind Ayden's curled legs and wrapping an arm round his chest. Ayden inched back against him with a contented hum, grabbing Freyrík's arm and hugging it in both his own.

"Are you ready?" Freyrík asked, nuzzling his cheek against the back of Ayden's head, closing his eyes as the hair tickled his skin.

"No," Ayden said. "Are you?"

"No."

"Lay with me one more time?"

Freyrík's breath caught, and he pressed a kiss to Ayden's hair. "'Tis not the end, you know. You'll *not* die today."

In the misery of the following silence, he felt Ayden's fingertips stroke along his forearm, back and forth, back and forth. He wished he could see Ayden's face, hear his song the way Ayden heard it.

"I know," Ayden finally said.

He turned in Freyrík's arms then, rolling face to face and placing a tender kiss upon Freyrík's lips.

Freyrík's flesh awoke with fervor, his heart quickening in his chest, but he forced himself away, groaning his regret.

"There isn't time," he said, but Ayden's hand was snaking down between them, groping at Freyrík's loins, and Freyrík found himself lacking the strength—and the heart—to argue.

When Ayden kissed him again, he tangled a hand in Ayden's hair and swore to himself that this was *not* goodbye.

"We'll be fast," Ayden mumbled against Freyrík's lips, freeing Freyrík's member from his nightclothes and stroking it to arms with two quick tugs.

Freyrík's own hand abandoned Ayden's hair for greener pastures, playing across the heaving muscles of the elf's chest and stomach, the hard planes of his hips, the curve of his thighs and the flesh that stood at firm attention between them.

He heard with one ear the sounds of servants readying his clothes, his bath, his breakfast, and whispered against the shell of Ayden's, "Do not sound so pleased." They were meant to be fooling people, after all.

Out loud he growled, "Don't fight me, elf," and took his hand from Ayden's man— *elf*hood just long enough to slap Ayden's buttocks. Ayden growled and grinned against Freyrík's lips, and Freyrík grinned back; this *definitely* bore remembering in the future.

"Again," Ayden whispered, and Freyrík merrily complied. Ayden cried out, added a whimpered "No, please!" for good measure, then threw himself against Freyrík once more, ravishing lips and neck and chest with tongue and teeth as they pumped each other toward completion with singular intent.

Freyrík reached climax first, a feat he'd doubted he could manage in the midst of his anxieties. 'Twas over quick and not so satisfying as their previous encounters, but at least it drained his tensions.

And perhaps that was all Ayden had hoped for this morn, but now, watching the elf writhe beneath him, Freyrík meant to give him more if he could. He bent to task, engulfing the whole of Ayden's member in one sudden swallow.

Ayden gripped at Freyrík's head with both hands and moaned, and though Freyrík had already had his own pleasure, there was more to be found in the salty-bitter taste of Ayden's skin, the scent of autumn leaves mingling thick in his nostrils with elven musk, the pressure of heated flesh against his lips and tongue and bumping the back of his throat. And Ayden's moans, *gods*, the *sounds* he was making, little whimpers and groans barely checked behind clenched teeth and thrashing limbs, hitched breaths and the whisper of Freyrík's name upon his tongue.

Freyrík felt Ayden's hands tighten in his hair an instant before he felt Ayden's ballocks tighten against his chin. He reached up, fumbled for Ayden's lips and clapped his hand atop them to hold back what cries Ayden could not. Then Ayden was spurting down his throat, back arching off the mattress and bared teeth digging into Freyrík's palm as he rode out the waves of his ecstasy.

Only when the twitching had stopped and Ayden's flesh had grown soft in his mouth did Freyrík release the elf's member, dragging his tongue along the way.

Ayden moaned again and pulled Freyrík into a kiss. "See?" he whispered, as mindful of the servants beyond the curtain as Freyrík was. "Naught but a matter of moments."

Freyrík nodded. "Do you feel better now?"

"No," Ayden said, but this time a wry smile graced his lips. "Do you?"

"No." One more kiss, and then, "I must go now and prepare to open the Fest. Remember your hate when the guards lead you out, but do try to seem already broken."

"Worry not, Rík," Ayden said, cupping Freyrík's head and stealing a final kiss, "for I am well and truly under your command."

Freyrík made it through his welcome speech, though he could not remember what he'd just said as he stumbled from the edge of the pavilion to the dais a mere five paces back. There awaited his brother's throne, which he'd gladly cede back to Berendil, and all the resident members of the royal family. They were smiling and clapping demurely, and the crowd was roaring—thousands upon thousands of them, a packed mass of waving, cheering flesh—so he was fair confident that whatever he'd said, he'd said it well.

Alas, he was equally confident that all would not stay well, for the morning's "entertainment" was about to begin. Oh, the crowd would love it, of course they would, and the bereaved would have their so-called justice. But his own heart would spill out onto the earth with each drop of Ayden's blood, each snap of the lash, each cry from Ayden's lips—

And here Ayden was, being led into the pavilion by half a contingent of guards, wrists shackled and bare feet hobbled, head low but eyes burning with hatred as they swept the jeering crowd.

Freyrík had so far managed to pretend that the whipping posts did not exist, but as Ayden was marched toward them, he could deny them no longer. The two wooden stakes had been recast in steel as precaution against Ayden's magic, and they struck Freyrík somehow as crueler that way, more deliberate: a weapon unmistakable.

The guards positioned Ayden on the little pile of topsoil between the posts, making tell their wariness by refusing to remove his shackles 'til they'd locked his sword hand into the cuff bolted to the right post. Only then did they remove the dungeon irons from his hands and feet, and chain his left wrist to the other post.

From where Freyrík sat, he could observe both the whole of the crowd and Ayden's face in profile, and he was relieved to find the guards' excess precaution unnecessary. For though Ayden never ceased his murderous glare, he stood pliant in their hands, just as Freyrík had asked.

Once secured, the execut— the *flogger* stepped forward, knife in hand, and cut away Ayden's clothes. It took but moments to strip away this first layer of dignity, and the crowd's whoops and hollers turned all at once mocking and suggestive. Freyrík recognized the looks of sneering desire on so many faces in the crowd, male and female alike, and beneath his buzzing anger and the desperate desire to protect, there flared an unmistakable burst of jealousy.

Yet Ayden seemed unruffled by it all, standing naked but wrapped in his pride, tall and shameless before the crowd. Not that he could have hidden himself if he'd wanted to, what with his arms chained out at head height like a man in prayer—*or surrender*, Freyrík thought with a grimace. But he recognized the expression on Ayden's face, and it screamed to all who dared to look, *Get your eyeful, you sons of darker whores.*

Good for him. He would need that strength very soon.

The flogger stepped away from Ayden and turned to face Freyrík with a bow. Freyrík nodded, gestured him over as tradition demanded. As the flogger fell to his knees at Freyrík's feet, Freyrík rose and laid a hand upon the man's head. The whip was held out before him to take, to sanctify.

'Twas not an especially cruel instrument, at least as whips went: its three braided tails would spread the force of each strike and thus cut less deeply, though the knotted ends would be punishing. But he'd not permitted them to soak it wet, nor had he left the hardened leather hooks tied to the tails. 'Twas the best he could do without compromising their pretense.

For a moment he feared he'd not bear to touch the thing, or that he'd fling it into the crowd, but the flogger was holding the whip out with all the patience in the world, and Freyrík's hand wrapped round the handle of its own accord.

He sighed out his relief and thrust the weapon toward the cheering crowd, shouting, "Here be your instrument of justice, people of Farr! Here be your retribution! Blood for blood, and life—"

He faltered, swallowed hard. How had he not considered this before? The people knew there would be no death today, but the words of the ceremony had gone unchanged for centuries.

Best then that he say them, and pray to the gods no evil would come of it.

"And life from death!" he finished, unfurling the whip and cracking it once upon the pavilion floor.

The crowd's cheers crested full into the roar of a thousand darker beasts, and as the flogger rose to his feet and accepted the whip from Freyrík's hand, Freyrík leaned forward and whispered, "Remember your orders. Do not render him worthless."

The flogger saluted sharply and took up his position along the edge of the pavilion, behind Ayden, where all could see his work in profile.

Freyrík let the crowd celebrate a few moments longer, then raised his hands for silence. A hush fell over the fairgrounds like a blanket of snow, and a young man Freyrík remembered from audience—the one who'd lost two brothers and gained three wives at far too tender an age—moved to stand by the flogger's left side. He unrolled several inches of a fat scroll, but he must have been illiterate, for a second man came to stand beside him, some minor officer-lord by the insignia on his uniform.

Freyrík kept his eyes locked on Ayden's profile as the officer read off the names of the sixteen dead. Ayden turned his head to lock eyes in return, and Freyrík gave him a single small nod. He could not hold Ayden, or soothe him through this, but he could, *would* be there for him, share his strength from a distance, think soothing thoughts and pray that Ayden could hear them.

Ayden nodded back, as grim-faced as Freyrík felt, and did not look away.

The man finished his recital of the dead. Freyrík rose and spoke the warrior's prayer by rote, for the first time grateful that he'd had call to recite it so often in the past.

The boy unfurled more scroll, and the officer-lord beside him read out the first of the surviving next of kin.

"Kyr Feigr, brother to Sverd Feigr," he called.

Beside him, the flogger drew his arm back and laid the first stripes across Ayden's shoulders.

Ayden flinched but made no audible sound, his gaze holding Freyrík's throughout. Freyrík struggled to mask his face as he laid eyes upon the three shallow cuts across Ayden's back, three angry weals marring pale skin. But Ayden merely rolled his eyes as if to say, *This? This is what you were fretting about?* The others on the dais would surely see that as defiance, but Freyrík knew better. 'Twas all he could do not to laugh, to sob, or more likely both at once.

The officer-lord proceeded to the second name on the scroll. "Riddari Feigr, brother to Svert Feigr," he called, and again the whip came down across Ayden's back.

Again Ayden flinched, held his shout and Freyrík's gaze, but Freyrík did not miss his hands curling into fists round the chains that bound them.

The officer called a third name, then a fourth, then a fifth. The crowd watched rapt, collective breaths held, as silent as Ayden had managed so far to remain. Freyrík almost wished he'd scream, befang him, and stop wasting strength on stubborn pride when he'd need it just to stay alive before long.

"Burr Feigr, second son to Svert Feigr."

Another strike, another silent jerk from Ayden, another three shallow cuts across Ayden's back. Soon they'd not be so shallow, for once the tails struck welted skin, 'twould split deep and bloody. And already the pain in Ayden's eyes was as naked as his flesh.

The easy course, the *bearable* course, would be to turn away, but Ayden was bearing far more than he, and 'twould be cowardice most reprehensible to abandon him when he was clinging to Freyrík's gaze as if by fingernails, grasping at the one thread of love in all this misery that he might shut out the rest of the world. Freyrík owed him that at the very least.

"Víf Feigr, first wife to Svert Feigr."

Ayden's eyes squeezed shut as the whip struck, but still he held his cry. Only a hundred and ninety-six to go . . . Freyrík pressed a surreptitious hand to his mouth, feeling ill just at the thought of what was yet to come, praying he'd not vomit in front of all these people. At least the flogger was holding true to his word, striking at half force: enough to look convincing, not enough to brutalize.

"Kván Feigr, second wife to Svert Feigr."

This time, Ayden shouted.

The crowd roared back a thousand-fold.

Freyrík hushed them quickly with two raised hands, meaning to get this over with as fast as possible. Let them cheer their bloodlust elsewhere. The whole thing sickened him.

The officer-lord continued to read, and much to Freyrík's horror, the flogger's strikes grew harder with each new name as the excitement of the crowd drew him in.

Freyrík lost count as the cuts upon Ayden's back grew deeper and his cries grew harsher and louder, until at last Ayden's knees buckled and he fell half to the planks, held up only by his chains.

The flogger drew the whip back, leaving bloody trails in the dirt at Ayden's feet. Another crack; a desperate scream ripped from Ayden's chest. Ayden's head jerked back, then forward, lolled on his neck. Tears spilled down his cheeks as blood spilled down his back and thighs, and though Freyrík willed him to lift his head, to look him in the eye again, the poor creature seemed far too lost in his pain to turn focus to anything else.

Freyrík's fingers curled round the armrests of his throne, so tightly that his nails dug into the gilded wood. He battled the urge to throw himself between Ayden and the flogger, to put a stop to his lover's agony, to put end to this vile madness.

Another strike, cutting deep. Another broken scream. Something splashed Freyrík's cheek and he jerked as hard as Ayden had, wiping at it with his fingers. *Gods,* 'twas— He swallowed convulsively, fighting to breathe round his rising gorge.

'Twas Ayden's blood.

Somehow he kept rein on the scream welling in his throat as he scoured his hand on his breeches, scrubbed his sleeve across his cheek until the skin felt raw. But Ayden gave voice for both of them, for a dozen, for *hundreds,* it seemed, and Freyrík found himself wiping tears from his cheek along with the blood.

Befang it, *nothing* was worth this—not his crown, not even his *life,* and damn Ayden anyway for loving him enough to endure this even when he clearly couldn't. And neither could Freyrík, it seemed; he couldn't watch this another moment, couldn't let this happen anymore, couldn't—

He realized he'd risen halfway to his feet only when he felt Ayden's eyes upon him, bloodshot and drenched with the agony of sixteen deaths. But he was lucid, gods befang him, and seemed to focus upon Freyrík with the last ragged scraps of his strength.

He held Freyrík's stare a moment longer, then shook his head ever so slightly.

Freyrík fell back into his chair.

Then the lash struck again; those green eyes squeezed shut and the connection was broken, the strength gone, Ayden dragged back screaming into the depths of his torment. Freyrík had to close his eyes against it, turn away before the pleading began, before he gave in and rendered worthless all that Ayden had already sacrificed.

*No.* He forced his eyes back open, cast his gaze once more upon Ayden's writhing form. He would *not* take the coward's way out. If Ayden found the strength to turn to him again, he *would* be meeting loving eyes. Freyrík would stay calm, and silent, and steely in his resolve until this ritual ended.

One way or another.

Ayden had known much pain in his eight hundred years, but never like *this*. 'Twas like . . . 'twas as if . . . 'twas beyond categorization, beyond endurance.

All he could do was run.

He was a strong runner, true, but the humans kept finding him, catching him, dragging him back with hateful shouts, buckets of water, the jagged teeth of the lash. It seemed forever that he knew naught but the agony of the chase, the terrible desperation to escape . . .

And the even more terrible realization that he could not.

He begged then, pride be damned, when all other exits failed him. But of course that failed him too. He could barely even remember why he was doing this, subjecting himself to this. He tried to turn his ears and eyes toward the man whose life his blood was buying, but even that was gone. Wherever Freyrík was, 'twas not with him; there was no more room for anyone, anything, but pain.

A loud *SNAP* in his song—shattered notes, shattered measures—and the world too shattered round him, falling away in a thousand jagged pieces. Yet the pain remained; the pain always remained.

He thought he might have screamed.

"Stop that," Ella said, splashing him in the face. He sputtered, ducked beneath the water.

Water?

"Just enjoy it, Ayden." Ella floated by him, sunning on the dammed-up waters behind Vaenn's gristmill. "It's not supposed to hurt here."

"But it does," he said. There was blood in the water. Why was there blood in the water? "How did I get here?"

Ella dived beneath the surface, then popped up beside him, pushing her dripping hair from her face. She nudged him in the side and he drifted on the sun-warmed water, away from the safety of the bank and toward the dam.

"You fell," she said. "Freyrík dropped you, and you fell."

Something nipped at his back. Then another something, and another. Sunfish. Blood in the water.

He thrashed away—from the fish, from the dam, from everything. Treaded water. "No," he said. "No. He didn't drop me; I let go."

Ella shrugged. The fish chased him, biting again. "It matters not," she said. "The real question is: what are you going to do about it?"

Pain blazed across his back, so intense he forgot to breathe, forgot to tread. He sank; the fish attacked him, razor-teeth searing flesh from his bones as he thrashed, flailed, prayed to every god he ever knew to make it stop, to end the pain, to kill him if that's what it took. He didn't even mind that he'd forgotten which way was up, that he couldn't breathe, because at least if he died here it'd be over.

A hand grabbed him by the hair and dragged him to the surface, shook him hard.

"Breathe," Ella commanded, and the ugly harshness in her voice startled Ayden into gasping. "I *said*, it's not supposed to hurt here. You *know* how to stop it, Ayden. Do it."

He clung to her shoulders, squeezing tight as the fish bit and the sun burned, letting her support them both. "Where's Rík?" he asked—*begged*—sniffing back tears. Gods, he was terrified. Why did he hurt so much? "Where is he?"

"Gone."

He shook her and sobbed, "Bring him back!"

"I can't. They took him from you."

Something splashed him in the face, but it wasn't Ella. Pain cleaved across his lower back, the tops of his thighs, and he arched into it with a scream.

"Please!" he cried as Ella hauled his head from the water once more. "*Please!*"

But she was gone then, and he was alone, slumped and gasping on the shore in a growing puddle of water and blood. He looked up and saw boots. Humans. Heard their cheers as the very sun reached forth and raked flaming claws across his flesh.

*Humans.* They'd done this to him. Taken Freyrík from him. Taken his home, his sister. Taken his father. He looked down and saw a rope in his hands, anchored to a willow tree off the bank. 'Twas woven of hemp and human sinew, bound together by hate.

He felt himself sliding back toward the water, the flesh-eating fish, and clung to the rope lest he drown.

He knew not how long he struggled there, clutching his life-line with both hands and both feet and even his cracking teeth, tasting three hundred years of blood and loathing against his tongue as agony burrowed behind his eyes, beneath his skin, deep inside his bones.

And then a woman squatted down beside him.

"I am Víf Feigr, first wife to Svert Feigr," she said. She fell silent, waiting for him to look at her. She would be disappointed; he had no strength to lift his head. He couldn't even prop it up; if he let go of the rope, he'd die.

"You killed my husband," she said. "He was a good man. I loved him. I thought you should know that." She reached round him then, pressed two fingers to his ravaged flesh. Her touch burned like lye, and he screamed.

When he could open his eyes again, she was holding her fingers up before him, coated in his own blood. She flicked them once, hard, and drops of it spattered to the dirt.

"You shed his blood, I shed yours."

She blinked away. Another woman took her place.

"I am Hraeddr Vord, first wife to Dýr Vord." She leaned in close, so close he felt her lips brush the shell of his ear. "My husband was a beast," she whispered, "and you killed him."

Then she reached round, touched two fingers to his wounds. She was gentler than the one before, but still she made him whimper. Fresh tears ran down his cheeks as she held her fingers up and flicked his blood to the earth, saying, "You shed his blood, I shed yours."

Then she leaned in once more and whispered, "Thank you."

A third woman took her place, holding hands with a boy, nearly a man. The child was weeping silently, his song echoing the wail of the rope in Ayden's hands.

"Go on," the woman said, nudging the boy forward. He took a small, reluctant step, wiping at his eyes. Green eyes, as familiar as the unruly black hair atop his head, as familiar as

*Father's dead, Ayden! They* murdered *him!*

the lips trembling with grief. His song warped with the need to avenge, and that was familiar too.

He pulled her to him, clinging tight as she wept against his chest. There was no pain yet, no true comprehension of the tragedy, but he sensed it lurking nearby, waiting to strike.

*No . . .* he *would strike first. He would kill them all.*

"I am Lóga, first son of Reidi," the boy said.

"Don't," Ayden whispered as the boy reached out with trembling fingers. Tears choked his voice and he cleared his throat, but new ones rushed in to replace the old.

The boy's upper lip curled in a sneer. He thought Ayden begging for mercy, which his hatred forbade. His hatred would forbid many things— too many things, just as Ayden's had: Beauty. Love. *Life.*

"Don't. Don't take this path," Ayden whispered. "Don't . . . It's not—" —worth it.

The boy's sneer deepened, and he reached round and dug his fingers into Ayden's wounds.

Ayden let go of the rope.

# Chapter Twenty~Seven

...And woke up on his belly next to Freyrík, a sunbeam warm across his cheek and the mournful cry of a violin painting worlds in his mind.

He pried open one eye and saw naught but the cloth-covered expanse of Freyrík's thigh. An attempt to lift his head earned him a thumb's width of movement and more pain than his mind could contain; the notes shrieked right off the scale and plunged him into silence.

Awareness returned slowly. The violin had gone silent, and Freyrík's hands, no longer occupied with godly tasks, were draped across his arm. The light had moved, brightened. So had the pain; it had hammered in pegs and set up camp. He would have to be more careful.

A soft murmur, hesitant: "Ayden?"

Behind it he heard a new melody, achingly heartsick, swimming round his head.

"Mmm." His throat hurt as if striped with blades, and rent his voice to shreds just as surely.

The cool rim of a glass pressed to his lips—*ow*; he must have bitten them—but he took a careful sip that seemed to help, and whispered into Freyrík's thigh, "Why so sad?"

One hand on his forearm disappeared, then reappeared on his head and stroked through his hair. "I'm not sad," Freyrík lied, his words as soft as his petting fingers. "You should be sleeping."

"And you at Fest," Ayden said, though he let his eyes close, let Freyrík soothe him back toward slumber.

"It's over. You've slept through."

Gods, he'd slept *three days*?

The hand on his head stilled, then slipped into his own and squeezed. "I was beginning to think . . ." Silence, and then, "Never you mind that. Just rest."

He was too tired to argue. But also hurting too much to find sleep. Freyrík's guilt lay heavily about his shoulders, and try though he might to keep still and quiet to balm the man's conscience—he'd done the right thing, after all, the *only* thing—'twas beyond his coping now. So he drifted in and out on churning waters, desperately seeking the silence once more and clinging tight to Freyrík's hand.

". . . supposed to be sleeping! Your potions are faulty and so, I am starting to think, are *you*."

Ayden moaned, rubbed his face against the bedcovers to blot the sweat away, tried and failed—rather spectacularly at that—to find a less agonizing position. Freyrík's hand slipped round his fingers as they fisted in the sheets.

"Nay, Your Highness, I assure you—"

"As you have done many times these last days, yet I see no results!"

Who was Freyrík trading such harsh whispers with?

"You said this draught would see him sleeping half a day or more, that this one would take his pain away. Yet he wakes in mere hours, and still he suffers beyond bearing!"

Ah, the royal physician.

"I, I cannot explain why its potency fades so quickly, Your Highness, but I assure you there is nothing wrong with the—"

"Then give him more."

"But I daren't, Your Highness! He has already taken twice the normal dosage; more too soon could kill him."

He felt Freyrík stand from the bed, felt those reassuring fingers slip from his own. "Damn your befanged excuses and find me something that works!"

"Rík . . ."

Freyrík's song slid an entire octave at Ayden's barely-audible address, from the high-pitched whine of fury to the lower sustain of eager attention. He crouched beside the bed, eye to eye, and stroked Ayden's cheek with his fingertips. "Yes?" he whispered. "Tell me what you need."

"The physician . . ." And before Freyrík could move away to drag the poor man over, he added, "is doing his best. The pain lessens each day. Do not blame him—"

For your guilt.

Confusion clouded Freyrík's eyes as surely as his song. Then wonder, then worry, and his hand moved to press against Ayden's neck, forehead, checking for fever or perhaps delirium. The physician took advantage of this relative calm by mumbling something about testing new concoctions and then sneaking away, if the fading of his song was anything to go by.

Ayden doubted Freyrík even noticed, for the man's whole attention was on him.

"Are you . . ." Freyrík began, then stopped.

Ayden wondered what words were poised upon his tongue that he felt the need to trap them there. Perhaps Freyrík thought the flogger had broken him.

Perhaps he had, at that.

Whatever Freyrík's question, he did not voice it. "I cannot bear to see you suffer so," he said instead, stroking again at Ayden's cheek. "I watched you like this once before. I did not even know who you were then, and still it pained me. All I wanted to do was hold you."

Ayden gritted his teeth and inched his hand up toward Freyrík's, capturing it in his own and pressing it to his cheek. "Now you can," he whispered into the man's palm.

Freyrík sighed, a sad and watery little sound, and mustered up an equally sad and watery little smile. "For a little while longer, anyway," he said. His hand trembled as his thumb stroked a line back and forth along Ayden's cheek.

Ayden closed his eyes beneath the touch and said, "You of all creatures should know the value of a little while."

He could hear it, the moment when Freyrík's thoughts shifted from tragedy to treasure, and then Freyrík was climbing into bed, so careful Ayden felt not the slightest jostling as he inched up close. Ayden curled his arm round Freyrík's thigh, wishing they could be closer, press skin to skin. But the whip had wrapped too many times, marking his sides from ankle to armpit and rendering such contact painful beyond bearing.

No matter; they would make do with what they had, just like always.

It seemed to last forever, the vigil Freyrík sat by Ayden's sickbed. Ayden's fever broke on the fourth day, gods be praised, and by the fifth he slept more than half the night before the pain managed to wake him. By the sixth he was making his ginger way to his feet for trips to the privy, and by the seventh, remarkably enough, the physician came to remove half the sutures he'd used to close wounds that had reached bone. Ayden daren't sit yet, but he was eating again, and conversing with relish, smiling and sometimes even laughing or pulling Freyrík in for a kiss.

Freyrík knew he should be happy. He just didn't know how to make it so.

He sat heavily at the writing desk he'd had moved beside his bed, meaning to work but unwilling to take his eyes from Ayden for more than a minute or two. At least Ayden was sleeping now, free for the moment of pain or night terrors.

A page interrupted his thoughts with a soft knock, stepping forward and bowing. "Lord Lini wishes a moment of your time, Your Highness."

Unwilling to disturb Ayden, Freyrík met his secretary in the drawing room.

"I'll not keep you, Your Highness," Lord Lini said once the bedroom doors were closed. Even so, he spoke softly. He spread three documents upon the nearby tea table and offered Freyrík a quill. "I need your seal and signature: here, here, and here."

Freyrík signed without reading.

"And if I may, Your Highness . . ." Lord Lini focused quite fiercely upon sprinkling pounce on the wet ink as he said, "'Twould be best if you'd join the court tonight for the evening meal."

"Perhaps," Freyrík said, his eyes sliding toward his bedroom doors.

Lord Lini redrew his attention by clasping a hand to his shoulder. "Your Highness . . . Rík. You must show your face. Please, do not undo all that you and Ayden have paid so dearly for."

Of course he was right; he was *always* right. 'Twould be no point to Ayden's suffering if all the court saw Freyrík fretting over him like some woman.

"All right." He nodded, reached up to lay his own hand atop Lord Lini's. "Thank you, my friend, for looking after us both."

Lord Lini took his papers and left, and Freyrík returned to the bedroom to find Ayden awake and on his feet, naked but for a few remaining bandages, picking at the sliced fruit on the tea tray on Freyrík's desk.

'Twas hard not to stare, but not for the usual reason. Ayden had lost weight that he could ill afford to spare; every muscle and sinew stood stark beneath his glowing skin. And his wounds . . . *gods*, were horrible even now to lay eyes upon, for though much healed—many were already naught but fading scars—his screams yet rang fresh in Freyrík's ears, the memory of his blood flowing through Freyrík's fingers—

"Stop it," Ayden said, soft but with the unmistakable inflection of command. He tossed his peach slice back to the tray, wiped his hands together and crossed the room to fold Freyrík into a hug. Freyrík's arms were halfway to hugging back before he caught himself, but Ayden held so tight he thought the elf would gladly have suffered the pain for him.

Befang it, hadn't he done enough of that already?

"You should lie down, Ayden."

Ayden stepped away, scrubbed a hand through hair more wild than usual. "I'm sick of lying down. Come, have tea with me."

Freyrík followed him to the desk; a servant rushed over to pull out his chair and pour them both fresh mugs of tea. Ayden leaned his hip against the desk with but the slightest wince, and drank deep.

"Did I ever tell you," he asked between swallows, "that my father was a diplomat?"

Freyrík nodded, then wished he hadn't. In all their time together, through all their strange intimacies, Ayden had shared almost nothing of his past; Freyrík did not wish to dissuade him now.

"When I was but a hundred-year, and our two peoples had begun to open both borders and hearts to each other, my father traveled into your lands with the ambassador to Aegea. He'd go a year at a time, sometimes two. I . . ." Ayden paused, nibbled on a grape. "I did not approve," he said, smiling wryly. "I was young, hotheaded."

Freyrík grinned, trying and failing to imagine Ayden any other way.

Ayden did not smile back. In fact, it seemed as if he hadn't even noticed, his eyes fixed as they were upon the tea tray, his thumb rubbing absently against his mug.

"He loved his work. Believed in it. Even after Ella was born he'd go back, and back, and back again." Another wry smile, a slight shake of the head. "No wonder she does the same, eh?"

Freyrík opened his mouth to reply, but Ayden gave no pause for it.

"He was in residence at High Court during the Great Betrayal. In the days that followed, he remained there, determined to prevent the war. Who knows, perhaps he might have succeeded if he'd not been murdered two days later."

Ayden poured himself more tea and said nothing else for a long while. Freyrík thought to fill the silence, but he knew not with what.

"I hated him for a long time," Ayden finally said. "Thought him a terrible fool." His words were soft, strangely flat of feeling for all their power. "I hated humans even more. But I think . . ." He paused, licked his lips. Met Freyrík's eyes. "I know now that he was no fool."

He drained the rest of his tea and plunked the mug back on the table, winced, glared quickly at his own back as if 'twere its fault he'd just hurt himself.

"I'm tired," he announced, then turned abruptly and crawled back into bed.

Freyrík watched him settle himself, wondering what beneath the great shadow of the gods had just happened—if Ayden had really just told him what he thought he had . . .

"Do as Lord Lini says, Rík. He's a wise man. I'll be fine alone; I always have been."

Freyrík stood, walked round the table to the bed and gently draped the lightest bedcover atop Ayden's bare body. He'd done the same so many times with his sons, felt so much the same love and fondness, that he could not resist bending down to kiss Ayden's head.

Ayden smiled sleepily and closed his eyes.

"Are you ready to go home soon?" Freyrík asked.

"No."

Freyrík's heart leapt from his chest and straight into his throat, but he swallowed it back down, chiding himself for a fool.

"But you will anyway?" he asked, knowing the answer already.

"Yes." Ayden replied, eyes still firmly closed. Perhaps 'twas easier that way. "Soon. I'll be fit to travel in a day or two."

Gods, so quickly? The *Blód Sekt* had been terrible, but at least it had bought them a few more weeks—or so Freyrík had thought. He needed that time; he wasn't ready yet to say goodbye.

"Perhaps one day . . ." he said, chiding himself again even as he said it.

Ayden nodded against his pillow, opened his eyes and stared straight into Freyrík's. "Perhaps a diplomatic visit; you can have me summoned for negotiations." He huffed through his nose, no doubt finding such a meeting as unlikely as Freyrík did. "Or perhaps a secret meeting in the Feral lands; for you, I would go there."

Indeed, he already had.

Ayden pulled his hand from under his pillow and touched Freyrík's face, tracing brow and cheek with the pads of two fingers. When those fingers brushed his lips, Freyrík kissed them. Ayden's eyes were glittering; Freyrík feared the elf might cry, but perhaps 'twas only the wetness in his own eyes that misled him.

"I shall miss you, human."

Freyrík grasped Ayden's hand, pressed it to his lips and kissed it. He wanted to remember the scent, the feel, the taste of him: fallen leaves and cut grass, sunlit warmth and a tingle of salt on his tongue. More than anything, he wanted to remember the joy, but already that seemed gone from his grasp.

He clutched at it anyway.

"And I you, elf."

Then he made himself let go, and summoned his groom to prepare him for dinner.

Freyrík's groom was fastening on his collar of state when a page stepped in to his bedroom. "The First Wife, Your Highness."

Freyrík opened his mouth to say, *I will not see her now*, but it seemed the page was not finished: "And His Grace Duke Vald, Aegean Ambassador to House Farr."

Freyrík snapped his head up and gestured his groom to hurry. What could possibly be so urgent that the ambassador had seen fit to call on him in his private chambers? And why beneath the shadow was *Kona* with him?

Gods, Berendil.

"Send them in," he said, turning round as he heard Ayden stirring behind him. The elf was out of bed, naked but stepping into his breeches. Freyrík waved him over with a nod, brows raised in reminder: *act broken*.

Ayden nodded back, then ducked his head and followed one step behind as Freyrík strode into his drawing room.

His greeting for the ambassador died on his lips when he saw how crowded the room was, for the ambassador had brought company: four attendants, judging by dress, though Freyrík thought them guards by size and bearing.

Duke Vald and his men bowed deep, and behind them, Kona curtsied, though he did not miss her eyes raking up and down Ayden's bare chest.

"Your Highness," the ambassador said.

"Your Grace," Freyrík replied, polite as decorum required, but suspicious even to his own ears. "Lady Kona," he added, nodding curtly at her. "What is this?"

Her smile was icy triumph. "You should have gone to your brother when I asked," she said.

She clearly wished to say more, but the ambassador eyed her sideways and she silenced herself. Freyrík didn't know whether to be glad of that or not. What he did know was that for the first time ever, she frightened him. And so did the ambassador, and his men, and this whole situation. He found himself glancing round the room, plotting escape routes . . .

Yet he knew already it would not matter.

"Your Highness," Duke Vald said with a bow, then took a single step forward and unrolled a scroll stamped with the Aegis's seal. "By command of the Aegis Exalted, Divine King of Kings, Man's Ear to the Gods and the Gods' Mouth to Man, Holy Ruler of the Empire and Binder of the Sixteen Realms, you are hereby ordered to present yourself and your elven prisoner at High Court."

Funny, how silence could pack his ears so when he clearly felt his heart battering against his ribs.

"We leave on the morrow," the duke said, crisply re-rolling the scroll. "I shall escort you and your prisoner personally."

Freyrík nodded, though it sent the room spinning round him, and locked eyes with Ayden. And for once, even lacking elven ears, Freyrík heard clear the fear and despair that screamed back and forth between them.

Gods, he should have set Ayden free the moment he'd conceived of it. For circumstance had made of him a liar once more, and this time, he did not know if Ayden could ever forgive him.

Or if he could ever forgive himself.

Don't miss the next exciting installment in
the Song of the Fallen with *Crescendo*.

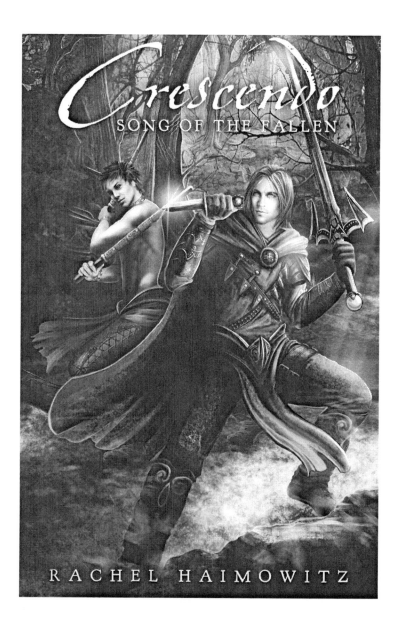

Dear Reader,

Thank you for reading Rachel Haimowitz's *Counterpoint*!

We know your time is precious and you have many, many entertainment options, so it means a lot that you've chosen to spend your time reading. We really hope you enjoyed it.

We'd be honored if you'd consider posting a review—good or bad—on sites like **Amazon, Barnes & Noble, Kobo, Goodreads, Twitter, Facebook**, **Tumblr**, and your blog or website. We'd also be honored if you told your friends and family about this book. Word of mouth is a book's lifeblood!

For more information on upcoming releases, author interviews, blog tours, contests, giveaways, and more, please sign up for our weekly, spam-free newsletter and visit us around the web:

**Newsletter**: tinyurl.com/RiptideSignup
**Twitter**: twitter.com/RiptideBooks
**Facebook**: facebook.com/RiptidePublishing
**Goodreads**: tinyurl.com/RiptideOnGoodreads
**Tumblr**: riptidepublishing.tumblr.com

Thank you so much for Reading the Rainbow!

RiptidePublishing.com

# Acknowledgments

No doubt everyone who reads these things has seen many an author state that while the act of writing is a solitary process, no book is ever created alone. This is especially true for Song of the Fallen, and I owe a profound debt of gratitude to Tal Valante, my editor, who—to abuse a metaphor—fertilized, midwived, and pre-natal-vitaminized this book into being. Her concept, editing, intelligence, humor, sharp ear, and occasional bouts of differential calculus helped to nurture this book and this author into much better versions of themselves.

The amazing Nathie also gets all my love and squee for reaching his talented fingers into my brain and yanking out the most gorgeous art ever to grace the cover of a book. How did I get so lucky?

A very special thanks to Jerry Haimowitz, who discussed everything from caltrops to polygamy on a fourteen-hour car ride; and who, long before that, all but shoved me through the doors of my dreams. Thanks also to Fran Haimowitz, who always (usually) (okay, sometimes) had that perfect word I was missing, and who kept me on deadline by asking, "Where's the next chapter, I want to read it!" with such enthusiasm. Huge thanks to Dr. Yitzhak Yuli, IDF Major (retired), for his military expertise, given so freely to an author he never even met; his advice, experience, and logic-checks helped to make one of the biggest scenes in the book one of the strongest, as well. Thanks also to my old friends Caz and Nicole, Ashley and Sarah, Stacy and Mary, for offering such great support, encouragement, and company.

# ABOUT THE Author

Rachel is an M/M erotic romance author and the Publisher of Riptide Publishing. She's also a sadist with a pesky conscience, shamelessly silly, and quite proudly pervish. Fortunately, all those things make writing a lot more fun for her . . . if not so much for her characters.

When she's not writing about hot guys getting it on (or just plain getting it; her characters rarely escape a story unscathed), she loves to read, hike, camp, sing, perform in community theater, and glue captions to cats. She also has a particular fondness for her very needy dog, her even needier cat, and shouting at kids to get off her lawn.

You can find Rachel at her website, rachelhaimowitz.com, tweeting as @RachelHaimowitz, and on Tumblr at rachelhaimowitz.tumblr.com. She loves to hear from folks, so feel free to drop her a line anytime at metarachel@gmail.com.

# Enjoy this book?
# Find more fantasy romance at
# RiptidePublishing.com!

*All My Crimes*
ISBN: 978-1-937551-93-3

*Scorpion*
ISBN: 978-1-62649-014-7

## Earn Bonus Bucks!

Earn 1 Bonus Buck for each dollar you spend. Find out how at
RiptidePublishing.com/news/bonus-bucks.

## Win Free Ebooks for a Year!

Pre-order coming soon titles directly through our site and you'll
receive one entry into a drawing to win free books for a year! Get
the details at RiptidePublishing.com/contests.